HIS WICKED SEDUCTION

LAUREN SMITH

Copyright © 2017 by Lauren Smith

Excerpt from *Her Wicked Proposal* by Lauren Smith, Copyright © 2017

Cover art by Kim Killion

Interior Acrylic Illustration by Joanne Renaud

Interior Art by Teresa Spreckelmeyer

The League of Rogues ® is an officially registered federal trademark owned by Lauren Smith.

This book was previously published in 2014 by Samhain Publishing. This is a republication of the original version.

ISBN: 978-0-9974237-6-1 (e-book edition)

ISBN: 978-0-9974237-7-8 (print edition)

ISBN: 978-0-9974237-6-1

❀ Created with Vellum

To everyone who has suffered the pangs of unrequited love, this story is for you. And to my brothers Grant and Andy and my sister Sara. I'm so lucky to have you all in my life. Siblings are the best gift there is.

CHAPTER 1

League Rule Number 2:
One must never seduce another member's sister. Should this rule be broken, the member whose sister was seduced has the right to demand satisfaction.

*E*xcerpt from *The Quizzing Glass Gazette,* September 30, 1820, The Lady Society Column:

LADY SOCIETY HAS TURNED *her eye this week to one of London's most notorious paramours, the Marquess of Rochester. Member of the infamous League of Rogues, the marquess is rumored by ladies of the ton as a fiery-haired devil capable of shocking delights behind closed doors.*

It has come to Lady Society's attention that no lady has held Rochester's interest for long. Does he secretly pine for someone of good breeding and good sense, perhaps?

Lady Society would like to learn the answer to this most fascinating question. Perhaps Rochester indulges himself to ease the pangs of unrequited love for some mystery woman. Should one hazard a guess as to the unlucky—or perhaps lucky—maiden who has stolen our dark marquess's heart?

LONDON, *December 1820*

She is going to be the death of me.

"Lucien! You're not even listening to me, are you? I'm in desperate need of a new valet and you've been wool-gathering rather than offering suggestions. I daresay you have enough for a decent coat and a pair of mittens by now."

Lucien Russell, the Marquess of Rochester, looked to his friend Charles. They were walking down Bond Street, Lucien keeping careful watch over one particular lady without her knowledge and Charles simply enjoying the chance for an outing. The street was surprisingly crowded for so early in the day and during such foul wintry weather.

"Admit it," Charles prodded.

Lucien fought to focus on his friend. "Sorry?"

The Earl of Lonsdale fixed him with a stern glare

which, given that his usual manner tended towards jovial, was a little alarming.

"Where is your head? You've been out of sorts all morning."

Lucien grunted. He had no intention of explaining himself. His thoughts were sinful ones, ones that would lead him straight to a fiery spot in Hell, assuming one wasn't already reserved for him. All because of one woman: Horatia Sheridan.

She was halfway up Bond Street on the opposite side of the road, a beacon of beauty standing out from the women around her. A footman dressed in the Sheridan livery trailed diligently behind her with a large box in his arms. A new dress, if Lucien had to hazard a guess. She should not be out traipsing about on snow-covered walkways, not with these carriages rumbling past, casting muddy slush all over. It frustrated him to think she was risking a chill for the sake of shopping. It frustrated him more that he was so concerned about it.

"I know you think I'm a half-wit on most days, but—"

"Only most?" Lucien couldn't resist the verbal jab.

Charles grinned. "As I was saying, it's a bit obvious our leisurely stroll is merely a ruse. I've noticed we've stopped several times, matching the pattern of a certain lady of our acquaintance across the street."

So Charles had been watchful after all. Lucien shouldn't have been surprised. He hadn't done his best to conceal his interest in Horatia Sheridan. It was too hard to fight the natural pull of his gaze whenever she was near. She was twenty years old, yet she carried herself with the natural grace of a mature and educated queen. Not many women could achieve such a feat. For as long as he'd known her, she'd been that way.

He'd been a young man in his twenties when he met her, and she'd been all of fourteen. She'd been like a little sister to him. Even then, she'd struck him as more mentally and emotionally mature than most women in their later years. There was something about her eyes, the way her doe-brown pools held a man rooted to the spot with intelligence—and in these last few months, attraction...

"You'd best stop staring," Charles intoned quietly. "People are starting to notice."

"She shouldn't be out in this weather. Her brother would have a fit." Lucien tugged his leather gloves tighter, hoping to erase the lingering effects of the chill wind that slid between his coat sleeves and gloves.

Charles burst out into a laugh, one loud enough to draw the attention of nearby onlookers. "Cedric loves her and little Audrey, but you and I both know that does not stop either of them from doing just as they please."

There was far too much truth in that. Lucien and Charles had known Cedric, Viscount Sheridan for many years, bonded during one dark night at university. The memory of when he, Charles, Cedric and two others, Godric and Ashton, had first met always unsettled him.

Still, what had happened had forged an unbreakable bond between the five of them. Later, London, or at least the society pages, had dubbed them The League of Rogues.

The League. How amusing it all was...except for one thing. The night they'd formed their alliance each of the five men had been marked by the Devil himself. A man by the name of Hugo Waverly, a fellow student at Cambridge, had sworn vengeance on them.

And sometimes Lucien wondered if they didn't deserve it.

Lucien shook off the heavy thoughts. He was drawn to the vision of Horatia pausing to admire a shop window displaying an array of poke bonnets nestled on stands. Her beleaguered footman stood by her elbow, juggling the box in his arms. He nodded smartly as Horatia pointed out a particular bonnet. Lucien was tempted to venture forth and speak with her, possibly lure her into an alley in order to have just a moment alone with her. Even if he only spoke with her, he feared the intimacy of that conversation would get him a bullet through his heart if her brother ever found out.

Charles had walked a few feet ahead, then stopped and turned to kick a pile of snow into the street. "If this is how you mean to spend the day then consider me gone. I could be at Jackson's Salon right now, or better yet, savoring the favors of the fine ladies at the Midnight Garden."

Lucien knew he'd put Charles out of sorts asking him to come today, but he'd had a peculiar feeling since he'd risen this morning, as though someone was walking over his grave. Ever since Hugo Waverly had returned to London, he had been keeping on eye on Cedric's sisters, particularly Horatia. Waverly had a way of creating collateral damage and Lucien would do anything to keep these innocent ladies safe. But she mustn't know he was watching over her. He'd spent the last six years being outwardly cold to her, praying she'd stop gazing at him in that sweet, loving way of hers.

It was cruel of him, yes, but if he did not create some distance, he'd have had her on her back beneath him. She was too good a woman for that, and he was far too wicked to be worthy of her. Rather like a demon falling for an angel. He longed for her in ways he'd never craved for other women, and he could never have her.

The reason was simple. His public reputation did not do justice to the true depth of his debauchery. A man like him could and should never be with a woman like Horatia. She was beauty, intelligence and strength, and he would corrupt her with just one night in his arms.

Within the *ton*, there was scandal and then there was *scandal*. For a certain class of woman, being seen with the wrong man in the wrong place could be enough to ruin her reputation and damage her prospects. These fair creatures deserved nothing but the utmost in courtesy and propriety.

For others, the widows still longing for love, those who had no interest in husbands but did from time to time seek companionship, and that rare lovely breed of woman who had both the wealth and position to afford to not give a toss about what society thought, there was Lucien. He seduced them all, taught them to open themselves up to their deepest desires and needs, and seek satisfaction. Not once had a woman complained or been dissatisfied after he had departed from her bed. But there was only one bed he sought now, and it was one he should never be invited into.

He glanced about and noticed a familiar coach among the other carriages on the street. Much of the street's traffic had been moving steadily and quicker than the people on foot, but not that coach. There was nothing unusual about it; the rider was covered with a scarf like all the others, to keep out the chill, yet each time he and Charles had crossed a street, the coach had shadowed them.

"Charles, do you think we're being followed?"

Charles brushed off some snow from his gloved hands when it dropped onto him from a nearby shop's eave. "What? What on earth for?"

"I don't know. That carriage. It has been with us for quite a few streets."

"Lucien, we're in a popular part of London. No doubt someone is shopping and ordering their carriage to keep close."

"Hmm," was all he said before he turned his attention back to Horatia and her footman. One of her spare gloves fell out of her cloak and onto the ground, going unnoticed by both her and her servant. Lucien debated briefly whether or not he should interfere and alert her to the fact that he and Charles had been following her. When she continued to walk ahead, leaving her glove behind, he made his decision.

Lucien caught up with his friend still ahead of him on the street. "I'll not keep you. Horatia's dropped a glove and I wish to return it to her."

"Plagued by a bit of chivalry, eh? Go on then, I want to stop here a moment." He pointed to a bookshop.

"Very good. Catch me up when you're ready."

Lucien dodged through the traffic on the road and was halfway across the street when pandemonium struck.

Bond Street was turned on its head as screams tore through the air. The coach that had been shadowing him raced down the road in Lucien's direction. Yet, rather than trying to halt the team, the driver whipped the horses, urging them directly at Lucien.

He was too far across the street to turn back; he had to get to safety and get others out of the way. Horatia! She could be trampled when it passed her. Lucien's heart shot into his throat as he ran. The driver whipped the horses again, as if sensing Lucien's determination to escape.

"Horatia!" Lucien bellowed at the top of his lungs. "Out of the way!"

He'd never forget the look on her face. The way her confused expression changed into unadulterated joy at seeing him, then to terror as she realized the curricle was headed straight for them.

Lucien crossed the street moments before the horses reached him. He tackled Horatia, knocking her to the ground in an alley between the shops. The curricle's wheels sliced through the snow and slush inches from his boots, soaking them with icy water.

For a long moment, Lucien couldn't move. She was alive. He'd made it. The curricle hadn't run either of them over...

Then his body seemed to realize it had a woman under it. A woman with the finest curves God had ever made to tempt a man. Her bonnet was askew, revealing long lustrous curls of deep chestnut hair. Her dark eyes, so innocent, fixed on his face in wonder.

"My lord..." she murmured in a daze. Her gloved hands rested on his chest, holding him at bay. He felt the tremble of her hands all the way to his bones, and his body responded with interest.

"What in blazes?" Charles rushed into the alley, gray eyes alight with fury. "Did you see who was driving that curricle?" Charles paused and took in the scene before him with a smile. "Horatia, love, how are you? Not too bruised I hope?" Charles had never in his life bothered with titles or propriety. Neither did Lucien for that matter. So it didn't surprise Lucien that his friend treated Horatia as he did.

"Oh Charles!" she exclaimed. She seemed to realize only now she was on her back in an alley just off Bond Street, with a street full of curious people peering in and Lucien on top of her.

Lucien gritted his teeth. "Oh Charles!" she'd said, but Lucien was always "My lord." It grated his nerves that she didn't offer such intimacy to him. It was his own damned fault. He pushed her away at every opportunity, just to keep himself from tugging her into the nearest alcove and kissing her. Something about her seemed to render him into the most barbaric state possible. He had little else on his mind other than how she'd taste, how she'd moan and sigh if he could just get his hands on her.

"Lucien…" Horatia stammered. His name on her lips was more erotic than a lover's sated sigh. "What on earth just happened?"

"I fear someone just tried to run me over, and you were, unfortunately, in the way," he explained, worried by the dazed expression swallowing her dark eyes.

"I say, Lucien, you might want to get off the girl, she's turning blue," Charles teased. "Besides, stay on top of her any longer and people are bound to talk. Wouldn't want to end up married just for saving her life, would you?"

Horatia was red-faced and Lucien wasn't sure if it was from lack of air or because she lay beneath him near a public street in such a compromising position. He rolled off her and got to his feet. Charles handed Lucien his hat and he set it back in place. He brushed off the snow from his clothes with one hand while offering the other hand to Horatia.

Her hesitation struck him like a blow. Finally her gloved hand settled into his and he helped her up, tugging just enough so that she stumbled into his arms. He couldn't resist smiling down at her.

If he leaned down just a few inches, he could kiss her, part her lips… For a moment, he lost himself in the dream of how she would taste. She stared up at him, unblinking with those damned lovely eyes that warmed until they were fiery with echoed desire. It would be so easy to—

"Ahem." The footman held out the box with a most pitiful expression on his face. "My lady…" he croaked as he showed her the package. It was soaked clean through, just as Horatia and Lucien now were.

She tugged free of Lucien's arms. "Oh dear!"

The spell he'd cast over her was broken as she rushed over, taking the box from the footman. "Oh dear, oh dear." The glitter of tears were sharp in her eyes when she turned to face him.

"My dress. It's ruined."

Tears for a gown? The behavior was more suited to her younger sister, Audrey. The loveable little chit was obsessed with fashion. Horatia, however, had always been quieter, and more academic in nature.

"Can't you buy another?" Charles asked.

"No... I cannot ask Cedric to spend any more than he has."

Ahh, there she was. The Horatia he knew was frugal to a fault. Cedric was as rich as Croesus but Horatia would never let him spoil her.

"Oh..." Charles replied, a little confused. He was a spendthrift, that was no secret.

Lucien took the box from the footman, eyeing it critically.

"It might be salvageable. We'll escort you home and you can have your lady's maid see to it."

Horatia glanced uncertainly between Charles and Lucien. "I'm not putting you out of your way? Peter and I are fine to go home on our own, aren't we, Peter?" She shot a determined look at her footman, who nodded hastily.

"We'll be fine, my lords."

"Nonsense," Lucien said. "You've had a shock and are soaking wet. We're escorting you home. End of discussion." He gripped her elbow with one hand and shoved the package back at Peter.

They must have presented an odd spectacle. Lucien and Charles flanking either side of the drenched Horatia like guards, with her footman following close behind carrying a sodden box in his hands.

Lucien ignored the curious stares and simply enjoyed the relief at being able to see Horatia home without another life-threatening incident.

When they reached the Sheridan residence, Horatia slid her drenched cloak off her shoulders and excused herself as she fled upstairs with the package. Lucien lingered in the hall, watching the flutter of her wet skirts, wishing he could follow her to her chambers and slip into the hot water of the bath she was no doubt going to take. The thought of Horatia, naked in a bath was only slightly less tempting than the dream he'd had the night before about her. She haunted his thoughts all too often of late.

"Shall we wait for Cedric?" Charles asked, joining him at the foot of the stairs.

"He isn't in?"

Charles shook his head. "The butler said he is looking for Horatia as it were."

Searching for his sister? What on earth for?

"We should wait," Lucien suggested. "Come, let's get some brandy."

His friend grinned. "Now that is more the activity I had in mind when we set out this morning."

They followed a footman to the morning room to wait for Cedric's return.

Charles settled into a large brocaded armchair, crossing an ankle over his knee. "Lucien, do you think Horatia will be all right?"

"I suppose..."

"Given her past, I mean," Charles explained. "With her parents and the coach accident. You were there. Do you think this will bring back the memories?"

Lucien shuddered. That was the day Cedric had lost his parents. They'd been traveling through town when two men had decided to race their curricles through the streets. Horatia, only fourteen, had been in the coach with her parents. The crash had been dreadful. Screaming horses with broken legs, several people who'd been too close wounded by the wreck. One young man dead, another terribly injured. Cedric and Horatia's parents hadn't survived the impact of the coach when it had rolled.

Horatia had been stuck in the coach with the bodies of her parents, unable to get out, dazed from the shock. She hadn't even screamed for help. When Lucien had reached the scene, he climbed up the carriage's side and opened the door. He called her name and she'd looked up at him, eyes full of terror. He'd pulled her out of the coach and into his arms. His stomach roiled at the memory of her body shaking violently against his.

"She's strong. She'll be fine." Lucien's words were more an assurance to himself than to Charles. He had to believe she'd not be too upset after this morning.

Thinking of her distraught left a hollow feeling in his chest. Despite his intention to ignore her as much as possible and pretend she didn't exist, she had possessed his every waking thought for the past few months. He knew exactly who to blame for this. The Duchess of Essex, formerly Miss Emily Parr.

His friend, Godric, the Duke of Essex, had kidnapped Miss Parr earlier that fall. The scheme hadn't gone at all as planned and Godric had found himself leg-shackled in matrimony a few months ago.

Lucien found himself smiling, which should have unnerved him, given that the hallowed state of matrimony was one he feared more than death. But damned if he wasn't a tiny bit jealous of Godric's easy happiness with Emily. The two were quite opposite in nature, and yet they were a love match.

The events after the kidnapping had thrown Lucien into Horatia's world again. All the effort he'd put into tactfully dodging dinner parties and balls were for naught. The League was so fond of Emily that not one of them could resist coming when she called. Cedric called it the "lapdog" effect—they'd been turned from perfectly dangerous rakehells of the worst sort to perfectly behaved gentleman in the presence of the Duchess of Essex. If only Emily and Horatia hadn't become such close friends, Lucien might have avoided her with more ease.

That Horatia was still unmarried at the age of twenty surprised him. How was it no other man had wanted to bed a creature with doe-brown eyes and such curves that were made for holding? Or spend an entire day planning jokes just to win one rich laugh from her soft lips? Knowing Cedric, however, there were probably several young bucks in the *ton* running scared at the thought of approaching him for permission to court his sister.

Lucien had tried to slake his thirst for Horatia between the thighs of other women, but it was no use. Only the previous night he'd attempted to bed a woman and found he wasn't aroused enough to perform. If word of that got out, he'd become a laughing stock. The irony of his rakehell reputation being damaged by an innocent woman was not lost on him. At this moment he dreaded his friend's arrival, considering the dream he'd had the previous night.

Horatia had been stripped of every scrap of clothing, all laid out before him, ankles and wrists bound to his bedposts by red silk. Perspiration slicked her skin as he moved up her body to nuzzle her perfect nipples. She arched into him, rubbing her sex against him, searing him with the wicked heat of her arousal. He thrust his tongue into her mouth, tasting her, and cupped her luscious bottom, raising it for the best angle of a powerful thrust. The dream had dissipated into mist, leaving him with an erection hard enough to pound a hole in the wall.

It would be a miracle if he could school his features and hide his guilt from Cedric after dreaming of doing such things with the man's sister.

Lucien glanced at the clock on the mantle. It was now

nearly noon. Cedric should have been here by now.

There was a serpentine crawling sensation beneath his skin that unsettled him. He'd had this feeling before, just before a storm was about to break. Worry knotted inside him, twisting his stomach until he could scarcely breathe. Dark clouds were on the horizon.

Charles frowned and leaned forward in his chair, concern weighing down the corners of his mouth. "Are you feeling all right?"

One deep breath. Two. The iron dread in his chest eased. "I've been better, I suppose. I just..." Lucien hesitated.

Charles reached for the decanter of brandy and poured Lucien another glass. "What is it?"

Lucien opened his mouth, but the door to the room crashed open, Cedric framed the doorway like an avenging angel, or a demon. He strode inside holding a note in one hand, knuckles white as he gripped his silver lion-headed cane in the other.

"What's the matter, Cedric?"

Cedric's rage was all too apparent. "That bastard!"

There was a moment of silence as Lucien shared a worried glance with Charles.

Charles stood and walked over to the cigar box on the side table against the far wall. "You'll have to be a bit more specific; there are a lot of bastards about." He ran the cigar underneath his nose. "Some are even in this room."

Lucien rose and paced towards the window overlooking the street front. He spied a comical scene of an overdressed dandy prancing about with a quizzing glass, examining various ladies' dresses as they passed by him. The man seemed to feel Lucien's gaze and raised his head. A cold chill swept through Lucien. Something about the man and his flat, cold eyes fired Lucien's nerves to life, leaving him unsettled. Had he seen the man before? A sense of foreboding raked his spine. The man turned away and disappeared through a door a few houses down opposite Cedric's townhouse.

Lucien forced his attention back to his friends. "So who is this bastard?"

Cedric threw himself into a red and gold brocaded chair and rapped the tip of his cane on his right boot. "Who do you think?"

Lucien's heart froze. "Waverly."

Cedric nodded.

"That isn't news to us. Someone tried to run Lucien over on Bond Street. Horatia happened to be nearby. Fortunately Lucien got her out of harm's way." Charles explained the morning's incident to Cedric, who spoke not a word as he listened. They all knew what Waverly was capable of. What was perhaps more worrisome was the man's complete lack of honor. He had no qualms about attacking his enemies from behind or, it would seem, their loved ones.

Lucien crossed his arms over his chest and leaned

against the wall facing Cedric. Beneath the man's fury, lines of worry stretched thin near his eyes.

"Is my sister all right?" he asked.

Lucien nodded. "She's as well as could be expected. I was able to get her out of the way, but she is terribly upset." Thankfully, only the gown had perished by Waverly's villainy. He tamped down on the urge to find the fiend and throttle him with his bare hands. Lucien knew that Horatia wouldn't appreciate him murdering a man on her behalf. His passions tended to rule him more than they ought to.

Regardless of the fact that she wasn't his, he could at least keep her safe. Horatia had to be protected at all costs.

"Cedric," Charles interrupted Lucien's thoughts. "Why did you go out looking for Horatia?"

Cedric's faced darkened again. "I was heading off to join Ashton and Godric at Tattersalls when one of my footmen found this letter tucked beneath the door knocker."

He held out the scrap of parchment in his hand.

With trepidation, Lucien took the note and read it. Charles stood behind him, bending to read over his shoulder. The note was on thick expensive paper. A black scrawling hand, unfamiliar to him, clearly not Waverly's, layered the surface of the note with sinister certainty.

Lucien read the words aloud for Charles to hear. "'Carriage accidents are a terrible thing, aren't they?'"

Lucien handed the note to Cedric who pocketed it. "It doesn't look like Waverly's handwriting. Are we sure it's him?"

Cedric shrugged. "Who else would dare to remind me of such a horrific event?"

"If it is the past he's referring to," said Lucien, "perhaps the timing here was deliberate."

Charles walked back around and threw himself into a chair, scowling. "He's threatened us before, but nothing has come of it. What's changed?" The earl's eyes glimmered like mercury, bright and ever shifting.

"Hell if I know." Cedric caressed the silver lion's head of his cane. "He's spent the past few years abroad. Now he's returned and renewing his threats."

Lucien wondered if his body had somehow known that something was set in motion. He could almost hear the clock gears ticking, but it was damned hard to know how to protect those he loved if he couldn't see from which direction the threat would come.

Cedric rose, rubbing his face with a hand. "Bad news aside, I would like to extend a dinner invitation to you both tonight—and I realize it is last minute, but Audrey is determined to see the entire League." He glanced between his friends hopefully.

Charles grinned. "You know I'm always eager to see your sisters!"

Cedric arched a brow. "Not too eager, I trust."

It was a damned nuisance. Every fiber of Lucien's

being demanded he break the League's second rule. He didn't want his lust directing him into a situation where he would be facing Cedric on a field at dawn or something equally ridiculous. With any other woman he would have bedded her and moved on. This was impossible with Horatia. Just thinking about her heated his blood and sent a throbbing ache straight to his loins. He shifted uncomfortably and adjusted his breeches.

"What about you, Lucien?" Cedric fixed a powerful stare at him. "Don't you dare give me any excuses."

Lucien had told Cedric ages ago that he didn't feel comfortable around Horatia. He'd said it was because she'd ruined an engagement proposal he'd made to an heiress years before. But it was a half-truth if anything. Horatia had been there, and the proposal had gone sour when Horatia dumped a bucket of water over his intended's head. But his need to avoid Horatia now had everything to do with wanting to take her to the nearest bed and... He shook his head, clearing it of such thoughts.

He began to protest. "Cedric, you know I—"

"Come now. You aren't afraid of my sisters, are you?"

Damn. There was no way he'd get out of it this time. "I'll come."

"Wonderful! I'll expect you at seven!" Cedric declared with satisfaction.

"Wonderful," Lucien echoed dully. How was he going to survive this?

CHAPTER 2

*H*oratia pressed two slim fingers to her temples as the bouncing form of her younger sister flitted past, distracting her from her latest book. It was not the way a young lady ought to behave, but trying to stop Audrey was like trying to command a storm. Horatia attempted to concentrate on the words, but between Audrey's chaotic squirming and memories of this morning's incident, she couldn't. The remnants of her fear tasted bitter in her mouth. She despised herself for being so weak as to let such anxieties rule her. One minute she'd been enjoying a walk, and the next there were horses screaming, curricle wheels spinning and icy cold water soaking her to the bone as she hit the pavement.

It was like her childhood all over again. Death had struck out at her without warning, and like last time, she'd been spared. But the event had awakened old fears. As before, Lucien had saved her life. He would never know how alive she'd felt when he'd knocked her back into the snow in the alley or how her heart had thrashed like a wild bird against her ribcage. His hard body above hers, pressing down onto her—he'd been so close she'd glimpsed shards of green embedded in the brown of his eyes like a dark forest beckoning her. Any fear she might have had at being trampled was swept away by the confusing wave of heat she'd felt when Lucien shifted above her, their hips and chests pressed together. Surely she'd nearly been compromised. If someone of note had seen Lucien on top of her it would have been scandalous.

She would never forget Lucien's face or his fierce, protective response. But that protectiveness was no match for her brother's, who'd rushed upstairs to check on her as soon as he'd heard. He had shown them a letter containing a vague threat about carriage accidents. Cedric was ready to pack the pair off to France and change their names to protect them. It had taken every ounce of diplomacy she possessed to convince him that she and Audrey were safer here.

"Oh Horatia, cheer up! Cedric said we will have a dinner party tonight with the League!" Her cinnamon eyes were intent upon her older sister's face. Audrey mistook Horatia's brooding for unhappiness and not the concern that it was.

"Audrey—cease that infernal bouncing." Horatia's

tone was sharper than she intended. She bowed her head, fingers pressing deeper into her temples as her frayed nerves sparked with pain. She looked up to see the smile on Audrey's face drop. "And stop calling them the League. You sound like that dreadful Lady Society in the Quizzing Glass."

"I'm sorry, Horatia, I just …" Audrey stammered, a pinprick of a tear in the corner of her eye. "With all that's happened today, I just wanted to cheer you up." She turned and slipped from the room, her energetic bounce gone.

Horatia started to go after her. "Audrey, wait—" Horatia stopped and sank back onto her chaise, her head still aching.

A moment later her lady's maid, Ursula, strode in. "What's all this now? That poor girl looked ready to weep for a week." Ursula was in her early forties, a plump but attractive woman with a threading of gray in her blond hair. She'd been with the Sheridan family for ten years and was the closest thing to a motherly figure Horatia had.

"She was acting like a child, so I snapped at her. I tried to apologize." Horatia only partially defended herself. She was at fault here, not Audrey. Her temper should never cause harm to others.

"And what put you in such an indelicate mood I wonder? I know the accident must have frightened you, but Lord Rochester was there and you're no worse for wear, are you?" Ursula went to the tall armoire and started searching for a gown to dress Horatia in this evening.

It was one of the many things about Ursula that Horatia admired—her ability to treat situations and problems with a cool rational mind, rather than an emotional one. Now that she'd determined Horatia had mistreated Audrey out of her own bad temper, she would no doubt discern what had upset Horatia, then decide upon a course of advice to give.

"No, you're right. I'm fine. A bit rattled, but it could have been worse," Horatia said.

In truth she was panicked about Lucien coming to dinner tonight. When she'd encountered the Marquess of Rochester this morning, well...it had been explosive. His touch, his gaze, his warm breath on her cheeks, all of it had lit a fire in the pit of her belly that refused to go out. If only they could have remained so close...

She couldn't help but dream about where it might have led. Would he have dared to kiss her? *Of course he would,* her inner voice replied, *he's a rake.* Had they been alone, he might have taken advantage of the situation and by God she would have let him.

It was a blessing he normally seemed determined to avoid her. Yet she couldn't help wanting to see him now, to catch his scent when he stood close to her, or the brush of their hands at breakfast when they both reached for the eggs.

As irrational as it was, she even craved the hungry way he looked at her with those smoldering eyes, lust simmering just below their hazel surface. Her heart slammed against her ribs and her palms slickened with sweat.

Ursula pulled out a violet colored gown with dark Parma slippers for Horatia to wear. "Your new Christmas gown was ruined after all, I'm afraid. No woman could be in a good mood after that sort of tragedy." Ursula's tone was half teasing. The other half was sarcastic.

"Yes, it is a pity about the gown."

The gown was a loss, but she could live with it. It was the sort of everyday drama one was prepared for. What she hadn't been prepared for was Lucien. Horatia had dug her fingers into his chest and stared up at him, oblivious to the cold of the ground. His gaze had been wild. It terrified her, to see the sudden change in his demeanor. It was a side of him she'd never seen.

She'd been forced to face the truth that there were things about him she didn't know. Secrets and passions ruled him. Is that why the men in the League were so close? Did they share something she couldn't understand? Was that why Lucien kept his distance? Maybe he wasn't in control of his passions. Maybe that's why he avoided her.

But I'm not the sort of woman who would test a man's control. Her inner voice chided her for being so foolish as to think she'd present a temptation for Lucien. She was no seductress. All he needed to do was crook one long finger and she'd come running. Pathetic, but true. It was a mercy she didn't seem to be worth the effort to seduce.

She let Ursula dress her. When she had finished, Horatia walked out of her room and towards the stairs. A black and white cat strolled into view, its yellow eyes wide and a dead mouse hanging limp between its teeth.

"Muff! You know better than to bring your presents inside!"

She darted after the cat. Muff ran down the stairs and past the main door into an unused parlor. The cat slipped between the marble fireplace and the fire grate, vanishing from sight, along with its prize.

"Oh honestly," Horatia growled as she pulled back the grate.

Muff had disappeared up into the fireplace, possibly even the chimney. The dinner guests would be here soon and she couldn't risk getting covered in soot. Luckily no servants would light the fire in this room tonight. Hopefully the cat would have enough sense to vacate the chimney before morning.

Muff was one of a pair of cats residing at the Sheridan townhouse on Curzon Street. The other cat, Mittens, was a black female. Cedric had bought them for Audrey as a Christmas present when she'd been a child. She'd also been given a pair of mittens and a muff, and had naturally named her cats the same. But that was the sort of thing Audrey would do back then.

The felines were quite ancient now. Horatia dreaded the day she'd find one or both of them passed away. They were her faithful companions, guardians of the library, defenders of the kitchen.

Horatia was more reserved and subdued than Audrey. She had few friends and often spent her days reading or riding. The cats would join her in a window seat or a chair and curl their tails around their bodies, purring with unconditional love. Being around them she forgot her troubles, forgot that she desired a man who was nothing but cold to her.

The front door knocker rapped. Audrey flew past the open study door, her face beaming with excitement. It seemed her sister had recovered from her scolding. Horatia hesitated before joining her in the hall. She knew Lucien would be there, and as always, she was torn between wanting to see him and dreading his callous disregard of her. Taking a deep breath, she went out to meet her guests.

Her eyes always found Lucien first. Among the group of handsome men standing in the hall, he alone enraptured her. With dark red hair just long enough to curl above his collar and burning hazel eyes, he was temptation personified. Horatia would happily fall at his feet and offer her body, heart and soul to him as tribute. But he'd reject her, just as he always did.

Lucien's gaze fixed on her while the rest of the crowd headed towards the drawing room. He remained still, tracking her every breath, every move. The gleam in his eyes startled her as a flash of heat went from her breasts down between her legs. Her face flushed. Lucien answered with a cold smile, as though he knew exactly what he'd done to her.

Lucien offered her his arm, and she hesitated only a moment before crossing the hall and dropping her fingers onto his sleeve. He tucked her arm more firmly in his, the warmth of his fingers burning her skin. She glanced about, wondering if anyone would notice, but no eyes looked her way. Unable to resist, she leaned into him, settling her arm in the crook of his, relishing the warmth where their bodies touched.

"Shall we?" Lucien's voice was soft and dark. A tone more suited for the bedroom than the hall.

Her throat went dry, but she managed a shaky nod.

AFTER DINNER LUCIEN and the other men opted to play whist, but he couldn't focus on the cards. The ladies in the far corner of the room had his attention. Ursula, one of the Sheridan girls' lady's maid sat in a chair, reading from a thick tome, oblivious to her young charges. Horatia and Audrey sat on either side of Emily, the young Duchess of Essex. Emily and Horatia were clad in shimmering gowns, while Audrey's was a light pink muslin. Their heads bent close as they whispered, making him think of three fairies who escaped from the court of Queen Mab in *Romeo and Juliet*. Occasionally one shot a glance at the men before returning to their secretive conversation.

Lucien would have paid anything to be a fly nestled on the wall close to them—to better see Horatia's lips part and form each word, just as much as he'd love to have those lips wrapped around his aching shaft, sucking him to sweet oblivion.

Christ. Lucien forced his gaze away from her.

"What do you suppose they're talking about?" Charles asked him.

It seemed he wasn't the only one dying of curiosity.

"God, I wish I knew," he admitted truthfully, just as Audrey broke into a fit of giggles.

Charles waggled his fingers at Audrey and blew her a kiss. Audrey blushed and quickly turned her back on them.

"You ought not to encourage her, Charles. She's young and impressionable." Lucien remembered all too well the perils of having a lovesick child follow him about.

"What is there to encourage? The little sprite hasn't the least bit of interest in me." Charles smiled wryly. He leaned back in his chair in a picture of relaxed ease.

"What? Are you sure? I always thought maybe she…" Lucien trailed off when he noticed Audrey's head turn in a very definite direction, and it wasn't towards Charles.

"Oh dear," Lucien kept his voice low. Audrey clearly had eyes for Godric's half-brother, Jonathan.

"Oh dear, indeed. We best watch out for fireworks. Cedric will rip Jonathan to pieces." The smug look on Charles's face nearly made Lucien laugh.

"You *want* him to get caught, don't you?"

Charles yawned. "This month has been a dead bore as you well know. After Tisdale gave his notice I just haven't been out as much unless it's with you. Watching Cedric chase Jonathan about town over Audrey's honor would certainly entertain me."

Lucien's humor fizzled. If Cedric ever found out that he wanted Horatia—in ways that would bring a blush to a courtesan's cheeks—Lucien was a dead man.

When the men finished their game of whist and downed the last of the brandy, they decided the evening was at last over.

"That's enough for me." Godric turned towards the ladies. "Come along, Em. Time to depart."

Emily didn't spare her husband a glance. She had one hand on Horatia's shoulder and another on Audrey's while she spoke to the pair of them in a huddle. None of the men really bothered trying to figure out what women whispered about. Lucien guessed it would always remain one of life's mysteries, like why a woman needed countless bonnets when they were such ugly and useless things. It was a damned nuisance trying to untie yards of unnecessary ribbons in order to touch a woman's hair while he was kissing her.

"That's an unholy alliance if I ever saw one," Cedric noted.

The Sheridan sisters were trouble enough, but adding Emily was like a lit match near a very large powder keg.

"I'd best collect my wife before she causes trouble," Godric replied.

Lucien didn't miss Godric's pleased tone as he had said 'wife.'

Godric stood, then walked quietly over and plucked her away from the group, scooping her up into his arms.

"Godric!" Emily kicked her feet in outrage. "Put me down at once!"

"I don't think so, my dear. It's time I put you to bed." Godric bent his head low so his face was inches from hers.

"Oh if you must." She tried to sound reluctant, but there was a breathless quality to her voice that fooled no one. For a moment, Lucien was struck with a sharp sense of envy. If Horatia weren't related to his friend, he would have been carrying her out the door in the same fashion, to find the nearest bed.

"Good night, everyone!" Godric called over his shoulder as he and Emily left the drawing room.

Cedric shook his head, but his eyes glinted with merriment. "By the way they act I swear you'd never know they were married."

"They are indeed fortunate," Ashton said. "To be so in love that marriage is a blessing rather than a burden."

"Perhaps we ought to leave as well?" Jonathan cast a nervous glance in Audrey's direction, who stared right at him mischievously. He had been staying at Ashton's townhouse to give the newlyweds some time to themselves before he moved in with them. Godric had settled an unentailed estate upon Jonathan, but had put it in trust until his brother was ready to settle down and run the property himself. Until that time, Jonathan would live with Godric and his new wife.

"After you, Jonathan." Ashton inclined his head to Lucien, Charles and Cedric, and bid the Sheridan ladies good night before departing with Jonathan.

Cedric looked hopefully at his remaining companions.

"You are both welcome to stay the night."

Charles agreed at once. "I'll send word to my valet."

Lucien, however, was reluctant.

Cedric's eager smile faltered. "I'll understand if you wish to decline, Lucien, but I do hope you will stay. After receiving that letter about coach accidents, it would be good to have a few of us keeping watch."

His friend looked so earnest that Lucien didn't have the heart to desert him. "Very well, then."

"Excellent," Charles and Cedric chimed in unison.

Lucien felt as though he'd made a grave error in judgment and would soon pay dearly for it. Still he would rather be here protecting Horatia. She was safer with her brother, himself and Charles keeping watch. Then again, she wasn't protected from every threat. Lucien felt the desire to slip into her bedroom tonight and crawl into her bed, pinning her beneath him and...

Damnation. Being in the same house with Horatia for an entire night was both his greatest temptation and his worst nightmare.

CHAPTER 3

*H*oratia still hadn't changed into her nightclothes. Restlessness had her up well past midnight. Knowing Lucien was somewhere in the house was unsettling, and she worried about that blasted cat. Muff should have been curled up on the extra pillow in her bed, but he was conspicuously absent. There was a chance a passing footman or maid had closed the grates around the fireplace and he hadn't been able to get back down.

Unwilling to let him stay in the cold chimney all night, Horatia abandoned her room and went in search of the cat. She tried to think of all of the other places he could be, and not the one place she wished *she* could be at that moment. In Lucien's arms.

It had been months since he'd last spent the night, and her brother was delighted to have him and Charles there.

If not for the League, Cedric would have been exceedingly lonely. She knew he loved her and Audrey, but he'd always longed for brothers. It was hard to miss the way he brightened whenever his friends came over for dinner, or how he looked forward to afternoons at his gentlemen's club, Berkley's. Perhaps it was because he could relax around them, and not have to play guardian.

After their parents died, Cedric had taken on a great amount of responsibility, not only to care for and raise her and Audrey, but matters of business and peerage as well. It was good he had such friends to ease his burdens and the pressures of family.

She slipped down the stairs to the ground floor and passed by the drawing room, where cigar smoke scented the air and muted laughter echoed against the partially open door.

At least someone was having a good evening. Irritation rippled beneath Horatia's skin. Lucien seemed to enjoy torturing her. Between his heated looks and cool smiles he was driving her mad. It was frustrating to not know how to act around him, whether to be warm or to keep her distance.

One of the men said something and Lucien's rich laugh teased her ears. Her insides shook with longing. She wanted to make him laugh like that, to be the center of his focus.

A small dark shadow flitted across the hall and dashed through the library door.

"Muff!" Horatia hissed, hoping to both summon and chastise the rebellious feline. Given the nature of cats however, she knew it was a fool's errand.

Horatia entered the library, lit a candle and started searching under couches and behind chairs. She almost missed the soft click as someone came in behind her and shut the door. The flame of the candle in her hand sputtered as she turned.

Lucien stood not five feet from her, watching her with hooded eyes. The aroma of brandy quickly reached her. The candlelight threw flickering shadows across his handsome face, highlighting a small scar near his brow.

In a few slow strides he towered over her. Horatia was suddenly very aware of his masculinity—the breadth of his shoulders, his height, and that the top of her head barely reached his shoulders. She knew herself to be tall, but next to Lucien she felt small, delicate and vulnerable. It was strange, but she liked feeling so helpless around him. Filled with longing, she barely stopped herself from reaching for him. He was too handsome, too virile. Whenever he was near he reduced her to a wild, wanton creature that would do anything for the chance to know pleasure in his arms.

"Horatia." Her name rolled off his lips like a fine dessert, sweet and decadent. "You ought to be in bed."

The wicked way he said "bed" made her lightheaded.

"I couldn't sleep."

He leaned forward, his body close to hers as he blew

out the candle in her hand. The sudden darkness around them made her catch her breath. A beam of moonlight broke through, lighting their faces. The smoke curled and danced up between them. Lucien's smile offered her a world of knowledge about pleasure.

"There's a lovely little remedy for sleep that I always employ. Do you want to know what it is?" His low voice set her skin on fire.

I shouldn't answer. I know what he's going to say. "What is it?" *Blast!*

The faint moonlight from the tall library windows lit his face as he leaned even closer to her.

He grinned down at her like a Cheshire cat. "I find the nearest beautiful woman, slip into her bed and wrap myself around her." His warm brandy-tinged breath fanned her face. Tingles of awareness spiked through her body and she stifled a gasp.

He raised a hand, drawing one elegant finger along her cheekbone. "Your face is warm. Have I made you blush? I'd like to make other parts of you blush as well." Lucien took the candle holder from her and set it on a shelf.

Horatia's knees shook. She stepped back and her head collided with the bookshelf behind her. Lucien closed the distance between them and braced his hands on either side of her face. His lips were inches from hers.

"Shall I kiss you, Horatia? I find you hard to resist when you look up at me with those dark eyes. They are begging me to kiss you. Did you know that?" His voice was a soft growl that made her breasts heavy and her nipples harden.

Incapable of speech, Horatia managed to shake her head. She wanted to throw her arms about his neck and drag his mouth to hers. She ached to run her hands through his dark red hair. Endless nights had been spent imagining what this moment would be like, when he'd be close enough to touch, to kiss.

Something deep inside her tore in anguish. He wasn't meant for her. Everyone knew he took only experienced, beautiful women to his bed. Lucien would never really consider her that way. She was acceptably attractive, but no diamond of the first water. With nothing to offer Lucien, he must be teasing her the way any rake did an innocent. He was the serpent, offering her carnal knowledge. Everything she wanted and couldn't have. It was an awful thing to be in love with such a devil.

Lucien moved his lips to her ear, using a finger to trace a loose pattern along her collarbone, down her chest and towards the valley between her breasts.

She inhaled, her breasts thrusting upward. "You've been drinking, my lord," she said. When he teased a finger below the fabric of her bodice, brushing a tight nipple, she gasped.

The grin he gave her was one of pure sin. "I certainly have…"

Horatia reached up and tore his hands away from her

bodice. She tried to knock his other arm out of her way to leave. "How dare you!"

Lucien grabbed hold of her, dragged her back against the bookcase and trapped her with his body. He fisted a hand through the loose coils of her hair, dragging her head back. Her eyes rose to meet his. A hunger churned in his gaze, swirling in eddies of changing colors.

"Tell me to let go of you," he begged in a ragged whisper. "Tell me."

She stared at him, unable to voice a protest.

"Christ. I'm not a saint, woman. I can't... Oh to hell with it."

The warmth of his breath tickled her lips before he devoured her neck in a slow languid kiss. Pools of wet heat built up between her legs and his tongue flicked out against her skin as he tasted her. She moaned. Lucien slid his hand down over her bottom, catching her in his grasp, jerking her hard against his stiff shaft.

Her legs shook against him, loose and unprotesting as he parted them with his thigh. He dragged her up the length of his leg so her toes barely touched the ground. The movement sent shockwaves of excitement through her and made her inhale sharply. Her hands fell to his shoulders, seeking to hold on to him. His lips found hers again and her palms skated up his neck into his hair, the strands whispering over her skin. She dug her fingers in and tugged on his hair. He growled deep in his throat and kissed her harder.

Saying no to him was the furthest thing from her mind. There was nothing beyond this moment—his kiss, the sliding touch of his palms, his fingers digging possessively into her flesh, cupping her bottom until a staccato rhythm throbbed deep inside her. It beat against his hard, muscular thigh, flooding her with awareness. She tried to rock against him, to create more friction. Anything to get closer to him, to satisfy her need for something she didn't fully understand.

"My God, you were made for sin," Lucien groaned as he tried to move his other hand deeper into the confines of her bodice.

She was made for sin? Was she nothing more than a body he'd like to bed? A temptation to release his needs upon? The words lit a flame under Horatia. She clawed his chest and sank her teeth into his shoulder to get free. Lucien jerked back with a low curse, letting her feet hit the floor again.

Undaunted, he said, "Careful with that temper of yours, my dear," and moved in to kiss her again.

Under other circumstances she might have melted in his arms. But he'd gone too far. Horatia brought her knee up into his groin.

Silence filled the room. For a moment Horatia wondered if it had made him a statue. At last a moan, several octaves higher than before, escaped his lips as he staggered back a couple of steps, then sank to his knees.

"Damn you, woman!"

"Serves you right, you...you horse's arse!" She covered her mouth, shocked at her own language.

Despite Lucien's pained groan, he chuckled.

"Touché, my sweet. Touché." He tried to reach for her again but Horatia bolted to the door.

"DAMNABLE CREATURE. I was going to apologize," Lucien muttered to himself as he hobbled over to a chair and collapsed.

The numbing affect of his brandy had worn off and guilt was wrapped around him like a death shroud. He'd been an absolute bastard. He should have known better than to drink when she was near. There had to be a way to make up for his lack of judgment.

He wracked his mind for some idea, some way to make amends. He'd apologize of course, but women were masters of holding guilt in trust and collecting interest on it. A trinket perhaps? A lovely bauble she could wear with a new gown... A gown! He'd buy her a new Christmas gown, one to replace the one that had been ruined.

Horatia never spoiled herself, other than to buy an expensive gown each December. The rest of the year she wore her usual silk garments, fashionable but rather understated. It was only during the holidays that she seemed unable to resist the allure of an enchanting dress.

He wished he could have seen her gown this year before it had been ruined.

He would buy her something new, something with a precariously low but still socially acceptable neckline, made from bright red silk, his favorite color and fabric. Even now he could imagine how it would feel under the light pressure of his hands as he caressed her, explored her. His loins tightened with lust and the pain of his recent injury inflamed all over again. He was being duly punished for his rash actions.

UPSTAIRS IN HER BEDCHAMBER, Horatia panted, her face flushed. She trembled with a mixture of longing and regret. Even when the man was a merciless rake she still wanted him. That was part of the allure she supposed, that threat of his passion manifesting itself in an explosive kiss, a demanding caress of covered places. Sleep would be impossible now.

Where was Ursula? Had she already retired? Her lady's maid never failed to stay up late to help her undress. But Horatia was too exhausted to worry about that. She wanted to sleep and didn't want to wake the house looking for her maid.

A light scratch at the door had her turning in relief.

"Oh Ursula, I hoped—"

Yet it wasn't her maid. Lucien leaned against the

doorjamb. He looked less foxed than before, which surprisingly didn't comfort her at all.

She tilted her chin up. "What do you want, Lucien? Haven't you done enough damage for one night?"

"I'm sorry, Horatia. I was indeed a horse's arse." He smiled a little.

"Well then, since we are in agreement, you may leave. I have things to see to. Besides, if Cedric found you here—"

"Things? What could you possibly have to do after midnight? Off to a secret rendezvous with a lover, I suppose?"

The very idea was ridiculous. She would never look at another man when he was all she'd ever wanted. It made little rational sense to love a man who had no real interest in her, yet here she was. When she'd been younger, Lucien had been exceedingly kind to her. He'd been the one to rescue her from her parents' coach.

Unwanted memories whispered at the corners of her heart, slicing her soul deep. Her parents lying broken and lifeless around her like marionettes with their strings cut. Their eyes, open yet seeing nothing, heads at awkward, unnatural angles. The coach on its side, massive splinters of wood embedded in bodies. People screaming. Then a burst of light as the coach door crashed open above her and she glimpsed a halo of fiery hair and warm hazel eyes. "Come now, sweetheart, reach for me. There's a good girl. Take my hands, Horatia, and I'll keep you safe."

Safe. It was all she'd ever wanted, and for a short time, he'd kept his promise. But when she'd ruined his proposal to a woman, he began to keep his distance. It only became worse when she'd had her come out two years ago. He'd taken one look at her when she'd entered Almack's assembly rooms and strode away, leaving her feeling utterly alone in a ballroom of familiar faces. Where he'd been only distant before, he'd now become cold. Her heart was cursed. But she could dream about what might be, so long as he remained unmarried. It was pitiful that she had only her dreams to look forward to, and even worse to love and desire a man who would never truly see her.

"Please leave." She tugged at the back of her gown, exhausted.

Her struggles didn't escape his notice. "Having a bit of trouble?"

Before she could protest he shut the door and rotated her so her back faced him, then proceeded to unlace her gown.

She tried to pull away. If anyone found them there'd be the devil to pay. "You shouldn't be in here, let alone helping me undress!"

He swatted her bottom and she gasped, shocked yet aroused at the same time. "Do you want out of this gown or not?"

She jerked free of him and he lifted his hands in surrender. "Fine! Sleep all night in that. I don't care."

He was nearly to the door when she spoke. Her voice small, tentative and unsure. "Lucien."

He hesitated, hand at the doorknob.

Slowly, she offered her back to him. It amazed her she could still trust him after what he'd done in the library.

Lucien resumed his work of freeing her from the gown. She knew his reputation, knew he'd been with scores of women. While that bothered her, she couldn't help but notice his fingers were clumsier than she expected.

"Shouldn't a rake be practiced at this sort of thing?"

Lucien answered with a growl of irritation, his fingers tugging at the knotted laces.

"Who trussed you up like this? These knots look to be the work of an expert seaman." With a final tug the bodice hung free about her, then he loosened her stays. Horatia's heart quickened as she crossed her arms over her breasts, hiding them. She'd been so focused on undressing she only now realized Lucien was in her bedchamber and she was half-naked. Never before had she been so vulnerable.

A harsh breath hissed through his teeth. His hands moved up to her neck, falling on the grooves between her shoulders and throat. She repressed a shiver of fear and delight. Would he kiss her again? Would he dare do more than that? Her body and soul screamed for more, begged to be held by him.

God, I am a glutton for punishment.

Lucien cleared his throat and awkwardly stammered, "I'm... I'm sorry about what happened earlier. I was not myself."

Horatia's heart thrashed. She turned to look at him over her shoulder. His eyes were fixed on the column of her throat, but his expression was unreadable.

"You are forgiven." She ought to have said she never wanted him to do something like that, but deep within her she knew she wanted him to lose control and kiss her like that again.

If only he hadn't been so cold, so ruthless when he kissed her, as though she was nothing more than another conquest in a long line of women begging for one ounce of his affection.

LUCIEN'S BLOOD thundered in his ears as his self-control waned. Horatia stood still as a statue, her breath faint as if she waited for him to act further. He shut his eyes, banishing the image of her naked beneath him until he could summon the strength to remove his hands from her and step back.

"Thank you," she breathed.

"You're welcome." He wanted to drag her into his arms and plunder her mouth with his, but the moment had passed. He snagged the reins of his remaining control and left her alone.

Lucien exited Horatia's bedchamber and hurried back to his own.

He questioned his sanity for touching her, kissing her, wanting her. He was a stout defender of the League's 'no seduction of sisters' rule. How many times had he threatened Charles upon pain of death to stay away from his own sister?

If Cedric ever found out I kissed her, and helped her undress... Lucien cringed. Men had killed over smaller slights to their sisters' honor. Cedric? He was a God-fearing man, but put in that position it would be wise to fear Cedric more than God.

Lucien had the door halfway closed when Charles burst inside.

"What the hell are you doing?" Charles shut the door, grabbed Lucien by his shirt, and shoved him backward. Lucien stumbled and hit the bed behind him.

"Care to explain why I just saw you coming out of Horatia's room?"

"It isn't what you think. We weren't—"

"Do not lie to me. You're worse at that than you are at whist." Charles's gray eyes were fathomless. "You weren't in there long enough for anything serious, but you *were* in there. I want to know why."

"I insulted her earlier this evening. I had to apologize."

"And you couldn't do that in the bloody hallway?"

Lucien folded his arms over his chest and glared back. "I didn't want her to slam the door in my face, so I went in after her. You know how women are. They hold grudges of biblical proportions if you don't apologize immediately. I've had enough upset mistresses to know when I need to beg forgiveness for the sake of peace."

"So you're treating Horatia like one of your kept women?" Charles arched a brow.

"Believe me, Horatia is the last woman on earth I would willingly seduce." The lie was heavy and bitter on his tongue. He'd started to seduce her mere moments ago. But he wasn't thinking straight. The damned brandy had him tied in knots. Reminding him of when he'd tangled his fingers in her stays. God he wanted to go right back to her room and shred her clothes from her body and take her to bed.

"There is no rule against being friends with a man's sister. Cedric would never shoot you over that. But you've been cold to her these last few years. Is friendship beyond your grasp?" Charles crossed his arms over his chest.

Lucien sighed heavily and leaned back on his bed. It was time to resurrect the old lie. Charles couldn't be trusted with the truth, it would be the same as telling Cedric.

"Do you remember, years ago, when I was courting Miss Melanie Burns?"

"Of course…" Charles voice trailed off.

Melanie Burns, one of the wealthiest, prettiest heiresses had nearly married Lucien. Instead, after Horatia's interference, she had refused his proposal and a month later was engaged to none other than Hugo Waverly. Rather than be truly angry with Horatia, he'd been thankful. She'd saved him from marriage to a woman who ended up his enemy's wife. For the next four years he'd been cordial, but maintained some distance. Then there had been her coming out when she turned eighteen. He'd never forget the first night she went to Almack's. Her hair had been artfully styled, her dress more elegant than her usual day gowns. She'd been utterly captivating that night and the only thing he could do was run. Put distance between them before he did something foolish. Resurrecting the proposal incident had been the only straw he could grasp as a reason to stay away from her. If he couldn't get his hands on her, he couldn't kiss her, couldn't make love to her, couldn't love her. It was for the best, though of late, it was working less and less.

"Are you saying Horatia had something to do with Melanie Burns?"

"Yes," Lucien answered flatly.

"How? She was a child back then."

"Horatia was with Cedric at my estate in Kent on a visit. Melanie Burns was there. I was in the middle of proposing when Horatia dumped a bucket of pond water over our heads from the gazebo roof. Melanie was humiliated, her dress was ruined and the little imp, Horatia, dared to laugh at her. No matter how much I apologized later, Melanie refused to marry me."

"Then she married Waverly. If he's more her type, you ought to thank Horatia, not punish her."

"There's more to it. Horatia professed her love for me. She was only fourteen," Lucien growled.

"A child's infatuation. That's no reason to be cruel," Charles replied softly.

"I told Horatia I would never love her. That she meant nothing to me."

A epiphany struck Charles's face. "You broke her heart."

"I couldn't help it. I was so much older than she. Now she's grown and I don't want her setting her cap at me. I'm not attracted to her and never will be." Lucien prayed with every fiber of his black-hearted soul that he sounded truthful.

Charles was silent for a long moment.

"Ash once told me that between love and hate there is a fine line. Sometimes you can cross it without even realizing it."

"You can't seriously be suggesting that I love Horatia! You know the sort of woman I need. She's too prim and proper for my tastes. I don't feel anything at all for her—certainly not *love*." A bitter taste filled Lucien's mouth at such a denial. He felt too much for her, and although it couldn't be love, it was stronger than lust and therefore more dangerous.

Charles frowned, his gray eyes surprisingly tinged with sadness.

"Are you so adamant to avoid her because of the second League Rule? Have you learned nothing from Godric and Emily?"

"Wouldn't you avoid a woman if it meant your friend might seek satisfaction against you? Charles, you know me. You know how I am with women. I couldn't stay around her for much longer and not desire more than friendship, and anything beyond that could end very badly. I don't have to remind you how protective Cedric is of his sisters. He's always taken Rule Two very seriously."

"You really cannot control yourself around her? Your only solution is to be cold and cruel in order to avoid temptation?" His friend seemed baffled, but then, Charles was the sort of man who was never tempted by forbidden things—he dove headlong into them.

"Unfortunately, that's exactly what I'm saying. The more I'm around her, the more I want to be with her. We both know I'm not the marrying type, so any time spent with her would have one conclusion and no one would like the result."

Charles raked a hand through his hair. "You're a fool, and you're hurting Horatia because of it. I can't stand to stay here, not when I'm tempted to box your ears."

"Charles." Lucien put a hand on his friend's shoulder

as he turned to leave, but Charles shrugged free as he turned to leave.

"Good night, Lucien."

Lucien stared at the door as it closed. A lump worked in his throat. Was Charles right? Had he been keeping his distance from Horatia to avoid more than bedding her?

Lucien loved women, but he didn't *fall* in love with them. It wasn't in his nature, and the women he'd had understood this. Horatia deserved a man who could be loyal. He could never have her, not as a lover or a wife. Cedric would never give him permission, and in any case there was the League's second rule. Still, the thought of having her, calling her his very own...

Why did it make his heart hurt so, knowing it could never be?

CHAPTER 4

When Lucien came down to breakfast late the next morning, he noticed both Horatia and Charles were missing.

"Where is Charles?" he asked, stopping himself short from asking about Horatia as well.

Cedric glanced up from his plate. "He's taken Horatia riding in Hyde Park to exercise my Arabians."

"Oh?" A stab of jealousy lanced through him like a hot poker. The idea of Horatia with someone else—especially Charles—made his vision turn crimson.

Audrey was quieter than usual. Her youthful gaiety, which so often amused him when he was over, seemed to be absent.

Cedric seemed to have noticed it as well. "I say, what's gotten into you, my dear? First Horatia is in a fit of the blue-devils, and now you are quite Friday-faced."

It was no secret that Cedric didn't like to see his sisters unhappy. It was something Lucien understood all too well. He had a sister of his own, and seeing her upset always set his teeth on edge.

"I wished to go shopping today, but Horatia went riding and you've business to attend to at Lloyd's, so I'm stranded here alone."

Audrey moped the way only a pretty young woman could, with her Cupid's bow lips plumped into a pout. When this reaction garnered no attention, she added a theatrical sniffle. Her eyes were glistening with diamond bright tears. It was always entertaining to watch Audrey try to work her magic on her elder brother when she wanted something.

Lucien immediately found a solution to dry her eyes. "With your brother's permission, I'd be happy to escort you. I have a few errands to run myself and would be delighted to have your expertise on the latest fashions."

All signs of tears vanished as Audrey looked expectantly at her brother. Cedric gave her a nod. "Very well, but take your maid with you."

Audrey dashed off to her room to retrieve her reticule, bonnet and cloak. When she returned she curled her arms about her brother's neck and kissed his cheek. Lucien stifled a laugh at the bemused look on Cedric's face.

"Anything to keep you in good spirits." He patted

Audrey's back and gently pushed her away. She left the room like a puppy with boundless energy.

Ahh to be that young again, Lucien thought.

Once they were alone again Cedric asked, "You're sure you don't mind escorting her?"

Lucien grinned. "Not at all. I do need her advice on a few things. The child does know her fashion." She was a clever girl, but she filled that brain of hers with far too much fluff on the types of gowns and the styles of bonnets. Then again, he shouldn't be wishing her intelligence was put to use elsewhere. Lord knows the little chit might end up a brilliant political hostess or married to a member of the House of Lords. He wouldn't give her credit for anything less and the very idea of her having any influence over a man in politics was terrifying.

"Very well then, I shall see you both later." Cedric drained his coffee, set the cup down and reached for his cane resting against the table's edge. Cedric never let the cane out of his sight. A reminder of vigilance, perhaps. He paused at the door's edge. "Remember to be on your guard, my friend."

Once Audrey was ready to leave, Lucien ordered one of Cedric's carriages to take them to Bond Street. With Lucien as an escort, Audrey would be free of the ogling of the charming Bond Street Beaux. They knew better than to stare at any woman in Lucien's company. He viewed them with no small measure of condescension, like the harmless popinjays they were. The real danger for

Audrey was being seen in public with someone like him. Rumors could spread like wildfire, and the press only fanned the flames.

Audrey flitted about on his arm, oohing and ahhing over every colorful window display they passed until she finally chose a fashionable modiste maker. Her lady's maid, Gillian, a quiet girl around Audrey's age dressed in a gray cotton gown, followed behind.

"Madame Ella is the best dressmaker in London," she said. "She made that lovely gown of Horatia's, the one that wretched driver destroyed."

It seemed fortune favored Lucien today. This was exactly the place he needed to be to buy Horatia a new gown.

He kept his tone soft to prevent being overheard. "Audrey, would you be interested in helping me with a special favor?"

She grinned at him. "Oh I suppose, but I shall demand a favor from you someday."

He had said nothing to give away his intent, yet she seemed to know she had him exactly where she wanted him. Were she a man, Audrey would have been a magnificent politician.

He tried to act casual. "As long as it is within the confines of the law and your brother won't challenge me to a duel, then you shall have it."

"Excellent. We have an agreement." Her brown eyes

twinkled with devilry, and he knew he'd come to regret this day. "What is it you need help with?"

"I'd like to replace your sister's ruined gown, but I don't wish to buy the exact same one she had before. I want something better. Something red perhaps…" His voice trailed off as Audrey's lips parted in shock.

"You want to buy Horatia a gown?"

"Er…yes." He held his breath, waiting for Audrey to reveal her knowledge of his secrets. Thankfully, she didn't.

Her expression changed from surprise to one of calculation. Her shrewd gaze was fixed on him, as if she knew something about him that even he did not. It was most unsettling.

"Very well. Red you say? Silk perhaps?" she suggested with a smile that was beyond any hint of innocence.

She couldn't know about his visits to the infamous Midnight Garden, or the games he'd played there, restraining women with red silk ties so he could take his time bringing them to screaming climaxes. He paid quite a handsome sum to keep his interests private. Yet the girl seemed to hint that she knew more than she should about him.

"Red is an excellent color on her, I agree. I haven't the faintest idea why she doesn't wear it more often." Audrey turned and went to embrace the stately, mature woman who had appeared near the back of the shop. "Madame Ella!"

"Miss Audrey! I'm so glad you're back. I kept those York Town gloves, the fawn colored ones you were so admiring a few days ago." Madame Ella brushed a loose coil of dark hair back from her face and retrieved a small glove-sized box. Audrey barely repressed a squeal.

Madame Ella curtseyed when she saw Lucien hovering in the doorway. "Good morning, my lord."

Lucien inclined his head and came over. He'd met her once before, a few years back when he'd come with his mother and Lysandra, his sister, to buy her wardrobe for her first Season. It seemed Madame Ella had an excellent memory.

Audrey took charge and commanded Madame Ella's attention. "We are here to order a new gown for my sister."

Madame Ella's brows knit in concern. "She was not pleased with my creation?"

"On the contrary. She loved it, but it met with an unfortunate fate." Audrey explained the previous day's events.

"I see. So what did you have in mind, Miss Sheridan?"

"A green ball gown with a red satin over dress. Embroider the gown's sleeves with holly designs, trim the hem with a flounce of white Belgian lace. And a green satin wrapping under her bosom." Audrey looked over at Lucien, measuring him intently before she added, "Also, trim the décolletage with sprigs of faux mistletoe."

Both Lucien and Madame Ella raised their eyes at this last request.

"Mistletoe?" Lucien asked Audrey in a hushed tone.

Audrey giggled.

"Don't you see, Lucien? She'll look so lovely in this dress, wrapped up like a beautiful Christmas present." Audrey wiggled her eyebrows suggestively.

"And they say I'm wicked," Lucien said to himself.

If the image Audrey had created in his head was even close to reality, Horatia would be a Christmas present worth unwrapping. With that mistletoe nestled against her breasts, he would be tempted to kiss every inch of her bosom to honor the tradition properly.

"Would she wear such a gown?" Lucien asked Audrey. He wouldn't mind the cost of the garment, but if Horatia refused to wear it, it would be an unspeakable crime against the gown, its maker, and Lucien's very ungentle-manly thoughts at that moment.

"She would wear it, if you asked her to," Audrey replied, her attention now fixed on the gloves she'd taken from the box. She rubbed one of them against her cheek, gave a sigh of pleasure and set them back in the box.

"And what do you mean by that?" Lucien felt breath-less as he awaited her response. Just what did she know?

Audrey shrugged. "She values your opinion. If you gave the gown to her and asked her to wear it then she would."

Her answer seemed so resolute that Lucien couldn't help but believe her.

"Then you have our order, Madame Ella. Just as Miss Audrey requested."

"It will be my pleasure, my lord. Miss Audrey has the finest taste."

Lucien patted Audrey's soft hand. "Indeed she does."

He instructed the modiste to send the bill for the gown and gloves to him. As they left the shop, he pulled Audrey aside, her maid staying discreetly a few feet away.

"You mustn't let Cedric know I bought the gown. Do you understand? Lie if you must, say you purchased it."

"Why should I—"

Lucien shushed her. "I can't buy a woman a gift such as that and not have the entire *ton* thinking she's my mistress, your brother included. Think of the consequences." When her eyes widened and she gave a curt little nod, he knew she understood. Her sister's reputation was paramount.

HORATIA CLUNG to her dark blue velvet cloak, pulling the ermine lined hood tighter against her face. Charles slapped the ribbons over the backs of the pair of horses, urging them to speed up. They were headed towards Bond Street, where no doubt Audrey had dragged Lucien to do some shopping since Cedric would be busy with other matters.

"Why are you in a hurry, Charles?" She leaned back in the carriage and glanced over her shoulder to check on Ursula, who rode in the back. "We barely rode at all in the park before you insisted we return them to the stables."

When Charles shot a look her way she saw his gray eyes were oddly turbulent, mirroring the stormy winter clouds above their heads. "I just remembered I need to take Audrey to see Avery. He's back in London, you know. I'd be in trouble if I didn't take her out on the Town for the afternoon with him. He does so adore your sister. You are welcome to come." He glanced her way again.

Horatia shook her head. She didn't feel the least bit sociable at the moment.

"You needn't drop me off at home. Ursula and I can hire a hackney to get back."

He scoffed as though affronted at leaving her alone. "Nonsense. I see Lucien up ahead. He's with your sister. I'll have him escort you home." The words came out in an oddly strained manner, as though he was torn on the matter. "You don't mind if I leave you with Lucien?"

"No, I do not. He will see me home safely, just as he's always done." Why she added the last part she wasn't sure, but she felt it necessary to reassure Charles.

Horatia put a gloved hand on his arm. He didn't even seem to notice. "Charles, are you unwell?"

He tensed. "No, I'm well enough. There's much to give me worry these days. Don't fret on my behalf."

She stared at him for a long moment, wondering if she ought to inquire further as to the nature of his distress. Charles was always close-lipped when it came to such things. Her brother always claimed Charles couldn't keep a secret, but Horatia knew better. When it came to matters of the heart, the Earl of Lonsdale could remain silent forever. She turned her attention to the streets again.

When they rolled up next to Lucien and Audrey, Charles called and waved them closer. He then got down to help Ursula off the carriage.

"Lucien, I need you to take Horatia home. Audrey and I have a lunch engagement with Avery, don't we?" He slanted a look at Audrey.

She blinked once before remembrance flashed across her face. "Oh yes!"

Before Lucien could protest, Horatia and her maid Ursula were dumped into his care as Audrey and her maid Gillian usurped her sister's spot on the curricle, and Charles tore off down the street.

"Did Charles just leave you behind so he could take your sister and my brother out for the afternoon?" Lucien asked in almost a stupefied tone.

"It would seem so." Horatia was just as mystified. She

blushed when she realized she'd been leaning into him as they watched the curricle drive off. With great reluctance she pushed away, not missing the way his hand lingered at the small of her back, as though he wished to keep her close. A little pang pinched her heart.

Lucien hailed his waiting carriage to take him, Horatia and her maid back to Curzon Street. He helped Horatia inside allowing her the seat facing forward. The carriage leapt into motion before Lucien had properly seated himself and was flung back onto Horatia. She cried out, more from surprise than any pain. He scrambled off her, apologizing profusely.

"Are you quite sure you are all right?" he pressed.

"I'm fine, my lord." She made her tone cool, determined to erase the memory of last night's bruising kiss and fiery touch. "You simply startled me. I'm not nearly as delicate as you seem to believe."

When he grimaced she suspected he was recalling his encounter with her knee. The thought did not displease her.

"Did you have a pleasant time with Audrey?" she asked after an awkward silence.

"Yes, she convinced me to buy her Christmas present early this year."

"How kind of you," Horatia replied, thinking back on her own gifts from him.

Every year Lucien bought her a book, which she secretly treasured with all her heart, despite her knowing he only did it not to show favoritism with Audrey. Her sister was everyone's favorite. Normally this didn't bother Horatia, but with Lucien it struck her deep in the chest. His hazel eyes were fixed on her now, as though he could read her thoughts.

"I bought your gift as well, but it shan't be ready for at least a few days. Madame Ella assured me it would be done in less than a week."

"Madame Ella?" Horatia's heartbeat skittered.

"I thought perhaps you would like a gown, since your other one was ruined."

"You bought me...a gown?" Her entire body tensed at the thought of wearing something he'd given her. It lit her blood on fire with excitement.

"Would you prefer to have another novel? I could cancel the order—"

"No!" Hope filled her so tightly she had trouble breathing. "A gown would be lovely. However, I hope you had the good sense not to tell my brother."

"Perish the thought." He flashed that all too appealing rakehell grin. "Your sister and I designed this confection especially for you this Christmas season and it would be a shame for it to go unworn."

Horatia bit her lip as excitement bubbled up within her. It was scandalous for him to buy her a gown, but she was secretly delighted. It meant he was thinking about her.

The coach pulled up in front of Sheridan House and

Lucien got out. He came around to her side of the coach and had the approaching footman assist Ursula down while Lucien helped Horatia down. Ursula and the footman disappeared inside, leaving Lucien and Horatia alone for a moment.

She offered her hand but he ignored it and moved forward to catch her by the waist, lowering her to the ground. Heat rushed through her in a violent wave as he let her slide down the length of his body. When he set her down, she raised her eyes to his face.

"The ice is fresh. I wouldn't want you to fall," he said.

A passing carriage's wheel dipped into a slushy puddle nearby, casting an icy spray. Lucien dragged Horatia into his embrace and shielded her from the splash with his body. He winced as the icy water soaked his clothes.

He was wet. Again. Why her own body shivered against his, she wasn't sure. Droplets of water dewed on his eyelashes and hung from the wet lock of hair that fell into his eyes. She stared at him, fascinated at the way the jewel-like drops clung to his dark, long lashes.

"Blast. I must have offended the gods of carriages in some past life." He gazed down at her, a wild wolf-like expression, both wintry and fierce filling his eyes. His passion could be her undoing if she let him. His lips were faintly blue and trembled. She ached to warm them with hers. A ridiculous notion, but damned if she didn't want to taste him again, just one...little...

"I should go," Lucien whispered.

"Stay."

"I shouldn't." His warm breath fanned her face and heated her blood.

"At least come in and have your coat dried by the fire."

I have only ever wanted to care for you, Lucien. Just let me care for you.

"Perhaps that is wise. I've no interest in getting a chill from wet clothes. Carriage gods be damned." Lucien made no move to step back from her as she turned, staying caged by him as they reached the door. His breath tickled her neck and she shivered from something other than the cold. The door swung open as the butler and a footman helped them both inside. A sigh escaped her as reality intruded on her once again and she was forced to step away from Lucien. Why did they always have to move apart?

ONCE INSIDE, Horatia took him to the morning room to warm up, but to their surprise the fire was unlit. Lucien peeled off his wet wool overcoat and looked at the cold fireplace with a raised eyebrow. For a moment she just stared at him. He glanced down, wondering what she was looking at. His shirt clung to his arms, highlighting his forearms and biceps. When he looked back to her, she'd gone wide-eyed and scarlet. Horatia hastily darted past him to the fireplace and pulled back the grate. He bit the inside of his lip to keep from grinning. She'd liked what she'd seen, he was sure of it.

A low and angry echoing sound announced either the presence of a ghost, or a cat up the chimney. "*Mreooooww.*"

"Muff!" Horatia got down on her hands and knees and peered up the chimney. "Come down right now!" She reached up into the sooty confines of the fireplace.

Horatia's backside was on full display to him as she tried in vain to coax down the stubborn feline. The icy chill he still felt dissipated beneath the heat that swept through him. How would her hips feel between his hands? How would his name sound as it was moaned from those lips? Lucien shook his head, trying to erase those images and, more importantly, discourage an enthusiastic response in his loins.

"Here, let me see if I can get him." Lucien knelt beside her. With the advantage of his longer arms, he could reach the crevice in which the renegade feline had lodged himself. "I see him. The question is whether I can reach him. You might want to shield your eyes, my sweet." The endearment fell off his lips without thinking. He reached up, grabbed the cat by the scruff of his neck and dragged him down. Lucien coughed as he dislodged a wave of soot and it rained down around him and Horatia. They both fell back out of the fireplace and onto the floor.

Muff hissed and lunged into Horatia's arms in his bid to flee. He dug his claws into her arms before propelling himself away, leaving a sooty trail of paw prints out of the drawing room. Horatia sneezed and tried to rise. Lucien caught her wrists but his hands came away bloody as he helped her to stand. Her forearms had been sliced by Muff's not-so-tender escape.

Horatia, covered in soot and clutching her bleeding arms, looked absolutely miserable. Something in Lucien's chest tightened. She was so brave; she hadn't made a squeak of pain. If it had been him he would have bellowed like a wounded bear. Not her though, not Horatia. She bit her bottom lip, blinked away the moisture in her eyes and all he wanted was to drag her into his arms and kiss her senseless.

"Come now, let's get that taken care of." He wrapped an arm about her shoulders and led her out into the hall and up the stairs to her bedchamber. He instructed a passing footman to bring warm water, some bandages and have the fire lit in Horatia's room, assuming the blasted cat hadn't gotten there first.

A few moments later, Cedric's housekeeper, a matronly woman with graying hair at the temples, entered the room carrying water and bandages.

"Here we are…" She winced at the sight of Horatia's injuries. "Oh my poor dear!"

"Thank you, Mrs. Stanwick. Could you bring us some hot tea?" Horatia asked.

The housekeeper's lips parted in surprise. "I shouldn't leave you alone…"

"It will only be for a minute. Leave the door open if

you must." Lucien's tone was less a suggestion and more a command.

"Very well, my lord, I'll be back shortly." Mrs. Stanwick set the bandages and hot water on the side table and went to fetch tea.

"You don't have to stay. I can see to it," Horatia said.

"Nonsense. I always took care of you when you were young, didn't I?" The words were out before he could take them back. The baffled look on her face, highlighted by her rounded eyes, made her seem so young. She was nothing like his usual women. He liked them fine-boned and full-figured. Horatia had ample curves and a lovely face, but she lacked that edge of cool passion that all of his conquests had.

Lucien pushed her to sit on her bed while he took the cloth towels from the footman. The footman started a fire while Lucien cleaned his hands of soot. The newly lit fire crackled and snapped over the logs. It warmed his back, putting him in a strangely gentle mood.

Her bottom lip shook a second before she opened her mouth.

"Shh…" He wetted a towel and cleaned Horatia's hands of the soot and wiped the dried blood away. After applying some salve to the cuts, he wound the bandages snugly around her arms. Then he then toweled off his face, as did Horatia. Lucien noticed she missed a few spots.

"What?" she asked when she caught him staring.

"Hold still." He captured her chin and tilted her head back.

Her knees broke apart, allowing him to step closer to her. He brushed the moist edge of his towel over the tip of her little upturned nose, resisting the sudden urge to kiss it. He wiped away a patch of soot, just above her collarbone. Horatia seemed to be holding her breath.

When he finished, he dropped the towel and placed his hands on her skin. He traced her bottom lip with the pad of his right thumb, feeling its fullness. Horatia's lips closed around his thumb as she kissed it. The warm wet caress of her tongue made his entire body tighten. Mesmerized, he pulled his thumb away and leaned down, closing the distance between her lips and his.

He coaxed her lips apart with an exploring tongue. Lucien's hands curled around her hips, holding her still as he pressed himself into the cradle of her body.

The barrier of their clothes didn't seem to matter. Horatia made a little sound of satisfaction as her tongue moved with his. For a brief moment he could forget she was innocent and everything he couldn't have. She was just another beautiful woman that he was going to reveal a new world of dark passions to. Her throaty purrs drove him to the edge. He slid his hands down her outer thighs, coiling up her skirts and petticoats, relishing the satiny skin beneath his fingertips.

Horatia gasped out and jerked back. Their mouths separated with a soft pop.

Reality crashed down. He stumbled back and tried to gather his wits.

Horatia blinked, her brown eyes warm and sleepy. Her pink tongue flitted out to lick her lips and he all but dragged her back into his arms.

She batted her lashes. "I'm sorry... You just startled me."

"No. It is better this way. We can't... This never happened. Do you hear me?"

"But..." Horatia touched her lips, her eyes drawn up to his face, unable to look away.

Lucien had to put distance between them, and not just physical. "Listen to me, Horatia. I'm a hot-blooded rake, I got carried away. You should not have encouraged me."

Her eyes flashed with barely hidden fire. "Encourage *you*? I did nothing of the sort."

"You licked your lips and gazed at me with longing. It makes a man unable to resist you. It was clear you desired a kiss and I felt compelled to oblige."

"You kissed me out of *pity*?" She looked torn between hurt and anger.

He hesitated, but only a moment. "Yes."

Horatia's voice shook and her eyes darkened with tears. "Pl...please leave."

"Happily." He left her room, slamming the door.

CAN'T that man ever shut my door normally?

Horatia buried her face in her pillows and took several deep breaths, but it did no good. She fought the urge to cry, but tears still ran down her cheeks. It was then that Mittens sauntered out from under the bed, jumped up and nestled against Horatia's stomach, purring.

There was something comforting about the animal's unconditional love. Only after stroking the cat's satiny fur did she finally calm down, but it was a long while before she could look rationally at the problem.

Over the years she'd heard whispers from maids and footmen about his sort. And of course, her brother's warnings always rang inside her head. *"Never trust men, Horatia. If someone asks to show you the garden at a ball, run and find me. You don't want to end up with someone like Lucien. They'll steal your innocence, break your heart and ruin any chance of a decent marriage. Word gets around and for us, reputation is everything."*

Lucien didn't want an innocent woman. He wanted a wild and wanton creature in his bed. If she were to ever catch his attention it would require something drastic. After today, she was positive that he had some small attraction to her. If she could just get close enough to him to make him act on it... But she couldn't get close to him. Most of the time he seemed to have enough sense to stay away from her. If only there was a way she could trick that stubborn marquess into seeing her as a woman, not his friend's sister.

Horatia's eyes fell to the open drawer of her vanity table. A silver loo mask lay in the drawer, a piece from a masquerade earlier that year. It spawned an idea. She needed to be someone else, the type of woman he would seek out.

But how to go about it? It would have to be in a location far away from her brother's watchful eye. Someplace dark, perhaps at night so she would have less of a chance of being seen. If she could interact with Lucien in a place where she could wear a mask, he might not know it was her. The risk was high that he would recognize her after talking to her, but if she had it her way there wouldn't be much talking.

All she needed was a chance to convince him that she was worthy of his attention. She wanted to be the seductress he made her feel like. Perhaps if she proved she was passionate, he would offer for her.

I'm such a peahen. The bitter thought struck her like a hard slap. Lucien wouldn't offer for her. He'd use her and then move on. Then again, he'd come close to marriage once. Why not once again? And a tiny voice in her head whispered that ruination at Lucien's hands would be worth it. Even if she spent the rest of her life as a lonely old spinster, one night with him outweighed a lifetime with someone she had no feelings for.

Forcing herself to focus on her idea, she evaluated her choices of clandestine meeting spots. This plan had all the earmarks of one of Audrey's schemes. Audrey! That was it. The moment her sister returned, Horatia would consult her. She wouldn't tell her what she intended to do, but she could solicit advice on how to bribe a footman from Lucien's household to divulge the Marquess's nightly activities and the places where he could be found.

For the first time in days, Horatia smiled with glee.

CHAPTER 5

$\mathcal{L}$ucien entered his townhouse on Half Moon Street in a rage, his jaw clenched and aching. Today had been a disaster. He'd let himself lose control, get too close, and he'd enjoyed every minute of it.

If it hadn't been for those warm brown eyes of hers, pleading for his kisses...

The door to the servants' quarters opened and his valet, Felix, emerged with a stack of freshly pressed white shirts in his arms.

"Felix, I'm going out tonight. Ready my things."

The valet nodded and hurried to Lucien's room. Lucien's hands twitched, feeling the urge to break something. He stormed into the drawing room and grabbed the first thing within reach, an expensive oriental vase. He arced his arm and—

"I say, Lucien, you all right?"

He spied his brother, Lawrence, a few feet behind him in the open doorway. Except for the fact he was five years younger, he was a mirror image of Lucien. Anger still boiling deep inside him like a dormant volcano, Lucien now aimed the vase at his meddlesome brother.

Lawrence stepped back, hands raised in surrender. "If you break that, mother will be most upset. She spent a fortune getting that back from Shanghai for you. To hear her tell it, she hired an entire caravan of elephants like Hannibal for part of the journey."

With a snarl, he set the vase back down on the cherry-wood side table and glowered at his smirking brother.

"I thought you were in France."

His brother gave a casual shrug. "I came back with Avery."

"Have you obtained lodgings?"

"Not as of yet."

"Then you must stay here," Lucien replied, but his heart wasn't in the gesture. He wasn't in the mood to entertain, not even his family. Was it so bad to want some peace and quiet to sort out the messy tangle of emotions that plagued him?

His brother flicked an invisible speck of dust off his coat sleeve. "I'm only here for a few days and I wouldn't dare to impose, especially since you seem to be having rather heated issues with your décor." Lawrence was well known for his sarcasm. Lucien had had words, and more than words with him over such remarks when they'd been younger.

"Just because we are no longer children doesn't mean I won't box your ears."

"You could try."

Lucien swung his fist good-naturedly at his brother, who danced back a step. They laughed, and Lucien found his anger deflated. God bless Lawrence.

"If you don't wish to stay the night, what brings you here?" Lucien asked. "I thought perhaps you'd go straight to mother." A terrible thought occurred to him. "She isn't here is she?"

Lucien half-expected the formidable Lady Rochester to explode out of a closet. His mother had on more than one occasion hidden herself to eavesdrop on her offspring, only to reveal her presence suddenly and scare the bloody hell out of her children. Linus, Lucien's youngest brother, refused to shut the closet doors in his bedchamber for that very reason.

She did so out of love of course. It was even a family joke. She'd been so besotted with their father that she'd insisted on naming every child with a name starting with L for love. Therefore they'd been named Lucien, Lawrence, Linus and Lysandra. Avery had been the only exception to their mother's naming scheme. He looked just like their father and so bore the same name as him. The other Russells favored their mother in looks.

"Mother's in Kent," Lawrence said. "She sent word to

you that she wanted to spend Christmas at home. Did you not get the letter?" Lawrence seemed genuinely surprised, since Lucien was the best of the Russell brood when it came to correspondence.

"I've been a bit preoccupied of late." It was an under-statement, a grand one at that. His study was littered with unopened letters, his mother's latest one no doubt among the clutter on his desk. Lucien stroked his jaw with his thumb and forefinger. "Does mother expect me to come visit her?"

"Lord, no. Not that she wouldn't mind, but I think she's happiest when left alone to torment Linus and Lysandra." Lawrence chuckled. "They're both with her now, God help them."

"What about Cambridge? Surely Linus has finished by now." A thread of guilt wound through his chest, knotting around his ribs. Had he been so consumed with his own affairs that he'd lost track of his siblings' lives?

Lawrence gave another shrug. "Only a short while ago."

"If you are leaving in a few days, you must dine with me tonight." Lucien's desire to be left alone had changed, and he hoped his brother would agree. Lawrence would be a welcome distraction and keep him from dwelling on hopeless desires.

Lawrence smiled deviously. "Actually, I have sched-uled an evening at the Midnight Garden. You are welcome to join me. Madame Chanson does miss your patronage."

The Midnight Garden was a discreet club, full of hidden scandals and romantic trysts. The most public secret in London. Madame Chanson tailored it to the needs of any individual, man or woman wealthy enough to pay for membership. She brought in the most beautiful ladies, hired only the most handsome men, and the decadence of the surroundings promised sinful pleasures of all kinds. She'd also acquired the good will and patronage of those necessary to keep it open.

Lucien had, until recently, been a frequent guest of the Garden. But since he had been thrown into Horatia Sheridan's life once more, and he'd not returned in search of pleasure. The one time he had ended in disappointment on all sides.

Perhaps that is what I need—a naughty tumble to erase the memory of Horatia from my mind. Lucien scraped a palm over his jaw before nodding. "I believe I shall. I've been too melancholy of late and my spirits need lifting."

His brother laughed. "As do other parts of you, I suspect."

Lucien ignored him. "What time is your engagement?"

"Nine o'clock. You'll need a mask. Madame Chanson is in a masquerade mood this month and she's requiring all her patrons to wear them. Rumor has it a delegation from Italy has arrived, and it's for their benefit."

Lucien frowned. Did he still have a mask? Surely he

did. He had gone to many of those parties at Vauxhall during the Season and a number of them had required masks.

"I'd best go find one." He started towards the stairs.

"I shall meet you at the Garden then, around nine," Lawrence called out.

"Felix!" Lucien called out.

The valet popped his head into Lucien's bedchamber. "My lord?"

"Change of plans. Set out my finest black breeches, black hessians and a black silk shirt. Also, do I still have a black domino mask?"

Felix's eyebrows rose. "Are we dressing you for a specific occasion, my lord? I was under the impression that abductions were not among your interests." The valet's eyes were cool, but Lucien caught the glimmer of amusement there.

Lucien sometimes forgot that what were considered secrets upstairs were sometimes common knowledge downstairs. No doubt he referred to Miss Emily Parr's adventure some months before.

"Abductions, when done properly, can turn out quite satisfactory. But fear not, Felix, tonight I'm off to the Garden. Madame Chanson requested all guests to wear masks."

"Ah. The Italians are back, no doubt. Well, you are in luck, my lord. I kept a nice half-face mask that you wore last year. It should look splendid with your chosen outfit this evening." Felix went to one of the dressers and dug through its contents until he found the mask. He set it down on a side table and slipped into the dressing room to fetch Lucien's evening clothes.

Lucien left his bedchamber for the small washroom where he had a tub. He pulled the bell cord to signal to the servants below that he wished to bathe. It would be a while before the bath was ready so he had a footman fetch some letters from his study to read.

Once ready he sunk low into the tub of hot water and let the tension ease out of him. Being around Horatia always wound him up into knots. He splashed his face and scrubbed at his skin, trying to remove the memory of her body against his. Soot still clung to his hair, and he washed it thoroughly as well, wanting nothing left to remind him of how close he'd come to losing his sanity.

The more time he spent around her the closer he came to acting on those base desires that would betray his principles, ruin her reputation and incite her brother's wrath. Yet the idea of coming to her and teaching her how to embrace her passions was too tempting. It was this that held the thrill for him.

He did not spend his days counting conquests like other men, but rather he prided himself on helping women conquer their own souls and bodies by accepting their needs and learning fulfillment in bed. Passion was a thing meant to be shared between a man and a woman, and he'd never liked the idea of a woman simply lying limp beneath him. Sex was a mutual exploration, a gift shared, not something stolen or taken by another. So while his reputation as a rake was forever assured, one would receive quite a different opinion about him from his women. To them he was a liberator, no matter how brief their time together.

After his bath, Felix helped him dress, and Lucien was out the door. A footman hailed a black cab so his presence would not be noted when he arrived. The Garden was not a place where the insignia of the Marquess of Rochester should be seen. Lucien kept his mask on, checking the ribbon as his hackney pulled up front of the stucco townhouse that was the facade for the Midnight Garden.

A footman hurried down to meet him and bowed his head respectfully. "My lord." The footman did not know his true identity, but all men and women in the Garden were greeted as lord and lady. If nothing else, it was good for business.

"Is Madame in?" Lucien asked the footman, following him up the steps. The young man nodded and opened the door for Lucien.

Day or night, the Midnight Garden was always dimly lit. It carried the ambience of a midnight rendezvous. Gilded wall sconces lined the entry way and halls splitting off to various rooms, of which there were at least twenty between the three floors. The walls were a deep burgundy with gold trim and the furniture was richly brocaded. Everything was selected to offer decadence and sensuality to the patrons who paid to enjoy their desires here.

For a good many years, Lucien had haunted these halls, seeking bedmates that would not fear him or his desires, and would trust him to master the pleasures of their bodies. Someday he hoped to find someone he could trust in return, but so far he had not. Since Emily Parr's abduction he'd been reluctant to return to his old habits. He wanted to find a connection between himself and his bedmate. The brief, wild couplings, or the slow pleasure of seducing a woman into being bound was not the same as savoring a woman he truly cared about. After his frustrating encounters with Horatia, however, he was desperate for relief.

Madame Chanson, a curvaceous woman in her late forties emerged from a nearby room with a woman Lucien recognized. Evangeline Mirabeau, the Duke of Essex's former mistress. Her eyes fixed on him, and he knew she recognized him as well. She gave him a cool nod. After her indirect help against a threat to Godric a few months ago, he had found a new, albeit limited appreciation for the French woman.

"My lord, you've returned! I had feared you would not, given that Lady Society has deemed you smitten and leaving your ways behind you. It gladdens my heart to see you return." Her voice was low and rich, a sultry voice that reminded him of his nights here. Her pale blond hair and gray eyes, which always seemed half-closed, made her appear as though she'd just woken up from a night of devilish bed sport.

"Madame Chanson, it is a pleasure to see you again. Do not believe everything you read. Lady Society is often wrong." He smiled at her and she winked. She had no trouble recognizing him with the mask on, his height and the rare color of his hair was a giveaway to those that knew him.

"You are in trouble with me, my lord." She teased him with an affection born of years of friendship. "I do not like that you have been absent so long."

"Perhaps later you might exact your punishment on me." He gave her his most rakish grin, one that made even the experienced Madame blush.

"Perhaps I shall," she replied. Madame Chanson never slept with the customers who came to her house, but she'd made an exception for Lucien. She'd all but begged him on more than one occasion, and he'd happily obliged.

Once a rake, always a rake.

"I heard that my brother has engaged a room this evening?"

"Oh yes, of course. Shall I escort you to his chamber?"

"Yes, thank you."

Lucien followed her down the corridor towards one of the finer rooms, one that had a terrace where a person could open the French windows to the gardens below.

Lawrence must have paid a great deal for the privilege. Madame Chanson rapped lightly on the door.

At the sound of Lawrence's muffled reply to enter, she opened the door. Lawrence was seated on a loveseat feeding grapes to a buxom young woman. Both were wearing masks.

"Brother," Lawrence said.

"Brother," Lucien replied in amusement.

The young woman straightened in Lawrence's arms. "My lord." The young woman greeted him with sly smile.

Lawrence chuckled. "Feel free to join us." He cupped the woman's right breast with a smile and she gasped in mock shock. "There are plenty of grapes."

Lucien turned to Madame Chanson. "Do you have anyone new who might interest me?"

She hesitated a moment. "Why yes...a young lady came here tonight, not half an hour earlier. A Lady of Quality, one might say. I offered her the services of my best men, but she wished for me to arrange a rendezvous with a man of equal social status. I told her there were several such gentlemen visiting the house, and if I could arrange it, she would spend the night with one of them. I did not mention names, but I did hint that you would be arriving soon. She seemed greatly interested when I described you. I know I should not have presumed to offer your company to her, my lord..."

Intriguing. It wasn't unheard of for married women to seek out pleasures when their own marriage beds grew cold. He had little interest in a jaded woman tonight. A young lady of quality though…one who was new to the atmosphere of the Garden was certainly of interest to him. "An innocent?"

Madame Chanson nodded. "I believe so. She hides it well, but I see the innocence in her eyes. I know such women aren't to your usual taste…"

Ordinarily the Madame would have been right. Innocent women had never been of interest before, and there was always the risk of them reading too much into their first encounter. But the masks meant this woman knew what she was seeking, and that put his mind at ease. He wanted someone soft and sweet, someone who reminded him of what he was denied. He could close his eyes and see Horatia, feel her body beneath his…

"I'm feeling adventurous, Madame. Please send her to me. Do not tell her my name."

"Of course." Madame Chanson curtseyed and swept out the door in a swish of purple silk.

Lawrence had resumed feeding grapes to his companion. Lucien removed his coat and waistcoat, flinging them over the nearest chair before reaching for the decanter of brandy on a side table. He had no problem being in the same room with his younger brother while the man seduced his current plaything. Lucien was even open to sharing, but tonight he needed a drink and his own woman. There was nothing more relaxing than to have a woman to hold and kiss when one's frustrations had been out of control. Unlike others, Lucien didn't take out his temper with boxing or drinking. He preferred a good woman and a sturdy bed. He often felt the world would be a better place if more men agreed.

There was a knock on the door.

"Enter."

When it opened, Lucien almost dropped his brandy. The young woman in the doorway wore a silver mask, but even at this distance he recognized her.

Horatia.

He'd spent too many nights picturing her seduction to forget even one inch of her form. He was relieved his mask concealed his identity.

What on earth was the silly creature doing here? It was full of wolves who'd pounce on her, just like he wanted to...

Madame Chanson's words came back to him. The young lady was interested in him when he'd been described to her. Had she come here, looking for a man like him to satisfy her own frustrated desires? Or had she been even more clever and discovered he was coming here tonight? Lucien found himself grinning. No matter her reasons, Lucien was going to show her just how foolish she was. He would make her regret this decision, and he would enjoy embarrassing her in the process.

Her evening gown of shimmering white silk had an over dress of silver netting. The bodice, cut low in a wide U, was made in a gauzy georgette that was pleated and tucked. The gown had short sleeves of the same fabric that seemed to increase the effect of her décolleté. The skirt, a silk in the same color, began just under her breasts. Though slightly pleated it skimmed her figure as she moved. In short, she was an utter vision and his body responded. She turned when the door shut behind her, startled, displaying the low neckline on the back of her gown.

"Please, come in," he purred, coming to her and taking her by the arm.

She gazed up at him, and he saw the flicker of recognition in her brown eyes beneath her silver mask. She knew it was him. Lucien glanced over at his brother who was far too occupied with his own woman to recognize Lucien's prey.

"I believe I may have been directed to the wrong room," she said, her chest rising and falling as she attempted to pull free of his hold.

Lucien tugged her up against the length of his body. "Nonsense, my little dove. Come, sit with me." Lucien pulled her onto his lap in the nearest chair. She all but squeaked in terror.

This shall be so much fun. He pulled her tight to his body, letting her feel every inch of his body that touched hers. She was rigid in his arms, but he'd soon change that.

"Frightened?" he asked in a low whisper only she could hear.

To his surprise, she gave a jerky little nod. "A little."

He couldn't resist smiling. "Sometimes a little fear with someone you trust can be a good thing."

Before she could argue, he tipped her chin up with one finger, exposing her neck with his touch. She swallowed hard, and he could see the pulse beating in her throat just as he bent his head and covered her neck with slow, soft kisses.

Horatia could barely breathe, let alone think. No doubt because her plan had worked and yet completely backfired at the same time. An hour ago, she had located the mysterious Midnight Garden. It cost her a pretty penny to pay one of Lucien's footman to tell her where the Garden was and learn that he would be there this evening. She'd arrived by hackney and paid Madame Chanson to secure her place as Lucien's chosen lady for the evening. She'd had to explain to Madame Chanson that her desire was only to spend the evening with Lucien. The Midnight Garden's owner had eyed her shrewdly and assured her that she would be with Lucien this night and no other. That had given Horatia some sense of calm.

She'd had the foresight not to give away her identity to the Madame, but she had not thought beyond that. Having no experience, Horatia was quite unprepared for Lucien's maddeningly quick seduction. She found herself on Lucien's lap, mere feet from his brother Lawrence, who she easily recognized despite his mask, as he entertained another woman.

"Why so tense, my dove?" Lucien's large hands massaged her shoulders, pleasure emanating from the force of his fingers rubbing her tight muscles. Horatia felt the heavy temptation to relax into that touch, to melt into him. It would be so simple to surrender. It was what she wanted after all.

"Are you scaring her, Lucien?" Lawrence teased between mouthfuls of grapes.

"Perhaps I am." Lucien cupped Horatia's chin, keeping her gaze level with his. "Are you still frightened?"

Despite the seriousness of his question there was a lift in the corners of his mouth that told Horatia he was barely containing his laughter.

"I am not used to having an audience, my lord," she managed to say, casting a nervous glance in Lawrence's direction. A treacherous blush rose in her face, only half-hidden by her silver mask.

Lawrence sat up a little straighter before leaning in their direction. "Tell me, brother, how on earth do you manage to bed the most naively charming women? She blushes like a bride!" He lost interest in his own woman and pushed her away when she leaned against him possessively.

Lucien's fingers slid down Horatia's back and dug into her hips, holding her still over his lap as he studied her.

"Would you prefer my brother to me? I daresay he would take you if you find me too frightening." Lucien's voice was like melted chocolate and just as sinful. Horatia looked between the two men, so alike in their black clothes, masks and dark red hair.

"I would prefer you, and you alone, my lord," Horatia

said. She saw the gleam of triumph in his eyes and wanted to slap him for his presumption.

Lucien clamped a firm hand around the back of her neck and urged her forward to meet his lips. He rewarded her with a deep thrust of his tongue, playing with hers in a sensual, suggestive rhythm that had her panting for breath when his lips moved to her neck and down towards her collarbone.

"Do you have another room, brother? Or must I convince you to take a turn in the gardens with your lady?" Lucien seemed to have no qualms about turning his younger brother out.

Lawrence inclined his head to the right towards a gilded door. "There's a bedchamber through that door."

Without looking at his brother, Lucien continued to explore the sloping indentations of Horatia's neck and collarbone with his lips and tongue. "Then take your woman and go there."

With a sigh Lawrence got to his feet and tugged his companion up to follow.

"Leave the grapes," Lucien added as Lawrence reached for the plate of fruit, leaving him to complain about whose money had paid for the room in the first place.

Horatia shifted restlessly as he returned to torturing her with his mouth. Her hands settled on his broad shoulders as she watched Lawrence and his woman leave the room and shut the door behind them.

"Now, shall we get comfortable?" Lucien slid her off

his lap, leaving her in the chair while he stood before her, legs braced apart as he removed his shirt and tossed it aside. When his hands fell to the fastenings of his breeches, Horatia's heart leapt into her throat. He smiled and reached out to hold her chin, tilting her head back to look up at him again.

"There's that charming blush. I find it lovely, but I wonder...do you blush from modesty or inexperience? Surely you suffer from neither of these, in your line of work?"

How *dare* he? Lucien knew full well her story was that she'd asked for someone of equal social status and here he was accusing her of... Horatia shot to her feet, unfortunately bringing herself closer to him than was wise. Any response she might have made was silenced by Lucien's mouth on hers. He caught her wrists, twisted them behind her body to hold them captive against the small of her back. He freed one hand to smooth down the silver netting of her gown over the swell of her bottom and then pulled her sharply against him.

"Feel how much I want you?" he murmured against her.

The better question, Horatia decided, was how could she *not* feel him? The bulge of him against her pelvis made her body respond with a sharp ache between her legs. Lucien released her and moved over to the loveseat his brother had vacated. He lifted up the plate of grapes and sat.

"Join me," he said, patting the empty space next to him.

"But," she began. She was regretting her brazen plan more with each passing minute. Surely there was a more rational way to get him to come around to liking her. Then again, perhaps not.

"Now." His command was not sharp, but did promise punishment if she refused him.

She darted onto the love seat, smoothing her gown with fidgeting hands. The gown's bodice clung to her breasts, making it harder to breathe. She'd had it made a few years ago, before her figure had filled out. It was the only dress she knew Lucien had never seen on her. Horatia had never been so aware of her body as she was now. The bodice clutched her breasts, her nipples rubbed against the fabric and the juncture between her thighs felt damp and tingly. He scowled at the obvious distance between them.

"Closer," he growled.

She shuffled over.

He didn't seem satisfied however until she'd come so close that her left hip was pressed snugly against his right. He wound an arm about her waist, jerking her even closer before releasing her. The warmth of his bare skin was impossibly delicious against the thin silk of her gown. The muscles of his bare chest were sharp and angular, carved and beautiful, like corded ropes of steel bound by a soft layer of skin.

"Do you like what you see?" Lucien teased.

Horatia was not sure if it was safe to answer that. Her gaze wandered over his body, imagining how it would feel to be in his arms again. She licked her lips, noticing his eyes fix on her tongue. He took a grape from the plate and slipped it into his mouth, then held up a second piece to hers. Horatia just blinked, unnerved by such an intimacy as being fed by him.

"Open for me," he coaxed.

His voice made her insides burn. It held an entirely different meaning than offering her mouth up to take a grape.

He had no idea who she was, and he was seducing her like a normal woman, not someone he avoided. She would risk her virtue if only to let Lucien rob her of her sanity with his passion. Foolish as her actions were, her need for him was far greater.

She took the grape from his fingers with her lips, moaning at the sweet flavor. But she barely had time to swallow before Lucien leaned forward and captured her mouth with his. The kiss began sweet, soft, teasing, but the sugary taste went straight to her head. A little noise of pleasure escaped her.

The plate of grapes toppled to the floor. Lucien gripped her hips and tugged her down to lie beneath him on the settee. With one expert hand, he rucked up her skirts and pushed her knees apart so he could slide into the welcoming cradle of her thighs. One of his palms stroked the outside of her leg, playing with the ribbons on her stocking. He deepened the kiss, covering her body with his and grinding his hips against hers in a slow rhythm. His tongue met with no resistance when it slipped between her lips. He tasted like an intoxicating glass of sherry on an empty stomach. But the couch was far too narrow for what their melding bodies needed.

Horatia laughed as Lucien tried to get his body better situated and almost fell off. He grinned and pressed himself down hard against her, once more trying to assert dominance over her. This time his one knee did slip off, causing him to roll to the ground.

"Blast it! We need a bed," he growled.

He ripped himself away from her then tugged her up onto her feet. The moment her body was free of his weight, some semblance of sanity returned, and Horatia fought his dominating grip on her body.

"Don't fly off yet, little dove." He purred like a cat luring a plump sparrow too close to the ground. "I've not had enough of your taste."

Horatia stumbled back but was saved by Lucien's firm grip on her wrist as he dragged her to the nearby bed.

"Lie down," he said, pointing.

Horatia balked, her feet tripping beneath her as she stepped back. "What?"

Lucien's response was to take her and put her there himself. She was still reeling from the shock of him tossing her onto the bed when he pulled out several long strips of red silk from his pocket. He caught her right hand and quickly anchored it to the bedpost. Horatia struggled to free herself but it wouldn't budge. Lucien tugged her other wrist towards the far bedpost and secured it as well.

Horatia had only enough slack in her bonds to strain a few inches off the bed. Panic set in, her breathing rapid and shallow. What was he planning? Should she tell him who she was? He would surely stop if he knew, and then she'd be safe. Unloved, but safe. It was almost as if he could read her thoughts as he laid his palm on her cheek and turned her face towards him.

"Do you trust me?" His eyes were dark and his voice rough, but in that moment she was spellbound. "I need your complete trust. I will bring you only pleasure, no pain." His face held passion but beneath that was nothing but a desperate need for her to trust him. And she did.

Still, Horatia's quick breaths would not ease. She struggled to stay focused on his face and not the fact that she was bound to a bed. Never before had she felt so helpless, so exposed. It was a risk like no other, to trust him now, like this.

"If I trust you, will you take care of me? I haven't..." She couldn't finish that sentence.

Understanding softened the intensity of the eyes behind his mask. "I promise you will be cared for. If anything hurts, tell me at once. Do you understand?"

"Yes, my lord." How desperately she longed to breathe

his name but she couldn't reveal herself and ruin the magic of this night.

"When we are done tonight, you will be well educated in the ways of passion," Lucien assured her, and with that he moved forward to undress her.

CHAPTER 6

*L*ucien began with her silver slippers, sliding them off and setting them on the floor. His palms slid up the length of her calves and along her thighs to unfasten her stockings and unhook her garters. He removed her stockings with ease and kissed the sensitive skin behind each ankle. He could feel every tremble, every shiver as his hands explored her body.

He forced himself to focus solely on Horatia and not his own arousal. Her pleasure had to come before his because he could not have her fully. He would push her to her limits, but he would not take her innocence. Not in the way that mattered for dowries and weddings at any rate.

Kneeling between her parted legs, he coaxed her to bend her knees up and widen. He needed to have her open for his tasting. He slowly slid his hands under her gown up to her hips and assessed her undergarments. Usually women in the Garden did not bother with much in the way of underclothes, but Horatia had enough petticoats on underneath to decorate a castle's battlements.

"A little overdressed for the occasion, aren't we?"

Horatia blushed. "I'm wearing what a proper lady should…"

"A proper lady? I have no interest in that. Not tonight, my dear. These petticoats must go." He slid off the bed and retrieved the small paring knife from the loveseat and returned to her. Her eyes widened and her chest began to rise and fall with frightened breaths. Her gaze narrowed in on the knife.

"Are you…" she began.

"I'm not going to hurt you. I don't wish to remove your gown, so I am going to cut the petticoats open." He brushed a hand along her waist. With quick precision, he split her petticoats up the middle until they fell open onto either side, but he didn't remove them. He dug his hands into the fabric and ripped them a little higher. Finally she was bare to his gaze, her gown pooling around her hips in a shimmering haze.

Lucien settled his hands at the top of her raised knees, gazing down at her sex. She was wet, swollen, and perfect. He enjoyed looking upon a woman's body, but never had there been such a strange sense of euphoria accompanying it. It made him hurt deep in his chest, to know she wanted him like this. This was perhaps the only time he could be with her, and he would savor every moment of pleasure he intended to give her, no matter how it agonized him later.

He began a slow trail of kisses along her inner left thigh. Her breasts jerked up against her bodice. He almost smiled, enjoying the jolt of panic he'd caused. She knew he wouldn't hurt her, yet she was excited and anxious as to what he might do. That was where the pleasure in bondage lay. He could do wonderful things to her and she had to accept it, couldn't rush it or demand it, merely accept it as it came. Though begging was always welcomed.

"What are you doing?" The bravado of her question weakened against the trembling of her voice.

"Why, you surprise me! Have you never been tasted?" He knew the answer full well, but he enjoyed the game of ignorance they played.

"T-tasted?" She jerked beneath his grasp, trying to dislodge his hands now holding her spread open beneath him.

In answer, he flicked out his tongue against the sensitive skin mere inches from her core. She trembled and tried again to push him away, but his shoulders were level with her knees, stopping her.

"But you can't!"

He used his hands to open her folds and took his first sweet lick. A strangled cry of shock ripped from Horatia and her head flung back. Her hands fisted in the sheets at the corners of the bed. Lucien licked again, swirled his tongue, her taste like a drug to his senses. The pain in his loins only intensified with the sensual moan of encouragement from Horatia.

"Again?" he asked, his warm breath teasing her inner thigh.

"Yes." Her hesitant reply was tinged with a need neither could deny.

He bent his head again, this time determined not to stop for any reason. He began to lick her, tonguing her sensitive spots, sucking on the swollen bundle of nerves until Horatia was shifting restlessly beneath him.

"I feel…I feel unwell," she said.

Startled, Lucien paused and looked up. Her eyes were closed and the silver sparkles of her mask glinted like a smattering of stars across her nose and cheeks as she panted for breath. A woman undone and on the verge of ecstasy. Never had he seen anything more beautiful.

"Does it hurt?" he asked, concerned.

"There's a…tightness in my stomach. It feels as though my heartbeat is there and not in my chest," she confessed.

She was so innocent she did not even recognize the arousal she felt.

"That's not sickness, my dear, but desire. It will not make you unwell. Be brave and I will show you how wonderful it can be." Lucien felt her muscles go taut beneath his hands.

He would have to coax her into relaxing. He slid up her body, settled his hips into the cradle of her legs and kissed his way up from the swell of her breasts to her mouth. After a deep, rich kiss she melted again, once more languid in his arms.

"There now. Feeling better?" He breathed in her ear as he licked it and then nipped the lobe softly.

"Yes," she admitted, her hips rising into his.

"Good girl." Lucien slid one finger deep into her wetness. She tensed again.

"Relax." He distracted her with the play of his tongue in her mouth and began a gentle rhythm with his finger. She settled into it beautifully. Her tongue became more demanding and he smiled against her lips while working a second finger into her tight sheath. Her hips tilted in response and her back arched, pressing her body tighter to his. Lucien increased his rhythm, enjoying Horatia's quickening breath as she began that delicious climb towards satisfaction.

THE HEAVY AND sharp ache in Horatia's womb built all over again. She was dying, her body burning, exploding, building up to a terrifying moment. She was climbing higher, her breath faint, her heart racing, her vision spinning out of control. She couldn't remember who or where she was. The only thing that kept her grounded was the red-haired devil on top of her. The fallen angel with the black mask who seduced her into delicious sin.

"So close. I can feel you trying to hold me inside you." He bit down on the skin between her shoulder and neck. His fingers plunged into her, faster, harder, unforgiving in their pace. It was more than Horatia could bear. Her last shreds of control slipped away and she cried out as she fell off a cliff and into nothing but a weightless sensation. Pure thrill. Why couldn't she hold Lucien, cling to him, to save herself by anchoring her life on those broad shoulders above her? Instead she was perishing beneath him. But maybe that was his intent all along. She was dying in splashes of pain and pleasure as a tingling heat spread through her wilting body.

FOR A BRIEF MOMENT Lucien almost believed he'd killed the woman with pleasure. Horatia had shaken so violently, had cried out so loudly, he'd regretted every action that led to it. He'd seen the fear in her soft brown eyes, yet he'd felt no rush of pleasure at having caused it. Instead, he'd been too frantic to free himself from his pants and sate his own aching pleasure with his free hand.

He shouted something unintelligible as he came and had to fight with all his might not to collapse on top of her as she finished coming. Somewhere along their journey he'd bitten her neck, the reddening bruise evidence of his possession. It sent a wave of primal pride through him, quickly replaced with worry as Horatia's eyelashes fluttered open. Their chocolate depths were hazy with the aftermath of their passion.

"I'm not dead?"

He tried to stifle a laugh before he kissed her quivering lips. Never before had he kissed to ease a woman's fears. He'd never had to. All of the women he'd been with before had been unafraid of him and were willing to explore their passions. Horatia was so new to this side of herself and to lovemaking that it must have frightened her. He didn't want her to be afraid, only excited. It was strange to yearn so deeply to please her, to comfort her, yet it felt so right. He could no sooner deny that the sun rose in the east than he could deny Horatia the comfort she so desperately needed after her first climax.

"Perhaps a little. The French call that *la petite mort* for a reason. But I assure you, you are very much alive," he said between comforting kisses.

Horatia let out a long sigh of relief rather than contentment. She looked like she had a thousand questions to ask him but not one made it past her lips.

"Still feeling unwell?" he asked after he'd removed his hand from between her legs and fixed his breeches.

"No. Quite the opposite in fact."

Lucien almost smiled but instead he reached around her to unfasten her hands from the bedposts, suddenly worried she might have hurt herself in her struggles. He checked her wrists, searching for bruises, but there weren't any.

An odd flutter blossomed within him. She had been the first woman to truly trust him like this, to surrender her body to his full control. The one woman he could never possess was the first woman he'd ever felt uninhibited with, completely and totally free with. Others had agreed to be bound, but none had reacted as Horatia had, as though the surrender to him was an act of pleasure for her as well. Her need to trust, his need to be trusted. She was a perfect match to him. Fate was a cruel and punishing mistress, Lucien decided.

"Did you find pleasure too?" The silver half-mask did little to hide the red blush over her face.

"Yes," he answered, offering her a smile.

She took stock of her destroyed petticoats bunched above her waist and raised her eyes to his.

"What am I supposed to do? I can't very well leave here with them like this." The torn under clothes hung loose and visible from beneath her gown.

Lucien studied her gown and then waved at her legs. "Lift your skirts, quickly, love. I'm going to cut as much of them off of you as I can to free up your skirts."

Horatia gripped her gown and hoisted it up as Lucien grabbed the knife, taking care to cut away parts of the ruined petticoats that hung too low. It was a messy fix, but surely she wouldn't be seen by anyone who would recognize her.

Once finished, he set the knife down and caught her hand.

"Care to take a stroll in the gardens? I know it may be cold, but I promise to keep you warm." Lucien didn't know why he was offering. It was far too romantic and would send the wrong message. He'd done what he'd meant to do, but in the hopes it would scare her away from him. Instead, she was *glowing*—damn her!

HORATIA PULLED her stockings back on and then her slippers while Lucien dressed. They proceeded out through the terrace door, stepping over patches of snow that had settled in clumps along the cobblestone walkway. Above them, the night sky was clear of clouds and the luminescent stars glittered. It never ceased to amaze Horatia how beautiful the sky was in winter. In the summer, one could see the countless stars, but the glow was fickle and undefined. Winter stars burned with a crystalline sharpness in the thick velvet sky. They reminded her of herself, stalwart in the light of eternal solitude. Horatia was pulled from her inner musings when she realized Lucien's attention was fixed upon her.

"Do you like the stars?" he asked, twining a lazy arm about her hips and tucking her into his side. She blushed.

The simple gesture sent ripples of pleasure through her. At that moment being with him seemed so unlike her tortured dreams or the harsh reality of their strained relationship. His black mask melded with the night sky so well that only his hazel eyes and his seductive smile shone through the darkness.

"I adore the stars in winter. They seem brighter somehow. Stronger, yet so very alone." She traced the constellations above in her mind.

"Have you ever studied them?" he asked, his gaze flicking from her to the heavens above.

"Oh yes. Astronomy is one of my guilty pleasures. Aud...that is to say, my little sister often made me feel quite silly for loving them, but she doesn't understand. Studying the stars is like studying the expanse of forever. I feel that when I look at the sky I am gazing into the mirror of creation and seeing the divine patterns that were formed long before I existed, and will continue to exist long after I am gone. It is humbling."

"But beautiful." Lucien's tone was so smooth that she shivered. Did he understand what she meant? Too often she'd been told by irritated suitors she tended to converse philosophically. It was perhaps why she'd been relegated to the shelf on the Marriage Mart, but she didn't care. Such opinions didn't matter, and those who held them were not worth her interest.

He grinned rakishly. "Would you be willing to tutor me, oh lovely stargazer?"

She returned his grin with a teasing smile. "I thought I was your little dove?"

He tugged her towards him so that her back was pressed against his chest. He nuzzled her neck, his lips dancing against her skin.

"You've quite surprised me tonight. I had not expected a scholarly philosopher. I find I like the depth of your mind. A change in your term of endearment was certainly required. Henceforth, you are my lovely stargazer."

"A bit romantic, but I shan't complain." She turned her head back towards his, letting him steal a deep kiss before she added, "Shan't complain at all."

She knew she was entirely a romantic creature. Lucien had helped make her so through those novels he gave her every Christmas. Each one was a love story.

"Well then, guide me through the heavens."

Horatia reached up a hand to point to the sky. "Do you see the trio of stars in a row?" She pointed just over the city's rooftops. "Just there?"

"Yes," he whispered, his breath warming her neck.

"That is Orion's belt. And the far northeastern star is his sword."

"Beautiful," he replied. She turned herself around in his arms to agree with him, but her nose brushed against his. He wasn't looking at the stars at all.

"You, my lord, are not looking."

"I am. I see the stars in your eyes."

The words were too wonderful, too perfect. Horatia, starved for his love, drank them in, knowing how foolish she was to do so. She'd waited half of her life for Lucien to see her as a woman, and even if he thought her to be a high paid doxy, it didn't matter. She could pretend he knew the truth, that he knew it was her. His arms tightened about her waist as she moved towards him for a kiss. Horatia was ready to indulge in her new guilty pleasure, Lucien's lips, but a pair of voices nearby startled her.

"Did you hear that?"

"Hear what?" Lucien's mouth grazed her neck, distracting her as they dragged along her silky skin.

She elbowed him as the faint cold breeze in the garden carried the echo of the voices again. "That!"

Lucien stilled against her back. "I recognize one of the voices. Come this way. Do not make a sound." He took her hand and led her through the maze of hedges until they were much closer to those speaking. Horatia did not recognize either man but their words cut her to the bone.

"I expect the Sheridan problem to be dealt with in a timely fashion." The man's voice was refined, but cold.

Dealt with? Horatia's mouth opened but Lucien clamped a hand over her lips.

"Aye sir, of course," the other man said, as though they were discussing a routine chore. "Everything is arranged, all that's lacking is opportunity. That requires patience. Fortunately, I have no lack of that commodity."

"Good. I appreciate a man who understands these things. There must be no mistakes. I have a bank draft here for the first part owed to you."

The second man growled low. "I told you no bank drafts. Coin only. My business cannot be traced back to either of us."

"I assure you this is not from that kind of account." The gentleman huffed as it became clear that was besides the point. "Very well. I see caution is also something you don't lack. I don't have enough in coin on me tonight. Let us meet back here tomorrow morning; the garden will be empty of tonight's visitors and no one will have arrived for the evening's activities that early."

"I shall be waiting. And the rest of the payment?"

"Not a penny until the conditions are met, and there is dirt falling upon a grave."

CHAPTER 7

*A*udrey Sheridan was alone with Lord Lonsdale at last. Lady Lonsdale, Charles's mother, had turned in for the evening, thinking Audrey had already returned home. But Audrey had returned under the guise of forgetting a glove, and she'd beseeched Charles to let her stay a while longer. It gave her more time to accomplish her mission. Namely, becoming compromised so that she might finally be married. It was a risk however, because she had no real interest in Charles.

She wished to marry Jonathan, the Duke of Essex's younger half-brother. But since finding a moment alone with him was next to impossible she had to settle on a more cunning strategy. If she managed to get Charles to compromise her, then she might convince her brother that she must marry soon. He'd never let her marry

Charles, of that she was certain. Her plan was to persuade him Jonathan was a safer choice.

Audrey had even spoken to Emily about her plan, hoping she would know how to help. She was quite knowledgeable when it came to outwitting her brother and his dashing League of Rogues. But Emily had warned her it carried too much uncertainty and risk, and asked her to wait. She planned to bring up the subject with their mutual friend Ashton, believing him to have the best chance of reasoning with Cedric.

However, Audrey was not a patient person. Horatia had inherited that trait, and Audrey envied her for it. No man ever coddled her or treated her like a babe still clinging to her mother's skirts. Men treated Horatia with respect. If Audrey could get married, then perhaps people would have to take her seriously as well.

"Did you find what you were looking for?" Charles's rich voice broke through her determined thoughts as he sat down next to her on the couch.

"Yes. I dropped my glove near the couch." They were settled in Charles's drawing room, completely alone. He hadn't even been suspicious when she'd asked to stay a while longer after finding her "missing" glove. The time had come for her to reveal her hand and see what level of mischief she could achieve.

Charles lounged on the red velvet cushions, his golden hair tousled as though he'd just woken from a pleasant nap. Audrey felt her pulse leap, though more with excitement and guilt than attraction. But she was a Sheridan. She took pleasure in the thrill of the game. This was no exception.

Audrey rose from her chair, and smoothed her rose-colored muslin gown, trying to keep her hands from shaking. She knew she looked fetching tonight. She prayed it was enough to seduce Charles. Her russet brown hair hung loose in a Grecian fashion, wound with periwinkle blue ribbons. Despite her efforts, her hands continued to shake as she approached the loveseat. He looked at her curiously.

"What's wrong, love? You've been awfully quiet this evening. You haven't even tried to tell me about the latest fashions from Paris."

Audrey held in a sigh. She was about to make him very angry, and she was already regretting it.

"Surely *you* don't care what styles of gown are most in fashion?" She wrinkled her nose as she slid into the seat next to him and gave him a coy smile.

Charles chuckled, but it was a hesitant sound, as though he'd sensed something had changed. "Right, er, well, it was good to see Avery again, wasn't it?"

Charles swallowed hard when Audrey moved several inches closer. He put his right hand down, as though hoping it would act as a barrier between their bodies. Audrey glanced down at it, then brushed a fingertip along the back of his hand in a sensual pattern. He jumped and yanked his hand back.

"Audrey," he warned when she scooted over the last few inches, now pressed right against him. She could feel the heat of his body radiating from his dark blue waistcoat and tan breeches.

"Shh, my love. Not another word." She leaned into his body, lips puckered.

Charles went rigid, then thrust out his hands, as though trying to ward off an evil spirit. His eyes were alight with panic and Audrey giggled, guiltily, enjoying the look of terror on the rake's face. This was the infamous scoundrel Charles Humphrey, the Earl of Lonsdale, and he was frightened of *her*? She ducked under his arms and hopped onto his lap, twining her arms about his neck.

He squawked like a startled goose and fell off the love seat. Audrey, with a death grip on his neck, fell flat on top of him. He grunted beneath her and tried to shake her off.

"Kiss me, Charles." Audrey captured his surprised mouth.

His struggling slowed. Audrey didn't know the first thing about kissing, but it didn't seem to be as romantic as she'd expected. Charles lay closed lipped beneath her, gray eyes glaring up at her. She blinked, released his lips and moved back a few inches.

"Are you quite done accosting me?" he asked.

Audrey frowned and forced her lips over his again, but still he refused to cooperate. She sighed, sat up and scowled. "You're supposed to at least kiss me back. I have no idea if I've done enough to be properly compromised." Audrey crossed her arms over her chest.

Charles leapt up so fast that Audrey toppled off his lap. He scrambled to his feet and moved behind the loveseat, as though the furniture would barricade him from her. She suspected this was the first time in his life he was the one trying to avoid unwanted advances.

"Properly compromised?" he snapped. "Audrey, what in God's name are you playing at?"

"I want to be married. I want to be happy. That's what I'm thinking." She smoothed her skirts and climbed back onto the love seat. He stumbled as he beat a hasty retreat from her outstretched arms. He bolted for the door, but Audrey was fleet of foot and threw herself at the door just as it opened, slamming herself against him and the door at the same time.

Charles stared down at her, blinking rapidly. "Have you taken leave of your senses, woman?"

"Certainly not! I know exactly what I'm doing." She tip-toed her fingers up his chest and he frantically, almost girlishly, swatted her hand away as though it were a fly he was trying to swat off.

"Audrey…you do not want to do this." He suddenly picked her up by the waist and bodily set her aside so he could beat a hasty retreat away from her.

"Get back here!" she said and dove for him.

He spun, trying to avoid her, and tripped over the arm

of a couch. With a little *oomph!* he landed on his back on the couch and she climbed onto him. "Now touch me. That's what you're supposed to do next."

"Good God, Audrey! You are a genteel lady! You should not be doing this!"

"If it will get me married, I will do whatever I must!" She tried to lean down and kiss him.

"I'm certainly not going to marry you. It's out of the question. Your brother—"

She giggled. "Oh I have no interest in marrying *you*. That would be ridiculous."

Charles ignored the barb to his honor. "Then why try to seduce me?"

"Because when I tell Cedric you compromised me, he'll see sense and let me marry."

"After he shoots me!"

"Oh it wouldn't come to that. At that point he'll just be relieved I've settled down with someone other than you."

"First you try to seduce me, then you tell me I'm not a marriageable option, then you suggest that anyone is a better option? You are not exactly winning my support, Audrey."

"Honestly! Charles, we both know your reputation and… What are you doing?" He caught her by the upper arms and in a quick move, flipped her beneath him on the couch.

"I ought to teach you a lesson," he growled. "If I'm not an option, then what is all of this nonsense about?" He pinned her against the cushions and he leaned over her, glaring.

"You're the last person Cedric would let me marry. He knows your reputation better than anyone. I will be able to suggest someone preferable, and he'll agree so I won't have to marry you."

"You're forgetting one detail. Your brother is one of my closest friends. He might believe me when I say you were the one seducing me." His hands on her arms were tight, but he didn't hurt her.

"He would never believe that *I* tried to kiss you," Audrey replied haughtily. "I'm the darling innocent child. You're the seasoned rake."

"You are too clever for your own damn good," Charles said darkly. "But I remind you—your brother would shoot me dead. Is that what you want?"

"A bluff. He would never shoot his friend," she insisted. "He just says that to scare away the weak and unworthy, like a test set up by a Greek god. The problem is, like those gods he makes them all but impossible to pass."

"If that is what you truly believe, then you really are a child. Your brother wouldn't hesitate to kill me if he thought I'd touched you inappropriately."

Surely Charles wasn't serious. Cedric would never do that...at least not to his friends. Audrey's eyes welled up. No one understood her frustration, especially her brother. Not one of her desired would-be suitors cared to seek her out after Cedric scared them off. It wasn't fair that she was relegated to the back of the room when it came to the attentions of men. How was she supposed to get married if no man would dare look at her?

She wanted not the marriage so much as the man. She hated hearing the other girls speak of their beaux. While other girls her age were ignorant of the ways of men and women, Audrey had paid close attention to Emily and Godric, and she wanted what they had. She wanted to be desired and loved. Cedric had given her all the love a brother could but it was not enough. Audrey had yearnings, both physical and emotional, which she no longer had the desire to resist. Marriage was the best solution, and Jonathan was the one man she wanted desperately. She would do anything to claim him.

Audrey had even sought advice from a source she trusted to be frank with her on such matters. Evangeline Mirabeau, the Duke of Essex's former mistress, was reputed to be one of the most desired ladies in London. She had agreed to meet Audrey for tea once a week over the last few months. She was an invaluable font of information and surprisingly, the two had become good friends. There was a fearlessness to her that Audrey admired and tried to emulate. Recently, Evangeline had tried to teach her the art of seduction so she might win over Jonathan. But first she needed to start with Charles.

Audrey needed to move this evening along to achieve her goal. Picturing in detail the tearing of her favorite gown, she managed to make herself cry. A lovely theatrical stream of tears ran down her cheeks.

"Don't you dare!" Charles barked. "Don't even think—"

Audrey blinked, causing more tears to flow.

"Bloody hell," Charles groaned. "Audrey love, you know I didn't mean to... That is to say..." Charles's words died on his lips.

"I just want to get married!" Audrey wailed and tugged free of his hands. She threw herself against the back of the loveseat and buried her face in the crook of her elbow, a scheme that had worked countless times on her brother.

Charles sat down next to her, patting her back awkwardly. "There, there, love. It will all work out. You'll see."

"You don't understand! Cedric frightens away all my suitors. No man wants to offer for me now. Even my dowry has ceased to draw the braver gentlemen to our door."

"And your solution was to compromise yourself? Audrey, that's not the most intelligent thing for you to do nor is it the healthiest for me. Why didn't you speak to Cedric about this?"

"And have him yell at me? Declare outright that no man is good enough? I'm desperate Charles. I have needs and urges..."

"Er...I don't believe you need enlighten me any

further on those, and perhaps you ought to never tell your brother such a thing. Ever."

"Oh it is *so* much easier for men. You can run out and find a mistress and—"

Charles cut her off. "Yes, it is easier for us. I don't envy you your position in life."

He seemed to understand. He was a rake for a reason. He understood women better than most, and he had to know they desired pleasure just as much as men. It was undeniably unfair that they had less freedom, at least the unmarried ladies.

Audrey had never believed that women were lesser creatures or deserved to be restricted. Something deep in her soul cried out at the injustice enforced by the church, by the courts, even by the newspapers. Not that she could explain that to most men. They had countless reasons for why women weren't their equals and each made Audrey want to scream in outrage. Her single outlet into that world was one she had to keep a secret, even from Cedric. Even from Horatia. But it gave her a voice where before she had none.

Yet if she were married, she could do so much more. She could change herself, and no longer simply be a protected sibling. Perhaps she could work for changes for other women. Deep down, it was what mattered most to her. Having the right to do as she wished, and seeing such a right given to others.

"So what was your plan? Have me compromise you and then convince Cedric to marry you off quickly?"

"I know how he thinks. Besides, I had Emily speak to Ashton, and she said he promised to speak to Cedric about seeing to my marriage. He was supposed to recommend Jonathan as a suitable match. This night was simply meant to speed matters along."

Charles smiled. "I suspected you liked him."

"Oh I do, very much! But he doesn't notice me."

"He does, love, he does. I assure you."

"Really?"

"Actually," Charles snickered, "you frighten him quite out of his mind."

Audrey jabbed him in the ribs. "That's not making me feel any better."

"If you want Jonathan, we will have to go about this carefully. Where your brother is concerned that's always sound advice. As far as Jonathan goes, you ought to do to him what you did to me tonight. Men like aggressive women. Corner him, kiss him, make him know that you want him." There was perhaps a glint of mischief in Charles's eyes, but it did match with Evangeline's advice

"Does that mean you're going to help me?" She widened her eyes, giving him her best doe-eyed look, one that melted any man into a puddle at her feet.

"Of course. However, if this starts to turn bad, you must promise not to let that overprotective brother of yours shoot me. I rather enjoy being alive."

"What are you going to do?" Audrey asked.

"I'm going to take you home tonight and it's going to look like you've been compromised. So much so that he'll no doubt want to kill me."

Audrey blushed when she caught his meaning.

"And how will we achieve that?"

Charles took her by the hand and pulled her to her feet.

"You'll see."

CHARLES HAD a carriage summoned and within a few minutes he, Audrey and her lady's maid, Gillian, were trundling along in the dark cobblestone roads towards Curzon Street.

"Come over here by me. We've got to fix your clothes and hair." Charles patted the empty space on his side of the carriage.

"Miss!" Gillian gasped and grabbed Audrey's arm to stop her. "You mustn't!" Gillian had been left in the coach during Audrey's adventure indoors, and a good thing too.

"Do stop being such a peahen, Gillian. Don't you want me to get married? I'd much rather be a lady of my own house. Think of it! You could be a lady's maid to the lady of a house. Wouldn't that be better?" Audrey prayed Gillian would have some sense of ambition.

Gillian bit her lower lip. "I will keep quiet, Miss

Audrey. But only because I know marriage would make you happy." She turned to face Charles. "You will not kiss her, nor anything else I do not approve of."

"Where were you a quarter of an hour ago?" Charles muttered.

A smile crept across Audrey's lips. Her maid, normally shy, was showing a rare bit of courage and she thoroughly approved.

When Audrey took the seat next to him, he immediately cupped her face, then spread his fingers outward into her hair, mussing it up. He artistically pulled a few tendrils and wisps free here and there before nodding to himself in satisfaction.

Audrey glanced down at her gown. "What about my clothes?"

Charles frowned. "My dear, I'm going to have to go one step further. It will require your consent of course."

"Oh?"

"Yes. Your hair is mused, but the clothes...well, and your lips of course."

"What about my lips?" Audrey touched her mouth, not understanding his meaning.

"You need to bite them hard to ensure the authentic appearance."

She did as instructed and bit her lower lip and pinched her cheeks for extra color. Charles began to crush her gown around her knees, wrinkling it. He tugged one of her sleeves down over her shoulder.

Charles caught her chin and examined her carefully just as the carriage rolled to a stop.

"That should do it," he said with an approving smile.

Audrey raised a trembling hand to her lips. They felt swollen, plump and then she understood what Charles had meant. She looked properly compromised, and she certainly felt compromised.

"What do you think, Gillian?" asked Charles.

"I think I'd have slapped you had I seen her come home looking like that."

"Perfect!" said Audrey.

"Ready to play your part?" Charles's amused countenance turned to one of annoyance as he assumed the false air of an angry rake as the carriage came to a stop.

"Just one more detail, I think." She ripped her gown near the shoulder, letting one strap fall off her shoulder.

Audrey donned her own mask of rage and let him drag her out of the carriage and up to her brother's door. She fought off a giggle as Charles beat on the door with a closed fist. Charles would be lucky if Cedric didn't shoot him after all.

CHAPTER 8

*A*lone in his study, Cedric slumped in a chair, legs stretched out in front of the fire. The embers crackled and spat, reflecting his mood. He had much on his mind, the safety of his sisters at the forefront. In one hand he loosely twirled his silver lion's head cane. It was an old habit, one that used to irritate his mother, God rest her soul.

The clock on the mantelpiece ticked in the heavy silence. The sound grated on his ears. He hated an empty house, truly hated it. Since his parents had died, it had just been him and his sisters. Often that was enough. But tonight he was alone and the dark thoughts that engulfed him were almost overwhelming. He shuddered, wracked with an uneasy sensation that something was wrong.

The cane fell from his fingers, thumping on the carpet below. He propped his elbows on his knees and buried his face in his hands. Was it possible that his life was slowly unraveling? Audrey had her first come out this year during the Little Season in London, and far too many suitors had tramped through his door throughout October and November. Thankfully he had managed to frighten all of them off.

Audrey had wept quite piteously for weeks after her last suitor had fled when Cedric threatened to pull a pistol on him. If the dandy couldn't stand up to a simple threat then he was not worthy of his sister's time. Audrey needed a real man, not one who would spout drivel at family dinners and holiday gatherings. And children! He wouldn't let Audrey bear the offspring of a spineless sapskull. That would happen over his dead body.

Then there was Horatia. How could he ignore that prickly problem? He wouldn't mind in the least that she remain under his roof and never marry, but he knew that was selfish, and sensed a deep unhappiness in her. If only he knew what could be done to make her happy. He'd seen brief moments of excitement flicker in her eyes ever since Godric's wedding, but he wasn't quite sure what had caused them.

The door to his study opened. The butler stepped through, sighted Cedric and addressed him.

"You have a visitor, my lord."

"Oh? Who is it?" he asked, getting to his feet. Perhaps the evening was looking up?

"Lord Lennox, my lord."

"Show him in."

Cedric grinned as Ashton strolled in. His friend was a welcome sight.

"Ash, you devil. What brings you here?" Cedric clasped his hand in warm greeting. Even though it had been only a day since they'd last met, it felt like ages. Melancholy often had that effect on him.

"I thought I might enjoy the evening with you. Jonathan is having dinner with Emily and Godric."

"And Horatia," Cedric added. His sister had told him she'd made plans to dine at Essex House.

"Oh? He did not mention..." Ashton's brows drew together. "He must have forgotten."

"It was last minute as I understand it. Care for a brandy?"

"Yes, thank you." Ashton shrugged out of his dark blue coat. Had Audrey been here, she would have oohed and ahhed over the silver waistcoat's finely embroidered pattern of birds in gold thread. A fleet of swallows, if Cedric was any judge. While Charles was the most interested in fashion among their number, Ashton was always elegant and presentable. Cedric, on the other hand, tended to put on whatever his valet laid out for the day. He didn't give much thought to his appearance beyond that, much to his valet's horror. The poor man likely wished he had a master more appreciative in the time and care taken to set his wardrobe to rights, but Cedric couldn't find it in himself to care.

Cedric poured him a drink and the two men took chairs near the fire.

"And where is young Audrey this evening?" Ashton inquired.

"She is dining at Charles's."

"Oh?" The single syllable held such heavy innuendo that Cedric blinked and watched his friend more closely. He was up to something.

"She's gone to his home for dinners before," Cedric pointed out.

"She's not a little girl anymore, Cedric. She's a young lady out in society. A dinner with Charles without a proper chaperone is tempting ruination." Ashton's heavy tone was full of warning.

Cedric bristled at the implication.

"She went to dine there at the Countess of Lonsdale's invitation and took her lady's maid with her." Charles's mother should have shielded Audrey from any impropriety, but he supposed including a chaperone would have been one step better. One could never be too careful.

"On a related subject." Ashton waited until Cedric glanced up. "It just so happens I've been meaning to speak to you about Audrey."

Cedric raised a brow as he sipped his brandy. The warm burn in his throat soothed him. "What on earth about?"

"I believe you should see her settled soon."

Cedric knew what Ashton meant, but feigned ignorance to buy him a moment to secure his temper.

"Settled?"

"Married." The word echoed like canon fire.

Cedric set his brandy aside to scowl at his friend. "Not that my sisters are any concern of yours, but why?"

"I've been speaking to Emily and—"

"Oh Lord," Cedric muttered. Would their suffering at the hands of that meddlesome Duchess never cease? As much as he adored Emily, she could drive him mad.

"Emily has a far better grasp of these matters than you or I, Cedric." Ashton moved to the edge of his chair, propping his hands on his knees. "And she has become one of Audrey's confidantes. Emily came to me, if that puts you in a more amiable mood. For my part I had no intention of bringing up such a delicate subject with you, but she insisted only I could do it."

"Did she now?" Cedric allowed his sarcasm to show.

"Yes, she did. She believes you are less likely to draw a pistol on me than the others for suggesting something as shocking as marriage." Ashton was no stranger to sarcasm either.

"Are you offering yourself in this discussion?" Cedric asked carefully, his fingers tightening around his glass.

"Of course not. Audrey's a darling woman, but I've no interest in settling down with someone like her."

"Too good for my sister, Lennox?" Cedric slammed his drink down on the side table between their chairs.

Ashton gave him a rueful smile. "You know my shipping line requires my constant attention and frequent voyages, and she is a lady who belongs in London if there ever was one. It would be most unfair to a sweet young bride. And you, my friend, are trying to make this about me, rather than her."

"Fine, fine. But you aren't telling me this without having a suggestion at hand, are you." It wasn't a question. Ashton would have thought this discussion through long before and come up with options.

"I had thought that Jonathan would make a suitable match. He's not too much older than she is. Eighteen and twenty-four is not so great a distance."

Cedric nearly spat out his brandy, which would have most certainly ruined the carpets. "Jonathan?" he sputtered. "You can't be serious!"

"I'm quite serious. You don't have any objection to him because of his background?"

The question was insulting. Cedric had never paid heed to titles and didn't care one whit about Jonathan's background. "No, of course not."

"Then what has upset you? He needs an easier way into society. Marriage to Audrey would secure his place very nicely."

"Secure his place? My sister is not a rung on a bloody social ladder!" he bellowed.

"I'm not saying that she is, so you may stop that infernal shouting." Ashton kept his cool as always. "Listen, Cedric. Audrey is very taken with Jonathan. She told Emily she has a mind to set her cap for him. Why not let her? Jonathan is a good sort."

"He's a St. Laurent." Surely Ashton knew better than to suggest Audrey marry a rakehell. She needed a good, loyal man who could handle her when her temper flared and more importantly, wouldn't seek the beds of other women. Surely there had to be one man in England that was a more appropriate match.

Ashton nodded. "Granted, Godric had a few rough years to be sure. But he's happy with Emily, and he's loyal to her. You know that."

"But who's to say Jonathan will be the same?"

"I've spent quite a lot of time with him lately, and he has taken his new life very seriously. He's no innocent, of course. As you said, he's a St. Laurent. But he is no longer actively pursuing women, not like we were at his age. If he married Audrey, I believe he would settle into the married life without any fuss."

"And here I thought you genuinely wished to see me tonight." Cedric narrowed his eyes. "No, instead you beat down my door to discuss Audrey's suitors and marriage! This might as well be a business meeting. Fancy the rising trend in salted pork? Or should I invest in Mr. Stephenson's new railway scheme in Stockton?"

"What's really troubling you, Cedric?"

"There is nothing troubling me." His grumbled

response made him sound like a wounded bear, but he didn't care.

Ashton leaned back in his chair as though settling in. "You are a terrible liar." Why that enraged Cedric, he couldn't say, he only had the sudden urge to blacken one of Ashton's eyes.

"And you are a terrible friend."

Ashton's eyes widening was the only indication of his surprise. "Perhaps you're right. I came here to discuss Audrey's future and I had no thought as to how that would affect you."

Cedric was increasingly uncomfortable. He knew his friend was right but, damn the man, he felt terrible for not having better composure.

"Would you like me to leave?" Ashton asked.

Cedric looked back to the fire. The tense silence became suffocating. Ashton rose from his chair.

"I'll see myself out." He nodded in farewell.

Only when Ashton reached the drawing room door did Cedric call out to him. "You haven't finished your brandy."

Ashton looked back at the lonely glass on the table. "It would be rude of me to leave it half full, I suppose."

"Impossibly rude." Cedric gave the barest hint of a smile. Ashton returned and made a great scene of sitting deep into his chair, as though he would not be leaving anytime soon.

"Now, since I'm not done with my drink, there is plenty of time for us to talk."

It took Cedric a few moments to properly gather his thoughts.

"I'm failing as a brother, Ash. Horatia is dreadfully unhappy, Audrey is distressed over my boorish treatment of her would-be suitors and the truth is that I'm doing everything within my power to not end up here alone." There was the crux of the problem. He didn't want to be left with an empty house, no family, just silence and servants. He feared it like nothing else in the world, save losing those he loved.

"Let us take one problem at a time, shall we? Firstly, you won't be alone. The League is constantly infiltrating your life, and on occasion your home, for our nefarious purposes." The twinkle in Ashton's eyes was a comfort beyond words. "Just because your sisters may someday leave does not plunge you into eternal solitude. You know you may call on any of us at any time should you feel the least bit melancholy. Now, as to Audrey, you know my opinion on the matter. Marry her off to a good man soon, and if it is Jonathan, you'll see her quite often. She loves you far too much to abandon you for any husband. Hasn't our policy always been the more the merrier?"

Cedric grumbled. "Dash it all. I hate how bloody sensible you are. I sound like some mulish fop who fears losing control over something he never actually had control of."

"You're not a fop. Mulish absolutely, but a fop? Never."

"You're very lucky that I like you. Otherwise I would be tempted to point a pistol at you after all."

Ash grinned. "Yes, yes. Now, about Horatia. What is making her unhappy?"

"That's just it. I have no idea."

"Not one?" Ashton seemed surprised.

"She mopes about, sighing and her eyes often seem red as though she's been crying. And then there was this morning with Charles."

"Charles again?" Ashton mused.

"He offered to take her riding, something she usually loves but at first she declined. It was only when I mentioned that Lucien and Audrey would be down soon for breakfast that she couldn't seem to leave fast enough."

"It seems you already have the answer to her unhappiness."

"I do?" What the devil was Ash playing at?

"Of course. Horatia has no problem with her sister, does she?"

Cedric swirled his brandy glass, considering the morning's odd turn of events. "Well, no, other than the usual sisterly squabbles."

"And the only other person you mentioned was?" Ashton prompted.

"Lucien? But why would she…" Cedric didn't want to consider what that meant.

"That is what we must discover," Ashton said.

"But Lucien barely notices her."

"Perhaps that is the problem. No one likes to be ignored, especially on purpose."

"But she's gotten along fine with it for years. It has only been since September when Emily first came here that Horatia started showing signs of unhappiness."

Ashton's eyes narrowed. "How very curious."

"Not really. Lucien blames her for ruining his match to Melanie Burns all those years ago."

This caught the fair-haired baron completely off guard. "Pardon?"

Cedric explained the long buried secret of that day in the gardens when he'd taken his sisters to Lucien's estate in Kent.

"She said she loved him? Perhaps that's it. She still does," Ashton suggested.

"How could she love someone who won't spare a moment's thought for her?" His sister was smarter than that. She wouldn't pin her hopes on such a man. Horatia was sensible, not a fool.

Ashton sighed. "Aren't you familiar with the term 'unrequited love?'"

"This isn't a joke, Ash."

"I'm not speaking in jest. It's probable that Horatia is still in love with Lucien. She has seen too much of him lately and has suffered his cold manner and it has made her upset."

"If that is the case then it is my fault. I've been pushing him to stay here more often and I haven't cared to think about his feelings in the matter, or hers it would seem."

"Do not punish yourself. There is every chance that Lucien sees Horatia as some form of temptation and treating her coldly is a way of keeping his distance."

"What on earth do you mean?"

Ashton took a sip of his brandy. "We have our rules, remember, and Lucien has a sister. He understands the brotherly instinct to protect those under his charge. It is possible that he fears Horatia will someday be a target, however unintentional, of his natural charm." Ashton stroked his jaw. "Therefore he is cold to her, in hopes her declaration of love from years ago never resurfaces."

"I don't follow. Are you saying he *desires* my sister?" The idea of Lucien even thinking of Horatia as he would any other woman made Cedric's blood boil. He refused to believe it.

The other man merely smiled.

"Never mind, Cedric. We won't worry any more about it tonight." Ashton took another sip of his drink.

A sudden pounding on the front door alerted both men to the world outside their thoughts.

"Now who the devil could that be?" Cedric muttered. He and Ash abandoned their brandy and headed into the hall where a tired footman was already moving to open the door.

Charles stormed in, dragging a disheveled, swollen-lipped and upset Audrey. Cedric, unusually observant about his sister tonight, immediately assessed the clearly dangerous situation. Someone had been kissing his sister, kissing her hard enough to give her that singularly bee-stung plumpness to her lips. Furthermore, she was upset, though not as though she meant to cry. No, she was livid, like a spitting mad cat.

"What on earth?" Cedric began.

"Sheridan!" Charles snapped as he shoved Audrey deeper into the hallway as the footman shut the door.

"Charles?" Cedric replied in shock.

"You have to do something about your sister! Marry her to the first oaf in Hyde Park if you must, but for God's sake, get her married!" After Charles's violent outburst the hall became deathly silent.

"Oh dear," Ashton said. This would not end well.

CHAPTER 9

"*N*ot a penny until the conditions are met, and there is dirt falling upon a grave."

Horatia's heart shot into her throat as she struggled to listen to the low voice on the other side of the garden hedge.

"Oh my God," Horatia hissed at the same time that Lucien growled, "That bastard!"

Lucien pulled Horatia by the hand back through the hedges and once more into their room.

"We have to leave now," he said in a tone rough.

"I can see myself home." She couldn't keep her voice from shaking.

"No chance of that, Horatia. I'm taking you to Godric's."

Horatia froze.

"How…how long have you known?" Her hands flew

to her mask, still firmly in place.

"How long have I known what?" Lucien asked as he grabbed his overcoat and cloaked it around her shoulders.

"How long have you known it was me?" She fought to remain calm, despite the wild gallop of her heart, and clutched his coat tighter around her.

"Since you walked in the door."

Horatia's stomach pitched straight towards her feet.

"What we did…that was…" She had no words to say anything more. "And you knew!" Her tone came out more accusatory than she intended. She had meant to seduce *him* after all.

"Tonight was a lesson for you to be careful around men," Lucien replied. "A lady of your standing shouldn't be here. What would Cedric think if he found out?"

"What about the garden? The stars? Was it all a lie?" Horatia's lower lip shook, but the anger she wished she could summon did not appear. She was bruised and hurting inside. Why was it whenever Lucien was around to wound her she lost the urge to fight? Was it because she cared so much about him that she didn't want to quarrel?

"Everything that happened tonight was a lie. Deep down you knew that. I gave you what you sought while retaining your virtue, at least in the most literal sense. Others would not be so considerate. I was playing along for your benefit."

"My benefit? Don't you dare cheapen what happened between us!" Horatia winced at the shrillness of her own voice. Her right hand raised as though to slap Lucien. "I won't let you!"

"Go ahead, my dear. Strike me for my villainous ways and my dastardly schemes. But we have more serious matters to attend to." Lucien waited patiently for her to slap him but Horatia, tears stinging her eyes, merely shook her head and took a step back.

"Even though you deserve it, I could never willingly hurt you." She turned away from him. This only seemed to infuriate him, however. He chased her to the door, grabbed her shoulders and spun her around.

"I don't want you to feel anything for me," he hissed. "Not love, not pity, not even kindness. Do you understand?"

Horatia managed a sad smile. "I understand. But it doesn't change how I feel." Her words seemed to light a fire within him.

He pressed hard against her, hands raking up and down her body. Lucien forced his mouth down over hers, scorching her with the violence of his kiss. Horatia melted into him, knowing he hated her for it. He cupped her bottom, jerked her tighter into him, demanding with his aggression that she scream and fight him off. It was as though he ached to wound her but nothing could compare to his betrayal of her heart.

"Fight me, damn you!" he snarled. "Strike me. Hate

me." But Horatia offered only soft lips and yielding caresses until he pulled away.

She raised her chin, unafraid and determined to prove it to him. "I won't. You're trying to frighten me on purpose. It won't work. You'd never hurt me."

The growl at the back of his throat was wild and warning her to stay away.

Glowering, he moved her aside so he could open the door, then pulled her along by the wrist until they were leaving the Midnight Garden's townhouse. Lucien called for the footman near the main door to summon a hackney.

When the coach rolled up, Lucien shoved her inside and instructed the driver to go to Half Moon Street. He didn't apologize. Didn't say a single word. He tore off his mask and when he caught her staring, he leaned over and ripped off her mask as well, then tossed both onto the floor. She kept her eyes on him.

"Stop looking at me!" Lucien shouted. Horatia flinched, but did not look away. "Did you hear me?"

"I suspect all of London heard you." Her tone was surprisingly cool. She was rather proud of herself, standing up to him so.

"Then do as I say."

"I may care for you, but that doesn't mean I have to obey you. Especially when you are being so rude. It's not as though we're married."

"Heaven forbid I ever suffer that fate."

Despite his cruel words Horatia could not do as he asked. She was unable to look away from the depths of his hazel eyes. He had no idea just how alive she was when he touched her. Even his roughness made her burn with desire. She longed to fight back, to match his passion, but until he loved her in return, she could not give in to that side of herself. There would be no turning back if she ever showed him the darker side of her nature —the secret, forbidden desires she longed to fulfill in his arms. It was better if he never know how truly alike they were.

They managed the rest of the coach ride in silence. When they reached Essex House, Lucien ordered her to stay put. She did obey this time, but only because she needed a moment to herself, to get control of her emotions.

Once Lucien left the carriage, the tears started. She sniffed and wiped her eyes, trying to swallow the painful lump in her throat. Tonight had been such a wonderful dream, until Lucien had ruined it. The pig-headed fool. How could he have faked such sweet emotions? Would he never again call her his lovely stargazer? Had that too been a lie?

God, I'm the one who's a fool.

She admitted twice tonight that she cared for him only to have him scorn her for it. Horatia wasn't a child anymore, but it seemed clear that Lucien still thought her to be the enemy. She wasn't even worthy of a second chance.

Her mind flashed back to that moment on the bed, when he'd driven her to a height of pleasure and comforted her as she experienced the frightening spiral of sensations. How was she supposed to reconcile that sweet, seductive man with the overbearing tyrant he'd become when his mask was off? He could be as different as light and dark and the constant switching back and forth was driving her mad.

Horatia hastily wiped her face as she heard a number of voices approach. She moved over to allow Emily, Jonathan, Godric and Lucien into the coach. It was a tight fit, the three gentleman all pressed on one side, allowing the ladies to have the opposite bench.

"Ouch, Jonathan, that's my knee!" Lucien hissed.

"Isn't this cozy?" Jonathan laughed. Godric grunted as Lucien jabbed an elbow into his ribs when trying to settle back into the seat.

Horatia found herself reluctantly smiling as the three grown men squirmed against each other like fidgety schoolboys.

"Are you going to tell us what this is about, Lucien?" Godric asked once the coach started moving again, this time towards Curzon Street.

"I shall explain once we're at Cedric's. It will be best if I tell everyone at once. That way if anyone has questions,

I won't have to repeat myself." His eyes warned Horatia to say nothing.

"Very well," Godric grumbled, trying again to settle in and looking more than a little surly.

Emily leaned over to Horatia and asked in a low whisper, "Where were you tonight? I thought you were coming to dinner?"

"It's a long story, one I can only share when we're alone. But would you cover for me? If Cedric asks, could you say I was at dinner with you?"

"Absolutely," Emily assured her. "I'll let the others know."

"What are you two whispering about?" Godric watched the pair of them curiously.

"Probably the overthrow of Parliament," Lucien said sourly.

"Don't be silly. That was weeks ago. We've moved on to Europe now," Emily replied with a dark grin.

Godric snorted. "Clearly you have too much free time on your hands, darling. I shall have to correct that once we return home." He flashed his wife a grin that Emily returned with interest.

"Now what are you *really* up to?" he asked.

"It is none of your concern, darling." Emily now dared to smile sweetly at her husband who frowned.

"You are my concern."

"Of course, darling." She agreed as though they'd had this discussion many times before.

"Emily." Godric crossed his arms over his chest.

"It doesn't concern me. Therefore it is none of your concern either."

When he started to protest, she kicked him in the shin with the tip of her boot.

"Ow!" He gasped in indignation more than pain.

"Oh I'm dreadfully sorry, did that hurt? How clumsy of me! This coach is awfully crowded."

"You will pay for that, my dear."

"And I expect I shall quite enjoy it." For a brief second, Horatia worried the newly married couple would forget that there were three other people in the carriage and engage in public displays of affection.

Horatia envied the love that so clearly bound Godric and Emily. Would she ever have that? The odds didn't appear to be in her favor.

When the coach arrived at Cedric's townhouse, Lucien leaped out and dashed up the steps. Godric followed, helping his wife down. Jonathan was next but waited patiently to assist Horatia. She noted the pair of masks lying on the carriage floor and picked them up, one black and one silver. She bit her bottom lip. Tonight the last of her childhood dreams had been crushed. Never again would she entertain such foolish thoughts of love and happiness. She wished she had the strength to cast away the masks, but her fingers wouldn't let go of them. She exited the coach, taking Jonathan's offered hand for support.

"Thank you," she whispered.

"You are most welcome," he replied, a smile of genuine affection on his handsome face.

Jonathan was a true gentleman, and it was a pity Audrey was so infatuated with him. Horatia ought to have fallen in love with a man like him. At least then she would be respected. Perhaps not loved, but she was going to have to accept that. She was doomed to never love again.

"It seems we are not the first to arrive," Jonathan observed as he joined her in the open doorway.

They were met by an unpleasant sight. Ashton had his arms about Audrey's waist, holding her back. Cedric was throttling Charles against the wall, his feet off the ground and poor Charles's face was a rather disconcerting shade of purple.

"What the devil?" Jonathan blurted out. Godric had already rushed to pull Cedric off of Charles.

"What in God's name is going on?" Lucien demanded.

Audrey delivered a sharp elbow into Ashton's ribs as she fought to free herself. When Audrey tried to deliver another such blow, Ashton spun her delicately into Jonathan's unsuspecting embrace.

"Hold her, man!" Ashton ordered. "And watch the elbows, they're like fire pokers!" Jonathan's arms locked about Audrey's waist, holding her captive. Now that Ashton was free, he sighed and rubbed a hand over his ribs.

"It seems Charles compromised Audrey this evening," Ashton said, finally answering Godric and Lucien's questions.

"What?" Emily's head whipped towards Ashton in disbelief.

Godric finally succeeded in wrenching Cedric away, and Charles collapsed to his hands and knees, wheezing.

"Cedric, we don't have time for this," Lucien cut in. "Something important has happened. Don't give me that look, it's more important that your sister's honor."

"What could be more important than that?"

"The safety of yourself and everyone you hold dear."

"What on earth are you talking about? You don't mean that note on my door, do you? I thought we'd agreed they were more idle threats?"

"I will be happy to explain, but we ought to send the women upstairs. There is much to discuss, and I haven't the time to deal with feminine hysterics," Lucien said.

His callous remark drew an arched brow from Emily and a glare from Audrey.

Godric came over, prepared for his wife to fight him. "I quite agree. It is a matter that cannot be shared with the ladies."

Emily held up a hand. "We will retire upstairs as you so politely requested. I would rather be in the company of hysterical women than ridiculous men. Ladies?" Emily indicated for Audrey and Horatia to follow her. Horatia was the first up the stairs, but Audrey still had to free herself from Jonathan.

"Let go!" she growled.

He looked down at her, holding her in his arms, as though surprised she was still there. Audrey stomped on his toes and he jumped back with a shout. She huffed and stalked up after Emily and her sister. Cedric trailed them all the way to Horatia's room and once inside he locked the the door. Audrey shouted vile curses no lady and few sailors should have known, some of it in French, ending with a hearty kick to the door. Unfortunately, her slippers were not the most effective weapons and she let out a yelp of pain. She hopped madly back and forth, clutching her bruised toes.

"Why on earth did you let them lock us away?" Audrey whined.

"Because you haven't been subjected to the indignities I have when those men downstairs don't get their way. It is most unpleasant to be manhandled, and far more undignified than this." Emily smoothed her midnight blue velvet skirts and sat down on Horatia's bed, looking at her expectantly. "Besides, I believe Horatia knows exactly what is going on."

Audrey looked to her sister as she limped over and joined Emily on the bed. "Well?"

Horatia sighed. "Very well. But you must not say a word until I'm finished. No, Audrey, not even a peep."

Audrey, whose lips had already opened up, stopped

and clamped back shut.

After a brief narration of the night's events, heavily edited for propriety's sake, Horatia waited for either of her companions to speak. Worry shaded Emily's eyes, turning them a deeper shade of purple. Audrey just blinked, gaped and blinked again.

"This is more serious than I thought. There is a death threat out on your brother?"

Horatia nodded. "Lucien seems to know who is behind it, but he cannot understand why the men were discussing it in such a place."

"The Midnight Gardens are renowned for secrecy," Emily said. "Everyone seeks it and so nobody listens upon another's private matters.

Horatia pursed her lips a moment. "There is another possibility. Maybe they wanted to be overheard?"

"But why?" Audrey asked. "What advantage would that give them? We know Cedric is in danger now and we can protect him."

Horatia met Emily's gaze, reading the other woman's thoughts. "Audrey, remember when Cedric took you shooting once? He had a groundskeeper swat at the underbrush to shake the pheasants out of their hiding places. Perhaps they are shaking the bushes and waiting for them all to fly out."

Audrey paled. "Oh dear, then that would mean he has some plan in place and likely knows how Cedric and the other men will react."

"Exactly," Emily said. "Since they will not recognize the trap, nor will they know how to escape it even if we warn them, it may be left up to us to protect them from themselves."

For a long moment none of the ladies spoke as they contemplated the dangerous task ahead.

"You really are in love with Lucien?" Emily asked, mercifully changing the subject.

The rush of heat to Horatia's face betrayed any denials she might have made. "I am. It's a stupid, foolish thing to love someone like him, but I can't help it."

Emily laughed, the sound delicate, but her eyes were sharp. "I fell in love with Godric the same way. I was convinced the entire time it was bound to end in disaster and heartbreak, yet it didn't."

Biting her lower lip, Horatia considered this. "Godric loves you, though. Lucien doesn't love me. I think he doesn't even really like me at all."

Emily snorted, though not inelegantly. "I think there's a fair chance he may fall in love with you. I have learned a few things about these men. Lucien wouldn't have kissed you if he hadn't wanted to. Not only that, but I've seen signs of possessiveness and jealousy where you're concerned, not disgust."

Horatia's heart fluttered in excitement though she tried to hide it. "You have?"

"Oh yes. He glowers at any man who kisses your

hand, and always escorts you into dinner whenever we dine together."

They were fair points, but they didn't exactly prove Lucien's undying love.

"Now, let's return to this assassination business. We know Waverly wants the League dead, and it seems now they mean to start with your brother. I'm sure Lucien was upset."

"I don't know that it was Waverly," Horatia said. "Lucien said he recognized the voice, but didn't say whose it was."

"Waverly is the only man I know that seems to come up in their conversations when they speak of enemies," Emily said.

"No wonder they sent us upstairs," Horatia mused. "No doubt those foolish men are making plans to go to war and want to keep us out of harm's way. It is a thoughtful gesture."

"Thoughtful?" Audrey objected. "They want to ruin our fun."

"I'd hardly call such a threat fun," said Emily. "But keeping us out, no matter how well intended, is a mistake."

"Well, we ought to formulate our own plan then," Horatia declared. "We are capable of far more than they give us credit." If her brother's life really was in danger, she wasn't about to let the men handle it alone. She would protect her brother on her terms.

"That is an excellent idea!" Audrey jumped to her feet as though they were planning a party.

Emily was already deep in thought. "It is. But first, I'd like to know why Cedric was trying to do away with Charles. This is the worst possible time for the League to be divided, and I can't help but remember our last conversation, Audrey."

Audrey flushed. "I…I know you said you would talk to Ashton about Jonathan, but I was having trouble waiting."

A laugh escaped from Horatia. "You always were too impulsive."

Emily pursed her lips as if bracing herself for disaster. "Audrey, what exactly did you do?"

"I convinced Charles to help me."

Horatia narrowed her eyes. "Help you *how?*"

"He may have introduced me to the finer points of kissing," Audrey confessed.

"Audrey!" Horatia gasped. Would her sister never learn that actions had consequences? Admittedly she wasn't one to talk, given her own night's events, but she knew Lucien would never be forced to marry her. Audrey and Charles might end up engaged if Audrey wasn't more careful.

"It was an intriguing experience, given that I have no real attraction to Charles."

"Audrey, you didn't let him kiss you?" Emily pressed.

No wonder Cedric had been murderous. "I warned you about—"

"Nothing happened, except that I kissed him. He didn't even kiss me back. To get this way—" she gestured to her disheveled appearance "—he fixed my clothes and hair and told me to bite my lips a bit. I wanted Cedric to think that I'd been compromised. I'd hoped he might allow me to marry Jonathan instead..."

Horatia sucked in a breath at her sister's brash behavior. *Am I the only sane Sheridan in the family?* As soon as the question passed her mind she stifled a groan of embarrassment. She was no better than Audrey, really.

"And he did it to help you?" Emily sounded dubious.

"Oh yes." Audrey nodded. "But he took some convincing. He was quite angry with me, especially after I accosted him in his own drawing room. The poor man hid behind a couch to escape me."

It was simply too amusing an image, Charles scrambling over furniture to escape the kisses of a pretty debutante. Horatia had to bite down on her fist to still her urge to laugh outright.

Emily was not so restrained. "I would have given the world to see that!" she said, gasping for air, laughing.

Horatia was wiping tears from her eyes. Audrey was back to her old self, imitating Charles's fall off the couch when she'd kissed him. She made a theatrical squawk and toppled to the floor with a thud. By now Horatia was laughing so hard she could scarcely breathe.

ONE FLOOR BELOW, Lucien and the other members of the League gazed up at the drawing room's ceiling. Arms crossed over his chest, he raised a brow as they listened to the strange noises from above.

There was a loud shriek, a thud, and hoots of unrestrained laughter.

"What the deuce is going on up there?" Charles asked.

"Probably jumping on the beds," Cedric grumbled.

"They're no longer children," said Lucien. "Someone should tell them."

"Do you suppose it was wise to leave them alone up there?" Godric asked. His head was tilted like a dog hearing strange sounds.

"They're fine." Now that he'd caught them up on more relevant events, Lucien had to bring them back to the point of the meeting. Lives were in danger. "Now, what are we going to do about this threat?"

"Waverly won't succeed," Cedric said with confidence. "We can defend ourselves."

"Nevertheless," said Godric, "it would be unwise if one of us wasn't keeping an eye on you and your sisters. Even if Waverly intends to kill you, they might get harmed in the crossfire."

"I don't intend to let them leave the house," said Cedric. "If they absolutely must, they'll have an escort."

"We mustn't forget how easily the defenses here were

breached in the fall," Ashton reminded the others. "That was a close call with the man who stole Emily. This is a house, not a fortress."

Lucien vowed never to feel that helpless protecting Horatia.

But Cedric could not be pulled so easily from his previous source of rage. "Before we discuss Horatia, I need to defend Audrey from that damned bloody cur," Cedric shot a finger at Charles, "who seduced her in a bloody coach!"

"I did not seduce her, Cedric." Charles raised his hands in defense in case Cedric lunged at him again. "I warned you she ought to marry soon. You're lucky she came to me first. Another man might have actually taken advantage of her."

"Are you saying you didn't touch her?" Cedric demanded.

"Touch? Yes, but I didn't kiss her. She asked for my assistance to make her look compromised."

"Look compromised? You *bastard!*" Cedric looked ready to go after Charles again. "Women have been ruined for such a thing as a lustful glance, and you go and muss up my sister? What if word got out to the Quizzing Glass of her appearance? Then she would never find a suitor."

Ashton stepped between the two of them, throwing up a hand to prevent Cedric from advancing.

"Come now, gentlemen." Ashton's steely tone stopped the two men. "Do we need to solve this in a ring?"

"I wouldn't recommend that," Godric said with a wry grin. "But if it does come to it, I'll stake ten pounds on Charles."

Both Cedric and Charles shared cautious looks with one another before declining, perhaps in part because none of the others would take that bet. Ashton dropped his hand when he seemed satisfied that Cedric would not resume trying to kill Charles. Lucien gave a sigh of relief. He had no desire to jump between his friends. Charles was a champion boxer and Lucien didn't want a blackened eye simply because he'd try to impose peace. If Ashton wished to risk his face, that was entirely up to him.

Jonathan, who had lingered at the edge of the group, suddenly spoke up. "Is this how all of your League meetings go? Perhaps we might focus ourselves back on the real problem and the importance of protecting the ladies."

Ashton turned to Cedric, his voice hard. "Quite right, Jonathan. Back to the matter at hand. I think it would be best, Cedric, if you take Horatia and Audrey away from London, at least until the rest of us sort this out."

"You want me to turn tail and run?" Cedric looked shocked and outraged at the very idea.

"You know I would never ask that of you." Ashton's voice was softer now. "But for your sisters' sake, yes.

You'd grab them and run to the ends of the earth if it would protect them. We all know this."

The fierce resistance in Cedric wavered against the persuasive power of Ashton's reasonable request.

Cedric slumped. "Where would you have me go then?"

Godric chimed in. "Some place Waverly would not immediately think to look for you."

Lucien's heartbeat kicked up as he realized the perfect place to keep Horatia safe. "How about my estate in Kent? You could take your sisters there and stay until the New Year. My mother is in residence along with Lysandra and Linus, so you'd be properly entertained." He didn't need to add that, should Hugo's men make discreet enquiries as to where they might have gone, Lucien's estate would be the last name on their lists.

Getting the Sheridan sisters out of London seemed like a very good plan. Anything to get them out of the line of danger, and Horatia away from him. Two birds with one stone, so they say.

"That's an excellent idea," Ashton agreed. "The rest of us can remain here and attempt to sort this mess out. Lucien, you'll accompany Cedric and his sisters, of course."

"What?" Lucien sputtered. That was the worst idea in the history of the world. Put *him* in his estate with Horatia where he knew every nook and cranny he could secret her away to? Damnation! "I could be of more use dealing with Hugo's men," he countered.

"It is your estate," Ashton reminded him in a firm tone. "And you were also the first one targeted in these attacks. You will escort Cedric and his sisters. Hopefully this issue will be resolved before Christmas. If not, then you will be with your family for the holidays."

That did not make the situation any more appealing. Lucien fought the urge to stamp his feet like a boy in a temper tantrum. Jonathan shared a sympathetic look with him, as though he seemed to know just what being around Horatia would do to him. Was that how Jonathan felt around Audrey; did he have an interest in the younger Sheridan woman, the way she did in him?

Here he was trying to do the decent thing and stay away from temptation, and Ashton was practically handing Horatia to him on a silver platter. He needed her to be safe—not just from the Waverly but from himself. Having her so close to his bed at home was the opposite of safe.

What other choice did he have though?

"Fine," Lucien said with poor grace. "I will go with Cedric."

He didn't want to spend hours in a coach with Horatia, and he certainly did not want to be stuck at his estate with her over the holidays. It was worse knowing that his mother would be there. She had an irritating way of meddling in his affairs, and he feared she would interfere with Horatia. His mother had a soft spot for the Sheridans, Horatia in particular. Letting his mother near Horatia would be more trouble than he wanted to deal with.

"When should we leave?" Cedric asked Ashton.

"As soon as possible. Do you think your sisters could be ready by first light?"

Cedric barked out a harsh laugh. "First light tomorrow? Absolutely not. You must at least give Audrey a day to pack or the little devil will harass me about it all the way to Kent."

"A day then, but I want the lot of you packed and in your carriages before the sun rises." Ashton was deadly serious. "Godric and I will go tomorrow morning to the Midnight Garden and see if we can't catch the two men from last night at their arranged time. I'd like to see for myself if there is any proof it was Waverly. We need to know what we're up against."

"Now that's all settled," Cedric growled, "would all of you mind getting the hell out of my house?"

"Capital idea," Godric said. His eyes then drifted to the ceiling.

"It's awfully quiet up there," Jonathan observed.

"Too quiet," Lucien agreed. Suddenly anxious, the six men proceeded out of the drawing room and up the stairs towards Horatia's room. The door was still locked. Lucien leaned against the wood and listened. Not a sound came from within.

CHAPTER 10

"*D*o you hear them?" Charles asked.

Cedric held a finger to his lips.

Lucien strained to hear even the smallest rustle or creak, but heard nothing. Cautiously, Cedric unlocked and opened the door. The bedchamber was empty. The windows were closed and latched and there was no sign of the women.

"Ash?" Godric said in a low whisper. Ashton nodded and proceeded inside, his sharp gaze leaving nothing unseen. There was no evidence the women had hidden themselves. No sign of hasty departure. They had simply vanished.

"Where the bloody hell is my wife?" Godric yelled into the aether.

As if in response, a footman came up the stairs and

handed Cedric a slip of paper. Dumbfounded, Cedric opened it and read it aloud.

My Dear Gentlemen,

We await you in the dining room. Please do not join us until you have decided upon a course of action regarding the threat to Lord Sheridan. We will be more than delighted to offer our opinions on the matter, but in truth, we suspect you do not wish to hear our thoughts. It is a failing of the male species, and we shan't hold it against you. In the future, however, it would be advisable not to lock us in a room. We simply cannot resist a challenge, something you should have learned by now. Intelligent women are not to be trifled with.

Fondest Regards,

~The Society of Rebellious Ladies~

"Fondest regards?" Lucien scoffed.

A puzzled Jonathan added, "Society of Rebellious Ladies?"

"Lord help us!" Ashton groaned as he ran a hand through his hair. "They've named themselves."

"I'll wager a hundred pounds that Emily's behind this. Having a laugh at our expense," Charles said in all seriousness.

"Let's go and see how rebellious they are when we're done with them." Cedric rolled up the sleeves of his white lawn shirt as he and the others stalked down the stairs to the dining room. They found it empty. The footman reappeared and Cedric wondered if perhaps the man had never left. At the servant's polite cough he handed Cedric a second note.

"Another damn note? What are they playing at?" He practically tore the paper in half while opening it. Again he read it aloud.

Did you honestly believe we'd display our cunning in so simple a fashion? Surely you underestimated us. It is quite unfair of you to assume we could not baffle you for at least a few minutes. Perhaps you should look for us in the place where we ought to have been and not the place you put us.

Best Wishes,

~The Society of Rebellious Ladies~

"I am going to kill her," Cedric said. It didn't seem to matter which of the three rebellious ladies he meant.

The League of Rogues headed back to the drawing room. Cedric flung the door open. Emily was sitting before the fire, an embroidery frame raised as she pricked the cloth with a fine pointed needle. Audrey was perusing one of her many fashion magazines, eyes fixed on the illustrated plates, oblivious to any disruption.

Horatia had positioned herself on the window seat

near a candle, so she could read her novel. Even at this distance Lucien could see the title, *Lady Eustace and the Merry Marquess*, the novel he'd purchased for her last Christmas. For some reason, the idea she would mock him with his own gift was damned funny. He had the sudden urge to laugh, especially when he saw a soft blush work its way up through her. He'd picked that particular book just to shock her, knowing it was quite explicit in parts since he'd read it himself the previous year.

"Ahem," Cedric cleared his throat. Three sets of feminine eyes fixed on him, each reflecting only mild curiosity.

Emily smiled. "Oh there you are."

"Are you finished with your little meeting?" Audrey asked, setting down her magazine and smiling up at her brother.

The way she'd said "little meeting" left Lucien with no doubt they were having fun at their expense, or perhaps it was her biting her bottom lip to prevent her laughter that gave her away. Regardless, Cedric's sisters had challenged the men and they were in no mood to play games. Especially Cedric.

"You." Cedric pointed to Audrey. "Bed, now!" His accusing finger then swept towards Emily. "Since when do you embroider? I distinctly recall you telling me once that such a thing was a complete and utter waste of time."

"Considering your rather callous behavior tonight in leaving us out of your decisions, I decided to renew the rather useless habit," Emily replied as though speaking of the weather. She politely held up the embroidery hoop, which was festooned with flowers around a simple phrase every single man in the room could read, *Never Challenge a Woman*. Lucien could only imagine how she must have embroidered that in so short a time.

"We left you out of it because this matter doesn't concern any of you ladies. Besides, it is a delicate and dangerous situation," Cedric said.

"Hmm," Emily responded, the feminine sound came out strangely condescending. "Perhaps we ladies are keeping you out of a dangerous situation and haven't bothered to inform you of our intentions. If you insist on keeping us in the dark, we will persist in our efforts to keep all of you alive regardless of your belief that we are incapable females."

Godric frowned. "No one said you were incapable. You know we don't think that, Emily."

Horatia came to Emily's defense. "She's right. You keep secrets from us that will only divide us and put us all at risk. You will explain yourself, Cedric. I will not leave this house until you tell me what you and the others have planned."

"Fine, tomorrow morning, I'll tell you, but not tonight. It's late and everyone needs their rest," her brother shot back.

"Nonsense, you can tell us right now," Emily insisted.

"Godric, collect your wife and take her home before I use her as a pincushion," Cedric threatened.

Godric, who tried to hide an appreciative smirk, seemed to find his wife's besting of the men most amusing. At Cedric's impatient tone, however, he jumped into action.

"Come along, Em. I believe you've made your point for now." He picked up the embroidered frame and tossed it on a nearby empty chair. He then wrapped an arm about her waist to pull her to him, planting a kiss on her brow.

"You wouldn't let him use me as pincushion would you, darling?" she asked, twining her arm through his after he released her.

"Never, my dear. He's just annoyed that he can't figure how you got out of Horatia's room when he locked you in, or come here undetected."

Emily cast an arrogant glance at Cedric's direction. "And he never will."

"But you'll tell me, won't you?" Godric looked down at his wife in adoration.

"Perhaps, if you entice me enough."

"Are you asking me to seduce you?"

"What else would I be asking?" Emily laughed.

"Oh for the love of all that is holy! Take her away Godric," Cedric pleaded. Shows of such tender teasing always seemed to distress him.

"He's right, Emily, we ought to go home." He tucked

her into his side as he escorted her from the room.

"I should be going as well." Ashton bowed to the others and departed in Godric and Emily's wake.

"Jonathan, would you be so kind as to return Audrey upstairs? She seems not to have heard me when I told her to go to bed," Cedric said.

Jonathan tried to argue. "Under the circumstances, tonight I would prefer not to, what with your reaction to Charles—"

"Unlike Charles, you have a sense of honor. I trust you enough to escort her upstairs."

Charles and Lucien watched the scene unfold with no small amount of amusement. Cedric seemed oblivious to the position he was putting Jonathan in. Lucien opened his mouth to say something, but thought better of it when he noticed Cedric's scowl.

"And you!" Cedric finally turned his wrath to Horatia but found himself unable to do anything with it. "Well, er, I'll get back to you." He turned to Charles and without warning, punched him square in the eye.

"That is for compromising my sister, you scoundrel. I hope it blackens well and warns women against straying from their moral compasses in your presence, at least for a sennight."

Charles groaned and clutched his face. "I was helping Audrey. If you don't understand that, then I will take my leave and see you again when your temper has cooled." He mockingly bowed to them and departed. Without another word Cedric left the drawing room, slamming the door behind him.

AUDREY WATCHED the two remaining men, Lucien and Jonathan, as they stood at the opposite end of the drawing room. Jonathan eyed Audrey with hesitation, then looked to Lucien, who shrugged indifferently. She bit her lip, trying not to smile. Watching him squirm was more than a little amusing.

"Miss Audrey, would you please accompany me upstairs? I should like to—" but Audrey cut him off.

"No, I don't think I shall," she declared. All of the men had been so boorish this evening she wasn't about to give ground, not even for him.

She reached for her fashion magazine again. Jonathan's eyes narrowed. She feigned a yawn, noting the way his nostrils flared and his fists clenched. There was a wicked pleasure to be found in getting under his skin. She knew he only wanted to cement his role in the League and she was making that difficult.

"She needs a firm hand, Jonathan. Show her who's in charge," Lucien encouraged as he leaned back against the wall, grinning.

Jonathan grimaced and walked over to Audrey's chair.

"Miss Audrey." This time his tone was clearly a warning. "You will come with me at once."

With a lift of her chin, Audrey declared war. "You wouldn't *dare* touch me, not after what my brother did to Charles." Secretly she hoped he would be daring enough. The thrill of making him work for her attention left her heart beating madly.

"Audrey, don't encourage him," Horatia cut in. Clearly she saw the storm brewing. Her sister abandoned her book and made to stand, but Lucien pushed away from the wall, blocking her. Horatia dropped back down into her seat as she met Audrey's gaze and gave a warning shake of her head.

"I would dare to touch you, and more, you rebellious little chit," Jonathan said. Before she had time to properly react, he scooped her up into his arms.

She kicked and squirmed. He was ruining the way she'd planned their encounter. It wasn't supposed to go this way. She wanted to be seduced! When her struggles proved futile, she retaliated in a way that worked against small children and unruly pets.

She rolled her magazine into a tube and started whacking him over the head while screaming, "Have at it, you fiend!" Despite the assault, Jonathan never flinched, even when she walloped him soundly between the eyes.

He glared down at her with such a level of irritation that sparks seemed to fly. "Fiend, am I?"

Jonathan marched out of the room with her in his arms and carried her up the stairs. When he reached her bedroom, he nearly kicked the door down. Audrey abandoned the magazine and resumed her struggles.

Lord he is strong, she thought with a sudden pang of desire. Being overwhelmed like this was something she hadn't counted on, nor had she expected to enjoy it so much. Perhaps there was something to be said about being manhandled. What if he lost control of himself and ripped her clothes off? She gasped at the dizzy excitement that overtook her.

He started towards her bed, and suddenly she was airborne. The horrid man had thrown her! She hit the mattress with a startled squeak and rolled right off the other side, landing on the floor with a painful thud.

"Ouch!" she gasped, her left hip smarting. She'd fallen to the floor twice already, a third time was not helping. She tried to get up and a small whimper escaped her lips. No doubt she'd bruised something this time. In an instant Jonathan was there, taking her once more into his arms and setting her more gently back down on her rose-colored bedspread.

"I'm so sorry, Miss Audrey. I got carried away, I didn't mean to…" A heavy blush of mortification spread across Jonathan's face. A lock of his sandy blond hair fell across his forehead and Audrey reached up to brush it back. He flinched from her touch, but Audrey was too entranced by the closeness of his lips.

Those countless conversations she'd had with some of the more open maids hadn't been forgotten. They'd enlightened her to many of the secret intimacies between a man and a woman. The way tongues could touch, the way a man's body would harden, even how a man and woman could kiss each other below the waist to increase pleasure. Audrey had absorbed their tales with fascination, and the hunger for her own experiences had only grown stronger.

But it wasn't until she'd met with Evangeline Mirabeau that she'd learned more specifically how to entice a man to bed her. The ways to coax him to respond, to lure him with lust…

Like a starving woman eyeing a plate of food, she curled her fingers into his cravat and tugged down. His startled mouth collided with hers and she licked the seam of his mouth with her tongue, trying to get him to part his lips. He resisted only a moment before he groaned against her and mounted her on the bed. His hands pushed her dress up past her knees and she spread her legs open beneath him.

He knew how to kiss and she was learning quickly. His lips and tongue danced feverishly against hers with a wild abandon she'd only dreamt about before.

"You taste so sweet," he said as he trailed kisses along her jaw towards her ear.

Audrey was caught in a thunderstorm of panic, pleasure and fascination all coursing through her body at once. More, she needed more now! She released his cravat and slid her hands down his neck, across his shoulders and under his waistcoat, then began to peel it off his shoulders. Never stopping in his kiss, he threw the jacket off and pinned her beneath him again.

One of his calloused palms stroked her thigh, a worker's hands she realized, and for some reason that pleased her. He did not merely exist, he lived, and that set fire to her blood and filled her with a strange recklessness. She wanted to be with him, to live the way he did, and experience things with him. This was no idle gentleman, but a man who earned his living, just as she wished to earn hers.

A pang of hunger streaked through to the juncture between her thighs. She tensed, startled at the frightening feeling of losing control of her body's reactions. Jonathan pressed himself deeply against her at the same moment, as though knowing how she would react. Audrey moaned and arched her body upwards as her hands roamed his tightly muscled body. He hadn't lived a life of leisure; he was corded steel layered with primal sensuality. A rough nibble of her lower lip, a grind of his pelvis against her core and she melted into him completely. One of her hands strayed below his waist, seeking the bulge in his trousers that he fervently pushed against her. He groaned helplessly. They were a symphony of ancient instincts, exotic sensations and thrilling sounds in a perfect moment that should have gone on forever. But it didn't.

Recalling what Evangeline had said to do, she moved one of her hands down to his groin and rubbed at the hard shaft pressing against the front of his trousers. He hissed against her lips, then almost snarled as he took her mouth hungrily. She tried to curl her fingers around as much of his covered length as possible and squeezed. She'd been told it was the best way to stimulate a man's interest so she made sure to squeeze as hard as she could.

Something seemed to shift a little in her hands, like Chinese baoding balls.

Jonathan gasped. His face had become a silent scream. But that face wasn't supposed to come until later, was it? Quickly she realized it was not a look of pleasure. Quite the opposite.

Jonathan ripped himself away from Audrey and dove for his jacket. Without a backward glance he sprinted from the room. Truth be told it was more of a bowlegged hobble. Audrey lay still on her bed for a long moment, struggling for breath, trying to ease the heavy panting and the disappointment she now felt. She'd come so close. What went wrong? One thing was clear however—kissing Charles had certainly not felt like that.

THE DRAWING ROOM was filled with candlelight, firelight and two people who should not have been in the same room. Horatia, not willing to concede defeat, had curled up in her window seat again, her silver gown tucked up around her slippers, knees nestled under her chin. She clutched her novel, *Lady Eustace and the Merry Marquess*, trying to focus on its pages and not the real life marquess sitting by the fire. In the short span of time between Jonathan's battle of wills with Audrey, and Jonathan's hasty departure soon after, Horatia and Lucien found themselves in a battle of their own. Though Lucien's gaze was on the fireplace's vermillion flames, she could sense his attention on her—as though his thoughts had become physical and caressed her skin, making her burn with awareness she wanted to ignore but couldn't.

"How do you find your novel? Amusing? Trite? Impossibly lurid?" The cold silence of the room succumbed to the surprising warmth in his voice.

She shouldn't have answered, but couldn't help it. "It may not be a literary masterpiece, but..."

"But?" Lucien turned in his chair, propping an elbow on the armrest and resting his chin in his palm, looking genuinely interested in what she had to say.

"Well, it is just that Lady Eustace is a most irritating heroine." Horatia idly flipped through the pages she'd already read before chancing a look back in his direction.

"I agree. Eustace is an inferior example of a female character. She lacks all the great qualities that would attract a man."

"And what, pray tell, would those qualities be?" Horatia closed the volume and eyed him curiously.

"Cunning, cleverness, intelligence," Lucien said.

"You don't prefer women to be sweet, demure and obedient?"

"Such a woman would be a dreadful bore. Perhaps a woman could be sweet, but if she was demure and obedient as well that would deprive a man of all the joys of a complex woman, and a woman ought to be complex. Simple things and simple people are quite overrated. Now let us return to this book. Surely the plot entices you to keep reading, despite Lady Eustace's disappointing lack of complexity?"

"Admittedly, it does. Eustace keeps finding herself in the most absurd predicaments. For example, on page fourteen, she gets locked in a tower. A tower! What woman is insipid enough to trust herself to a man's whims like that at the start of the story?"

"It is foolish to get locked in a tower, but as to trusting in a man...given certain circumstances, it can be most thrilling. Wouldn't you agree?"

His eyes were like honey, but his words had reminded her of the sting that often followed such sweetness.

"Thrilling, yes, but not ultimately satisfying, given that trust seems to end in betrayal." She returned to the book, trying to focus on Lady Eustace's mad flight from the marquess's castle in the dead of night. What rubbish! Yet the Merry Marquess's character also kept her attention, probably more than it should, rather like the very real marquess who sat only feet from her.

"Not ultimately satisfying? I seem to recall your screams of pleasure as my fingers—"

"Stop!" she hissed, slamming her book shut. "Or do you forget how that ended?"

He grinned devilishly. "You'll have to make me."

"Oh? Now who's the child?"

Lucien shut his eyes and licked his lips. "I can still taste you. Even though it's been hours, I can't help but wonder if my memory is doing you justice. Would you shiver beneath me? Moan my name in helpless pleasu—"

Lady Eustace and the Merry Marquess had its revenge by catching Lucien right in the face. He cursed, clutching his nose and shot a dark look at Horatia who still sat in the small window seat overlooking the back garden, eyes now fixed on the ceiling. Lucien got up from his chair and started towards her, a predatory gleam in his eyes.

"What are you doing?" Horatia flattened herself against the cold windowpane, hands braced behind her on the chilly glass.

"I think it's time I taught you a lesson, and since there's nothing else you can throw, this seems like the perfect opportunity." He strolled right up to the window seat, hands on his hips.

Horatia raised her chin. "Just being in the same room with you is punishment enough." She crossed her arms over her chest in what was meant to be an imposing pose, but it only seemed to draw his eyes down to her breasts.

"Being with me is a punishment?"

Horatia wondered if she'd said the wrong thing.

"I suppose the better question is why do you see me as a punishment if you claim to love me? And don't deny it. Even now your pupils are dilated and your breath is quickening."

He was right, the arrogant rogue. Her heartbeat was fast and her breath unsteady.

"Do you still desire me even after all that I've done?" He leaned down and cupped her face, brushing his lips teasingly over hers. Horatia swayed towards him, wanting more than that torturously brief contact between their lips.

"Why?" he repeated, his tone low as he nibbled her lower lip.

Horatia refused to answer. He knew full well why. He trapped her back against the window, the frosty glass burning her shoulder blades. His hands slid up her outer thighs, baring her legs to his touch and pooling her silver skirts around her waist. Lucien thrust one knee and then the other between hers as he knelt on the seat, caging her against the window. He spread her legs so he could lift her up against him and made her straddle his lap. Her knees clutched at his hips, molding her to him.

"You didn't answer my question."

"What question?" she asked in a pleasure-filled daze. She felt his body fill with silent laughter and for some reason that angered her, bringing a wave of clarity with it. Horatia leaned back and balled her fist, striking in the general region of Lucien's stomach. In a whoosh of air he doubled over and they both fell from the window seat. Horatia heard her gown rip as she fell off to Lucien's side. He lay on his back, one hand clutching the wounded area.

"Good God!" he howled. "I'm fairly certain you just obliterated my insides. Did your brother teach you to punch like that? Perhaps Charles was in more trouble than I thought; I should have taken up Godric's wager."

"It serves you right for being such an insufferable tease. You're lucky I admire your face so much or I'd claw your eyes out." Her own eyes narrowed as she scrambled to her knees, glaring at him.

"Getting to be quite the harpy in your old age, aren't you?" Lucien laughed.

"Harpy? *Old?*" Horatia's voice was embarrassingly shrill and she clenched her fists, ready to punch him again.

"You've had what? Three seasons? You're practically ancient, my dear. You even have the cats to play the part." Lucien looked to the drawing room door where Muff sat idly licking a white-tipped paw. The cat paused when he caught the two humans fixed on him.

"*Mrreow?*"

Unable to help herself, Horatia laughed. This clearly annoyed Muff and he walked off, his black bottlebrush tail waving like a feather plume. Horatia regained control of herself and got up to retrieve poor Lady Eustace from her spot on the floor. Several pages were bent, like broken wings. Horatia's throat tightened. She'd worked so hard to keep her books in good condition, especially the ones Lucien had given her. Why did the man always have to tie her in such knots?

LUCIEN PROPPED himself up on his elbows on the floor, legs crossed at the ankles, watching her through hooded eyes. He'd enjoyed rousing her, but the resigned hurt in her eyes now made him uncomfortable. She was trying to bend back the pages of the novel and her lack of success was distressing her.

"It's just a book. You can buy a new one."

Her brown eyes misted over. "It wouldn't be the same."

"Don't tell me that you've grown impossibly fond of Lady Eustace in the last few minutes." He was trying to tease her but she wasn't smiling.

"It's not Lady Eustace I'm fond of."

Horatia got to her feet, not seeming to notice the rip in her gown near the shoulder. The silver fabric sagged off her left shoulder, exposing part of the creamy mound of her breast. Lucien silently begged for the gown to drop farther. Would her nipple be a soft peach, or a sweet berry red? He ached to know its taste, to explore that nipple with his mouth, his tongue. Would she like to be laved, bitten or sucked on? All of these questions suddenly seemed vital. He had to know the answers. Lucien whimpered in protest when Horatia tugged the ripped sleeve back up, hiding that taunting bosom from him.

"If you'll excuse me." She made to leave but he lunged to his feet and caught the back of her gown, stopping her dead in her tracks. She reached behind her and gripped the wrist that held her gown, digging her nails into his skin. He didn't even flinch at the pain.

"Release me."

"Answer my question." He found himself grinning, knowing she would break. He wouldn't let her leave otherwise.

"You know the answer," she replied, releasing his wrist and crossing her arms. She turned her face away from him.

"You're no fun tonight," Lucien muttered.

"Since when do you ever want me to be fun, or even want me to *have* fun? As I seem to recall, your life's mission is to rip my heart and soul out and crush them under your boot heels. And congratulations Lucien, you've succeeded. Bravo. Now please let me go, so when I start to cry I may do so in peace. Please, save me the humiliation of breaking down in your presence."

Lucien would not have believed she was close to crying, her tone was too strong. But the almost invisible quake in her pale pink lips spoke volumes.

"I promise to let you go if you answer my question

directly." He lowered his voice, speaking more gently. "Do you still desire me after everything I've done to you?"

"What do you think?" Horatia blinked back the shimmer of tears in her eyes. "I feel like a mouse being toyed with by a cat. You're worse than Muff. You bat at me with your paws, claw me, excite and thrill me with your wild antics, but it is all a game to you. You seduce me because you're bored. You derive pleasure from giving me hope of returned affections, then lay ruin to my dreams. I'm begging you, Lucien. Either kill me now or leave me alone forever, but for God's sake stop this infernal dance. I am in agony every minute of every hour of every day, fearing what you'll do to my heart next. Put me out of my misery and be done with it."

Lucien was stunned. Never had he thought she would be so honest over something so private. Her warm brown eyes blinded him. The pain in her voice cut through him, leaving scars he justly deserved. She was right, he'd gone out of his way to ignore her these last few years, only to tease her when he couldn't stand to stay away, and what use had that been?

Why did he persist in torturing Horatia? In treating her so callously he'd taken a grim satisfaction from his ability to control his desire for her, though that had become more and more difficult as of late. Slowly he loosened his grip on her dress. A moment passed as neither of them moved and then Horatia, clutching her book like a shield, fled from the room and up the stairs.

Lucien shut his eyes at the distant sound of her door closing.

Something had changed tonight. He wasn't sure what, but he felt it deep in his bones. It was as though he'd been set on a course and turning back now was impossible. What was more he didn't want to. The only thing he knew was that his life's mission, as Horatia had called it, had changed.

Starting tomorrow he'd never again pester or tease Horatia, or be cold to her for that matter. He would maintain a polite but hopefully warm distance from her. And once this dreadful business with Waverly was over he would start looking for a wife. If Godric could settle down, then Lucien could too. It just couldn't be with Horatia.

Cedric would never condone that marriage. If Lucien were in his place, he wouldn't have allowed it either. Cedric had seen him sleep with two women at once, and knew Lucien had done things in bed even some of the League shied away from. Stupidly, he'd boasted of such conquests and the cunning methods of seduction he'd used.

No, Cedric would never allow his sister to marry a man like him. Nor would Lucien find a woman who would rouse his passions, but then he'd always known he'd be doomed to a loveless marriage. He'd find some quiet unobtrusive girl, marry her quickly and be done with it. If Horatia saw him married, then she'd be able to move on herself. *And the past will be truly buried,* he thought.

A sleek, furry, black body appeared in the drawing room doorway. Muff had returned. Lucien, too weary to go and summon a hackney to return to Half Moon Street, decided to stay here, warm by the fire, still burning with the memory of Horatia's form against his. He walked over to the couch against the wall, puffed a few pillows and threw himself down on it. The fire crackled, the only light in the room after he'd extinguished the candles. Muff gave an odd little chirp and pounced on Lucien's chest.

Lucien, like Cedric, was a lover of all animals and he scratched the wizened cat behind the ears. The responding purr was loud but soothing. As sleep started to close in on him, he wondered if he could spend the rest of his days as a bachelor, with nothing but a cat like Muff for company. Or perhaps he would spend his days at the Midnight Garden, whose ladies were always eager to make his dreams come true.

It wasn't ladies he dreamed about however, but one teary-eyed beauty in a torn silver gown. A Cinderella whose Prince Charming had not danced with her at the ball, nor kissed her before the clock struck midnight. In the dark moonlit palace of his dreams, he held a lone silver satin slipper and wept, for what he did not know.

CHAPTER 11

The next morning, Horatia donned a morning dress of twilled French silk in a dark rosy pink and went down the main stairs. The house was quiet, which meant that Cedric and Audrey were still asleep. Her normally soft steps became tiptoes as she trod through the house. She passed by the drawing room, paused in puzzlement and retreated back a few feet to gaze discreetly through the open doorway.

In the far corner, Lucien was stretched out on his back, asleep on the daybed. Muff, the little feline devil, was stretched out on his back across Lucien's stomach, one paw raised in the air, tail twitching at the very tip. Lucien had one hand flat over the cat's belly, his fingers surprisingly graceful as they caressed him. It was the sort of caress a person made half-asleep, or half-awake.

Horatia felt an ache rise in her as she watched. She

would never know if Lucien would stroke her this way in bed. Only then did it occur to Horatia that Lucien hadn't left last night. A flash of remorse shot through her. She'd been a horrible hostess. A room should have been prepared and a bed turned down for him. Lucien should not have suffered the discomforts of a daybed.

Horatia took a tentative step inside, but Muff shifted upon seeing her and began to purr. Fearing she'd wake Lucien, she retreated to the breakfast room where a hot meal was already awaiting her. The coffee was fresh and the rich scent danced out into the hall. Horatia, preferring tea, saw to preparing herself a warm cup with plenty of sugar. She'd only started to bite into her toast when a sleepy-eyed Lucien joined her.

Even as he yawned and ran a hand through his tousled red hair he was a god among mortals. He gave her a surprisingly sheepish smile which would have sent her straight to the floor had she not already been seated. It reflected a bashfulness for having done something devilishly intimate the night before. Horatia's breath caught as he tugged his rumpled waistcoat down and tried to straighten his cravat. Was this how his mistresses saw him after a night of passion? If they had they would have insisted on getting him straight back into bed. At least that's what she would have wanted. The thought made her blush but Lucien didn't seem to notice.

"Morning," he said, taking a chair opposite her.

"Good morning," she managed to reply. It had startled

her, this change, this lack of cold hostility or casual flirting. What was he playing at?

"Is the coffee still hot?" he asked.

"Yes, it's been freshly brewed." She leaned forward to pour him a cup.

"Wonderful. Two sugars, please," he asked when she started to slide the cup and saucer over.

She hastily dropped two cubes into his cup. Odd, she always thought he'd take it black and strong.

Lucien noticed her puzzled look and grinned.

"I can never stomach the stuff unless it is sweet. It has been noted, according to my brother Lawrence, as one of my greatest faults."

Horatia giggled, despite her intention to remain stoic.

"Then perhaps you should know that I once saw Lawrence put *three* sugars into his tea one afternoon last spring." She relayed this in a conspiratorial whisper. "He tries to do so when no one is looking."

"That cur! Tea I can drink straight, and the little weasel dares to needle me? Oh the things I endure!" he bemoaned theatrically, clutching his chest. "I will get even with him the next time I face him in the boxing ring." Lucien threw this out with dramatic flare.

Horatia winced at the image of Lucien striking his younger brother in the nose hard enough to draw blood. But men often did the most foolish things. Her own brother was clear proof of that.

"I trust you slept well?" Lucien changed the topic of conversation.

"Yes, well enough, but oh…you should have had the servants prepare a room for you, Lucien. To sleep on that daybed must have been wretchedly uncomfortable." She could feel her face warm as she spoke. It was a clear admission of her failure as a hostess. Thank goodness her mother wasn't alive to witness it.

He shrugged and sampled his coffee. "Nonsense, it was fine. A bit stiff, but nothing less than I deserved. Which brings me to the point I must speak to you about."

Horatia shook her head as she tried to stop him from saying anything that would ruin such a pleasant beginning to the day.

He held up a hand and any protests she had died on her lips. "Now hear me out, Horatia. What happened last night, everything I said, I apologize unreservedly. I was childish and cruel. I have no reason to ignore you or be so cold. So please accept my apologies and tell me you agree that we should let bygones be bygones."

He reached across the breakfast table, offering one of his hands. Before Horatia could stop herself she was sliding her fingers into his firm grasp.

"Friends?" he asked. This simple connection was more intimate to her than any kiss he'd given her before. It was a touch he'd offered out of friendship with good intentions, not because he was toying with her—and it scared her. It reminded her that she would always want more, but this she would take happily.

"Friends," she agreed.

"Excellent," he said. He eyed the newspaper lying near her elbow. "Is that the *Morning Post?*"

"Yes, would you like it?" She slid the paper over.

Lucien loved the news. Whether he was actually concerned with the latest political or social gossip, or merely using it as a shield at breakfast, she wasn't sure, but it was a habit he'd had as long as she'd known him. Horatia watched him take the paper and whip it up, hiding him from the world. She understood that need better than anyone. Every year she used his Christmas presents, the books he gave her, as a refuge of sorts. She'd spent more than one afternoon tucked away in the library reading, rather than join Audrey and Cedric on a tour of Hyde Park. It was easier to hide than to face the realities of the world. She didn't want to be husband hunting, not when she was already in love with a man.

"Care for toast?" she offered, pushing a tray in his direction. His paper wall wilted over his fingertips, allowing him to peer over the pages to eye the tray.

"Sounds lovely." He reached for the tray and after retrieving a piece he returned to his paper. Horatia blinked. Was it possible they were actually getting along? Unfortunately, her quiet reflection of this question was disrupted when Audrey and Cedric arrived in breakfast room, squabbling like children.

"A day? A single day? Cedric, I can't be ready by then! That's barely enough time for my maid to pack my hats, let alone my entire wardrobe! Must we go so soon?"

"I'm sorry. I'll ask the lurking assassins in the shadows to give you more time to prepare, shall I?"

"Don't be so dramatic," said Audrey. "It doesn't suit you."

"What's in a day?" Horatia asked politely, hoping to quell Audrey's rising temper. Her younger sister spun on her, seeking an ally.

"Tell him, Horatia. Tell him that one day to pack for Kent is not nearly enough time."

"Lucien, help a man out and tell her that she need not bring *every* article of clothing with her?" Cedric begged as he threw himself into the seat next to his friend.

"Why are we going to Kent?" Horatia asked. There was only one place in Kent she'd ever been to, and surely Cedric wasn't sending them there. Not after what she'd done the last time. She had been a child, but the embarrassment pulled at her as if it had been yesterday.

Lucien stirred a spoon in his coffee, raised it to his lips and met her gaze over the top of the rim. "You, Audrey and Cedric have been invited to join my family for the Christmas holidays. We leave for my estate tomorrow, before first light."

"See! No time at all!" Audrey punctuated her complaint with a glare at Lucien, who had abandoned his paper and was smiling rather too sweetly back at her.

Horatia knew that look well. Her little sister had better watch out, or Lucien would trick her into doing something she didn't want to do.

"Surely we would be an unnecessary burden, especially during the holidays." Horatia gave a pleading look at her brother, seeking his support.

"Sorry, Horatia, but Ashton has given me orders."

"Do you always let him dictate your life?" Audrey snapped.

Cedric didn't answer, but Lucien did.

"Your brother listens to reason from his friends when your safety may well depend on our guidance. I would not become too upset, ladies. My mother will insist on taking you to town shopping until you have more clothes than your trunks can carry. Wouldn't that be nice?" Lucien was nothing if not a charmer.

Audrey flounced into the chair beside Horatia and sighed. "I suppose I can endure that. I do so love Lady Rochester. She reads *La Belle Assemblée* you know."

Lucien smiled and Horatia's heart turned over. Everyone who knew Lady Rochester was privy to her obsessions, fashion being among them.

"Hmm…indeed," he murmured as he sipped his coffee.

Audrey started a lengthy discussion on the various modes of neck cloths and the proper styles for an evening out. The men responded with low grunts of agreement whenever she seemed to pause and wait for their attention. Not that she seemed to care what their response was, nor did they. Had she asked for a thousand pounds and a new horse they no doubt would have agreed as well, strictly to keep up appearances that they were listening to her talk.

Horatia finished her breakfast and quietly slipped out of the room, something she found easy to do whenever Audrey discussed fashion. Horatia would be packed and ready to leave in a mere two hours. But there was nothing she could do about the flutter in her stomach as she realized the four of them would be squashed most uncomfortably in a carriage for several long hours. Despite Lucien's new desire to be civil to her she still carried a deep-seated uneasiness inside. He had to be up to something, and she dreaded what he might have in store for her.

CHAPTER 12

Something wasn't right. Ashton shifted uncomfortably in his knee-high black boots. The actual gardens behind the Midnight Garden were chilly and his breath puffed out in small pale clouds as he waited in a concealed area of tall shrubbery to see where the two men from last night might rendezvous.

Lucien had been positive that he'd heard Waverly's voice as the one giving orders to the hired assassin. But it was easy to let prejudices color a man's memory. Ever since the League had confronted Waverly that night by the River Cam, when he'd attempted to drown Charles, Waverly had transformed from mere mortal to bogey-man. An innocent man had perished during their struggle and enmity had been born. It was only a matter of time before someone would pay for the life lost that night.

Ashton knew it was nonsense to lay the blame for every misfortunate at Waverly's door, but the man did seem to have a knack for spreading pain and trouble. Ashton had done his best to remain detached from such thoughts. Still, if Lucien had heard correctly, then Waverly was finally trying to make good on his threat.

Ashton could still hear Waverly's cruel shout from the shore opposite them after they fished Charles out from the river. "You'll pay! Each and every one you! Not one of you rogues will know peace or a long life! Do you hear me? You are all damned!" Their enemy had been clutching the body of the man who'd died. It was a sight Ashton couldn't erase from his mind, nor the guilt lurking behind it. Perhaps he was right. Perhaps they were damned.

It was Charles who suffered the worst. He still sometimes woke in a fit of screams, unable to recognize a soul around him and crying out about the water filling his lungs. When they happened to be under the same roof for a night, Ashton was adept at quieting Charles and doing it so quickly that he never woke up anyone else. It was why the poor man always slept so late.

Godric joined him, crouching down, his boots crunching in the snow. "I don't like it, Ash. This place is far too quiet." The two of them had arrived first thing in the morning to see if anyone had witnessed Waverly or if any evidence existed that could lead to the man or his hirelings. So far, they'd come up with nothing, not that

Ashton expected differently. Most of last night's visitors had crept away by coach or foot in the early hours before dawn to return to their daily lives.

"I don't either. It's too bold, too much of a coincidence that Lucien overheard them." Ashton knelt into a low squat, balancing on the balls of his feet as he traced a gloved fingertip over the indentions made by a boot. A pattern of prints had led away from the meeting spot last night just through the area where he and Godric now waited and hid.

"Do you think he has another target in mind?" Godric asked.

"You mean have us scrambling to protect Cedric, when it is another of us he plans to kill?" Ashton raised a brow. "It is certainly possible. I wish I knew how to better protect us. If we scattered it would diminish our strength in numbers, but we'd be harder to find. If we kept ourselves together, it's easier for him to focus his resources. Either way we will be in danger."

"Sometimes it is a pity we have a standard of morals. I for one would love to put that sniveling piece of filth in his grave." Godric's eyes were sharp as jade daggers.

"If I didn't have some concern for the state of my immortal soul, I would have ended his life back in Cambridge," Ashton agreed solemnly.

Godric placed a hand on his shoulder.

"Our souls were stained enough that night, and we had to rescue Charles from a watery death. If we had it to do over again, I would still let Waverly escape. I'd choose Charles's life over Waverly's death every time," Godric said.

"It's not a choice I regret, but Waverly is a menace. Something has to be done."

"Agreed." Godric rubbed his gloved hands together to warm them.

"It is half past ten now," said Ashton, examining his pocket watch. "We should send word to Lucien before he and Cedric leave. I think that the rest of us should remain in London, but keep in close contact. I want everyone to report in to your townhouse Godric, every night by ten o'clock. I don't want anyone getting hurt by not paying attention."

"I'll have Jonathan move in with Emily and me so you won't have to worry about him," Godric suggested.

"He's fine where he is. I'd actually prefer to keep him under my roof. He has excellent instincts. I think I'll have Charles move in for the holidays as well. I'll keep them both with me until this is over, and we can continue our investigation here."

"Then we'll only have to defend against Waverly on three fronts."

Godric and Ashton started walking back through the hedgerows when a man in a cloak and cap exited the nearest door, heading straight towards them. They ducked behind a tall cluster of trees as the man strode past them, cloak unfurling behind him like a black flag.

He walked directly to the spot just beyond where Ashton and Godric had been moments before and seemed to be waiting, most impatiently.

"Do you think that's one of the men?" Godric nodded at their suspect.

"I think it highly likely," Ashton whispered. "Stay here and watch the door to the Garden's house. I shall endeavor to get a closer look at our mystery fellow."

Ashton used the cover of more bushes to conceal himself as he crept along the nearest path created by the shrubs. Through the thick foliage he could make out the fluttering of the man's cape as he paced back and forth. There wasn't a clear enough view through the bushes for him to get a glimpse of the man so he had to chance raising his head or peering around the last bush when the path ended. He opted for peering around rather than over the bush.

A fallen twig snapped beneath his boot and the sound drew the pacing man up short. He spun, and their eyes met. Not long, but long enough for Ashton to see cold caution change to decisive action. The man drew a pistol from his cloak and fired. The shot rang out like a crack of thunder and a spike of fire surged through Ashton. He cursed and clutched his left arm. When he pulled his hand away, his black leather glove gleamed with the sheen of blood.

"Ash!" Godric ran in his direction, glancing about for signs of the shooter, but the man had vanished. He hadn't returned to the Garden house, nor had he gone in any direction they could see.

"Should we go after him?" Godric asked. "I didn't see which way he went."

"Nor did I. Must have had an escape route planned."

"Clever bastard," Godric said. "Why did he shoot at you?"

Ash shrugged, wincing. "He saw me peer around the edge of the bush and reacted. I think he fired because he recognized me."

"Good thing he missed."

Ashton stumbled and gripped Godric by the sleeve for support. "He...he didn't actually." Blood began to flow freely down his left arm. The pair quickly ducked back inside the Midnight Garden.

"What? Ash, you're bleeding! Hell man, why didn't you tell me you'd been shot?" Godric's face turned white as marble.

"Pardon me if my mind is a bit fogged with pain at the moment," Ashton replied sarcastically. "Hurts like the very devil too. Do you mind if we get out of here before I lose any more blood?"

"Right, of course. Come on." His friend gripped him by his good arm and helped him over to the door leading back into the Garden's house.

The owner of the Midnight Garden, Madame Chanson ran over to them. "Did I hear a gunshot?" she asked in a panic.

"Yes. It seems the man we were looking for didn't wish to be found."

"Should I contact the Bow Street Runners?"

"He's already long gone, I'm afraid, and there's your anonymity to consider. Could you summon my carriage immediately? And have a doctor sent to my residence quickly." Godric gripped Ashton's right arm firmly to keep his wounded friend on his feet. As he spoke, he removed his cravat and tied a makeshift tourniquet.

Godric's carriage pulled up and he helped Ashton inside. The bullet, whatever sinister path it had taken, had left a nasty wound in Ashton's arm.

"My home isn't far, we can wait for the doctor there. Emily can fuss over you until then."

"You'd subject me to your wife's fussing?" Ashton gave a pained chuckle as he clamped his right hand over his wound.

"Of course I would."

"Have I wronged you somehow? Why would you let Emily tend to me? I might lose my entire arm in her desire to play nursemaid."

"I fear more what Emily would do to me if she's not allowed to help."

Ashton groaned in pain and his vision blurred. Godric shouted for the coachman to go faster.

"Stay awake, Ash," Godric barked as Ashton gave in to the temptation to close his eyes for a moment.

"Trying to," Ashton muttered. "In all of the times

we've gotten into scrapes, I've never been shot. You hear of soldiers speak of it with some degree of pride and bravado. The experience, I've decided, is highly overrated." His frowned down at his bound arm. "Perhaps you ought to distract me?"

"That I can do. So I spent all of last night trying to seduce my wife into telling me how she and her companions escaped their room last night and into the drawing room without us seeing them. But despite my best efforts, she disclosed nothing. What are your theories?"

Ashton gritted his teeth, trying to formulate an answer.

"I would say that they convinced one of the servants to let them out and they snuck down to the dining room while we were still in the drawing room. Once we went upstairs they moved once again and waited there for us."

"That is what I assumed as well. Though I still cannot figure out how Emily embroidered that phrase *Never Challenge a Woman* so quickly. I know she hasn't been doing any needlepoint." Ashton smiled but his expression changed into a wince as the carriage rolled to a stop at Essex House. A footman was at the carriage door. He opened it and helped Godric take Ashton out and up to the house door.

"Thank you, Timmons. We're expecting a doctor. Have him brought in immediately."

Godric threw Ashton's good arm around his shoulders and helped his friend get inside.

Emily was waiting at the top of the stairs and with a panicked cry she rushed down to help them.

"What happened to him?" she asked.

Godric motioned for her to open the door to the drawing room. Emily did, then called for a maid to bring some water and cloths.

"Lay him on the couch, Godric." Emily indicated a blue and gold brocaded bit of furniture. She hastened to help Ashton sit down. He took a deep shaky breath that made Godric and Emily share a look of concern.

"We've sent for a doctor," Godric told her.

"That's all well and good, if he doesn't bleed out before then," Emily snapped.

Godric took hold of Ashton's shoulders and looked his friend in the eye.

"Do you plan on bleeding out, Ash?" he asked, partially in jest. Ash shook his head in a wobbly sort of way.

"No, Your Grace." He chuckled. The blood loss was making him feel a little silly, not because he was losing much of it, but because the sight of blood sometimes made him lightheaded. Besides, his friend bickering with his wife was far too amusing.

"See? He'll be fine, darling." Godric wrapped an arm around her shoulders and tucked her into his side.

"Don't you *darling* me, Godric. If he dares to die in my drawing room, I'll revive him only to kill him again myself!" Emily helped remove the old binding on his arm and then peeled off Ashton's coat. "Followed shortly by yourself."

The maid returned with cloths and a bowl of water. Emily made short work of removing Ashton's shirt, then used a thick strip of cloth to make a fresh tourniquet. Godric helped her, taking note of the wound's condition.

"Looks like it went clean through. No bone damage that I can see," Godric said, but Emily was too busy cooing to Ashton as she placed a wet cloth to his forehead.

Ashton stared up at her, admiring the way she tended to him. Godric was a lucky man. He couldn't help but wonder if he'd ever be so lucky. He'd always viewed relationships with the intent of what he might gain in the way of business and it had won him many partnerships in bed, but never love. Perhaps he was becoming a sentimental fool.

It's just the blood loss, nothing more. A man faces death and he starts thinking all sorts of wild things.

"How did this happen?" Emily asked.

"Ash and I were at the Midnight Garden, hoping to catch the men Lucien overheard last night. They said they would meet there this morning. The hired man caught sight of Ash spying on him and shot him before fleeing. We didn't even have a chance to give chase."

"Did you see who it was?" Emily stroked Ashton's pale blond hair back from his face. He leaned in to her gentle touch with a soft sigh.

"No one I recognized, though the reverse may not be true."

Emily shut her eyes. "Do you still believe Waverly is behind this?"

He nodded. "Many dislike us, a few despise us, but only Waverly has ever proclaimed to want us dead."

EMILY WAS SILENT A LONG TIME. She sat down next to Ashton, keeping the cool cloth to his head.

Ashton held an important part in Emily's heart. He'd championed her cause to Godric, and had been the first to see that she and Godric were in love with each other. Without his cool head and warm heart, the pair might never have believed enough in their love for each other.

Ashton began to close his eyes and Emily slapped him forcefully across the cheek.

"Don't you dare fall asleep, Ashton!"

His stunned gaze at the assault seemed to amuse Godric. It took quite a lot to shock Ashton.

"You slapped me?" he asked, shocked by Emily's behavior.

"And I'll do it again if you shut your eyes," Emily threatened.

Ashton had the gall to let out a hoarse chuckle. "Now I know how Charles must feel on a daily basis. Still, I'm sure the benefits more than compensate for it."

Despite her concern, Emily smiled. No doubt if Ashton had enough energy to tease her, he wasn't dead yet.

A footman appeared at the drawing room door, informing them they had a visitor.

"That will be the doctor." Emily guessed as she jumped up and ran towards the door. But it wasn't. It was Anne Chessely, Baron Chessely's daughter and one of Emily's closest friends.

"Anne?" Emily said in disappointment.

The crestfallen look on Anne's face wasn't hard to miss, even from where Godric stood. "Should I go? I would not wish to intrude." Anne chewed her bottom lip, looking doubtful as Emily ushered her inside.

"No, please come in. I was just expecting someone else." Emily attempted to hide the truth, but Anne was too clever by half.

"Was that blood outside in the snow on the steps? I see it here too." Anne pointed to a trail of droplets leading towards the drawing room.

"Er, what?"

"That *is* blood." Anne abandoned her muff and bent down to dip a finger into the nearest splotch. Her gloved fingertip came back bright red.

"Emily, you didn't *kill* Godric did you? I mean, I'm sure you had a good reason, but it's foolish to leave a blood trail." Anne's gaze swept the hall, seeking the truth.

"Murder? Heavens no, Anne. Wherever do you come

up with such nonsense?" Emily tried to lead her away to another room, but Anne, who was fairly strong for a woman, pulled free and opened the drawing room door.

Emily froze behind her, fearing Anne would faint as she took in the scene of Godric tending to a half-naked Ashton. A bloody shirt lay on the ground near his feet.

"Oh my…" Anne exhaled in shock.

Ashton turned his head in her direction, bright blue eyes now dim with pain.

"Miss Chessely, I do beg your pardon for my lack of proper attire. As you can see I was shot this morning. Hurts something dreadful," Ashton finished in a breathless apology. "So, if you don't mind, some privacy would be appreciated."

"Forgive me, Lord Lennox, it is I who intruded." Anne backed up so quickly that she trod over Emily's toes. Emily squeaked and jumped out of the way.

"Sorry," Anne muttered as she retreated into the hall, away from Ashton and all that blood. "What happened to Lord Lennox? Did he fight in a duel?" she asked in a scandalized whisper.

"Don't be silly. He's too levelheaded for that. No, this is a much longer story I'm afraid. Would you care to come to the morning room for some tea?" Emily offered.

"If it's not too much trouble."

Just then the footman, Timmons, came in through the front door, with a doctor in tow. The two men went straight to the drawing room and shut the door. Emily breathed a sigh of relief.

"That was who I was expecting when you came," Emily explained as she and Anne entered the morning room. "I'm sure the wound isn't that serious. At least it didn't appear to be once Godric got it cleaned up." She glanced back at the way the doctor had gone. The blood had panicked her, but now she was sure Ashton would be fine. If he had the breath enough to tease her and speak to Anne, the man was not ready for the next world yet. Didn't Lady Society in her articles always say that no bullet could kill a rogue?

A maid brought them a tray of tea and Emily quickly narrated the disturbing events of the previous night as well as this morning's close call with Ashton. Emily always felt free to speak with Anne, especially in matters concerning her husband and the League.

It had been Anne who had first told her, or rather warned her, about the League of Rogues. Anne was acquainted with Cedric and knew about the others only through reputation since she and the League both avoided the social events of the season like the plague.

Cedric had courted Anne briefly, the year before Emily's abduction. He'd had no success in seducing her and sadly had abandoned the endeavor entirely. Emily thought it a pity, but Anne didn't want to marry. She was content to live with her father and breed Thoroughbred horses for racing. She kept her fortune and her land this way, but she was also lonely. At least, Emily suspected she was.

"So, where are the other rogues?" Anne asked as she sipped her tea.

"Charles, Jonathan, Ashton and Godric are all still in London. But Cedric and Lucien are on their way to Lucien's estate in Kent. But you must tell no one of this."

A flicker of emotion passed over Anne's face so briefly that Emily thought she might have imagined it. Was it possible that Anne felt something for Cedric after all? She'd never indicated anything but mild irritation at his attempts to woo her. But the moment he'd stopped calling on her, Anne had started showing up at the Essex doorstep with surprising frequency. Anne never asked after Cedric, at least not directly, but she did ask where the other League members were each time she came over.

"Will you and your father be spending the holidays in London?" Emily asked.

"Yes. I wish we weren't though. The snow is much prettier in the country this time of year and I usually like to take a ride on Christmas morning."

Emily sighed wistfully. "That sounds lovely. It is a pity that Cedric will be in Kent. I might have persuaded him to take us out on the town in his curricle with his pair of Arabian mares."

At the mention of Cedric's Arabians, Anne's eyes brightened.

"Is it true that he won them in a wager from a sheikh?"

"Has he not told you the story himself?" Emily was genuinely surprised. She knew that part of Cedric's purpose in courting Anne was to achieve his desire of breeding his mares with Anne's stallions.

"I'd only heard the rumors from the papers." Anne looked put out at this.

"When you next see him, I'll have him tell you. I could never do the story justice." That was certainly the truth. At the time Cedric had told her the story, she'd been fairly distracted by Godric and the rest of the League, what with being their prisoner at the time.

"If we weren't so worried for his safety right now, I would insist you and I go to Kent. But as it is, Godric is one minute away from locking me in a blasted tower for my own safety."

"I imagine Lord Sheridan was not fond of going to Kent?" Anne asked astutely.

Emily nodded. She was surprised Cedric hadn't fought harder to stay in London, at least by Godric's account. Cedric was incredibly brave and it must have killed him to turn his back on a fight, especially where Waverly was involved.

When the ladies had finished their tea, Anne rose and started for the door.

"Anne, would you and your father like to come to

dinner this evening? I know it's short notice. I promise to have my hall cleaned of blood by then," Emily jested.

Her friend smiled and gave a little nod. "My father and I would be delighted. See you tonight."

Anne departed and Emily turned her attention back towards the drawing room. She squared her shoulders and walked in, eager to check on Ashton and her husband.

CHAPTER 13

The Russell family estate in northern Kent, four miles east of the village of Hexby, was in an uproar. Jane, the Marchioness of Rochester, was on the verge of strangling her second youngest child, one Linus Winston Russell. Despite her own knowledge that she had birthed that troublesome boy twenty-one years before, sometimes she swore he hadn't matured past the age of eight.

The young man in question was balanced precariously on a rickety ladder in the entryway of Rochester Hall. He held a sprig of what Lady Rochester feared was mistletoe. That child was in for a thrashing when she got hold of him. She'd found his handiwork all over the house. Every single doorway, window, and alcove was adorned with that dreaded poisonous plant. The chaos and impropriety that would ensue from his little prank could bring down the very stones of Rochester Hall.

Lord knew, her brood were wicked enough that they didn't need the help of mistletoe. It was in their blood, and sadly, not a trait taken from her husband's side.

Linus, having a full head of red hair like all of her children, was at the moment wiping a sheen of sweat off his brow before he resumed reaching for the upper door-jamb to affix the mistletoe. The forest green waistcoat and buff breeches he wore were well tailored to him—the body of a man, her baby boy no longer.

Lady Rochester blinked back a rebellious tear. How had her child grown up so fast? Hadn't it been yesterday that he'd put a frog in Lysandra's bed and tacks on Lucien's study chair? It had to be the holidays bringing up all this silly emotion. She stormed down the stairs to deal with her youngest's antics.

"Linus Winston Bartholomew Russell!" She bellowed the name in such an imperious tone that Linus dropped the mistletoe with a cry of alarm and scrambled to steady himself on the now wobbling ladder.

"Mama?" He hesitantly turned to face her as she glared up at him from the ground, her foot tapping with anger.

"Get down here at once," she barked.

Linus practically fell off the ladder, his boots smacking loudly on the marble floor.

"Just what do you think you're up to?" she demanded.

"Nothing." He tried to nonchalantly kick the mistletoe under a cabinet with a booted toe. As if she wouldn't notice!

Lady Rochester grabbed him by the ear. She was two seconds away from hauling him up to the old nursery when the knocker on the front door clanked four times. Linus grinned at his apparent reprieve and tugged free of his mother's hold.

"I'm not done with you yet. There *will* be a reckoning." She gave him one of her death glares before her face transformed into a heartwarming smile suitable for guests. She waved off the butler, who was advancing towards the entryway. "I'll answer it, Mr. Jenkins." She opened the door to find a welcome surprise. Her eldest child, Lucien, was there as well as his close friend, Viscount Sheridan, and his two sisters.

"Mother!" Lucien greeted her warmly, bending down to kiss her cheek.

"Lucien, my dear boy, so wonderful to see you. But it would have been more wonderful if you had sent me a note in advance. Especially if you were bringing guests." This last bit was delivered in a low warning tone.

Lucien lowered his head. "We apologize for the short notice, Mother, but it was important to come straight away." Lucien offered Horatia his arm to escort her inside and Cedric did the same for Audrey.

"Oh?" Lady Rochester's eyes narrowed.

"It's a long story, Mother, but I will explain later. May

we have some tea? The trip was devilishly long and tiresome."

"Yes, of course. Right this way. Lovely to see you all, Lord Sheridan, Miss Sheridan, and Miss Audrey." Lady Rochester let Cedric kiss her hand before she embraced the two girls warmly. Then she led them to the nearest parlor where a strapping young footman awaited her orders—Gordon, if she remembered correctly. One of the recent replacements she'd had to acquire.

"Tea and scones if you please, Gordon," she said.

The servant nodded and departed to see to her wishes.

Lady Rochester caught sight of her youngest trying to sneak past the open doorway of the salon unseen. "Linus!" He froze mid-step, shoulders hunched in resignation before he sighed and came back into the parlor. She fixed Linus with a look that promised misery if he tried to escape again. "Greet our guests."

"Good afternoon," he replied, bowing towards Cedric and his sisters.

Lady Rochester did not miss Audrey's look as she tried to fight the urge to laugh. Linus and Audrey were quite good friends, as good as men and women could be without the complications of their genders getting in the way. Perhaps co-conspirators was a more apt description. Still, they were now at that age where it would be unwise to leave them alone together.

Lucien sat back in the chair he'd chosen, perfectly at

ease. Lady Rochester watched as the eldest of her brood of hellions interacted with the youngest.

"How are you, Lucien?" Linus asked.

"Well. And you? How was Cambridge?"

"Fine. But I am glad to be through with it," Linus admitted.

"I'll bet." Cedric sniggered. It wasn't a secret that he'd loved everything about school, apart from the schooling.

Gordon returned with a tea tray and Linus moved to sit down next to Audrey on the loveseat. With no small amusement, Lady Rochester studied their interaction out of the corner of her eye, whilst they believed everyone else was looking away and talking. Audrey prodded him with a sharp little elbow. He eyed the offending weapon, and the second the opportunity presented itself, he pinched her arm in retaliation. Audrey let out a strangled little sound that came out somewhere between an *eek* and *ouch*.

She blushed and held her teacup in defense. "The tea is rather hot."

"Really?" Lady Rochester eyed the teapot, trying not to laugh at the mischievousness of youth. "Now Lord Sheridan, may I offer you rooms at the Hall through the New Year? It would be lovely to have you all here to celebrate Christmas. The house will be happily full, you see. I've just invited the Cavendishes to come from Brighton."

"We'd be delighted to stay, Lady Rochester," Cedric answered.

"The Cavendishes will be coming?" Audrey asked excitedly.

The Cavendishes were old family friends of both the Russells and the Sheridans. It wasn't too hard to guess what Audrey was excited about. Eligible men were always exciting for a young lady.

"The entire family will be here. I'm hoping that Mrs. Cavendish and I might manage to marry off one of our children before either of us dies." She threw the statement out with inner glee, waiting for the fireworks to begin.

"Mother!" Lucien choked on the scone he'd been eating.

"Oh don't give me that horrified look, Lucien. I quite gave up on you years ago. But perhaps I can convince Lysandra to set her cap for Gregory Cavendish. He's quite a handsome young man, and well-inlaid you know."

Linus watched her in terror. "Mama, just because he's a bang-up cove, doesn't mean Lysa will have him, or even that he'll have her." Linus seemed most insistent on defending his sister, probably because he believed there was no worse fate than marriage.

"A bang-up cove? Where do you learn such language?" Lady Rochester sighed and looked up, imploring the heavens to explain why she'd been burdened with such obstinate offspring.

Linus grinned and reached for a scone. They both knew vexing her was one of the true joys of his life.

He piped up as he swallowed the last of his scone. "Lord Sheridan, may I escort Miss Audrey outside? I'm sure she would like some fresh air after the long carriage ride here."

"Not without a chaperone," Lady Rochester intoned.

"But Mama," Linus whined.

Audrey put a hand on his arm indicating him to shush.

"My sister shall chaperone us. Won't you, Horatia?"

"Yes, of course," Horatia replied.

"If I'm not worried, Lady Rochester, then you shouldn't be," Cedric reassured her.

"I suppose that is safe enough."

"Come on then," Linus offered his arm to Audrey. Horatia followed the pair out of the salon and into the hall. Linus and Audrey immediately bent their heads together, whispering now that they were out of sight of Lady Rochester.

Horatia groaned as she heard Audrey giggle wickedly. Linus must have had a scheme afoot and he was determined to rope Audrey into it. Knowing Linus as she did, which unfortunately was quite well, Horatia guessed it would be a prank of some sort. From time to time Linus and Audrey shot looks over their shoulders at her, as though worried she might be eavesdropping on their plotting.

Horatia raised her hands in surrender. "As long as I

am not the victim of whatever you're planning, I won't spoil your fun."

"I make no promises," said Linus. The rascal was one year her senior in age, but not nearly as mature. It was why he'd always taken more to Audrey. Horatia couldn't even begin to count how many afternoons she and Lysandra had been the target of pranks from this unholy alliance.

"Linus, where is Lysa?" Horatia asked. She'd rather seek out her friend than linger in their presence. Her role of chaperone was nonsense, everyone but Lady Rochester seemed to know that.

"Last I saw, she was in the library." With that, he and Audrey darted up the stairs and vanished from view.

Horatia found herself alone in the massive entryway of Rochester Hall. It was a beautiful Georgian country house with sandy stones on the outside and marble within. She admired the tapestries on the walls depicting various scenes of pastoral bliss. Gazing at the scenes, she lost track of time, remembering the last time she'd been here. The memory was still so fresh that she felt it emerge from the gloom of her memory and envelop her fully.

CHAPTER 14

*R*ochester Hall, Kent, 1815

It was a perfect day in May with the heady scent of blooming flowers filling the gardens. Horatia was idly picking her way through the maze of tall hedges as she searched for Linus and Audrey. At fourteen, she was too old to enjoy hide and seek but she still humored the other children. She had counted to one hundred and was now having a devilishly hard time finding the others on the vast grounds of Lord Rochester's estate. *Lord Rochester,* she sighed aloud at the thought of his name. He was twenty-six years old, her brother's close friend and unbelievably handsome.

She also knew Lucien was a rake; she'd heard that whispered in the servants' hall among other places. At first she'd thought it odd that the Marquess had been likened to a gardening tool, but after listening to her brother talk to his friends, she'd learned a rake had another meaning with no botanical connection whatsoever. After a bit of pleading with one of the laundry maids at their townhouse in London, she'd learned what a rake in this particular context meant.

From that moment on she'd been hopelessly entranced by the marquess. At fourteen she knew she was too young for him, but her heart didn't seem to care about age. She'd nearly squealed with joy when Cedric had come home the day before and told her they'd be visiting Lucien at his estate for the weekend.

Unfortunately, when they arrived, Horatia learned that a beautiful young heiress named Melanie Burns was also visiting. It was with no small amount of indignation that Horatia had been ushered by an elderly maid to the nursery—*of all places!*—while Cedric, Lucien, Lady Rochester and Miss Burns took tea that morning. By the afternoon, Lysandra was practicing her embroidery and the other children, Linus, Audrey and herself had been sent outdoors to play in the gardens while the weather was still fair. Horatia heaved a sigh but it was cut short when a pair of large hands clamped down over her eyes.

"Guess who?" a rich voice asked in a soft playful chuckle. Horatia's heart stopped for a moment, then fluttered like a hummingbird.

"Lord Rochester?" She knew it was him. She could be blind for a thousand years and know that voice, and his scent of sandalwood and pine. Being near him reminded her of Christmas somehow, even in the spring.

"How on earth did you know it was me, you little hoyden?" Normally being called that would not have pleased her, but when he released her to tug her brown curls, watching them bounce as she gazed up at him, what he called her hardly seemed to matter. Her head tilted back. He was so gloriously tall, like Achilles from *The Iliad.* With deep red hair and warm hazel eyes, he was a god, or very close to it.

Horatia felt her body twist inside in ways she didn't understand. With anyone else this onslaught of physical sensations would have scared her senseless, but with Lucien it did not. Whenever she was with him she trusted him, adored him, and nothing could rip that trust away, not even the awakening of the woman in her.

"Are you enjoying the sun, little Horatia?" He reached down and ruffled a hand through her hair, the price she paid for refusing to wear one of those dreadful bonnets.

"Yes, the weather is lovely," she answered in what she hoped was a mature tone. She even dared to raise her chin defensively, but Lucien laughed as though he saw right through her.

"I spend all day talking about business, politics, and other dull topics with adults, don't you dare grow up on me." He grinned and reached for her hand. She gave it to him without hesitation. "Now, let us take a turn about the garden and speak of anything else. What do you say to that?"

"Only if you promise to tell me of your wicked conquests," Horatia said boldly, with a glint in her eyes.

Lucien's grip on her hand tightened and he jerked her to a stop. He looked down at her in shock.

"And just what do you know of my wicked conquests?" he demanded, a little on edge.

"Not much I'm afraid. No one tells me anything." Horatia worried her lower lip with her teeth, afraid her boldness had gotten her in trouble.

"And it will stay that way," he replied as he resumed their walk.

"Then what shall we talk about?" Horatia almost had to skip to keep up with him. As they rounded the corner of the nearest hedge, Lucien froze. Miss Burns was sitting on a stone bench, hands folded on her lap. She was complete to a shade, her gown a lovely blue that favored her pale blond hair and brown eyes. Horatia swallowed down a wave of jealously, knowing she would never grow up to be as beautiful. Her own chin was too sharp, her nose too pert; she had none of those classic features that Miss Burns displayed from beneath her bonnet.

"Pardon the intrusion, Miss Burns," Lucien said, smiling at the young woman. It made Horatia's chest ache. Something felt wrong. It felt...it felt hard to breathe.

"My lord, how nice to see you." Miss Burns smiled back. Lucien's grip on Horatia's little hand loosened.

An overwhelming sense of dread flooded through her. Her instincts screamed that this wasn't right.

"Er, you ought to go on ahead, Horatia. I'm sure the other children are looking for you." He released her hand and gave her a brotherly pat on the head, sealing her fate. He might as well have slapped her, for all the pain his disinterested dismissal gave her.

"Yes, do go off and play," Miss Burns said before turning her wide smile back to Lucien who joined her on the bench.

Horatia felt as though a rug had been pulled out from under her. Lucien was no longer paying any attention to her, however. He reached over and put his hand on one of Miss Burns's, the pad of his thumb stroking her wrist slowly. Miss Burns blushed and giggled.

Horatia fled.

Another moment of that and she was certain she would die.

She ran so frantically that she didn't watch where she was going and crashed into Lady Rochester. The lovely matron caught Horatia's chin and turned her face up.

"Whatever is the matter, dear?" she asked.

Horatia was nearly on the verge of tears. "It's nothing," she gasped, trying to breathe.

"It is most certainly not that. Now tell me what's upset you. It must be something serious if a well-possessed young lady such as you is distressed." Lady Rochester had always been so kind to her and Audrey. It was as though she knew she couldn't replace Horatia's mother but had tried to anyway, and Horatia loved her for that.

"It is Miss Burns. I cannot stand her. And he *likes* her!" There didn't seem to be any clearer way to put it.

"By he, you mean Lucien?" Lady Rochester asked.

Horatia managed a shaky nod. "He's with her right now. They were holding hands."

Lady Rochester's eyebrows rose. "Are they? Oh dear. Well, we can't have that."

"What?" Horatia hadn't expected that from Lady Rochester. Miss Burns was her guest after all.

"We cannot allow Lucien to get involved with her sort. That will not do."

"Her sort?" Horatia repeated dumbly. Was she secretly from a common background? Or worse, French?

Lady Rochester sighed and took Horatia's hand.

"Miss Burns is pretty, wealthy and accomplished, but she's not a good woman. I am friends with her mother, but her? I do not want her as my daughter-in-law. She despises children. I once saw her twist Linus's arm to get him to behave. There is discipline and there is abuse and being a good parent is knowing the difference. I shudder to think what my grandchildren would suffer at her hands. That is why we must stop them."

"We're going to stop them?" Horatia asked, hope rising in her chest.

"Of course we are. My son is too blinded by Miss Burns's charms to know the needs of his heart."

"How?" Horatia was serious now. Lucien was the need of her heart and she would do anything to protect him from such a horrible woman.

"I don't know. We'll have to think of something. Now dry your eyes, there's a good girl, and go find the others. I am sure that Linus and Audrey are up to no good. I expect you to prevent any mischief they have planned." Lady Rochester smiled at her, always treating her like the adult she wished she was.

Horatia once more entered the gardens and avoided the path that would lead her back to where Lucien and Miss Burns were sitting. Eventually she came upon a white painted gazebo adorned with a rose covered trellis on one side. Marring the scene of bliss was a little boy near her age and half her maturity. Linus. He was climbing up the trellis with a large metal pail of water. It sloshed as he scrambled up to the gazebo roof and out of sight. Audrey was at the bottom of the trellis waiting for him to return. Her white apron was covered in dirt and her cheeks were rosy as she watched the champion of mischief climb back down.

"Linus, what are you doing?" Horatia demanded.

Linus laughed. "We're going to drop these pails of water on the next person who comes into the gazebo." His tone was haughty as he showed off the second bucket he held.

"You will not. Your mother told me to put a stop to whatever mischief you were up to. Now get back up there and take that other bucket down." Horatia stamped her foot.

"No. You do it," he challenged. "Unless you're scared."

"Fine. I will." Horatia stormed past him and started up the trellis. "Both of you, back to the house." She slipped a few times, getting cuts and scrapes on her hands where thorns bit into her skin. She was nearly to the top when she heard voices. Linus and Audrey stuck their tongues out and ran off, abandoning her to whoever was coming her way. She would get in trouble for climbing up here, even if she was trying to foil Linus's sinister plot. Better to hide. She scaled the last few inches onto the roof. The pail of water was near the hole in the middle of the roof. Horatia saw Lucien and Miss Burns approach the gazebo and come fully inside until they were in its center directly below her. Horatia held her breath, afraid to move in case they heard her.

"Miss Burns, may I ask something?" Lucien began.

"Yes," Miss Burns's melodious voice answered back. Horatia watched the scene unfold with a mixture of horror and revulsion.

"We've known each other for two months and I've grown fond of our times together. As improper as it is to ask you without first speaking to your father, would you consider marrying me?"

Horatia knew Lucien must have been giving Miss Burns one of his most handsome smiles.

"You wish to marry me?" was Miss Burns's not-so surprised reply.

Horatia thrust a fist into her mouth to keep from screaming. He couldn't marry her, he just couldn't! He had to be stopped from making a mistake. Horatia grabbed the pail of water and tipped it over. The water sluiced down in a messy waterfall over Miss Burns's head. Then, unable to stop herself, she dropped the bucket down the hole as well. By God or the devil's grace it landed on her perfectly, fitting her like a medieval helmet.

"Bloody hell!" Lucien hollered as Miss Burns let out a harpy-like shriek that reverberated through the metal.

Unable to stop, Horatia giggled. Miss Burns pulled the bucket off only to trip down the stairs and fall face first into a flowerbed. With another shriek of rage she tore off back into the gardens. Lucien ran a few steps as though to pursue her but then looked up, his eyes meeting Horatia's through the slats on the gazebo roof.

"Horatia Sheridan, get down here this instant!" He stormed out of the gazebo.

Horatia climbed back down from the roof, her body quaking with fear. When she was within reach of him, Lucien gripped her by the waist and wrenched her from the trellis. Horatia felt more thorns tear into her but she dared not make a sound, not even one of pain.

"What did you do that for?" he snarled, hazel eyes blazing.

His tone terrified her and she gulped. "I…" She fisted her hands in her skirts and stepped away from him.

"Spit it out!"

He would never harm her, not physically, but the idea of him being angry at her made her heart jerk against her ribs.

"You can't marry her," she begged.

"What?" Lucien looked angry and confused.

"She's awful. You can't marry her. You can't."

"Whom I marry is my business and mine alone. Do you understand? It is none of your concern."

"But I love you." She had never spoken that thought aloud before, never even knew that she felt it that strongly. But once she said the words, she knew they were true. At fourteen, Horatia had fallen in love with Lucien.

The words silenced Lucien, but not for long. "You don't know the first thing about love. You're a child," he spat.

She looked up at him with pain in her eyes, humiliation bleeding through her, enhancing the splintering of her heart. She put a hand to her mouth to silence her cry of agony, both of body and soul.

"I…I'm sorry," she said. Tears blurred her vision and pain laced her every movement.

Lucien wasn't looking at her, he was looking straight

ahead. Miss Burns had returned to the gazebo and had seen everything. She flashed them both a hateful glare and turned away.

Lucien cursed under his breath. "Do not bother to apologize. What you've done today can never be forgiven."

He turned on his heel and chased after Miss Burns.

Horatia sat on the gazebo floor for several long minutes, trembling. Something deep inside her chest seemed to break, and it was only after she finally remembered to breathe that she realized it must have been her heart.

CHAPTER 15

*H*oratia hated how that memory always managed to choke her at the worst times. She blinked and turned at the sound of a polite cough. Lucien was leaning against the wall a few feet away, watching her.

"ARE YOU ALL RIGHT?" he asked, pushing away from the wall and coming towards her.

"I'm fine."

Lucien frowned and cupped her chin in one hand, turning her to face him.

"I can always tell when you lie," he said, as if the knowledge of this surprised him.

"Yes. I hate that." She needed to get away from him. She needed room to breathe.

He dogged her steps as she left and picked a room at random to try and hide from him. She shut the door and slid the lock into place, relaxing when he tried the knob and couldn't get inside. Leaning back against the door, she listened to him walk away. Her heartbeat slowed in her chest.

Suddenly one of the study bookshelves swung open. Lucien emerged and eased the bookshelf back into its place, grinning. Horatia gaped. Rochester Hall had secret passageways? How had she not known about them? She truly ought to have been nosier as a child.

"Why do you hate that I can read you so easily?" he asked.

Horatia studied the room with a slight frown. This was Lucien's study. His scent filled the air and a messy pile of letters littered his large desk. She couldn't have picked a worse room to try and escape from him. He was everywhere. And she would not be able to hide from him anywhere on the estate. There were likely passageways all through the house connecting all the rooms.

"Lucien, could you please just leave me alone? You've made your peace with me, and I with you. Can we not leave it at that?" She turned her back to him but he chuckled, coming closer.

"My dear Horatia, I fear you and I are England and France. We quarrel and battle and therein lies the pleasure of our relationship." He brushed back a loose curl that had draped over her shoulder. She flinched, though not from displeasure. Even the barest hint of heat from him was something she could not endure for much longer without wanting to turn in his arms and beg for a kiss.

"I am tired of battling with you, Lucien. It has caused me nothing but grief." She moved towards the window behind his desk, looking over the snow covered gardens. The flowers were all withered and sheathed in ice, and it struck her how much she sympathized with those flowers. Her heart felt much the same, withered and frozen. But Lucien wouldn't let her alone. He was right there behind her, warmth emanating off him in sweet waves, heating her back.

"Then I will leave you, but only if you allow me to honor tradition first. I've heard it is bad luck to ignore such things." His breath fanned her neck, sending shivers of anticipation through her. Who would have thought the word *tradition* could be so seductive? Horatia whirled around to face him, her nose brushing his as she hadn't realized how close he was.

"Tradition?" she asked.

Lucien's eyes flicked up to something over their heads. A sprig of mistletoe, pinned to the wood above the large window.

"But if someone were to come in and see us..." she trailed off as she focused on his lips.

"This is my study. No one will disturb us. Besides, you locked the door." He reached up to brush his knuckles across her cheek, and then his fingertips danced down to her neck where they wrapped around the back of her head. He massaged her scalp in slow tender movements as he pulled her closer. When she was flush against the length of his body, his other hand banded securely about her waist. She moaned and he caught the sound with his lips, plundering her with a possessive tongue.

"I've wanted to do this all day," he said between languid kisses.

"You have?" she asked faintly, leaning more into him than was wise or proper.

"God yes!" The hand about her waist dropped to her bottom and clenched her tight, pushing her against the evidence of his desire. "Have I told you how good you taste?" he murmured, brushing against her lips in a teasing fashion. Horatia shook her head the slightest inch. "You taste heavenly, yet sinful." He licked his way to her left ear, pulling the lobe between his teeth.

Horatia's knees buckled. She clutched his upper arms to keep from collapsing like a rag doll. Lord, the things he could do to weaken her! Hadn't she only just resolved that morning to move on?

"Lucien," she gasped.

"Lucien, yes or Lucien, stop?" He flicked a fingertip

over the hardened nub on her right breast through the silk of her gown.

"More," was all she could manage.

With a growl of desire he backed her up into the corner between his bookshelves and the wall. He dipped a hand down to her skirts, rucking them up to grip one of her thighs. With a swift stroke he bared her leg and had it wrapped around his hip so he could push closer into the welcoming cradle of her body. Her head fell back, allowing him access to the underside of her chin and her neck. He devoured her skin with kisses like a starving man.

The closeness of their bodies was both startling and enchanting. Horatia lost herself to Lucien's seduction. How could she have ever wanted him to leave her alone? For one single kiss she'd walk through fire, for a heated glance she'd brave her darkest nightmares. All Horatia could think beyond more, more, was that she would do anything for him. Even after all these years that hadn't changed—so how could she have convinced herself otherwise?

LUCIEN COULDN'T STOP HIMSELF. Her hands fisted in his hair and her silken mouth welcomed his tongue with a reckless intensity he'd never experienced from any woman before. He'd had countless lovers and mistresses, but none had so completely abandoned their control as Horatia did. She did not lose herself. She was still Horatia, from the soft brown waves of her chestnut hair to the tips of her blue slippers. But when she kissed him, she threw caution, morals and hesitancy to the wind in a way that had him desperate to possess her.

He'd always prided himself on his own self-control. Of course, lately he seemed to have little of it and Horatia had been testing what remained to its limit. He wanted to sink so deep into her that he'd never leave, wanted to lose himself in her eyes and drown in the symphony of her breathless cries. He'd thought of nothing else the entire carriage ride to Kent. Each time a curl of her hair was jostled by the bumpy road, he'd watched with envy as it caressed the tops of her breasts. When she'd fallen asleep, her lips had softened into a cupid's bow. Usually she kept those lips pursed into a tight line around him. The things he wanted those lips to do made him groan helplessly as he pushed himself even harder against her.

Through the haze of his desire, Lucien was suddenly aware of a voice calling his name, and it wasn't Horatia. It was like a pail of cold water dropped on his head, followed by the pail. It was Cedric, outside the study door.

"Lucien, you devil! Where'd you run off to?" With regret he stepped back from Horatia, holding a finger to his lips to indicate silence.

"Quick, under my desk," Lucien said in a hoarse whisper.

~

HORATIA TOOK refuge under the desk, never more thankful it was a large bulky beast and not a spindly-legged dainty creation. Tucking her skirts under her, she curled up just as Lucien unlocked the door before moving around to the front of the desk, to block the small bit of open space between desk and floor. Horatia held her breath as her brother opened the study door and entered.

"There you are! I thought perhaps we'd have a game of billiards to pass the time before dinner. What do you say?" Cedric offered hopefully.

Horatia heard Lucien clear his throat. "Uh, yes. Excellent. You go on. I'll be there directly. I just have a letter I need to see to first."

"Are you all right, Lucien? You look a bit flustered."

"Of course. It's a natural reaction to my mother's rantings about marriage, no matter who her current target might be."

Cedric laughed. "That I can well understand. I shall wait for you in the billiard room." She heard the door click shut.

Lucien exhaled a long slow breath. Horatia echoed it with one of her own. She didn't want to think about what would have happened had Cedric found the door unlocked. Lucien helped her out from underneath the desk. He held her still as he inspected her with a critical eye. Then his hands moved to her hair, tucking stray wisps back into place and securing pins.

"Better," he said as he worked.

"Have you had much practice at this?" She regretted the words the moment they left her.

Lucien raised one brow. "Do you wish for me to deny it?"

She could never ask him to deny what he was. She loved all of him, even the wicked parts. "No."

"There. I think that should do." He stepped back to examine her, cool and distant once again. These mood swings of his were impossibly frustrating.

"You can use the secret passage. It opens up down the hall. I apologize. I ought not to have done this to you. You don't deserve to be manhandled in my home. I promise it won't happen again." Before Horatia could find it in her to reply, he was gone.

"That's a promise I wish you hadn't made," she told the empty study.

Horatia waited in Lucien's study and found herself gazing at the bookshelves. There was one section, near the window that caught her eye. Six books were placed neatly in a row, and each title was familiar to her. Among them was *Lady Eustace and the Merry Marquess*. These particular six titles were a matching set of the books she'd received the last six Christmas holidays. Curious, Horatia crooked an index finger into *Lady Eustace's* spine and pulled the volume off the shelf. She opened it, finding an inscription on the title page that read "Gave to Horatia Sheridan, 1819." He was documenting his gifts to her? To what end?

She examined the other five books, finding similar notations inside, and each book looked well read. Horatia had the most astonishing vision of Lucien reading each book as she did, as if to try and see what she would experience in each book. It was a decidedly happy thought, to know he took great pains to connect with her, even in such an indirect fashion. The sting of his promise to not repeat his seduction lessened in light of these small treasures.

When Horatia finally left Lucien's study she did not find herself alone in the hallway. Lady Rochester was exiting the chamber across the hall.

"Horatia." She waved for Horatia to come to her. Horatia swallowed uncomfortably as she approached Lucien's mother.

"You're blushing, my dear," Lady Rochester observed. "You needn't worry that I shall press you as to the reason why. I suspect that my son is involved."

"Linus?"

Lady Rochester shot her a look that seemed to ask what genus and species of fool Horatia took her for.

"We both know that you've loved Lucien since you

were a child. Let us not deceive ourselves in this any longer. Now, come this way. You and I are going to have a little talk."

"But..."

"Don't protest, Horatia. I'm an old woman and I'm used to getting my way."

Horatia tried not to show her incredulity. Lady Rochester may have been in her fifties but she seemed anything but old. She followed Lady Rochester to a room a few doors away to a small, personal chamber of Lady Rochester's.

"Have a seat, Horatia. For heaven's sake, try not to look so ill. I do not mean to bite you." Lady Rochester seated herself in a pale blue chaise across from her.

"So you are still in love with my son." Horatia didn't reply. "Do you wish to win him?"

"I think it is fair to say that I shall never have any chance of winning him."

Lady Rochester smacked her armrest with surprising force. "Nonsense. He's perfectly susceptible to being won over by the likes of you."

"The likes of me?" Horatia did not particularly like the sound of that, given the context of their conversation.

"You are smart, beautiful and a challenge to him. He may not realize it, but he won't be satisfied until he's had you. Am I correct in assuming he has not fully claimed you?"

Horatia felt her head spin, she who never once had

the inclination to swoon in her life. "I'm sorry, Lady Rochester, but your question—"

"Oh come now, Horatia. We are women of the world. Society would have you believe otherwise but these topics should be discussed, and frequently. I have never encouraged my children to hide their curiosity or enjoyment regarding the act of lovemaking. Hang polite society and their close-minded nonsensical propriety. A little more boldness and a lot more candor on such matters, and people would have a far easier time of match-making."

Lady Rochester's faint hint of a smile reminded Horatia of Lucien. He favored his mother in looks and characteristics.

"So he hasn't compromised you then. Fully I mean?"

"No, Lady Rochester, we haven't..." she finally managed to say.

"That will make this much easier for us."

"What will?" Horatia found herself asking.

"He's not yet had you. He clearly desires you. If we use that lure of forbidden fruit to our advantage, and I may yet have a wedding before I reach my grave."

"I don't wish to trap him into a marriage. He would despise me. I would not do even one thing to incur his wrath again."

This statement had a great effect on Lady Rochester. "What have you done to incur his wrath before?"

Horatia laughed bitterly. "I'd imagined the whole

house knew. You really do not know why Lucien has been cold to me these past six years?" Lady Rochester shook her head. "You recall the last time I was here, when I was fourteen?"

"Naturally. I often wondered why you and Audrey did not return when Cedric came to visit after that. But then your brother always was a tad overprotective, and I've seen fathers and brothers do similar misguided things in the name of good intentions. "

"The day that you found me in the gardens distraught by Lucien and Miss Burns, I found Linus placing a pail of water on top of the gazebo and went up to take it down. But Lucien chose that moment to take Miss Burns into the gazebo to propose marriage. I acted rashly, childishly, and dumped the bucket over her head. She ran away and Lucien yelled at me. I told him I loved him and he laughed in my face. He blames me for Miss Burns's refusal to marry him and I have suffered every moment since. That is why I cannot win him."

Through the entire explanation Lady Rochester was still and quiet, but by the end of the tale she was uncommonly pale.

"Lady Rochester, are you well?"

"My dear, it was me. God in heaven, it was me," Lady Rochester said.

"What do you mean? What was you?"

"When Miss Burns came into the house, wet and furious, Linus and Audrey saw her. My boy teased her by waving an empty bucket and I assumed he had dumped the water on her. Then I saw her strike my son. I told her then in no uncertain terms that she was to leave Rochester Hall immediately. I said that if Lucien were to continue to court her or propose to her, and if she did not refuse him, I would destroy her, and I left her with no doubt that I could do so. I had no idea my idiot offspring would connect you and her departure in such a foolish fashion."

Horatia didn't know what to say. For the past seven years she had believed herself solely responsible for what had transpired that awful day. The view of her world tilted on its axis like a wobbly globe and she couldn't help but wonder if she was one awful spin away from careening off her stand.

Lady Rochester came over to Horatia and wrapped her arms around her shoulders. "I will make it right. I'd had such high hopes you'd marry one of my sons and I'll be damned if I just sit back and not correct my mistakes. You and I will show Lucien how wonderful you are and I promise he will come to his senses. Then I might have grandchildren to dote upon in my old age."

Horatia blinked back tears. Lady Rochester had said this with such conviction that for a moment Horatia completely and totally believed she could do exactly that.

"Now, let us dry our eyes and find your sister. I'm sure what we all need is a good outing. To Hexby, perhaps. There is a decent modiste's shop and a talented milliner that I'm sure your sister will approve of."

Lady Rochester escorted Horatia into the main hall and insisted she wait there until Audrey could be located. Quite alone now, Horatia had a moment to compose herself. She listened to the distant sounds of Lucien and Cedric laughing as they played their game. It was so good to hear them both enjoying themselves.

CHAPTER 16

$\mathcal{I}$n a private room of the gentleman's club Boodle's, Sir Hugo Waverly lounged in a chair, swirling a glass of brandy as he listened to the report from Daniel Shefford. Shefford had been his man for years now. Loyal, highly skilled, and one who would do anything he asked for king, country, or his more... personal whims. Shefford stood in front of Waverly, calmly narrating the events that transpired the morning before last when Lord Lennox had narrowly escaped death.

"I managed to track down the man you sent me to meet at the Garden. He said Lord Lennox was waiting in the Garden. He suspected it was because you had been overheard last night. Our man there confirmed that Rochester was at the Garden last night. It seems a likely scenario."

"Rochester was there?" Hugo frowned. Was there no place in London he could find refuge from those damned rogues? How was he supposed to conduct his business without tripping over one of those men?

"And what did he do when he saw Lennox?"

"He took a shot at him. I was told by the Madame of the Garden, acting as a concerned friend of Lennox, that he was shot in the arm. It did not appear to be fatal, but it was no scratch either."

It was fortunate that Lennox had suffered only a minor wound. It was only a matter of time before Lennox and his friends were rotting corpses in the ground. But not before the proper time.

Shefford crossed his arms over his chest. "I returned to my station outside the Sheridan house. It seems the Sheridans have left London, and my source there informed me that their destination was Rochester Hall in Kent."

"Lord Rochester was awarded the honor of playing nursemaid to Sheridan's sisters? How amusing. I daresay that makes things much easier, having the League divided. Did one of your men secure a position?" Waverly asked.

Shefford nodded.

Two months ago, Shefford had acquired five men to infiltrate the League's ranks. Most had already done so and were already feeding him valuable information, and unless told otherwise, that was all they would do. One, however, had so far only been able to find employment at the gentleman's club they frequented, but that particular person had unique potential and, unlike the others, just the right amount of desperation. "Excellent. Now I should like for you to send a message to Sheridan and Lonsdale. I think it is time we leave them both a little gift."

"Do you wish to send this message to Lonsdale's house on Curzon Street?"

"Yes. I'm sure that fool Lennox is watching the Sheridan townhouse carefully, since it is close to his own. I want you to get inside both houses and do what you do best."

Everything was falling into place. In time, the center of the League would be destroyed and their power disbursed to weaker men and less unified heirs. Then? Then the rest would be easy.

"I will deliver an appropriate message, sir. Will that be all?"

"Yes, on that matter. We still have more serious matters to discuss." Waverly returned his attention to his drink.

Killing the League would be easy, though he could never do so in haste without risking exposure. But haste was not his goal. He had more pressing concerns, such as protecting England, it was how he had earned his knighthood. Running spy rings across the continent was no easy feat. Even one of Rochester's brothers was involved in the various tentacles of his operations. The irony of this was not lost on him.

It was what truly mattered to Waverly, protecting the things he cared about. The League had taken so much from him. Two lives were gone because of them. He considered them a threat to himself and therefore a threat to England.

Normally a threat to the nation would be dealt with swiftly and mercilessly. But that was not his intention here. These men deserved…special attention. He knew it was a weakness to indulge in such melodrama and subterfuge. Worse, it was reckless. But then, such risks made life worth living. They were a vice, but one that had sustained him, gave him purpose. A tree of hatred grew inside his heart and would soon bear bitter fruit.

He turned his attention back to Shefford. "Now, where are we on the Spanish matter? It's been almost a month since Panama declared its independence. We need to know what repercussions this will have across Europe. I want men in every court and noble household we can reach. If Spain wishes to go to war to reclaim Panama, we might have an opportunity to pry loose Spain's grasp on their other colonies and destroy their strongholds."

"Of course." Shefford changed topics effortlessly, but Waverly was barely listening. Already his mind had returned to thought of the League and his plans for them.

CEDRIC BENT over the billiard table and aimed at a ball. "Tell me the truth, Lucien."

"About?" Lucien lounged back against the table's edge, arms crossed.

"Are you quite all right with Horatia being here? I know I have been pushing you to accept her into your life again, but I can stop. I had hoped enough time had passed and perhaps we might put this all behind us." Cedric pursed his lips as he took the shot. He pocketed the green and grinned. Cedric was competitive and excelled at nearly all games and sports.

"You have every right to push me. I'm being obstinate and foolish." After everything they'd been through, resisting Cedric's sister was not going to break them apart, not if he could help it.

"I am relieved to hear you say that," Cedric admitted.

Neither man spoke, both lost in thought. Lucien was visited by the awful memory of the day when Cedric's parents died.

Lucien knew that Cedric had been watching over Audrey at the Sheridan townhouse on Curzon Street when a footman had come running. Cedric once told him that everything seemed to slow from that moment on. The footman was flushed and sputtered about a carriage accident and finally blurted out, "Dead, sir. Both Lord and Lady Sheridan are dead. Your sister suffered a broken arm, but is alive. Lord Rochester was nearby and helped in rescuing your sister."

Lucien would never forget that moment when he'd brought Horatia home after the accident. Cedric had taken two steps towards the door and his legs gave out, sinking to his knees. Lucien had seen to Horatia's care then went back to the accident to see to the care of the bodies.

The bodies...no longer were they Lord and Lady Sheridan. He couldn't allow himself to think of them as such. Not until later.

When Lucien had returned, he found Cedric sitting in the drawing room on a brocaded couch, a favorite place of Lady Sheridan's when she used to embroider or read. He held a tiny, ten-year-old Audrey in his arms. She'd said nothing, would say nothing to anyone for a full three months after. The light in her little brown eyes had dimmed so much that they'd feared daily she might slip away.

He would never forget holding Horatia in his arms. She cradled her broken arm, which had been splinted and bandaged. She cuddled up to him, and would not let go of him until Cedric began to whisper to her softly to comfort her. Horatia had never told him from that day to this what had happened in the carriage before or after the accident. Some memories should never be remembered, and Lucien hadn't pushed her.

Cedric had been lost himself, so young to become the head of his household. He knew nothing of raising children, and poor, sweet Horatia had abandoned her childhood the day after her parents' funeral to help Cedric raise Audrey. Lucien had been at Cedric's side, helping him get his father's estate in order and taking over the title and the responsibilities. No one else save his sisters had ever witnessed his grief. He'd borne it well to his other friends, but Lucien had seen Cedric cry as though he were a boy barely out of leading strings. That bond, that strength of their friendship had to withstand everything. If it couldn't... He would not entertain such dark notions.

Lucien's thoughts returned to the present, though not to the game. "Horatia has grown up these past few years."

"She's not the child she once was," Cedric agreed. "Not for a long time now." The melancholy note in his voice made the air in the room heavier.

"She's certainly not. Old enough to consider marriage. Has no one asked for her?" Lucien attempted the casual question and lined up and took his shot, sinking a red.

Cedric's head shook. "No. There were a few at first, but she has that quiet way about her, you know. Most men find the idea of a woman with her own thoughts off-putting. They didn't continue to court her. I didn't have to scare them off as I do with Audrey's. I know too many men who prefer agreeable chatterboxes for wives. What about you? I know you haven't asked for a woman since Melanie Burns. Have you given up?" Cedric abandoned his cue and turned his full attention to Lucien.

Lucien cleared his throat. "You know... After September..."

"After Emily Parr, you mean?" Cedric supplied with a low amused chuckle. "We should mark a new calendar with that date—Before Christ, Anno Domini, and now After Emily Parr."

"Quite. But after watching Emily and Godric fall in love, I realized that I had never loved Melanie. We simply played our parts exceedingly well. The charmed and the charming. I think I loved the idea of being in love with her. Does that make any sense?"

Cedric laughed, fixing his brown eyes on Lucien, eyes that reminded him so much of Horatia just then. It was more than familial resemblance alone. Both Cedric and his sister often smiled with their eyes, it was in their natures.

"All too much sense. You were besotted with an ideal, a woman raised on a pedestal. One can worship women on pedestals, but those women can never love one back the same way. A flesh and blood woman on the other hand is another matter entirely, or so I'm told." Cedric's wry chuckle spoke volumes.

Lucien nodded. "Once I realized that, it occurred to me that perhaps I ought to be more thankful to Horatia for her timely interference."

Cedric grinned. "That is perhaps quite the most intelligent thing I've heard you say."

The two men finished their game in companionable

silence. It was one of the things Lucien liked best about Cedric. He was not a man who over-talked. Charles was prone to narrating fantastical tales, Ashton always waxed the philosophical. But Godric and Cedric were more often quiet, either lost in whatever game was being played, or consumed by thoughts of their own. Lucien valued that, the gentle support of good friends. One did not need to be wining and wenching to enjoy oneself. Those days were long past and he was glad. He was grateful to have such good friends.

A commotion from the hall alerted them to the presence of others.

"It seems the shopping party has returned," said Lucien. "I daresay we should make ourselves scarce." But before either man could scamper to a more hidden location, Audrey came barging in, with a disgruntled Linus in tow.

"Cedric! You must correct Linus and tell him that my new bonnet is fetching. He says it looks like a poorly constructed bale of hay." Audrey pointed to her rather broad brimmed hat that used a most peculiar style of thatch work.

"I believe my exact words were 'a hastily gathered haystack.'" Linus grinned at Audrey's flabbergasted expression, but his amusement was short lived. Audrey grabbed the pool cue from Lucien's hands and jabbed the fat handle into Linus's ribs, causing him to double over.

"And that is my *cue* to leave." Lucien chuckled and slipped out, leaving Cedric to handle his sister and Linus.

"That's awfully rotten of you, Russell, to abandon me to death by billiard cue!" Cedric called out as he dodged the stick Audrey swung around, attempting to impale Linus with the pointy end.

Lucien expected to find Horatia somewhere in the hall, but it was his mother who was lying in wait for him. She looked more dangerous than a cobra nestled in a basket.

"I should like a private word with you, Lucien."

Her tone did not bode well. It was too close to the one she used to lure him into a false sense of security before he was paddled as a child. He was well beyond his paddling years, but should his mother entertain such thoughts again he would most assuredly escape out the nearest window or door before she could get her hands on him.

He'd often wondered if perhaps there was some secret pamphlet that a mother received upon the birth of her first child that bore instructions on how to instill fear in one's child with only a look. If there was, his mother had been a quick study. Perhaps she had written the latest edition.

"Lucien, don't dally. Attend me now." His mother proceeded to her personal rooms. She seated herself and waited for him to follow suit. He did so, reluctantly eyeing the door he'd foolishly shut behind him.

"What is it, Mother?" A nervous churning settled over him as he recognized the determined look on her face.

"It has come to my attention that I've made a grave error. One that has had unseen ramifications for the past several years."

Lucien was dumbfounded. His mother was admitting to a mistake? Surely cows were hurtling over the moon and pigs were discovering the luxury of wings. He eyed his mother cautiously, waiting for her to continue.

"On the day that you proposed to Miss Burns—"

Lucien was on his feet, not wanting to hear his mother say another word.

"On that day." Those were the words she said. The tone, however, said, "Sit down."

Lucien glared at her and returned to his chair.

"I encountered Miss Burns after the accident in the gazebo. Linus saw her and began to tease her with an empty bucket. She struck him, Lucien. She struck your brother, and it was not the first time she'd done this. I informed her that she was to refuse to marry you or I would make sure she would regret it. She was unkind to those beneath her and especially cruel to children. I would not tolerate such a match, nor such a woman to bear my grandchildren. I am telling you this now because I've only just discovered that you've blamed an innocent party all these years."

Lucien felt as if he'd been shot as her words sank in. *You've blamed an innocent party all these years.* Miss Burns had rejected him, told him if he couldn't stand up to a mere child to defend her, then he wasn't a man worth marriage. He'd been furious at the time, but he'd seen the truth of Miss Burns's character later when she'd married Waverly.

He couldn't tell his mother that Miss Burns barely mattered anymore. He dared not confess it was a convenient excuse to keep him away from temptation, though one that had become ineffective as of late. The pain his mother's words struck was entirely his own fault. He'd only just begun to try to undo the wrongs he'd done to Horatia and to have his mother throw his sins back in his face was worse than he could have imaged.

"I can see that you need some time to come to terms with what I've said." She got up. "I will leave you now. But Lucien, do not postpone your apology to her."

Lucien looked up at his mother. "What could I ever do to make right seven years of coldness?"

Lady Rochester's eyes were softer and more motherly than he'd seen in years.

"A kind word to begin with. Despite your attempts to drive her away, she has clung to the memory of your kindness like a piece of driftwood in a storm. The fight has worn her down, but some tenderness will ease her suffering and strengthen her faith in you again."

Lucien realized, not for the first time in his life, that his mother was well and truly wise. For all her obsessions over the latest fashions and horrifying attempts to marry off her children, she was a woman of great understanding and intelligence.

"Thank you, Mother," he whispered.

Lady Rochester inclined her head, put a soft hand on his cheek and then left him alone. Lucien collapsed back into his chair. What was he to do? Where was he to start? But before he could ponder his course of action he was arrested by a distracting and ludicrous sight out the nearest window overlooking the expansive gardens.

"What in God's name?" he muttered and stepped closer to the window.

CHAPTER 17

he afternoon seemed to stretch for hours. Linley's back ached from hiding in the mews outside Jackson's Salon. The dark suit he wore was borrowed and slightly too big, as were the waistcoat and breeches. The entire ensemble was nearly threadbare and didn't keep out the chill of the winter wind. With each gust, he hastily gripped the edges of his white-powdered wig on his head, keeping it secure.

He prayed that the man he was sent to watch would appear soon. His fingers were turning blue and his blood was like ice in his veins. His quarry, the Earl of Lonsdale, a skilled boxer, could spend hours in the salon. There was no telling when Linley would get a chance to escape the cold and seek shelter inside. He rubbed his hands together, attempting to generate warmth. It didn't help.

A sudden wave of exhaustion swept through him. He didn't want to be here. His master had made him come here. Sir Hugo Waverly. A true bastard if there ever was one. Tom tried not to think about it but failed.

He was the man who'd taken advantage of him... and stolen something precious from him. Stolen everything, really. Including his freedom.

The month following his master's assault, Waverly's wife had dismissed him without references. That alone had threatened his future and now he had someone who depended on him. But Hugo could always make it worse. It had been easy for his master to take advantage of his desperation and force him into this job. This new identity. This new life of shadows and subterfuge.

My poor baby girl. He thought with aching sorrow of Katherine, the child he cared for. His Kate was the most important thing in Tom's life. Waverly had threatened to take her away, and Lord only knew what he would do with her...

Unless he gained the confidence of the Earl of Lonsdale and infiltrated his household. Tom sensed something darker and more horrifying was afoot but he was helpless to stop whatever his master had planned. His orders were simple, though far from easy—get hired by Lonsdale to replace the valet who'd recently left his employ and regularly report back to Waverly.

Tom didn't want to lie to anyone, and certainly not

the earl. After a week of discreet surveillance, he'd learned enough about Lonsdale not to want to betray him. He was a rake but not a cad. He was a man who would offer a hand in aid of those who needed it. Tom had seen him more than once toss several coins to paupers as he passed and never had a harsh word for others, even when men deep in their cups tried to start arguments. But to save little Kate, Tom would have to damn himself and do wrong by one good man for the sake of a bad one.

THE BIZARRE SIGHT of Audrey and Linus chasing a stray goat dressed in a lady's spencer was one Lucien could not draw his eyes away from. The garment, once a lovely shade of baby blue, was now torn in several places and beginning to fray at the edges.

Lucien watched from the window as Audrey screamed bloody murder. She dove at the goat and fell to the frozen ground as it bolted away. Linus had taken up a garden hoe and was charging at the animal but a shout halted his blow. Horatia arrived, hastily dressed for the cold, and urged Linus to back away from the angry goat.

Lucien chuckled at the bleating creature whose wild eyes promised retribution on anyone who dared accost it further.

Horatia bent over and held out a carrot, coaxing the stubborn thing to eye her less viciously. It took a few cautious steps closer, then nibbled the carrot. When Horatia set the vegetable down the goat did not pay any attention to her as she casually extracted the spencer from it. She then returned the ruined garment to a distraught Audrey.

Lucien held his breath from his vantage point, enjoying the sight. Horatia's hair was a bit windblown and her cheeks flushed with the thrill of the chase. Horatia's womanly body with ample curves was made for passionate lovemaking and wicked fantasies. She was, in truth, the woman he'd always wanted, always needed. Even in light of his mother's revelations, it could never happen.

She was Cedric's sister, and the League had rules.

Lucien couldn't trust himself with her. He wanted to make love to her by candlelight, to better see the shadows playing across the curves of her body. He enjoyed restraining a woman and rousing her to peaks of pleasure. Never to hurt, no. But he loved to have power over a woman, and more importantly, her trust. He could learn every sensitive place and dark desire she harbored so he might fulfill it. He never once left a woman unsatisfied after a night tied to his bed, and he refused to enjoy himself until his lover had first been fully sated.

Now, this finely honed talent would go to waste. The one woman he longed for was the one woman he could never have. He wanted to be with her in ways he'd never been with other women, to show her a side of himself he'd always held back from others. Perhaps Horatia's allure was derived from her unattainability. Forbidden fruit. He could only pray she was safe from him, so long as he exercised that damned self-control that had frayed at the edges lately.

Lucien tore himself away from the window as he heard Audrey's shrill voice echoing in the main hall.

"I swear, Linus, you are the worst sort of man! How could you put my best spencer on a goat?"

"I thought the little fellow looked chilly."

"It already has a coat. What more does it need?"

"'Tis the season of giving. You should be thankful I exercised my goodwill to ensure the goat's warmth."

"The season of giving? I'll give you something!"

There was a thump and a responding shout of pain.

"What in God's name did you put in that...rocks?" Linus bellowed.

Lucien came out of his mother's room in time for Audrey to dodge around behind him, using him as a shield from Linus's revenge.

"Save me, Lucien!" Audrey begged, her little hands fluttered about his shoulders, along with a rather heavy reticule.

"Hand her over, Lucien. It's high time I took my hand to her backside." Linus sounded positively medieval as he glared at the woman.

"You ruined her spencer on that goat, Linus, and I'm sure it was an expensive one." Lucien crossed his arms and glared back at his youngest brother, lucky to have the advantage of age, since Linus equaled him in height.

"That jacket was six weeks' worth of pin money I shall never get back," Audrey said. "Perhaps I ought to have it from your quarterly allowance?" Audrey smiled impishly.

Linus reddened. "Why you…" He took a step forward but Lucien halted him with a firm palm.

"I think that is an excellent idea. You shall pay back the full amount of the spencer, won't you, Linus?"

Linus growled but gave a curt nod and stalked off.

"Oh and Linus," Lucien called after him. "You have one week, or I shall pay her myself and deduct it from your allowance,"

Audrey clapped her hands and danced about Lucien. "Oh you are such a dear! My champion!" Audrey stood up on tiptoe to kiss his cheek before she dashed off, no doubt to further incite his brother and cause more trouble. So be it.

"That was awfully kind of you." Horatia's voice gave Lucien a start. She'd been hidden near the door to the back garden.

"It is only fair. Linus is over twenty now. He ought to be growing up. The years for pranks are over, but he seems determined to learn this the hard way. I can't understand why he still acts like a child. Mother coddles him too much, I suppose."

"Audrey's provocation doesn't help matters," Horatia added. "They played too often together as children to really adjust to their more mature roles in life. It's one of the reasons I never worry about my lack of diligence as their chaperone." Horatia confessed this with a small little smile.

Lucien's chest tightened as a wave of guilt struck him. An awkward silence settled between the pair. Horatia's warm smile wavered and then wilted as the silence lengthened.

"Pardon me," Lucien said gruffly and turned to leave. He couldn't bear to be near her anymore. Caught between deserved guilt and wicked desire, he was damned if he claimed her and damned if he didn't.

Lucien called for the footman, Gordon, to send a message to the stables that he wanted his horse then went in search of his greatcoat and riding gloves. A ride would do him good. Cold air and solitude would cool his ardor and give him time to think. Thankfully, Horatia did not follow him.

A groom brought Lucien's stallion to the hall steps. The beast twitched its tale. Lucien nodded to Gordon and then mounted up. He trotted from the main yard and crossed the snowy meadow to the east of the hall. His horse plodded along on the icy snow, carefully treading until the snow became thicker. Then Lucien coaxed it into picking up the pace. Then wind whipped through his coat as he cantered through the meadow.

Gray clouds formed a thick winter wall, leaving the land ahead of him a shadowy world between intermittent snowfalls. There was something beautiful about the desolation of Kent in winter, especially this year. More often than not, snow was rare, but this year the grounds were covered with it. The decay of life lay inches below the snow, unobserved. That world held secrets, like the moment before a swimmer breaks the surface for breath, the seeds in the ground waited to breathe, to reveal themselves. Lucien felt much the same, waiting to breathe, waiting to break free.

He remembered the multitude of kisses he'd stolen from Horatia, both in anger and desire. Now, without anger to fuel his emotional blindness, he could see the truth. It wasn't merely desire, nor lust for forbidden fruit, it was something more. Something secret lay hidden beneath the flames of his passion.

I shouldn't, but... He watched his breath blossom in a pale cloud as he examined his confusing thoughts about his feelings for Horatia.

Lucien's horse had slowed to a complete stop now, something the beast had never done before without encouragement.

How odd.

He dug his heels into the horse's side to give it a kick of encouragement. The horse whipped its head around violently. Lucien kicked again, and this time the horse bucked and whinnied. Lucien clung to the reins as he sought to keep himself in the saddle. The horse reacted even more fiercely and this time Lucien was unprepared. He was flung from the horse, his arms tangled in the reins as he landed with a crunch on the icy ground. Pain exploded through his head and body. His vision spun in slow circles, then started to fade...

CHAPTER 18

*S*eeing Ashton wounded had shaken the very foundations of Charles's existence. He needed to restore some sense of order to his world, to reassert his strength and defense. He stood in the ring of Jackson's Salon practicing his boxing technique. Sweat gleamed on his forehead and dampened his hair.

He fought like a man possessed. Punch after punch, opponent after opponent, and still he battled on, ignoring his aching muscles. As he punched and ducked, all he saw was Ashton. Pale from blood loss, resting in Essex House as he recovered from his injury. The doctor had assured everyone there was little to worry about and that Ashton would recover control of his arm in time.

Many of the men in the best circles enjoyed to play at boxing, but not Charles. He took the art seriously. A pugilistic match was his way of fighting back against his fears and insecurities.

Conquer the ring and you conquer your demons.

Today, he sported a blackened eye, one he'd deserved but not gotten in the ring. Charles grinned as he withstood the ribbing by the other gentlemen at Jackson's. They'd all assumed he finally lost a fight and he was not about to tell them the real reason.

His current opponent was a man named Everard Ralph, a young pup compared to Charles, eager to test his mettle against Jackson's unofficial reigning champion. The two traded blows for a good twenty minutes before Ralph began to weaken.

"Had enough?" Charles asked. His usually light tone was on edge.

Ralph stumbled back a step as Charles pressed his advantage.

"Enough, Lonsdale, enough!" Ralph gasped as he dodged another jab from Charles. "Lord, you fought like the devil himself today."

He was a decent enough fellow with the sort of grin that made virginal maidens swoon and widows leave their calling cards in his coat pockets. He had nothing on Charles though. Charles had been a rakehell since the age of seventeen and the more blackened his reputation became, the more women seemed to "stray" across his path. However, the game was beginning to change.

It was one thing to abduct a girl like Emily Parr and

revel in the delight of such a devilish scheme. But it was another thing altogether to get into his carriage after a night of carousing and find a lady waiting inside to be compromised by him. That was not how the game ought to be played. He was supposed to give chase and the lady to flee, but for the past couple of years he felt as though he was the one fleeing.

Matchmaking mothers schemed when he entered ballrooms and seemed to hear wedding bells when his name was announced at Almack's. Despite his notorious reputation, he was always able to obtain vouchers to the club's assembly rooms, probably because the risk of allowing him entrance was worth the opportunity for someone to catch him.

When Charles had relayed this unfortunate turn of events to Ashton, the man had said in his usual wise way, "Perhaps a bit of respectability and restraint would dim your allure to the unmarried ladies." At the time, Charles had scoffed. "Ash, you and I both know I am capable of many things, but respectability and restraint are not among them." To which Ashton had pointed out, "It has done wonders for Godric. Look at him and Emily."

Charles had huffed and stalked away.

"Thank you for the match, Lonsdale. It proved most instructive." Ralph offered a hand to Charles. Charles shook it before leaving the ring and retrieving his towel. He wiped his face and contemplated the poor state of his clothes. His valet had just left his service to marry a maid from a neighboring household. Charles liked to be immaculately dressed and would need a new valet quickly. It was just one more problem on a growing list.

He needed a drink. Now. With this in mind, he headed for his gentleman's club, Berkley's. None of his friends would be there tonight, which was a blessing. He was not fit for company. He was in a foul mood and would soon drink enough to reach a state of oblivion for the rest of the evening. He could also ask around to see if anyone knew of a valet looking for a new position.

In half an hour, he was sitting alone in a private room, glass in hand, listening to the fire crackle in the hearth. Voices outside in the halls sounded merry, so contrary to his own spirits. The door to the room opened as a servant entered. There were many young men and errand boys employed by Berkley's. Charles rarely interacted with them, unless he was determined to get deep into his cups and he needed them to keep the brandy coming.

"Afternoon, my lord. Care for another decanter?" the lad asked. He was small for his age, with light hair hidden by a cap, and blue eyes. His features were perhaps a little too delicate, his frame a bit odd in places, all the signs of awkward youth. He'd grow into his body like all men did. Funny, he'd never given much thought to the servants here before. Something about this boy however, grabbed his attention.

"Have I finished the first already?" Charles seemed

surprised. He looked to the side table where the tray of brandy and extra glasses were. Sure enough it was empty. The lad brought the second to Charles and topped his glass with the warm amber liquid.

"Thank you." Charles hastily tipped the glass back and downed its contents.

The boy's eyes went wide with shock.

Charles merely chuckled. "Ever had brandy?" he asked.

The boy shook his head, a lock of hair escaping from his powdered wig to fall across his eyes. Just then, something melancholy stirred inside Charles like twisting shadows. Had he ever been that young? If he had, he couldn't remember when.

"How old are you?" Charles asked the boy.

"Twenty, my lord."

"Twenty? That's a lie if I ever heard one. You're far too —scrawny." Charles knew he was a little too drunk to curtail his tongue. The boy's eyes narrowed.

Charles raised his hands in defense. "My apologies, lad. I'm determined to get foxed and you are the victim of my being two out of three sheets to the wind. Come, sit. I trust they have no need of you downstairs for a while." Charles pointed to an empty chair by the fire. He hadn't thought he'd wanted someone to keep him company, but the young man looked as though he could use a rest. His eyes were shadowed with dark circles from lack of sleep.

Charles could give the lad a rest and ease his sudden desire for companionship tonight.

"Oh I couldn't, my lord!" the boy protested. "It's against the rules."

Charles dug into his pocket, retrieved a handful of shillings and held them out.

"I'm a member of this club. As such the rules bend when I need them to. I request that you see to my needs. One of those needs is that you sit and keep me company."

The boy heaved a sigh and took the offered shillings with a grateful smile. It seemed he was in bad need of coin. He knew a man's pride could keep him from taking charity.

"What's your name?"

The boy hesitated. "Linley, my lord. Tom Linley."

"Tell me, have you worked here long?"

Linley shook his head. "Only a few months. I used to work as a valet, but haven't been able to find new employment. My old Master would not give me a reference."

"Oh?" Charles sat up a little. "Why's that?"

Linley scowled. "He and I did not see eye to eye on the upkeep of his wardrobe. Clothes are there to help define a man's character, and my master did not respect the importance of that."

This young man had ideas akin to Charles's own mind. A proper wardrobe was crucial for a man to make a powerful impression upon society. This lad could well be the answer to his valet problem.

"Do you like your employment at Berkley's? Be honest. I shan't tell the club owners what you say." As he waited for the boy to answer, he was seized by a strange desperation to save this lad. Why he couldn't say. Perhaps he wanted to pass on the kindness his own friends had shown him. Linley was in sore need of someone to look after him. It wasn't hard to deduce that the lad's father was out of the picture and there didn't seem to be any brothers.

"It isn't wise to trust a man deep in his cups," the boy said warily.

"Ha! Never have truer words been spoken!" Charles laughed and spied a smirk from the lad. "Now, I am drunk enough to consider offering you a position, but sober enough to swear on my father's grave my intentions are good and I won't forget my promises in the morning. Would that interest you? I would pay double whatever you are getting paid now."

"But my lord, you do not know how much I'm currently paid!" the boy exclaimed, eyes widening to the size of saucers.

"Believe me, Linley, whatever you are receiving here, it is nothing compared to what I'd pay for a decent servant. I have need of someone to attend to me while I'm about town. For me a valet is more than a personal attendant."

"Surely you possess footmen for such duties?" Linley inquired.

"I do, but their duties keep them homebound. They're hard working, but not much fun to be around. There's only so much professionalism I can stand. I'd rather hire a scamp like you to entertain me." Charles had noticed Linley's articulated speech and controlled grace, something that only came from a person raised in a good environment. "You seem to be educated enough to provide amusing conversation."

"I am the son of the lady's maid to the Dowager Countess of Haverton," Linley supplied.

"Haverton? I know the earl, he's a good man. Now, what say you, Linley? Care to take on the job?" A delightful buzz was warming his veins as he mellowed. Linley was already proving a useful distraction.

"Before I agree...permit a question, my lord."

"Go on."

Linley fidgeted in his chair. "I am not the sort of man who would agree to—well I wouldn't allow you to *use* me." The young man's face flushed as he sought the words to clarify his meaning. "I mean, I have no interest in men and will not allow you to...to use me for physical sport. If that is your intention, then I must respectfully decline."

"What? Don't be ridiculous," Charles laughed. His sexual interests had always been towards women and he was amused by the man's assumptions. "I know I have a certain scandalous reputation, but it isn't for that. Mr. Linley, the truth is you remind me of myself when I was younger. Scared, alone and in need of a friend." He paused, shocked at how the truth came so easily. "I offer only a position and some companionship. Nothing else. Have I passed your test?"

Linley studied him before he replied. "I should like to know exactly how much I'd be paid and where I would expect to lodge. Also, I have a problem." Linley's brows furrowed. He paused to draw a slow breath. "I am the sole caretaker of my young sister, a babe only one year old. I must have a means to care for her as well."

Charles contemplated this news with a surprising level of seriousness. He did want the lad to work for him, and a baby seemed to be part of the terms. There was certainly room at Charles's house.

"Very well." He lightly smacked his hands on his thighs and stood up. "I should like you to start right away. No sense in you staying here a moment longer. I will speak with the management to secure your release on good terms. You may accompany me to dinner tonight at the St. Laurent house. Afterwards we can see about moving you into my townhouse and finding a nursemaid for your sister. I daresay my housekeeper would be up to the challenge whilst you see to your duties with me. Her own child just left for school and I fear she's becoming lonely." Charles set his glass of brandy down. "I am willing to offer thirty-five pounds a year as your salary. What say you to that?"

Linley's eyes grew round as he mouthed the words back in wonderment.

"May I take your befuddled reaction as an acceptance?"

Linley nodded mutely.

"Excellent. Have a drink of brandy, in celebration of your new employment." Charles handed Linley his glass and Linley took a small sip, sputtering almost immediately. Charles laughed and slapped Linley on the back as the boy coughed.

"Haven't much experience with liquor?" he asked.

Linley's face drained of color. "Only to receive the beatings of those too deep in their cups."

Charles's chest tightened. He despised those who used drink as an excuse to unleash their demons on others.

"If you don't mind my asking, sir, how did you come by that shiner?" Linley asked quietly.

"This?" Charles touched his purple eye. "I got this after I aided a friend of the female persuasion."

"Someone tried to harm you when you helped a young lady?" Linley looked doubtful.

Well, if this young man was going to be his valet, it would be best if Linley understood what kind of adventures—or rather misadventures—he could expect to see in his service.

"The lady was a sister of my close friend." He paused,

uncertain of how to explain what sounded like terrible behavior. "She wishes to marry someone, but her brother is being a bit of an arse, if you will. So she asked me to make it look like she'd been compromised so that her brother would be willing to discuss her marriage to this other fellow."

"Oh?" Curiosity gleamed in Linley's eyes. "Did she succeed?"

"Somewhat. Her brother has agreed to discuss marriage, once he's done with some, er...business." Charles found himself limiting his comments. One could never be too careful. Waverly had a vast reach in the London underworld and Charles knew better than the others how low he would stoop to achieve his evil ends.

"That is fortunate, for the lady I mean," said Linley. "She is lucky her brother is so kind and understanding."

"I wouldn't go that far. I got this after all." He pointed again to his eye. "But it will all work out in the end. I trust in that."

The resigned look the boy had entering the room earlier was now gone. Charles felt a warmth in his chest that seemed to spread through his body and it had nothing to do with the brandy. Helping the boy had made him feel good in a way he hadn't felt in ages. It reminded him of how the other members of the League once saved him.

Linley cleared his throat. "Thank you for the opportunity, my lord."

"Think nothing of it, lad."

Linley made an odd little noise before trying another sip of his brandy. It seemed to go down easier this time. Charles took in the companionable silence as he waited for Linley to finish off his glass.

"Well, we'd best be off if I'm to dine at Essex's tonight. First, we'll see to your employer, then I shall need to return home to change."

HORATIA STARED at Lucien's riderless horse as it galloped around the side of the house and found its way back to the stables. Even as fast as it was moving, it seemed to be favoring its left foreleg. The reins hung limply in front of it.

Where was Lucien? She ran to snatch her cloak and left through a side door close to the stables. She dashed outside and took hold of the horse's reins. The horse fixed her with a baleful stare. It was then that Horatia saw the trickle of blood near the back of the saddle. She loosened the girth and raised the saddle with trembling fingers.

A sprig of barberry was embedded into the horse's skin, the thorns causing a painful wound on the animal. If Lucien had sat back too hard he would have forced the thorns deeper. Horatia gazed out towards the field. Where was Lucien? Perhaps the horse had escaped him when he'd returned.

She brought the horse to the stables where a groom took the reins.

"He had some barberry tucked under his saddle," she informed him.

"What?" The groom looked mortified. He removed the horse's saddle to inspect the damage. "Blast, the thorns must have caught on the saddle blanket somehow. Did his lordship find this?"

"No. I thought Lucien was here. Did he not return?"

When the groom shook his head, Horatia felt her heart leap into her throat. She ran to the nearest occupied stall where a stout horse was feeding contentedly. She pulled out a loose bridle and quickly fixed it before dragging it from its stall.

"I'll saddle him quickly. Allow me to go with you." The groom hastily threw a blanket and saddle over the horse's back and strapped him in. "You'll need help if he's had an accident."

Horatia shook her head. "No. If he's had an accident I need you to get the doctor from Hexby immediately. We can't waste any time." She raised a hand when he started to protest. "You'll be able to ride faster to the village to get the doctor."

"Very well." The groom frowned but did as she asked.

Once mounted, she guided the house out of the stables and looked along the ground for hoof prints. Only one set of tracks led away from the hall. Horatia followed them, urging the horse to gallop. Its heavy large hooves pounded through the snow steadily.

Lucien, where are you?

After what seemed like acres of endless white, Horatia spotted a dark shape in the distance. As she drew closer she realized with horror that it was Lucien's body.

"Oh God!" she gasped. "Faster, damn you!" she shouted at the draft horse and it increased its pace.

When she was within a few yards she slid from the saddle and ran to Lucien. He was face down in the snow, cloak wrapped about him. Horatia rolled him onto his back and paled when she saw the bloody gash above his forehead. His eyes were closed and his pale lips parted.

She couldn't lose him now, not after everything that had passed between them. Memories flashed across her eyes—the way he'd twist his lips up in a wicked smile, the brush of his lips against hers, the sweetly whispered words he'd spoken to her when they'd shared the room at the Midnight Garden.

"Lucien!" She bent her ear to his lips, praying to feel the warmth of his breath. It was there, but barely. Horatia put her palms on either side of his cheek, letting her warmth seep into his cold skin. Once her hands grew too cold she dragged his body into her lap and held him close, rubbing him, praying her body heat would have some effect. After what felt like an eternity, Lucien's dark lashes fluttered. When his hazel eyes focused at last, it was not on her face but on her bosom, which was mere inches from him. He managed a weak smile.

"Heaven looks quite lovely from this angle." The smile changed into a playful leer, even as Horatia's eyes narrowed.

"I'll ignore that because you are alive." She cupped his cheek and pressed her trembling lips to his forehead in a thankful kiss. She could have wept with relief, but she pushed the tears back. He wasn't out of the woods yet. She needed to get him back to the house and have the doctor see to him.

"Scared you, did I?" Lucien teased but still she couldn't stop shaking. "More than I'd care to admit. What happened?"

"Not sure, I was riding and suddenly my horse threw me."

"There were thorns under the saddle blanket digging into your horse."

"Thorns?" Lucien struggled to sit up.

"They must have snagged on the blanket as it was being saddled." Horatia allowed him to pull away as he unwound his cloak and tried to stand. He wobbled so unsteadily that she threw one of his arms over her shoulders to support him as she led him to the horse.

"Can you mount him?" she asked.

"I'd rather mount you," he said with a grin. His gaze seemed to grow unfocused again.

Horatia gripped the horse's neck and mane as she pulled herself up in the saddle.

"This is not the time nor the place, you fool." Horatia pinched his arm, bringing him back to reality. "Now, focus! Can you get up or not?"

"Hold him steady and I shall find out." Lucien managed to swing himself up. He immediately slumped against her back, his head falling on her shoulder.

"Stay conscious, Lucien. Hold on to me." He wrapped his arms about her waist and she urged the horse back to Rochester Hall.

It seemed to take ages to reach the house. There were a few more moments when Lucien threatened to slip away into unconsciousness. Horatia knew little in the way of medicine, but she'd been told she should not allow him to fall asleep with a head wound.

"Stay awake!"

"I'm trying." His frustrated voice vibrated against her ear. "You're too damned warm. I just want to hold you and fall asleep..." His words softened into a drowsy murmur.

"What would keep you awake?" she hissed. "If I could turn around I'd happily slap you—" His hands slid up from her waist to her breasts, cupping them and then gently kneading them. Horatia arched in shock, though not without pleasure.

"Now this is keeping me very awake."

"Take your hands off of me!"

He squeezed her breasts and chuckled, then shifted even closer to her from behind. She felt a distinctive prod against her backside.

She glanced up at the skies. Even in grave bodily danger the man was a cad. "Fine. If it helps you stay awake...but I swear to God, Lucien, the second we're in sight of the house, move your hands, unless you want my brother to see!"

That comment had him drop his hands straight back to her waist, but he stayed awake the rest of the journey home. The sting of disappointment that he hadn't tried to push her further surprised her. Did she want him to just walk all over her and force her to admit she wanted, no, craved his touch? Yes. She loved it when he did that.

When she drew the horse up by the main doors she was relieved to see a carriage and a separate pair of horses had beaten them there. The two riders she recognized at once.

"Avery, Lawrence, help!" The two younger Russell brothers leapt from their horses and ran to her.

"What happened?" Avery reached up to help her down. She let him catch her waist and drop her gently to her feet.

"His horse threw him. I found him out in the meadow a good deal away." Horatia pointed to Lucien who slumped immediately without her body for support. "He was unconscious, and he has a nasty head wound. Before I left I sent the head groom for the doctor in Hexby."

"Well done, Miss Sheridan. Come on, Lucien. This way, towards me." Lawrence coaxed his drowsy elder brother down from the horse.

Avery seemed reluctant to release Horatia. "And you, are you all right?"

"I'm fine, really. Help Lawrence."

The brothers carried Lucien inside like he'd staggered home drunk from a tavern. Horatia handed the bridle to a groom, then took off after them.

The entry hall of Rochester Hall was full of people. Lady Rochester had apparently been in the midst of welcoming the Cavendishes, who had arrived at the same time as Lawrence and Avery.

"Get out of the bloody way! Wounded man coming through!" Avery bellowed as he and Lawrence carried their brother through the crowd towards the stairs leading to Lucien's bedchamber.

Lady Rochester started to follow them but Lucien shook his head. "I'm fine, Mother. Please, stay with the guests. Horatia will see to me and send you up when I'm settled." His tone, while breathless, brooked no argument.

"I'll be up to see you soon, my dear," she promised him.

Horatia tried to follow after Avery and Lawrence, but Lady Rochester grabbed her arm, demanding answers. In a breathless rush she explained the events in an attempt to calm the crowd at large. Strangely, the act soothed her for the moment as well.

"He looks well," Sir John Cavendish said. "Don't fret. If he's walking and talking he'll be fine. I suffered worse during the war."

Sir John Cavendish and his wife Marie were old family friends of the Sheridans and Russells. Until Sir John had moved his family to Brighton four years ago, the three families had often spent the holidays together.

His calm words drew a trembling nod from Horatia. He was right. Sir John was always right. She'd never met a more level-headed man.

"Sir John, how lovely to see you again." Horatia greeted him with real warmth and embraced the lovely and Rubenesque Marie. The Cavendishes had two children, Gregory and Lucinda with them. Lucinda was Horatia's age with blond hair and blue eyes. She was a more feminine version of her impossibly attractive brother Gregory, who had been schoolmates with Avery at Eton and Cambridge, being only year apart in age.

"Excuse me, I must go and see how Lucien is." Horatia managed to slip away from everyone and dash up the stairs.

Lucien's door was open and he was lying in his bed stripped of his wet clothes. His eyes were closed and his chest bare with the blankets pulled up only to his waist. His muscles were smooth and sculpted and for a second her mind blanked before reality crashed in. Three pairs of eyes studied her and Horatia felt her face heat up.

"I..." she stammered.

Lucien stirred. "Horatia?" His voice was hoarse. "Yes?"

Lawrence stood back, allowing Lucien's seeking gaze to find her.

"Come in, please. I wish to speak with you. Alone." He shot pointed looks at both of his brothers.

The two exchanged a look of disapproval, hesitating until finally Lawrence gestured towards the door that he and Avery should leave. Lawrence, still frowning, made a grand show of leaving the door ajar. Lucien in turn scowled comically at the open door.

"If only he knew he was mere inches from you at the Midnight Garden," Lucien chuckled dryly. "I daresay he'd faint if he knew he'd offered to ravish you there."

Horatia blushed, even as a smile pulled at her lips. The memory of that night should have been painful, embarrassing, but it wasn't. There was a part of her that relished it. Perhaps that was the price of falling in love with Lucien. His wickedness was rubbing off on her.

"How do you feel?" Horatia lifted her skirt a bit so she could sit on the edge of the bed. She leaned over and stroked his hair back to better examine his wound. It had been cleaned and looked more likely to bruise than to develop an infection like she'd feared.

Lucien shut his eyes and rubbed his thumb and forefinger over his closed lids. "I think I'll live."

As she tried to pull her hand away, he caught it, kissing the inside of her palm. He glanced up at her, his hazel eyes dark and warm. "I have you to thank. If not for you I might still be out in the meadow. Who knows what might have happened?"

Horatia shuddered at the sudden sense of dread she felt overtake her. Unable to control herself, she threw her arms about his chest and buried her face in the crook of his neck, trembling. She wondered how she could hurt so much over losing him when he'd never belonged to her. It seemed that loving someone that was never hers made her fear losing him all the greater. Losing Lucien to death would have been worse that losing him to another woman.

His arms settled around her body, pulling her closer, keeping her against him when he should have been pushing her away. When she'd mastered herself again, she bravely raised her head, her nose brushing his cheek. His arms around her chest tightened, and his breath hitched.

"You should thank God I'm weak as a newborn kitten, my dear. Otherwise I'd be thanking you properly for saving my life, and that blasted door would be bolted shut," Lucien murmured as he placed a soft, lingering kiss on her jaw.

Horatia's blood heated at the images his words created. An all too familiar ache started within her. She tore herself away when his hands moved to her breasts.

"No," was all she said. She cleared her throat and wiped the remains of tears from her eyes, then smoothed her skirts and left for the open door. She paused in the hallway and turned back to him.

"I wish you a speedy recovery, my lord." She dipped into a curtsy, something she'd never done to him before and left. The absence of his arms around her already made her hurt with longing, but she dared not linger.

CHAPTER 19

*D*inner at Rochester Hall was always a grand affair, which was just the way Jane liked it. There was something wonderful about having her children and friends gathered around her table, eating, drinking and talking. The table in the formal dining room sat thirty people when all the leaves were inserted, but tonight it was perfect for accommodating the more intimate party of thirteen.

The doctor had come and gone, assuring Jane her son was well enough to dine with them if he wished and that he'd only suffered a minor concussion. With instructions to rest for the next few days, he'd exhibited the stubbornness he'd inherited from his father and come down for dinner. Jane snuck a glance at him, still concerned about the pallor of his complexion.

She had arranged the seating so that the younger children were all paired together. Cedric and Horatia sat across from each other by the head of the table on either side of Lucien. Lucinda and Linus were next, and on down the line were Avery, Lawrence, Audrey, Gregory, Lysandra and finally John, Marie and herself.

She'd noticed a great many things throughout the evening and wasn't sure whether she ought to worry about how the close quarters of the three families over the holidays would affect everyone. Linus kept sneaking glances at Lucinda across the table. For her part, Lucinda politely attempted to include him in her conversation with Cedric, but Linus would only spit out a quick reply and look away, anything to make it look as though he had no real interest in the girl.

Jane wasn't fooled, but she was worried. Although he was one and twenty, Linus was still young enough to act rashly. His interest in Lucinda Cavendish, if acted upon, could force both of them to the altar, and for Linus she feared that would be too soon. As much as she desired at least one of her brood to marry, he was not ready, and no one desired a marriage due to scandal. He was still immature, and it would drive his wife positively mad if he married now.

It wasn't surprising to see Linus intrigued by a woman. He was a Russell after all, and had her passionate blood in him. However, the most interesting development of the evening was Lysandra. Jane's only daughter had always seemed like a miraculous anomaly after so many troublesome boys, yet Lysandra managed to be just as vexing as her siblings. The girl had no interest in fashion and spent far too much time in the library. Not that books weren't a healthy pursuit for a woman. It was important to be intelligent. She saw it as a woman's duty to be smarter than most men, but a woman could not marry books, nor could books give Jane the grandchildren she longed for.

There was nothing so important at a particular point in a person's life than seeing their children grow, marry and bear their own children. Grandchildren were a special treat, and Jane was envious of her friends who had them. She longed to hold a sleeping baby in her arms once again, and breathe in the clean sweet scent of its skin and whisper sweet lullabies. She would see all of her children married and producing children if it was the last thing on earth she ever accomplished.

As dinner progressed, Jane saw something new in her daughter. There was a flush in her cheeks, a brightness to her eyes and a startled look as though Lysandra had woken from a dream of pale pastels to see the world in its true vibrancy at last. Only the desire of the heart could form that new sight. And the way Gregory Cavendish threw back his wine with reckless abandon told Jane everything she needed to know. Lysandra was officially a Russell if she was wreaking such havoc on the dashing young man with mere glances. He would be an excellent match for her daughter.

Jane resisted the urge to preen at the knowledge that she and her friend Marie would soon be family after their children had married. It was only a matter of time.

However, whatever had happened between the pair —and something had, she sensed—it had not gone as planned. One could never take back a kiss that was given, or perhaps stolen as the case might be. Jane only prayed that her daughter's hot-blooded actions had not been too bold. It would be most unacceptable to have to marry her daughter for reasons that would be obvious in a few months time. For her sons to marry under such circumstances was almost expected of them. Not one of them had even a smidgeon of self-control, but Lysandra ought to be stronger. She was a woman after all.

As an array of desserts was brought out, Jane turned her attention to Lucien and Horatia. They were speaking amongst themselves and Jane hated that she couldn't hear a single word.

It was so obvious that Horatia loved him. What would it take for Lucien to realize the same? No other woman could hold such a depth of emotion, nor handle his tempers the way Horatia did. The woman ought to be awarded sainthood for her bravery in loving such a man.

I must not interfere...well, not too much.

Tonight there would be dancing and playing on the pianoforte, and Jane would rally allies for her mission of pushing Horatia into Lucien's arms.

Once dinner had ended, she stood and addressed her guests.

"I thought we might all move to the ballroom for the remainder of the evening and have a bit of music and dancing." This suggestion was met with approval and the group moved together towards the ballroom. Jane intercepted her three younger sons, trapping them in the dining room alone with her once the others had gone.

"Mama, what are you on about?" Linus asked, forgetting that she still owed him a tongue lashing for his mischief earlier that day.

"Sit down, all of you." She'd spent twenty years perfecting that tone of voice and Avery, Lawrence and Linus all but dove for the nearest chairs. Once seated she began to pace back and forth, knowing full well she was behaving like a commander of His Majesty's armed forces.

"I have decided that tonight you three must seduce Horatia," she announced.

Avery blanched, Lawrence frowned, and Linus, who'd been balancing on the back two legs of his chair, fell over with a crash.

"What?" Lawrence started to rise.

"Did I say you could stand?"

Lawrence promptly dropped back down.

"Have you gone mad, Mother?" Linus asked, righting his chair and sitting back down. "Shall I send for Dr. Lambert in Hexby?"

"Good heavens, no." She laughed. "I am sane as ever and plan to be here as long as I must to see that all of my children are happily married so you might as well get accustomed to my presence."

"Is that what this is about?" Lawrence crossed his arms in such a way that he suddenly reminded her of her late husband. He was the gentlest man there ever was, but he could certainly appear as cross as the devil himself when he wanted, a trait Lawrence had inherited. "You wish for one of us to marry so you've gone and selected Horatia in the hope that one of us will like her?" The disapproval in his tone was as clear as cannon fire.

"Don't be foolish. She's in love with Lucien."

"Then why have us seduce her?" Linus asked. "It seems to me you should have cornered your firstborn for this." He leaned back in his chair, forgetting his accident not one minute ago, a placating grin stretching his lips as though he were humoring a small child. Jane was on the verge of exasperation. Had none of them inherited her wits or cunning?

"I swear, by the way you three act, I might have dropped you on your heads when you were babes. If Lucien sees you all vying for Horatia's attentions, he will become jealous and act on his feelings for her. He needs encouragement and sibling rivalry in this house has never been in short supply. I believe it is time we put such energies to good use."

"Clever," said Avery, who had been quiet so far in all this.

Linus huffed. "Who says Lucien has feelings for her? I thought after Miss Burns and the gazebo disaster he did not favor her at all." His irritable tone was probably the result of guilt since he had caused the aptly named disaster.

"Miss Burns left that day because of something I said to her, Linus. I have only recently informed Lucien of the truth. He has changed his opinion of Horatia for the better, I believe."

"A change of opinion does not herald wedding bells, Mother," Lawrence said.

"He cares for her, and he desires her," Jane insisted. Lawrence and Linus grumbled in disbelief.

Avery sat up in his chair. "Actually, I believe mother may be right in this. I am more than ready to believe Lucien feels something for Horatia."

His brothers whipped their heads in his direction.

"And how do you know that?" Lawrence asked.

Avery grinned. "Remember that night you met Lucien at the Midnight Garden, Lawrence?"

Jane let out a horrified gasp but Avery ignored her.

"How the devil do you know where I was?" Lawrence asked.

Avery continued to smile. "Do you recall the woman in the silver gown and mask Lucien was so interested in?"

"Of course," Lawrence answered. "She was quite beautiful. There was a charming naiveté about her that—oh God."

Avery's smile deepened. "Yes, that woman was Horatia. She paid Madame Chanson to send her to Lucien that evening."

Jane gave a little cry and half-fainted into a chair. She peeped up at her son from beneath her lashes. None of them were paying attention to her. Instead they were more interested in Avery's source of information. Did they not even realize what their wild, reckless behavior was doing to her nerves? Well, if they were going to act like devils, then by God, she'd make them use their devilish talents to suit her ends.

Lawrence felt ready to toss his accounts. He remembered every detail of that night and his jealousy when Lucien had offered to let the woman, Horatia, choose him over his brother. Lawrence had all but shoved his own woman off his lap, in the hopes of taking Lucien's prize. A woman he'd never once thought of romantically. It was hard to accept.

"Are you telling me that the woman I practically begged to steal from my brother that night, the one he shamelessly seduced in front of me was…"

"Indeed," Avery said. "But I must return us to the point of this revelation. Lucien knew it was her the entire night. He was very clear in declaring his desire for her and she for him."

His mother had roused herself to sit up from her theatrical swoon and was once more engaged in the conversation. "Did he...did they... Horatia told me they hadn't..."

"No, not at all," Avery reassured her. "Well, not fully." He then made twiddling motions with his fingers.

Linus got up and held out his arms, expecting their mother to faint for real this time.

His mother screeched. "Dear Lord, I've raised a pack of libertines and hedonists! Indulging in passion is one thing, but this?"

Lawrence ignored his mother's exclamations regarding the damnation of her sons' souls and focused instead on his younger brother.

"Avery, how did you come by this knowledge? You weren't at the Garden that night."

"I have my sources," Avery replied cryptically. It wasn't even the first time he'd made that comment to them.

"You and your bloody sources. One of these days you will get yourself into trouble," Lawrence warned him. "The war is over. Don't you think your line of work ought to end too?"

"Wars never end," said Avery. "Only the battlefields and objectives change."

Avery's missions to the continent were a well-kept

family secret, highlighted by the fact that they knew so little of it. It was dangerous work, and he didn't want Avery bringing danger and trouble to the family's front door.

"Lucien and Horatia must marry," his mother said. "At this point my conscience won't allow otherwise. 'Not fully' indeed..."

Lawrence pondered this. "Do you really suppose he'll want her more simply because of jealousy?" They were not boys anymore, no longer fighting over toy soldiers in the gardens. Women were a serious business.

"Knowing the three of you, if you do your best to tempt her to passion, he will notice and respond."

"Not with bullets I hope," Avery mused. "To be called out by my own brother...that would be highly embarrassing."

"Don't worry, Avery," Linus sniggered. "I shall attend your funeral. It will be a lovely service. I'll have the headstone read, 'Here lies Avery Russell—Stealer of Hearts and Secrets.' I'm sure you'll have at least a few people who will mourn your loss."

"Hush, pup!" Avery snapped.

Lawrence stretched out his legs and crossed them at the ankles. "I'd be more concerned about Cedric." There would be no avoiding him. Lawrence knew how protective the man was of his sisters. "He'll be bound to see our amorous overtures to his sister. Imagine his reaction."

"Leave him to me," his mother said.

Lawrence supposed she would enlist Audrey's help to keep Cedric distracted. God save them all if it didn't work.

Jane waited until she had her sons' full attention once again and gestured for Avery to speak.

"Now, let's get down to specifics, Mother. What do you expect us to do that will make him jealous?" Avery looked up at his mother with false wide-eyed innocence, the rogue wanted her to say it! He didn't think she would be capable of laying out her scheme in explicit detail. He was quite mistaken.

"Don't give me that sweet-as-a-lamb look, child," Jane warned. "The three of you have sinned enough to fill the second circle of hell all on your own, and leave no room for others. You will do what you do with any gentle born lady. Compliment her. Seduce her. Fuel the fire deep within her. Lure her into passion. But do nothing to worry me in a month's time. Understood?" Had she been in a better mood she would have laughed at the flush of embarrassment on their faces.

"What? You expect me to play ignorant of such things? I gave birth to five children, and I assure you that I did not do that all on my own. Your father played a significant role in bringing your miserable existences about. There's that little book from India I believe you all own? The one with all the illustrations. Don't pretend you don't know it, because I've read it as well."

"Mother! For God's sake!" Lawrence begged, cutting his mother off.

Jane allowed a smile to curve her lips.

"It isn't as much fun when you are on the other end of unpleasant thoughts now, is it?" She clapped her hands together. "Now then, off to the ballroom. And remember, do what I charged you or you will beg for mercy, and I shall have none to give. I brought you into this world, and should you displease me, I shall happily remove you from it." She made the threat in such a sweet tone that all three of her sons shuddered.

THE MOMENT AVERY, Lawrence and Linus entered the ballroom, Lawrence turned to his brothers, speaking so he could not be overheard.

"What do you say we try the shell game?"

"Who will be the main player?" Avery asked in a low whisper.

Lawrence spoke up. "I will. You both remember what to do?"

The shell game was something the three of them had done together many times. No matter the form the game took, each knew his role. Linus and Avery nodded and the three of them separated. Linus went straight towards their unsuspecting prey, while Avery and Lawrence broke off opposite directions.

CHAPTER 20

*H*oratia perched in a chair against the wall, listening to Lady Rochester's performance on the pianoforte. Cedric attended her, turning the pages as he followed her progress on the sheet music. Audrey was dancing with Gregory Cavendish, the two of whom seemed to be making the most of the wide expanse of the ballroom. Avery and Lucinda were dancing near them and Lysandra was dancing with her youngest brother.

A smile tugged at Horatia's lips. It warmed her to see Audrey so happily engaged. Her first season had been quite a disappointment after word of Cedric's overbearing nature circulated among the young bucks of the *ton*. Audrey had wept for days when no flowers or cards had been delivered to her. There was nothing so cruel as to watch one's sibling suffer. Marriage was all the poor girl wanted, and with Cedric's watchful eyes she simply didn't stand a chance.

Horatia spied Lucien across the room with Lawrence and their guests. He seemed much recovered, although still pale. There was a haunted look to his eyes that tugged at her heart. Lucien ran a hand through his hair, mussing the sleek red waves as he spoke to John and Marie. Sir John laughed loudly, his voice carrying over the music.

Lucien had it in him to be a great, warm and loving man with a rare and irresistible charm. Horatia's eyes burned a little. She wanted to cry because he was hurt, and she wanted to weep with relief that he was healing from his injury.

She was so focused on Lucien she did not notice an entirely different Russell vying for her attention.

"Horatia?" Linus inquired, adding a polite cough.

He stood in front of her chair, peering down with an expression on his face that made her anxious. With him, schemes and pranks always followed that sort of look.

Horatia realized he seemed to be waiting for her to say something. "I beg your pardon?"

"I was asking you to dance. Would you like to?" Linus offered her his arm and a charming smile. It snapped Horatia out of her Lucien-watching daze.

"You wish to dance with me?" She hadn't meant to sound so incredulous, but Linus had never showed the least bit interest in dancing with her before. It made her wonder what exactly this prankster was up to.

"Of course! You are an accomplished dancer, and I've been known to dance a quadrille or two when the occasion arises."

He waggled his eyebrows, and she stifled a giggle. Linus was a devil, but a charming one.

"And a waltz?" Horatia asked as Lady Rochester's tune changed to a sweeping, light-hearted melody. "How do you fare with them?" At a formal ball in Almack's an unmarried lady would not be allowed to dance a waltz without the Patroness's permission. However, Lady Rochester didn't set such standards amongst friends. It was something she enjoyed about the Russell family and Rochester Hall. She was free from such plaguing social niceties.

"Waltzes are my specialty. You must let me prove it to you." Linus winked at her as though he was confessing a secret.

"By all means then. Let us take our places." Horatia took Linus's offered arm. She still suspected that he was up to something, but couldn't begin to guess what.

He ushered her onto the floor and spun her in a slow twirl before pulling her back into his arms. She shoved a palm against his chest, attempting to put some distance between their bodies.

"I don't believe we have to dance quite so close," she cautioned him.

"Nonsense. A man never backs down from an opportunity to hold a pretty lady close."

"Pretty lady?" she echoed. "Really Linus, you are quite odd tonight. What game are you playing?" Her tone, while soft, warned him she knew he wasn't sincere. There had never been a hint before now that he was interested in her romantically.

"Sometimes a man wakes up one day and realizes what he's had in front of him all along." His eyes strayed away from her for the briefest second, a betrayal of his true thoughts. She was not the woman he longed for, but for some strange reason, he was pretending she was.

As the waltz gathered speed, Horatia became almost dizzy from the constant turns. She'd barely gotten used to the rhythm with Linus when he deftly spun her away from him and a different man caught her on the dance floor.

LUCIEN ENTERTAINED HIS GUESTS, enjoying the playful banter of the elder Cavendishes. Sir John had been a good friend of Lucien's father and hearing Sir John's stories of their reckless youth always filled him with a deep warmth. He very much missed his father and still mourned him despite the years that had passed.

"Your father would be proud of how well all of his children have turned out," Sir John nodded seriously at

Lucien. "He loved each of you so much and must be smiling wherever he is."

Marie's eyes grew watery and she leaned against her husband. "Oh John, dear, you're making me very sad. You mustn't speak so, not on tonight of all nights." She curled her hand through the crook of Sir John's arm and glanced apologetically at Lucien.

"Are you excited to bring Lysandra to London next year for the season? I believe she will win many suitors."

Lady Rochester chortled. "She might win interest initially, but I doubt any gentlemen will interest Lysandra."

When Marie and Sir John's faces scrunched up with confusion Lucien laughed.

"She's a bit of a blue stocking. More interested in books. I think she'd rather conduct experiments on a suitor than dance with him."

Lawrence joined their group. "You're talking about Lysa?" He shook his head. "Woefully true, I'm afraid."

"Oh dear." Marie laughed softly. "But I suppose when the right gentleman comes along she will be as befuddled as the rest of us are when we fall in love."

The group dissolved into other discussions and Lawrence diverted Lucien's attention with an unexpected comment.

"Horatia's looking quite well tonight."

Lucien fixed his brother with doubting eyes. "Quite well? She looks spectacular, as always."

Lawrence's expression became unreadable. "Of course, you're quite right. That reminds me, Linus would like a private word with you. He's in your study."

"A private word? What does he want?"

His brother shrugged. "I believe he wishes to ask you to court Horatia. He knows she had feelings for you in the past, but he wishes to make certain you have none in return, so that he may pursue her."

"Like hell he will," Lucien snarled and stomped off to find his brother. Horatia was still dancing with Avery and would be safe enough from his youngest brother for now.

"Avery?" Horatia stammered in surprise at the new dance partner holding her. The middle Russell grinned back at her.

"And how are you faring, lovely Horatia?" The devil dared to charm her. He alone looked the least like his siblings who all favored their mother. Avery favored his father in looks and therefore always seemed one step removed from the rest of the Russell brood.

"I am well enough, and you?" She tried to keep her focus on the conversation, but her mind was on other matters.

"Perfect now that I have you in my arms."

Horatia gawked at him before she recovered herself.

"Wha—what?" First Linus, now Avery? This was all very strange.

The waltz's tempo changed, and Horatia found Avery's hand delicately stroking her waist in soft but sensual sweeps that startled her into a deep flush.

"I believe my brother has been a fool. You have pined for him too long, my dear. Why not give another of us a chance to woo you?"

"Honestly, this is quite—" She couldn't finish because he cut her off.

"I see, you still care too much for him. Well, I suspected that might be the case. He is waiting for you in the hall. Do you care to meet him?"

She gave a little furtive glance over her shoulder and saw that indeed, Lucien had left the room.

"He really wishes to see me?" It was too much to hope that it was true.

"Of course. We convinced him that he shouldn't deny what was in his heart."

"Very well, then I should like that."

Avery drew them both near the ballroom's door, which was ajar and he twirled her through the darkened doorway. Horatia would have stumbled but a pair of arms caught her, clasping her to a hard, warm body. In the dim light of the hall she looked up at the man who held her scandalously close.

"Lucien?" she whispered.

The man who held her glided gently down the darkened hall with steps that still held the echoes of a dance to them. The servants hadn't lit the lamps—or someone had blown them out. A shiver of apprehension settled over her.

"Lucien, we shouldn't leave." She jerked at his hand, her slippers digging into the carpet as she tried to slow him down.

"Come now, Horatia. Lucien and I are not so alike, are we?" Lawrence's amused laugh froze her dead in her tracks. He tugged again on her arm, and she nearly stumbled.

"Lawrence, let me go. We ought to return to the ball-room. This isn't—where are you taking me?" Her pulse leapt as Lawrence chose a door halfway down the corridor and opened it, taking her inside. Horatia tripped over a wrinkle in the carpet and fell against the nearest piece of furniture, which happened to be a bed. Lawrence had brought her into a bedroom...alone.

"Lawrence, what's going on? Why did you bring me here?" She struggled to get up, hearing her gown rip at the hem as she tried to push away from the bed.

Lawrence ignored her questions. "This will do very well, I think. We don't have much time to do this and it must be done correctly."

Horatia righted herself and turned to face him. Her heart stuttered as he smiled and made a show of leaving the door open a few inches. There was no light in the room save for a pair of candles above the fireplace.

Shadows fell across Lawrence's face as he stripped his overcoat off and dropped it over the back of the nearest chair. Horatia took two slow steps towards the door, but he mirrored her movements with an amused expression.

"Going somewhere?" he teased.

"Lawrence," she said softly, a new sense of uneasiness filling her. She was cornered and a little bit frightened. At that moment she did not trust him at all. "Let me leave." Horatia hoped he would listen to reason. "Surely you must see that this isn't at all proper, even for your family."

He leaned against the wall by the door, arms crossed over his chest as his eyes raked over her body. "My family is improper even at the best of times, and my dear sweet Miss Sheridan, you've become the newest toy for my brothers and me to fight over. Congratulations! Lucien is a fool not to want you, but I am no fool."

"You wouldn't...You couldn't!" Horatia watched in almost dazed shock as Lawrence removed his cravat and unbuttoned his shirt.

This couldn't be happening. He was a friend, someone she'd trusted and respected.

"You won't touch me. You won't." His widening smile made her shudder. "Come any closer and I'll scream..." Truth be told she'd do a lot more than that, but her instincts warned her to keep that intention to herself. No sense in warning the man what she was capable of.

He watched her with an expression so primitive that Horatia scrambled to get away as he pushed himself from the door and advanced upon her. She wished to God her hands would stop shaking. She knew his reputation was just as bad as Lucien's. She also remembered him in the Midnight Garden, and how he'd been seducing the woman he'd chosen that night. She would not be his next conquest. She could not!

Part of her was still stunned that it was Lawrence who would treat her this way. He'd always been so protective, almost as much as Cedric. What had changed in him that would bring about an attempt at forced seduction such as this?

As if reading her mind, Lawrence said, "I know it was you that night at the Midnight Garden. You were the beautiful woman on my brother's lap. I can still see that vivid blush beneath your silver mask when I shut my eyes. I've been haunted by dreams of your supple body beneath mine... It quickens your blood, does it not? The idea of that struggle for exquisite pleasure?"

Lawrence seemed to voice exactly what was happening in her body, but she was envisioning a different surrender to another man entirely.

Horatia was terrified now, and tried to do the sanest thing possible, which was scream at the top of her lungs. But the sound was strangled on her lips as Lawrence advanced on her. He grappled with her, curling one hand around her mouth, and she reacted.

Horatia bit down.

He yelled in surprise and stepped back. "Christ,

woman! I'm not going to hurt you!" His look of genuine shock startled her, as though he hadn't really intended to touch her and even more stunned that she'd been frightened enough to bite like a cornered polecat.

"Horatia…" he said, as though trying to calm a startled horse. "Listen to me. He's coming. We need to pretend to kiss—" He lunged, catching her and pinning her against the wall.

She couldn't shake him off. Panic blurred her vision. He's coming? Was Avery or Linus going to join in this madness? She was trapped and helpless! He made no move to undress her, but his warm breath came out in soft pants.

"Just let me kiss you for one bloody second, woman! It's for your own good!" He ducked his head in towards hers.

Horatia slammed her head forward, her forehead colliding with his.

Lawrence staggered back a few steps, holding a hand to his forehead. "Holy hell! If you'd only let me explain…"

Horatia didn't fare much better from the blow, stumbling backward in surprising pain.

Just then Lucien burst into the room with a dark scowl the likes of which Horatia had never seen on him before.

"You bloody bastard!" Lucien's voice became a snarl as he lunged at his brother.

The two collided and smacked against the wall.

Lucien had murder in his eyes, but Lawrence looked as though he'd been expecting Lucien to come into the room and throttle him.

Horatia shouted, "Lucien! Stop! Please! Just take me to my room...please."

Only the last word seemed to reach him. He released his brother, muttering a filthy string of insults. Lawrence straightened his clothes as Horatia walked up to him. Her palm itched to slap him, but not before she said what she needed to say.

"I don't know what you were trying to do tonight, Lawrence, but know this—you will face my wrath and it will make Lucien's fury look pale in comparison." She was barely able to keep herself from shouting at him. His eyes narrowed and the challenge snapped what control had remained. She slapped Lawrence as hard as she could, the harsh sound echoed through the room.

Despite the reddening mark on his face, Lawrence did not make a sound. Horatia raised her trembling chin high and marched to the door. She paused when she realized Lucien had not followed her. He still eyed his brother with murderous intent.

"Lucien, leave him. I need you."

He tore his gaze away and followed her to the door, pausing only to shoot one last furious look at his brother before he wrapped a protective arm around Horatia's waist and escorted her to her chambers. A footman stepped forward, a concerned look on his face.

"My lord, I heard a commotion. Do you or Miss Sheridan require anything? Shall I send for Miss Sheridan's lady's maid?"

"No. No need. It's Gordon, isn't it?" Lucien was still getting acquainted with his mother's new staff.

"Yes, my lord."

"Thank you, Gordon. No need to send for Ursula, but if you would be so good as to keep the other servants clear of my room and Miss Sheridan's. She needs to be attended to and I do not wish for her reputation to suffer."

The footman squared his shoulders. "Of course, my lord. I will take it up on myself to see that you are not disturbed." The footman bid them good night and slipped down the hallway, vanishing through one of the doors that led to servants' quarters.

The moment her door was shut Horatia fell into the nearest chair, body shaking with the aftermath of her scare. She had the sudden urge to cry, but choked down the sobs that tried to bubble up in her throat. She meant to thank Lucien for his intervention, but instead she burst into tears, unable to maintain her strength any longer. It wasn't so much what Lawrence had done, or almost done, it was something deeper, something more painful that she didn't fully understand. Looking at Lucien was like salt in a fresh wound. Why was she always falling to pieces around him?

LUCIEN APPROACHED HORATIA, hating the distance between them, and scooped her up out of the chair to hold her to his chest. She fisted her hands in his waistcoat and buried her face in the crook of his neck. The intimate seeking of protection and reassurance made his heart turn over. Even after being cold to her for so long, she still trusted that he would care for her. She amazed him.

Lucien banded his arms about her back, tightly grasping her to his body. He layered gentle comforting kisses on the crown of her hair, shushing her with warm soothing sounds. His rage at Lawrence and Linus was still strong, but Horatia was more important right now, and she needed him to stay with her. He would punish his brothers for luring him away when she needed his protection. Even Avery was involved somehow. They would all be dealt with on the morrow.

"Why did he...why did he have to do that? He has no interest in me, so why? He was cruel to toy with me, and to what end?" she asked between choked sobs.

"I don't know, love. I don't know." And for a long while after that neither of them said anything. He wished he had answers. He would by tomorrow, and Lawrence would be fortunate if he still drew breath once Lucien was done with him.

Lucien held her tight, amazed by how good she felt

even now—every curve, every scent, every sweet breath she exhaled. He couldn't picture ever letting her go, or that he could exist in a world where she wasn't his.

SHE CRIED herself out until she was exhausted. Horatia sagged in Lucien's arms and he picked her up and carried her to her bed. Somehow being put on the bed banished her tears and the need to cry any further. Her thoughts drifted away from Lawrence and back to the eldest Rochester.

"Feeling better? Why don't I fetch Ursula to undress you and put you to bed?" Lucien suggested.

Her hand shot out and locked around his wrist. "No. Please stay."

"Someone needs to get you settled and undressed." He frowned, oddly even more attractive in the way he was determined to care for her.

"You can undress me." She smiled at him. "You've had plenty of practice."

"Horatia, you do realize how inappropriate it would be for me to..." He waved his hand up and down, gesturing to her clothes.

She rolled her eyes and sighed. "Inappropriate is your forte, Lucien. I want *you* to undress me. I trust you."

After he set her down, he began to undress her with

tenderness akin to tending a newborn babe. There was nothing sensual or seductive in his movements.

Horatia wiped her tear-stained cheeks with the back of her hand, wondering if her complexion had become splotchy. She gazed down at Lucien's bent form as he removed her dancing slippers and slid his hands up her legs to unroll her stockings. His hair caught the lamplight so that the waves of dark crimson were glossy and inviting. She ached to thread her fingers through the strands, to see if they matched her memory of that night at the Midnight Garden.

Her fingers stretched towards him just as he moved to stand again. Horatia dropped her hand onto her lap as he began to slide her gown down over her shoulders. She was too weary to protest when he lifted her and dragged the gown down and off her until she was clad only in her stays and chemise. He reached out and unlaced her stays, peeled them off and let them drop to the floor. Her breath hitched as she crossed her arms over her breasts, hoping to hide her body with the filmy chemise.

Lucien then went to the armoire and searched through the clothes until he found a thick flannel nightgown and held it out to her. She took it and prepared to remove her chemise. He turned his back, uncharacteristically gentleman-like. It made her smile, if only a little, as she pulled the nightgown down over her head. He turned back around and the look on his face made her breath catch. He looked devastated, yet relieved, as though everything she'd been feeling on the inside was now painted across his handsome features. Her knees gave out and she sat down on the bed, thankful for the support it gave her.

As Lucian sat on the bed's edge beside her, he gently turned her sideways and began to pluck hairpins from her untidy coiffure with a gentleness Horatia had not thought possible. With the last hairpin set on the nightstand, Lucien wound his fingers through her wavy mass of dark hair with his fingers. The feel of him coaxing tangles loose and sweeping through the strands sent a wave of longing through her. When his hands finally drew away, Horatia faced him and his fathomless eyes.

"Lucien..."

"Yes?" The word wavered on his lips.

"Please don't leave me tonight." Her request shocked her. She'd only meant to thank him for saving her.

"Horatia, you know I ought not to stay..." His voice trailed off helplessly, but he didn't retreat. Instead he leaned down and stroked her hair away from her face.

"I would feel better if you stayed. Safer." She reached out and cupped his cheek with her hand and brushed a finger over his lips, recalling the way they felt on hers. He raised his hand and caught her wrist, rubbing his thumb over the sensitive skin of her inner wrist, just over her now racing pulse.

"Please stay. I need you here." Horatia felt like a child again, trapped in the shattered, splintered remains of her parents' carriage, hearing screams of pain, realizing later they were her own. She needed him to comfort her, to stay and hold her now as he had then.

Something in her plea made him nod, and he pulled back the covers of her bed.

"Go on then, get in." He urged her under the covers as he pulled them back. Lucien got up from the bed then and began to disrobe. Horatia's breath hitched as he removed his shirt and locked her bedroom door.

Usually, there was a natural air of control and command about him, but he seemed robbed of those qualities tonight. His legs shook, and he breathed more rapidly, as though he were being tested and found himself on the verge of failure.

The lamplight played over his sculpted form as he stood clad only in his drawers. She could spend a lifetime memorizing the feel, the shape, the taste of that body and it would never be enough to satisfy her. Lucien was a wicked addiction, and she had no hope, nor any desire to be free of the drugging influence of his body.

As he approached the bed she moved back a bit to give him plenty of room to join her. He blew out the lamp, enveloping them both in darkness as he settled into the bed next to her. He plumped a pillow behind his head and then without hesitation brought her body against his, his arms anchoring her to him.

For better or worse, he was here with her, comforting her in a way he had not done in seven years. It was worth

Lawrence's rash actions to have been awarded this quiet, intimate moment with Lucien. She savored his warm breath fanning her neck and the heat of his body against her own. She was barely aware of anything except him as sleep crept in.

LUCIEN LAY AWAKE, all too aware that sharing a bed with Horatia was dangerous. Only her scare with Lawrence had allowed him to maintain his restraint for her. He focused instead on his brother. What the hell had Lawrence been thinking? Lucien knew his brothers better than he knew himself. Lawrence would never have hurt Horatia, or any woman. Why then had he put her in such a terrifying situation? A prank? That was more Linus's game. Lucien replayed the evening in his mind, searching for any hint, any detail to explain his brother's actions. Lawrence had lured him out on the pretext of meeting with Linus who supposedly had amorous intentions towards Horatia, but when he'd arrived at his study the room had been empty so he'd started back to the ballroom. When he glimpsed Linus ducking into a room at the end of the hall, he'd started to follow until he'd passed by one room that hadn't been occupied a few minutes before.

That was when he'd stumbled upon Horatia and Lawrence.

Lucien would never get that sight of them out of his head. Fear clawed at his insides and worry knotted his stomach. Whatever scheme his brothers had been involved in...tomorrow they would pay. Lucien would see to it, no matter the reasons. Horatia belonged to him, not Lawrence or any other man. And no one harmed what was his. A woman as wonderful and kind as Horatia deserved to be cherished, protected and...loved.

He pulled Horatia tighter against him. She shifted, murmured something and lay still again. It did not escape his notice that her body fit well with his, as though she had always belonged to him.

Only then did he realize that for many years now he had belonged to her, and this epiphany troubled him greatly.

Nothing good would come of feeling this way towards her. The rules of the League could not be broken, and friendships could not withstand such a trespass. Lucien didn't want to choose between Horatia and her brother. He silently prayed that he wouldn't have to.

CHAPTER 21

*L*awrence flung himself into a deep armchair within a private parlor, his brothers flanking it on either side. His head hurt like the devil. He'd likely have a knot on his brow by the morning. Avery frowned and stared down at him while Linus paced back and forth. The rest of the guests had all gone to sleep and the three Russells were alone now to discuss the possible victory of their plan.

"Well, Lawrence, how did it go?" Linus asked.

Lawrence growled in response. He didn't want to think about what he'd just done. "I have a bad feeling that Lucien is going to put a bullet through me tomorrow. And if Cedric catches wind, it might be two."

"What?" Avery eyes widened.

"I went too far. It took Lucien too long to find us." Lawrence rubbed his eyes wearily.

"Just how far is too far exactly?" Linus asked.

"In trying to delay things I was perhaps a bit too convincing of my intentions and frightened the poor woman. She smashed her head into mine when I tried to kiss her. It was never my intent to scare her. I thought I could convince her to play along and kiss me back so Lucien would get jealous, but she panicked before I could explain." Lawrence flinched at the shock in his brothers' faces. "Lucien arrived just in time. Or at the worst possible time, I suppose. What the devil took him so long?"

"You really did that to Horatia?" asked Linus. "You almost…"

"Of course not. But she thought I was going to. She was terrified and I feel…" He scrubbed his hand down over his face. "God. I doubt she'll ever forgive me. I hope I didn't do her lasting damage. Lucien better marry her, or I've ruined a lovely friendship for nothing." Lawrence got up and stalked over to the nearest cabinet in the parlor and took out a bottle of brandy.

"I need a drink," he declared. His two brothers joined him, all grim over the spectacle they'd helped to create that night.

"Do we know how Lucien took it?" Avery asked Lawrence.

"No. He took her back up to her room. I haven't seen him since. I ordered the servants to stay clear of her room until after breakfast. I hope he means to stay the night with her. If he does, we'll most likely have won. We all know what a soft-hearted man he is, especially if he thought it would cheer up a disheartened lady."

"That's certainly true. He's much too tender-hearted to let her alone tonight after..." Avery trailed off.

"After Lawrence almost ravaged her?" Linus supplied helpfully.

"Russells do not ravage," Avery stated. "We're far too gifted in natural persuasion. There's no need to force a woman when after a few well placed caresses she'll give you whatever you ask for."

"Don't encourage the lad, Avery," Lawrence said noting the look on Linus's face. "He's in enough trouble already with Miss Cavendish."

Linus whipped his gaze from Avery to Lawrence. "What do you mean *I'm* in trouble?"

"After she saw you dancing with Miss Sheridan she took it rather personally. You did not ask her to dance, after all."

Linus's lips parted as he sputtered. "But we were... damn! Was she very upset do you think?"

Avery grinned. "I believe she spent the evening time glaring at you. I was surprised you didn't turn into a pillar of salt. I'm afraid you've rather bungled it." Avery patted Linus's shoulder in a rough but affectionate gesture. "Perhaps you can woo her again on the morrow?"

Lawrence continued to sip his brandy, watching the

byplay with amusement, but his guilt at his actions from earlier still niggled at him.

"I suppose I'll have to. I mean, I owe the girl that, after kissing her. I suppose I ought to speak with her father as well. I know I'm a bit young to offer for her but... Perhaps we may enjoy a longer engagement period until I am ready to accommodate a wife."

The hopeful look on his youngest brother's face stopped Lawrence from re-filling his glass.

"Steady on, Linus!" Avery cautioned. "What's all this talk of making an offer? You need not, especially at your age."

Lawrence eyed his brother curiously. "But you kissed her?" The almost calf-mooned expression in Linus's eyes was a little disturbing. He'd seen it before, and always in the young.

"Yes. It was a rather chaste one, though. I believe it was her first," Linus mused aloud, a blush tingeing his cheeks.

"You like her!" Avery said shrewdly.

"There is...something undeniably sweet about her." Linus admitted.

Lawrence groaned. His brother was on the way to falling for a woman. One woman. But there were so many out there to taste and feel and explore. He shouldn't be limiting himself so soon. Linus had to be saved from himself.

"Sweet as she is, one kiss does not herald wedding

bells," Lawrence said as he set down his brandy glass. "If it were, I would be married a thousand times over to a hundred different women. Fathers may expect offers after a single kiss, but we Russells do not go quietly into the leg shackles of matrimony."

"Then why are we helping Lucien with Horatia? Won't they end up married?"

"That is the plan," Avery said.

Linus frowned, entirely perplexed. "Then why—"

"Lucien is past his prime. He ought to settle down. It might as well be with someone who adores him. Miss Sheridan is the perfect young lady to prepare him to become a father to the much needed heir to the marquessate."

"We don't need an heir," Linus countered. "There are three more of us in line."

"Don't tell me that *you* want all that responsibility, Linus," Avery chuckled.

"Better that Lucien has a passel of boys and an army of girls," Lawrence said. "That way there's an heir and plenty of grandchildren for Mama to fawn over and the rest of us will be left to our own devices." The mere thought of Lucien having children eased Lawrence somewhat. What a wonderful sense of relief he would have when Mama finally left him alone. He'd do anything to achieve that freedom, even incur his brother's wrath. Though in light of recent events his liberty might be short lived.

"I suppose that does make sense, after a fashion. Mama would love all those grandchildren," Linus chuckled.

Lawrence poured brandy for his brothers and they raised their glasses for a toast. "To Lucien, Horatia and all the grandchildren Mama will ever want!"

CHARLES BID his friends at Essex House good night before collecting his new servant, Tom Linley. Charles leaned back against the plush squabs of his coach as Linley scrabbled up to sit next to the coachman. He gave instructions to go to the house where Linley's baby sister was located. It was close to midnight and the baby's nurse would most likely be unamused at the disruption. Charles was prepared to pay to smooth any ruffled feathers that might arise from their late arrival. When Linley finally joined Charles inside the coach, he raised a quizzical brow.

"I asked him to take us to Bennett Street, my lord," Linley said.

"Bennett Street?" Charles sat up. "Where exactly do you live?"

"I rent a small room above the Dandy House, my lord."

"The Dandy House? You mean to tell me that you live above a gambling hell?" Gambling hells were not hellish, despite the title, but they were often rowdy and occasionally dangerous places. It was appalling to think of Linley trying to raise a baby in such a location.

"It was all I could afford, sir." Linley's face darkened and Charles felt he'd made a mistake in reacting.

"I was merely surprised you lived there. I will admit I have been to the Dandy on several occasions. Some of my friends and acquaintances are officers and they especially like the high stakes. It amuses them. I was just astonished to learn that you've been able to keep a child there."

Linley relaxed, but flinched when Charles tried once more to pat his arm.

"I'm sorry. I didn't mean to startle you."

"'Tis my fault, my lord. My last master only touched me when he needed to thrash something to ease his temper."

"Who was your previous master before you came to work at Berkeley's?"

"I should not say. It would not be proper to speak ill of him," Linley protested.

Charles flung up his hands. "Easy, lad, I won't demand you reveal all your secrets. Not tonight anyway. We all have devils on our backs." Charles fell silent, a rare contemplative mood capturing him.

Neither he nor Linley said anything more until they reached Bennett Street. Linley tried to insist that Charles wait in the coach, but Charles leapt out and eyed the gambling hell with mild interest.

It had been awhile since he'd tried to gamble away his vast inheritance. Men in crisp red uniforms and those of an aristocratic bearing milled about the club's front entrance, talking and laughing. A few men recognized Charles and waved. He hailed them and followed Linley down the nearest alley and to a back door.

Linley went right inside and Charles followed, rather enjoying this curious little adventure. Charles listened to the raucous noises on the other side of the thin walls as they climbed the back stairs. There were shouts and the cackles of women, cheering on the winners and consoling the losers. Such things had never caused Charles concern before, but he was suddenly seeing his lifestyle through the eyes of the young lad ahead of him. Someone who was bearing a great responsibility by caring for his baby sister all on his own. It was admirable, and right now he felt quite the opposite.

Linley paused at a single door at the top of the stairs and rapped his knuckles in an odd pattern. After a moment the door opened a crack.

"It's me, Mrs. Bertie," Linley said.

The door opened more fully, allowing Linley inside. When Charles moved to follow him a rotund woman in her mid-thirties blocked his path.

"Eh, Linley, who's this, love? I thought ye stayed clear of them lords who fancied lads..." Mrs. Bertie's implication that he had such intentions made Charles wince.

Charles had no qualms with what other men did in

their private lives, but abuse was easy to come by, and sometimes where wicked desires and vices were involved, people got hurt.

"That is Lord Lonsdale. He's an earl, Mrs. Bertie, so please be on your best behavior and let him inside." Linley strode straight for the wooden cradle against the wall. A bundle stirred where Linley bent his head over the cradle's edge. Mrs. Bertie eyed Charles with deep suspicion before stepping back and allowing him in.

"So, Linley love, ye were late, I expected ye hours ago. It'll be costin' ye double since I missed time with them gents downstairs."

Mrs. Bertie seemed unfazed by Charles's presence and turned her attention back to Linley who had started to gather his few belongings into a cloth sack.

"I...I can't pay you extra tonight Mrs. Bertie, but in a week I will have enough to settle my debt."

"I want my money now!" Mrs. Bertie hissed in annoyance.

Linley blanched just as Charles stepped between the woman and the lad.

"My dear, charming Mrs. Bertie, I am sure we can reach an agreement. The lad is now under my employ. I will advance him his wages to see you well paid for your services." Charles took Mrs. Bertie's hand and palmed several coins into her hand. Mrs. Bertie's eyes widened in shock before she leaned around Charles to look at Linley.

"Whatever he be using ye for lad, let him!" Mrs. Bertie

whispered these last two words, but Charles still heard her and he raised his eyes heavenward, giving a silent plea for patience.

"Er, thank you for everything, Mrs. Bertie. But we really must be going now." Linley shouldered the cloth sack with one hand then scooped up the squirming bundle with a natural ease.

Linley juggled the babe and bag as he started towards the door. Charles followed him out, chuckling at the shocked expression on Mrs. Bertie's face as they headed down the stairs.

Once they were in the coach Linley dropped his bag onto the floor and saw to the care of the baby. The child's tousled golden curls were feathery light and seemed to shine, even in the dim light.

Charles ruffled a hand through the curls of the babe's head and continued to watch her the rest of the way back to his townhouse on Curzon Street. There was something about the baby, something familiar, just at the edge of his memory, but for the life of him he could not recall what it was.

The coach stopped out front of his townhouse.

A footman rushed out to meet them as they descended from the coach.

"Timothy, you look awful, what's happened?" Charles demanded as the white-faced footman took their coats.

"It's dreadful, my lord, dreadful. Come inside."

Timothy led the way, all the while Charles felt his blood turning to ice in his veins.

When they entered the townhouse, several of the servants were standing there, all looking just as distressed as Timothy. A young upstairs maid stepped forward and held out a bundle of cloth.

"My lord, we found this in your tub." After he'd taken the bundle from her she wiped away tears and spoke again. "It was drowned, my lord."

Drowned? Charles peeled back the cloth and sucked in a harsh breath. A black cat was lying dead in his hands. The little body was stiff, cold and still damp. Despite all this, he recognized the cat's markings. It was Muff. One of the two cats from the Sheridan house.

"The poor thing!" Linley's eyes were bright as he held Kate's bundled body closer to his chest. The baby was asleep and Linley raised her higher in his arms as he spoke.

"Who would kill a cat?" Linley asked as he protectively shielded the baby.

"An enemy. An enemy who wants to send me a message."

"What message?"

"He wants me to know he can get to me and to my friends. The cat never left the Sheridan house. Someone grabbed him and brought him here. My enemy, the League's enemy, may be ready to strike."

"The League?"

341

"Yes. You might as well get used to the name. My friends, Viscount Sheridan, Baron Lennox, the Duke of Essex and the Marquess of Rochester and I are sometimes referred to by the society pages as the League of Rogues. We adopted the title in jest, but it seems to have stuck."

"So this enemy, he wishes to destroy this League?" Linley asked.

"Yes."

"Do you know who he is?"

Charles gave a slow nod as he looked down at the body covered in the cloth. He had a wretched feeling deep inside that Muff was the first casualty in the war that had been simmering for years.

"Sir Hugo Waverly. I believe he means to kill us all eventually," Charles predicted. A heavy shadow fell across Linley's face. "The worst of it will be breaking the news to Cedric and his sisters. They're damned fond of this little scamp. It's a blessing they're in Kent. I couldn't bear to watch the girls hear the news. Women crying is the worst thing imaginable. I never say or do the right thing to stop the blasted waterworks." Charles tilted his head back, heaving a sigh.

He tried not to think about how the cat had died. The choice of execution was no coincidence. Charles shuddered, remembering the sensation of cold water strangling him, smothering his nose and mouth, blinding his vision as he sank beneath the dark waters, weights attached his legs, and his hands bound so he couldn't swim. Yes. There was no doubt who committed this sin against an innocent creature.

"I wish we could bury him, but the ground is frozen. We'll have to cremate him. It might help console Lord Sheridan and his sisters to know that the poor creature was cared for," Linley suggested.

"That is a very considerate idea. We'll handle it tomorrow." Charles ran a shaky hand through his hair. Waverly was upping the stakes.

"It seems you may have chosen an ill time to take on a new employer, Linley," Charles muttered. Linley buried his face in the blankets around little Katherine, planting a kiss on the babe's forehead as though to ward off evil. But Charles knew better. Tender kisses and thoughts of love would not save anyone from Hugo Waverly.

CHAPTER 22

*D*reams were wonderful things, no one could dispute that. But the moment when an intangible vision of one's desires becomes a reality? That is something infinitely more powerful and breathtaking than the moonlit inspired visions woven in the night. Now here Horatia was, waking beside Lucien. She blinked a few times to clear her vision and glimpsed snow falling outside the large window opposite her.

The flakes had clumped into penny-sized blotches, drifting down like feathers. It was still early. The light in the sky was reduced to a heavy gray by the voluminous winter clouds. Horatia lay nestled next to him, the heat of Lucien's body warming her back. She rolled over, settling deeper into the feather bedding as she studied him in the dim morning light.

Lucien was stretched out on his stomach. One hand

was fisted around the bottom of his pillow, scrunching it up beneath his cheek. His other arm dangled off the side of the bed. The wide expanse of his shoulders and back were exposed as the sheets rode low on his hips. His face was turned towards her, his dark lashes spiking across his cheeks as he slept. Although Lucien was thirty-three, Horatia could see the boy in his features as they softened with sleep. She ached to brush her hand along his brows and trace the strong, straight aristocratic nose down to his sinful lips.

The lines of his body were carved with muscle. A long, pale pink scar dipped along the side of his chest and stopped at the top of his hip. Without thinking Horatia ran a curious fingertip along the raised surface of the mark. Lucien stirred at her touch, and his eyes opened. Horatia wished she knew the smallest details about him —the things a lover or a wife would know—such as whether he woke easily or not.

"Lucien, are you a light sleeper?" she asked.

His gaze warmed as he seemed to consider her question.

"Why do you wish to know?" He remained still, watching her, the closeness between them overwhelming her senses.

"I was curious," she hedged.

She realized her finger was still touching him near his left hip. She didn't pull her hand back.

I should stop touching him, she told herself. But instead

she let the rest of her fingers splay defiantly on his skin, the touch intimate and possessive. Lucien did not shift his gaze away from her.

"I am a light sleeper. And you?" It seemed he was aware of the intimacy of the moment, and the conversation.

"Sometimes when I am worried or vexed I have trouble sleeping."

"You slept soundly last night," Lucien observed.

"That is because..." Horatia felt her cheeks flush.

"Because?"

"Because I feel safe when you are near." She could not tell him how she really felt. That being near him made her both restless and peaceful, that she trusted him with her body, heart and soul. When he was with her the dark memories that haunted her could not penetrate the ring of light he shone about her.

Lucien did not reply. Instead he propped his head up on one hand and removed Horatia's inquisitive hand from his hip. He studied her fingers and palm, his thumb teasing patterns on her skin. He spread her fingers and placed his own palm against hers, matching their hands, though his fingers were much longer than hers. Then he laced their fingers together and pulled her towards him.

Again, Horatia was struck by their closeness, and it left her struggling for breath. What if he pushed away again, as he always had before? The idea was unbearable.

She had to emotionally take a step back through conversation.

"Lucien, how did you come by that scar?"

"Which one?"

"The...the one on your hip." She couldn't believe she was in bed with Lucien discussing his hips. If it weren't for her breathless fascination with his body, she would have laughed at the prudish shyness she was feeling.

"Oh that." Lucien laughed and placed a soft kiss on the back of her fingers.

Horatia shivered at the warmth of his lips. The man was irresistible. Her heart cracked at the seams, bursting with love and sadness all at once.

"I received that particular scar when I was at university. Ashton and I had only just met, and we didn't like each other."

"You and Ashton? But you are such good friends!" Horatia couldn't envision a world where Lucien and Ashton disliked each other.

"True. But at first, he and I did not see eye to eye. Ashton believes in rules and principles. To him I was the most unscrupulous fellow he'd ever met. I dare say he wasn't completely wrong about that."

She leaned into him, enchanted with the way he talked. "And what does that have to do with your scar?"

Lucien's face flushed uncharacteristically red. "Well, it is rather embarrassing."

"Well, now I must hear it."

"I was a student at Cambridge, and I got it into my head to seduce the young wife of one of our professors. He was interested in well...gentlemen, and she was quite lonely." Lucien grinned wickedly. "Call it payback for poor examination results I'd received. I don't know how Ashton found out what I meant to do, but he followed me one night. I was halfway up the trellis to the lady's room when Ashton jumped out of the bushes and startled me. I lost my hold and the wooden trellis sliced me open as I fell."

Horatia gasped. He chuckled at her shock.

"Quite. I was in a bad way when I landed, and Ashton was far too noble to abandon me. He helped me onto my feet and when he saw how deep my wound was he helped me to the nearest inn and found a doctor. Somewhere between my fall and the seven sutures I'd received without one drop of brandy to dull my pain, Ashton decided he liked me after all. He thought I ought to behave more like the gentleman I was, but he also knew I couldn't always fight my more untamed nature. He reconciled himself to the idea of our friendship and we've been as we are ever since." Lucien's mouth once more settled on Horatia's skin, this time on her wrist to kiss the sensitive skin where her pulse thrummed even more quickly.

She had a thousand questions, but when she felt his tongue flick out, all rational thought faded. With a slow sensual slide, he pulled her body flush against his.

"Horatia, I'm not good at this," Lucien whispered, his lips mere inches from hers.

"Good at what?" Her voice was a tad tremulous as she feared what he might say.

"Being a gentleman. In London I promised that you would be safe from me, yet I let Lawrence hurt you and now I'm sharing your bed, and having the most wicked sort of thoughts about you."

Her heart leapt inside her chest. "Oh?"

He let his lips brush hers, smiling as though he enjoyed her stunned response.

"Oh yes. I keep thinking about that night at the Midnight Garden and how brave you were to face me. How sweet you tasted! And right now, I wish it had been me last night who had you alone in a bedroom at my mercy." Lucien nipped her bottom lip and the spot between her legs ached.

"Lucien, I'm always at your mercy." Horatia brushed her hand through his dark red hair as he teased her further. "And you do have me alone in a bedroom."

"Mmm, I do, don't I?" He framed her face with his hands and plundered her mouth in a way that left her dazed and throbbing. "What do you say we—" Someone knocked at the locked bedroom door.

Horatia scowled. "Drat. That must be my maid, Ursula. She's early."

Lucien released her and slid out of the bed with a slow sigh.

"Perhaps it is for the best. I... Damn. This is a mistake, Horatia. I can never bloody think straight when I'm with you." Lucien's voice was hoarse as he quickly dressed.

WHEN LUCIEN OPENED the door the maid eyed him with disapproval. He'd faced far worse, however, he didn't want this woman bringing trouble to Horatia.

"I trust you will be silent about what you've seen here?"

"Of course, my lord," Ursula said without warmth. "My lady's reputation means everything to me. I dare not ask what your intentions are."

"My intention is to continue to see Horatia without anyone knowing. For her benefit, not mine. I am not ashamed to be with her, but her brother finding out would put everyone in a difficult position."

The lady's maid nodded. "Lord Sheridan would certainly be furious. I would not like to be the cause of his temper. I will keep silent so long as you treat her well."

Lucien nodded in farewell to Horatia, then slipped out into the hallway to ring for his valet, Felix.

He had to erase the image of her in bed from his mind. The way she looked so warm, soft and perfect, her hair tumbled in waves around her shoulders, her eyes still a little dreamy with sleep and her lips pink and ready for kisses... It was enough to drive a man mad.

After he'd bathed and dressed, Lucien stumbled upon his three brothers exiting the breakfast room and headed for the closest door that would take them outside.

"You three, stop!" he barked. It was time for a reckoning.

They caught sight of him and bolted like rabbits. Lucien managed to snag Linus by the collar of his long black greatcoat.

"Avery, help!" Linus clawed at his brother, who dodged away as he and Lawrence eyed Lucien the way one would a man-eating tiger.

A killing rage stirred in Lucien's blood and he was more than ready to unleash it after what had happened to Horatia.

"I want a word with you, Lawrence," Lucien growled. "*All* of you, in fact."

Linus kicked out but Lucien's grip had rendered him helpless. Avery and Lawrence looked to one another and nodded, coming back to Lucien. Lucien loosened his grip on Linus but did not release him completely.

"Last night. What you did, Lawrence, that had better been part of some silly plan you've concocted, because if I learn you meant to do Horatia harm you will never be welcome in this house again."

"Easy there, Lucien," Avery said gently, as though speaking to a spooked stallion.

"It was Mama's doing!" Linus gasped out. "She's to blame!"

"What?"

"Be quiet!" Lawrence hissed.

"Mama told us to seduce Horatia so you would become jealous and want her more." Lucien let Linus go, causing him to fall to his knees.

"You tried to make me jealous? The three of you kept her away until..." Lucien fixed his gaze on Lawrence, who gulped audibly.

"You were supposed to find the two of us much sooner!" Lawrence said. "I was trying to explain, but she kept... I never meant to take it so far."

"Tell that to the young lady you frightened. God, Lawrence." Lucien stepped past Linus. "I thought you had more sense. Did her pleas mean nothing to you?"

"I regret every second of it," Lawrence snapped. "But it's done. You stayed all night with her, just like we expected you to."

Lucien hauled back his fist when a voice from down the hall stopped him.

"Everything all right here?" Cedric asked as he came down the hall, pulling on his gloves and coat.

Lucien changed his movement to a stretch and rubbed his hair. "Yes. Everything is fine." Lucien scanned Cedric's heavy coat and gloves. "Where are you off to?"

"To build the forts. You know, for the snowball battle your mother arranged? Your brothers and I are to build two forts on either side of the garden. The ladies will be out in an hour or so to join us."

"The ladies?" Lucien was baffled. It had been ages since his family had a snowball fight, not since he was sixteen at least. What was she up to?

Cedric grinned. "Who else? Last night we decided that should we have a decent snowfall, we ought to have a battle. Men against women, of course. Even Sir John and Lady Cavendish have agreed to join in. The numbers favor us, but I imagine that a few of the gents will defect to the enemy side when our chivalry gets the better of us."

Thankfully it seemed Cedric hadn't overhead any of their discussion. Lucien could deal with his brothers later. For now he just wanted some peace and to spend time with Cedric.

"Well then, lead the way, Avery." Lucien called for a nearby footman to fetch his coat and gloves. Avery, Cedric and Linus headed outside, but Lawrence lingered behind.

"Lucien, about Horatia—" Lawrence began.

Lucien cut him off with a raised finger, but Lawrence threw out a hand and stopped Lucien from brushing past him.

"I would never have done anything more to her. I swear it. She's...well, she's Horatia." Lawrence's tone conveyed his meaning where his words failed.

Lucien moved the hand aside. "Never, and I mean

never touch her again. If you make her uncomfortable for even a moment..." He didn't finish his sentence because it would end with a threat and he didn't wish to ruin his day with such black thoughts.

Lawrence studied his brother's face. "Mother was right. You really do care for her. She's a good woman and will make a wonderful wife and mother."

The sudden vision of Horatia holding a child, *their* child in her arms stilled his heart. Pain, such sweet pain and longing, blazed to life inside him. But Cedric would never condone the match—he always seemed to forget that when he was near her.

"Speak of it no more. I expect you to find a moment later today to make your apologies to Horatia. And if you ever let mother coerce you into something so foolish again, I won't save you, whatever the consequences," Lucien warned.

"I'll apologize to her." Lawrence slid his coat onto his shoulders and looked as though waiting for his brother's permission to leave.

Lucien shoved ahead of him and donned his own coat and gloves. "Come along, Lawrence. These snow forts must be soundly built, and if we leave Linus in charge he'll make some delicate nonsense that will look impressive but blow over in a stiff wind." Focusing on the upcoming frivolities, he prayed he could shake loose the longing he had for Horatia. Last night couldn't be repeated ever again.

$\mathcal{A}$n hour later, Horatia and the other ladies were assembled on the east side, admiring the fort the gentlemen had built for them. It was a waist high wall that arched around in a half circle about ten feet across, providing ample protection for the women now huddled behind it preparing their arsenals. The vast gardens behind Rochester Hall had been molded into a white battlefield ready for the coming war.

Lady Cavendish was helping Lady Rochester manufacture their ammunition. Horatia, Audrey, Lysandra and Lucinda were in a tight circle, all wearing red fur-lined cloaks with heavy hoods pulled up. Audrey had remarked that they were the most fashionable army in Europe. They discussed the various traps and places to avoid in the garden, areas where one might become cornered and savaged by the weapons of the enemy.

"Should we try to lure them out from their fort?" Lucinda asked.

Horatia glanced over her shoulder to the opposing fort fifty feet away. The men were hunkered down out of sight, save for the occasional surfacing head that glanced warily about. Her gaze met with Gregory Cavendish's as he peeked out over their fort's edge then ducked back down. They looked like a pack of squirrels, popping up and down like that. Horatia grinned at the thought of such noble gentlemen behaving so out of character.

"I think luring is not a bad idea," Audrey declared. "But we must go about it smartly. Only when one of them is decently separated should we set up a trap. Otherwise they could easily overwhelm us."

"And someone ought to be carefully guarding the fort," Lysandra reminded them. She broke from the group to show the other ladies something she'd covered in a brown cloth blanket. She pulled it back to reveal a simple yet cleverly constructed wooden trebuchet approximately four feet long that was counterweighed by a heavy pouch of stones. "This should help whoever is remaining here."

"Is that a trebuchet?" Horatia asked, both amused and appreciative of Lysandra's ingenuity.

Lysandra grinned, glancing in the directions of her brothers. "I thought we might need a bit of extra help seeing how they both outnumber us and can throw farther. I found a book in our library detailing its construction and I had a scaled down replica built last summer. I had a devil of a time keeping Linus from finding out."

She took a snowball from the ever growing pile her mother and Lady Cavendish were making and set it in the sling attached to the trebuchet's long wooden arm. Then Lysandra prepared the pouch of stones and as all of the ladies watched, she aimed towards the men's fort and then dropped the pouch. The trebuchet hurled the snowball in a beautiful arch before it crashed into a tree a few feet behind the men.

"Oi! Who threw that?" Linus's head popped up, scowling in their directions as he hollered.

Horatia bit down on her lower lip to keep from laughing.

"Sorry, Linus! We're just practicing." Lysandra waved a snowy gloved hand in his direction, then turned back to the ladies. "As you can see, we may need a larger snowball, but it's a decent way of forcing them to keep their heads down."

"Excellent thinking!" Lucinda said and the other ladies nodded.

Sir John Cavendish called out from across the garden at that moment. "I say, are you ladies ready to begin?"

"We are!" Lady Cavendish returned to her husband.

"Good, good. I've been informed that I must now state the rules," Sir John said. "Which are as follows: Whoever captures the enemy fort is declared the winner. Captives may be taken and marked with red ribbons provided by your side's leader. There is no bargaining for captives, they remain captive until the end of the battle and lastly…there are no other rules. Begin!" Sir John bellowed before ducking down below his fort.

The ladies fell behind their snow wall as a massive volley of balls came their way. Audrey shrieked as a slush of snow and ice landed on the top of her hooded head. There was a chorus of distant laughter from the other side. Audrey stood up to shout at them since the weapons were supposed to be fashioned of fluffy snow, not hard packed with slush and ice, but Horatia jerked her back down as another flurry was unleashed. The balls flew past the empty space where Audrey had been standing moments before.

"Why those wretched devils!" Audrey hissed as she crawled over to the trebuchet. "Quick, someone distract them while I add more counterweight."

"But the balls will fly too far!" said Lady Cavendish.

"Not necessarily."

Lady Rochester peeked over the edge of the fort, her face alight with a delightful smile.

"Tally-ho!" Lady Rochester whooped most inelegantly and waved her arms as she acted as a decoy so Horatia and Lysandra could return fire. Unfortunately the fifty feet of distance between the two forts seemed to ensure that their throws would fall short.

"See? We've nothing to worry about. They can't even

reach us!" Linus taunted as he stood up brazenly to take his time in aiming at his mother. Audrey meanwhile adjusted the aim of the trebuchet and with a curt nod at Lady Rochester, Audrey dropped the heavier counter-weight and let fly their snowy vengeance. The women watched in glee as a snowball the size of a man's head smacked Linus square in the chest, knocking him to the ground.

"What the deuce?" They heard feebly from behind the fort.

The ladies all burst out laughing.

LUCIEN and his fellow warriors were all gazing at Linus's prone body. At last he got up and brushed himself off.

"Didn't we pace it at fifty feet?" Lawrence asked. "I thought Avery said they wouldn't be able to throw anything that far?"

"Or that heavy," added Avery.

"Perhaps not that far," said Linus. "One of them must have snuck up closer and we didn't see them. Search the trees for scouts. Mother has a surprisingly powerful arm."

Sir John's lips twitched. "Do you mean to tell me that you lads purposely put the ladies at a disadvantage both physically and numerically?"

"Clearly you have never engaged our women in a snowball fight, Sir John," Lucien said with a low chuckle.

"They cheat and therefore any measures we take are simply precautions to protect ourselves against the inevitable."

His brothers nodded in agreement.

"They are ruthless," Avery said in all seriousness.

"How should we go about getting them away from their fort?" Gregory asked.

Cedric peeped over the edge of the snow wall as he voiced an idea. "We ought to send a scout of our own. One who can see just how their supplies stack up and how they are organizing themselves. The rest of us can remain here."

"I'll go," Gregory volunteered.

"Head south and make a large sweep around back," Lucien advised. "We don't want them guessing what our game is."

Gregory had barely left when the women pressed their advantage. Several flanked from one side, distracting them from among the trees, and every so often out of nowhere either a white cannon ball or a storm of smaller ones rained down at once, seemingly dropped from Heaven itself.

A little while later, Gregory returned with a prize. Lawrence and Avery were the first to spot them and laughed at seeing Lysandra following behind with a red ribbon around her wrist.

"Got a captive on my way back from the enemy encampment," he declared and indicated for Lysandra to sit down behind a tree a few feet away. "Tried to sneak up on me, but her shot missed and I threatened to put my snowball down her hood if she didn't surrender."

"Well done. What's the status of the opposing forces?" Avery demanded.

"Lady Rochester and my mother are producing the ammunition. Luce and Miss Sheridan are the primary hurlers, but as we planned, they cannot reach us from there. They left the fort to flank you."

"We know. We've only just beaten those two back."

"So how the devil are they hitting us so hard?" Lucien asked.

"It seems the ladies have the use of a small trebuchet." Gregory stifled a laugh when his captive huffed.

"So that's how they're raining death upon us," said Linus.

A large ball hit the side of the fort, making the rampart buckle.

"Bloody hell. They'll be firing real cannonballs soon," said Lawrence.

Linus flicked a calculated glance at Lysandra, then studied the other men crouching down behind their wall. He then he dug out a white handkerchief from his coat pocket and leapt to his feet.

"What on earth are you doing?" Lawrence asked.

Linus jumped back a few steps and then bolted towards the ladies fort, waving the handkerchief as a sign of surrender. Lucien watched him tear off across the snow-covered lawn.

Traitor. He shook his head at his youngest brother's quick defection to the other side.

～

"HAVE MERCY, LADIES! I SEEK SANCTUARY!" Linus shouted as Horatia and Lucinda jumped up, ready to pound him with snowballs.

"You bloody traitor!" Lucien hollered across the garden.

"Got to follow the progress of technology! Why fight with sticks when the other side has bronze weapons?" He dove behind the cover of the ladies' fort as a vicious barrage of snowballs from the enraged men followed him.

Linus rolled on the ground and landed up on the balls of his feet like a practiced warrior. Horatia found it impossible to keep from laughing at him. He could be very impressive when he wasn't playing pranks, and she couldn't miss the excited gleam in Lucinda's eyes regarding their new ally.

Horatia shouted for them both to duck and they covered their heads as a barrage came crashing down on them.

"Always causing trouble, aren't you?" Lucinda giggled to Linus.

"I wouldn't be me if I didn't," he replied, then popped up to retaliate. "Take that, you cheating curs!" He hurled three snowballs one after the other. He was their very own knight errant ready to lay siege to his former allies.

Lucien bravely stood up across the yard. "Silence, pup! We'll capture your fort and you will have to surrender the lovely ladies whose skirts you hide behind!" He spoke like a villain from a comedy play.

But all Horatia felt was the love and joy she always had for him. Like drinking too much wine, she was light-headed and eager to find a way back into his arms. Even at a distance his answering smile was intimate, as though meant only for her. She uttered a silent prayer deep in her heart that the one dream she'd longed for most would come true.

The snowball battle lasted close to two hours but after that the excitement died down, and the chill in the air and the damp cold of the snow had started to set in. They declared the battle a draw and Horatia was happy that the others agreed they should return indoors. She wished she could have more time with Lucien—but it wasn't to be. She followed the rest of the party inside, her heart sinking lower with each step.

CHAPTER 24

The rider from London arrived in the early evening, just in time to prevent everyone from going to dinner. Lucien took the note, and he and Cedric returned to his study to read it in privacy. Horatia and her sister lingered in the corridor outside. She thought it might involve news from his friends in London.

Pressed against the wooden door to eavesdrop, Horatia flinched when she heard Cedric curse. There was a heavy thud, as though something had hit the wall. Lucien muttered something she couldn't hear, then there was a growl from her brother before footsteps approached the door. Both Audrey and Horatia scampered back, hoping to conceal their feeble attempts at eavesdropping.

When the door opened, Horatia's stomach clenched as

she saw Cedric's face shrouded by a mask of pain and barely controlled rage.

"What is it?" Audrey asked as she glanced between Cedric and Lucien.

"Charles sent some bad news," Lucien answered carefully. He glanced around, making sure that it was only the four of them. Horatia knew it must be a private League matter if he didn't wish for his brothers or anyone else to overhear.

"What happened?" Her throat constricted.

"Ashton was wounded when he and Godric were investigating the threats we overheard," Lucien said. "Someone shot him, but he'll be fine."

Horatia watched him closely. "That's not all, is it? You're not telling us everything." She'd been too afraid to ask her brother or Lucien, but she'd sensed there was more to this situation than either had let on. Were they all in more danger than she'd originally believed?

"I'm sorry. Someone killed Muff." Cedric's low sharp tone made Horatia flinch.

Audrey screamed. "No!"

"Waverly somehow managed to breach our home." Cedric's fists tightened as he spoke. "Someone killed Muff. They drowned him and left him in a tub at Charles's house."

"But why?" Audrey whimpered, tears threatening to spill over.

"Because he could. He wanted us to know our homes

aren't safe. And he's succeeded. No one is going back until this is resolved." Cedric's tone was dark in a way that Horatia had never heard before.

"How do you know it was Waverly?" Horatia asked. Her voice cracked, but she got the words out.

Neither her brother nor Lucien replied for several long moments.

"We have no proof," Lucien said. "It's more of a feeling."

Cedric added his own dark thoughts. "He tried to drown Charles once. Now he's drowned a cat. It's obvious enough it's him."

There was a vengefulness in his brown eyes that frightened her. He was buried in a rage she understood all too well. She could barely think herself, the anger and grief churned to violence inside her.

Audrey threw herself at Cedric's chest and wept. Cedric folded her in his embrace.

"Take her to her room, Cedric," Lucien said. "I'll have dinner sent up."

Cedric nodded in silent thanks before leading Audrey, still sniffling, up to her bedchamber.

"Horatia?" Lucien was at her side now, weariness carved lines in his face. He'd always seemed confident and self-assured to her before, but his look now was entirely new to her. He appeared vulnerable.

"Yes?"

"Is there anything I can do for you? I know you were

fond of Muff and that this news must be an awful shock to you."

"No...thank you. I would just like to be alone now." Her tone was dismally cool, she didn't have the strength to even feign that she was fine.

Lucien seemed hurt, as if that tone had been meant for him.

"Of course. I will leave you alone. Send for me should you need anything." Lucien left her alone in the dim hallway. The evening dinner bell rang, but sounded so very far away.

Heat surrounded her, a stifling kind that strangled her throat and made it hard to think. She broke out into a sweat and stumbled towards the door that led to the gardens. She needed fresh air. She couldn't breathe inside. She craved numbness. The cold winter air was the only way to achieve it. Without a coat or gloves, she forged a path through snow that was halfway up her calves. Just a few minutes outside and she could process this horrific news. Someone had broken into their home. A place of safety. What if it had been Audrey or her and not poor Muff? Muff...her charming companion. Gone.

She tried not to think but memories shot through her —Audrey's cherry red cheeks, so young and cherubic as she held up the pair of tiny kittens for Christmas. Muff falling asleep in Audrey's lap listening to Cedric sing Christmas carols. The black and white ball of fur struggling to climb the stairs behind Cedric—little paws batting his Hessian boots for attention. She told him all the stories of the constellations and the charmer that he was, Muff would rub his furry whiskered cheek against her chin, purring loudly.

Horatia tripped in the snow, falling on her knees. Pain lanced up towards her heart. Her parents had given them to her and Audrey the Christmas before they'd died.

Muff was more than a cat. He'd been a part of her and one of her last connections to her parents. And now one more part of them had been taken away, violently. Would Audrey or Cedric to be next? Or herself? Which of her loved ones would be a target for one man's hatred?

Horatia lay down in the snow, too tired to care about the cold.

All I want is peace, please, let me have peace. Her dark lashes brushed across her cheeks as she shut her eyes.

But horrible thoughts haunted her. How scared had Muff been when his killer had captured him? Had the aging cat fought or had he been too weak in his grasp? Had his death been quick? She would never know.

A violent shudder shot through her at the thought. Who could be so cruel?

An explosion of panic and fear speared her through the chest. It wasn't just a way to hurt her family. It was a message, as her brother had said. He could get to any of them. She and her siblings weren't safe. No place was safe. He could always find them.

The vision of her parents dead in that coach flashed

across her mind's eye just as the vision of a drowned cat, fur damp and body stiff merged with it. Her father's neck broken, her mother's pale pink lips coated with blood. Their bodies like a pair of broken marionettes abandoned by a child.

She'd touched them, her mother's cheek, her father's hand. But they'd been gone, and she couldn't bring them back.

Was her own life soon to be forfeit? Perhaps it was only a matter of days before hands would reach out of the shadows and snap her neck, leaving her lifeless body for Lucien or Cedric to find.

She struggled to breathe, but her gasping didn't help. There was only suffocating terror and pain.

"Horatia!" A soft cry, distant as the stars themselves.

Something yanked her up. She fought, screamed, bit, but she was so weak and cold that after a minute she had to yield. Noises intruded upon her numbed ears—the crash of wood, the scuffling of boots, the huff of breath. She felt cold softness beneath her. Horatia shifted uncomfortably while forcing her eyes open.

She was in a dark room, one she didn't recognize. The décor did not at all match that of Rochester Hall. A man huddled before the fireplace as he added few logs to the fresh burning kindling, stoking them with a poker. When he turned to face her, she saw it was Lucien.

Without a word, he came over to the bed where he'd set her down, and eased her onto her stomach. He dug his fingers underneath the neck of her gown and began plucking buttons out of their slips. His hands were hot, piercing against her cold flesh and Horatia winced.

"Does it hurt?"

Horatia shook her head as she tried to speak. "You're so warm," she managed at last.

"Good. That is the idea." He reached the last button of her gown and he peeled it away, easing her cold limp arms from her sleeves before he dragged the garment off her completely. Lucien did not stop there. He removed her stays, chemise, stockings, and slippers.

Ordinarily Horatia would have been clutching at a blanket to hide some of her nakedness but her inner pain and weariness had numbed her to such inconsequential concerns. Lying on her stomach, she gazed straight ahead listening to the sounds of Lucien stripping himself of his own clothes behind her.

There was nothing sensual in his movements. In fact, he nearly tripped getting his shoes off. The second he was down to his bare skin, he reached for a thick woolen blanket draped over the foot of the bed and he wrapped it around him like a cloak. Only then did he turn his attention back to Horatia as he scooped her up and carried her to the soft thick rug near the fire.

He sat down and braced her body back against his, securing the blanket around their bodies. Between the fire before her and the fire of his skin behind her, the chill in her bones melted away, followed by sharp prickling as her nerves came alive again. She shifted against Lucien and his hot breath quickened against her cheek.

"Easy, love," he whispered in her ear. "You have no idea how long you were out there, do you?" The tenderness of his voice, the soft endearment so pure on his lips had her quaking with bottled up emotions. "Let it out darling, let it all out. I'm here."

It was this promise, undiluted by the outside world and its concerns that crippled Horatia's protective barrier. She broke down, burrowing into him as though she could forge an unbreakable connection between their bodies and she never wanted to be without him or his comforting touch again. Her dry eyes pooled with hot, heavy tears and Lucien rubbed each drop of moisture away with his fingertips.

"It hurts," Horatia gasped as the weight of everything descended upon her. Like knife shards embedded in her lungs, each breath she sucked in was ragged and icy.

"That's a good thing, my love. It means your heart is still alive. Just let it all out." Lucien brushed his lips along her tear-stained cheek and absorbed her shaking with his body.

The two times in her life when she needed someone most, when she'd been her weakest, he'd been there. She'd often wondered why she loved Lucien and no one else, even when he'd been determined to be cold to her. This moment, this embrace, was everything that mattered. A man who would do this for her was the only man she could ever have, ever want.

As her shaking subsided, Horatia turned about in Lucien's arms. He gazed down at her in tender worry.

"Make love to me," she pleaded.

"No, darling, not like this." He feathered his lips against her temple and stroked her hair back from her face. "You've been through too much. I'll not add to that pain."

"I want you, Lucien. Each second you aren't kissing me is killing me inside." Horatia cupped his face. An auburn tinged night beard had started to graze his cheeks, and the roughness of it was an enticing contrast to the smooth skin of his chest.

Lucien smiled ever so slightly. "I know I'm a wonderful kisser but no one has ever perished from a lack of it as far as I can recall."

Horatia, her body filled with desire and a desperation for some sort of release, pulled free of his arms and stood up, entirely bare before him. She walked around him and approached the bed.

"I don't recognize this room," she said softly as she eased onto the bed.

Lucien followed her movement, his eyes focusing on the peaks of her breasts, the chill in the air tightening her nipples.

"I found you too far away from the house. I brought

you to the gardener's summer cottage," Lucien explained. He got to his feet, blanket still loosely cloaking his body.

"The gardener's cottage?"

There was a hungry look in his eyes as he approached, but still it seemed he meant to resist her.

"Yes, it's always empty in the winter." Lucien's voice was even lower, huskier than before.

"So we are alone, without fear of discovery." Horatia started to reach for the blanket about his body.

"Are you trying to seduce me?" A wicked smile played about his mouth.

"That depends. Is it working?" Horatia ran her foot up against his calf and he tensed.

"Your feet are cold, love. Shall I warm them up for you?"

For an answer, Horatia tugged harder on the blanket. Lucien dropped it at his feet, baring his body before her. It seemed her entire life had been leading up to this moment. Bodies and souls finally bared to each other. She stared up at him, examining his finely formed body, at last able to see all the parts of him that had been hidden.

The inner savage in her was unbearably close to taking over. She held out a hand and Lucien took it, kissing the inside of her palm before she tugged him to the bed's edge. Horatia pushed back as he advanced, their bodies miming an ancient dance of conquest and submission as he crawled over her. Lucien dropped his head to hers, their mouths meeting in a slow kiss that lit fire to every nerve in her body. Horatia's hands slid up to his flexing biceps, clenching his muscles as he released her mouth to trail kisses down her throat.

"I didn't know a collarbone could be so desirable," Lucien murmured as he licked the grooves of her upper chest.

Horatia laughed until his mouth settled on the tip of one breast. He savored her, suckled her, teeth nipping her with sparks of pleasurable pain before he circled her with his tongue, leaving her writhing beneath him.

Horatia moaned as his lips danced to her other breast. She ran her fingers through his thick red hair, tugging as he feasted on her.

"Never let it be said that I neglected you, darling," he teased before taking her other breast into his mouth.

Her nails dug into his arms, Horatia's back arched, yearning for more of him. At the pressure of his hands on her inner knees, her thighs fell apart. A flash of déjà vu, a masked man, the devil of pleasure, an angel of sin between her legs.

"Oh God, if you do that...that thing again, I'll kill you," she gasped as his mouth trespassed down her waist and towards the dark triangle between her legs.

"You mean if I do this?" He assaulted her senses with a devastating lick, then fastened his mouth around that same tight bundle of nerves. Horatia bucked. Lucien pinned her deeper into the bed as he pushed her over the brink of sanity.

"You devil…" She forgot entirely what she meant to say as his tongue traced erotic patterns and she careened over the edge in a fall she thought would never end.

In time she became aware of Lucien moving higher, his mouth back on hers again. She could taste herself on him, the thought sinfully erotic. She groaned as his weight eased down over her. The pressure of his body was a welcome one; he pinned her to the bed when she felt light enough to drift away in the winter breeze. His shaft was hard against her inner thigh and he rocked forward, the tip of him sliding over her with a rhythm her body's instincts knew better than she ever expected.

"Yes, Lucien, yes."

"I don't want to hurt you, not ever again…and this might."

"If I never hurt again, I won't know I'm alive," she reminded him. She was desperate and needed to feel him. Her hands slid down the ridges of his hard abdomen until she wrapped her hand possessively about his length. He groaned against her lips with feral pleasure.

"You play with fire, darling, and I don't wish to burn you." He tried to pull back. Horatia slid a hand down to the base of him and back up to his tip.

"Burn me. Consume me, Lucien. It's the only thing I've ever wanted." Horatia kissed Lucien so deeply that her assault seemed to drive him wild. He snatched her hand away and confined her wrists above her head. Poised at her entrance, he began to work his way inside, gentle and slow, so unlike what she'd come to expect from him.

Horatia lifted her hips, forcing him too deep too soon and he muttered a curse and tried to lift away. She locked her legs around his hips, keeping him close. His hips jerked forward in a shallow thrust. The sudden intrusion of his shaft inside her burned and a piece of her was forever lost in the wake of his penetration. But she was glad. She was changed. She was his.

SHE IGNORED his apologies as passion sparked his movements into life inside her.

Lucien now held her prisoner beneath him, a slow steady pace of thrusts testing her limits. He feathered kisses across her cheeks, nose, lips and chin, as though unable to stop himself from branding his essence on her in every way possible.

The pain dulled in the wake of a tension that was steadily building. The sensation she'd once mistaken for nausea was back, stronger than before. Horatia reveled in it, understanding now what it meant and the throbbing between her legs eased with each of Lucien's thrusts.

Even though her wrists were trapped, she raised her hips, welcoming him deeper into her. Lucien released her wrists to glide his hands down her sides and underneath her, cupping her bottom, lifting it up. The angle changed things dramatically, and his shaft struck some new place deep within her. The cry that left her lips was one of startled surprise and Lucien hastened to repeat the move again and again, her cries a primal encouragement to continue. Sweat dewed on their bodies as Lucien's pace picked up.

"Lucien, I think I..." Horatia was silenced with a dominating and possessive kiss that ended in the most brilliant burst of pleasure in her life. She heard a scream and only later realized it was her own. Lucien shouted her name as he jerked against her. He continued to shake and rock, trembling above her. Horatia would never forget the look in his eyes—so bright with passion, fire, tenderness and confusion.

"My God, Horatia. I've never—didn't know—it could be this way." He seemed afraid, like a young boy faced with fear for the first time. Horatia ran her fingers through his hair and raised her head up to kiss him.

"Don't be afraid, Lucien. I'll hold you."

It was too soon to hope that he'd come to love her, but she knew that he cared. This was no casual affair. This was about making love, about forging a connection. Lucien settled in her arms, their bodies still linked as her hands brushed against him. He buried his face in her dark brown hair. A cool breeze tickled their bodies and Lucien disentangled himself from her.

"Please don't leave," she begged in a ragged whisper.

"Never, my heart. Never." He pulled back the covers of the bed so he could slip inside and join her, cocooning her body with his own. The only sounds were their mingled breathing and the snap and crack of the fire in the hearth.

Everything has changed. But what would Lucien do now? Not wanting to dwell on the possibilities, she burrowed into his arms and settled down to sleep.

$\mathcal{A}$shton sat in his study on Half Moon Street. Letters of a financial nature were strewn over the surface of his oak wood desk. The numbers on the letters blurred as pain lanced up his left arm, which still hung limp and useless in a sling about his neck.

What a bloody nuisance being shot was. He had lost so much of his strength that his footman had to do many routine things for him and his valet, once a minor irritation, had become indispensible. He couldn't put a shirt on, let alone tie his neck cloth or button his trousers without assistance.

It was most humiliating. Everyone treated him like a child in leading strings and he was tired of it. And he'd only been injured a few days. The doctor had given him instructions to rest for the next *five weeks*. The idea was intolerable. He, of all people, could not afford to rest. There was so much to be done aside from his business; namely tracking down Waverly and ending this battle before it could progress to a full-fledged war.

With a heavy sigh, Ashton reached for the nearest letter, the movement sending a stab of pain through his bad shoulder. He pinned the letter down on his desk with his hand in the sling, ignoring the ache it caused and used his other hand to break the seal. He cursed under his breath until the seal gave way.

The letter was from his banker at Drummond's Bank, Mr. Jared Simms. Simms had given Ashton a detailed report of his funds currently tied up in the consols. It was a sound investment. Consolidated annuities were government bonds that paid three percent dividends twice a year.

Ashton had put fifty thousand pounds into them and the return had been a mighty fortune that he spent wisely and cautiously. Unlike his friends, he had not been born into money. His entire life he'd amassed a grand fortune so where his political clout could not win the day, his bank accounts could. Though he did not flaunt his wealth, he did not hesitate to use it when it could gain a clear advantage.

He was currently caught up in a bidding war over a company called Southern Star Shipping. Ashton owned his own shipping company, Lennox Lines, but acquiring Southern Star would put his ships deep into the

Caribbean trade markets and the routes closer to Africa, an area he had yet to penetrate.

This was not his only interest in the line however.

For months he'd heard rumors that Waverly was involved in questionable shipments, bringing lord knows what into England. Ashton suspected slaves might be involved but it could be a number of things. If he could gain control of the line, he could clean up the ships, put new captains and crews on them that he trusted, and begin to eliminate Waverly's illicit sources of income, piece by piece. It was the one thing he knew he could do better than Waverly and if it was his best weapon, he needed to use it. A man couldn't hire killers to take out the League if he didn't possess any money.

He would have possessed Southern Star by now, but a rival shipping company had been matching him bid for bid. The end result was his solicitor, Mr. Danforth, contacting the owner of Melbourne, Shelley and Company to meet with Ashton in less than an hour to discuss the matter and come to an arrangement.

A knock on his study door made Ashton look up. His butler, Wimbley, a balding man of middle years, stepped inside.

"What is it?" he asked, looking back down at the investment report.

"There's a visitor to see you my lord. A lady," Wimbley clarified.

"If it is Her Grace, tell her I shall be with her shortly."

He had no idea what Emily was doing here, except to berate him again for putting himself in danger.

"It is not Her Grace, my lord. She says her name is Lady Melbourne and that you are expecting her."

"Lady Melbourne?" Melbourne's wife had come? He'd asked to see her husband. "Show her into the Rose Parlor and have tea brought in. Tell her I will be with her directly." Still, he supposed he could work this to his advantage.

"Yes, my lord." Wimbley disappeared.

Ashton hastily organized his desk before checking his appearance in a nearby looking glass. His cravat was snug and his trousers unwrinkled. His silk navy blue vest was crisp and his shirt pressed. He looked decent enough for company.

Perhaps his hair was a tad long for the conventional styles favored among society but he'd been too busy of late to have it cut. His eyes, which had been glassy with fatigue and pain of late, were bright again with his irritation at having to deal with this proxie.

Ashton looked every inch the dapper rogue, save for the white cloth sling holding his left arm. Showing weakness in any way was not what he wished in a business setting, but his arm could not be helped.

He left his study and walked up the stairs to Rose Parlor. It was perhaps a bit improper to have a parlor on the same floor as his bedroom, but he only used the Rose Parlor for two things—intimate meals with his mistress, when he had one, and when he did not, it was a place of seduction.

He found that the dark hues of the room seemed to lull the ladies into a receptive mood. Rose-colored gauze curtains laced the windows, casting the room into tempting rosy dimness even in the morning. A fire was always lit in the hearth to keep up the impression of an evening rendezvous. The Rose Parlor had never failed to help him in his conquests.

If he was to deal with his competitor's wife, it seemed logical that a bit of seduction might help his cause. Ashton was no fool. Unlike other men, he learned long ago how powerful a woman could be in a man's world of business and how men underestimated them. However, if he played the charming rake, Lord Melbourne would be but a pawn in Ashton's game and Southern Star shipping would be his.

Ashton opened the door, expecting to find a gray-haired matron. What he found instead halted him in his tracks. A woman, who must have been in her late twenties, perched on the edge of the red velvet settee close to the fireplace. Her raven-black hair and almond-shaped gray eyes were framed by sooty dark lashes. She stared back, seemingly just as confused by him. It was clear that neither of them had expected the other to appear as they had.

"You are Lady Melbourne?" Ashton asked.

"Yes. Lord Lennox I presume?"

Her lips were a pale shade of pink and not as full as most women's, but their shape was somehow quite erotic. Rather than a pretty pout, she had a wide mouth, as though she was more inclined to smile, despite the cool gray of her eyes. Ashton rarely entertained thoughts regarding married women, but in her case he could make an exception.

"I am Lord Lennox."

"Good. We have much to discuss, my lord." There was a soft accent to her speech, a Scottish lilt. Not as heavy as a brogue and far more refined, as though she was trying to hide it. It was a revealing weakness and he acted upon it instinctively.

"What part of Scotland are you from, Lady Melbourne?" Ashton enjoyed watching her eyes widen. It was clear she preferred to hide her origins, something he understood only too well.

"I was born in Falkirk, my lord."

"Falkirk? *An Eaglais Bhreac*," he said with a smug smile.

"You speak Gaelic?" She looked doubly surprised.

"Only a few phrases and some cities and villages. I had an uncle who married a woman from Edinburough."

"Oh?" Lady Melbourne replied curiously. Ashton pressed on with his advantage now that she was off balance.

"What brings you here, Lady Melbourne? Not that I don't find your presence in my home charming, but I had expected to be meeting with Lord Melbourne."

"Lord Melbourne?" Her black brows rose in surprise.

"Yes. I had my solicitor contact the owner of Melbourne, Shelley and Company. Your husband, I presume, or perhaps father? It is he that I need to meet with. I assume he's related to William Lamb?" No longer surprised, her eyes seemed to glint with glee. He'd clearly missed some vital piece of information.

"I'm afraid *I* am the owner of Melbourne, Shelley and Company. My husband, only a distant relation to William Lamb, passed away last year. His company has been under my control for the better part of a year."

Ashton's jaw drop. A woman running a business? It wasn't unheard of...but still...

"You can handle business with the opposite sex, I presume?"

He didn't like that she'd gotten the better of him already. And the way she dressed was driving him to distraction. Her husband was dead less than a year yet she was not wearing the black crepe gown and veil expected of her. Instead, she wore a low-cut ruby dress that seemed to make her pale skin almost luminescent against the firelight. She looked more the seductress than the grieving widow. She knew her looks were an advantage and she wasn't afraid to use them. A dangerous lady. He'd have to remember that.

"And what of Shelley? Is he stationed in London? Perhaps I ought to meet with him instead."

A thin smile of victory teased her mouth. "That would

be a waste of your time, my lord. I bought out Shelley's stock months ago and am now the sole owner of the company my husband founded. We will be changing the name before the next quarter. So it is in fact me you need to see." She punctuated this statement with no small amount of pride.

Ashton glowered. He was not one of those men who believed in discouraging women from the arena of business, but with Lady Melbourne he wished to make an exception. With her in the same room, he could not concentrate, not when his mind and body were conspiring against him like this.

"I've noticed that you are injured, my lord. Please sit. How did you come by such an injury?"

Lady Melbourne had the nerve to offer him a seat in his own bloody parlor? Oh, he'd sit down all right, and pull her body beneath his... Ashton locked the thoughts safely away in a dim corner of his mind, then he sought to regain his natural civility.

"Thank you." He seated himself in a chair opposite the settee. "In answer to your question, I was shot recently." He waited for her to show disgust or some form of feminine aversion to the mention of bloodshed.

She did nothing of the sort. Minor surprise transformed into open curiosity. Must be her damned Scottish blood.

"Were you dueling, my lord?" she asked bluntly.

"Dueling is outlawed. Do not make such quick

assumptions about me, Lady Melbourne. I can guarantee you will be wrong on every account." His tone was so rough he barely recognized himself. It was the tone of his youth, before he'd learned to hone in his temper.

Lady Melbourne had awakened a very dangerous inferno in him. She raised her chin defiantly in a silent challenge to his temper, but the movement only brought her tempting lips closer to his. Ashton forced himself to back away from her as he spoke again.

"My apologies, Lady Melbourne. My arm twinges with pain and it has quite ruined my ability to play the polite host." It was the truth, though only part of it.

"I will accept your apology my lord—if you will satisfy my curiosity as to how you received your wound," she said. Her impertinence both infuriated him and astonished him.

"The business that led to my injury was personal in nature and I will not divulge it just to flatter your curiosity. Now come, let us speak of business, if you will."

She seemed as though she wanted to say something further, then thought better of it. "Very well," she sighed. At that moment a maid entered with a tea tray and Lady Melbourne took the pot from the tray and glanced at Ashton.

"May I pour?" It was usually a maid's job when a man did not have a wife or a lady of the house to perform the task, but the maid in this case took one look at him and scampered from the room without so much as a backward glance.

"Yes, of course," Ashton muttered curtly, once more resuming his seat as she poured two cups of tea.

"When your solicitor contacted my office I was informed that the business matter that concerned you involved the purchase of Southern Star Shipping."

"Indeed." Ashton didn't take his eyes off the woman as he took a sip of tea—and nearly spat it across the table.

The blasted woman had not added any milk, leaving it scalding hot. She seemed to be watching him for some reaction, some exclamation of pain, as he fought to remain calm and pretend that he hadn't just lost all feeling in his tongue due to sabotaged tea. The woman was ruthless.

"What puzzles me is why you crave the Southern Star ships." Ashton took another step in her direction, trying to recover lost ground. "As far as I can tell your business doesn't require them."

"Why does anyone want anything? I crave the power of the ships. And contrary to your no doubt thorough research on my interests, I do in fact need them for access to the Caribbean ports." It was a business answer, but not the truth, and for some reason her answer angered him. He could not negotiate with someone with such solid defenses around her. If only he could tear down those walls somehow.

"I propose a trade. If you tell me how you were shot I will cease bidding on the Southern Star."

This was unexpected. Another ploy to keep him off guard, perhaps? Ashton scrubbed his jaw with one hand, considering the proposal. Normally his affairs were kept private, especially those relating to the League, but he saw no harm in giving her a somewhat censored answer. He didn't trust her, however. Not one whit.

"You would relinquish the line to me that easily?"

She gave a graceful shrug of one shoulder. "There are other lines, of course. I have enough capital that I could build my own if I had to. Buying the Southern Star was simply a more efficient way to reach my goal."

Her answer satisfied him enough.

"I agree to your terms." He took a deep breath. "I was shot while investigating a place of ill repute for evidence that someone of my acquaintance had hired a man to murder my close friend. That same man found us there and opened fire before running off."

"You were shot trying to prove someone wanted to murder your friend?" Lady Melbourne seemed surprised.

"Yes." He would not tell her any more than that however.

Her reaction puzzled him further, as if his words had told her far more than he'd intended, and had told her everything she wished to know about him. "Very well. The Southern Star is yours, Lord Lennox. Enjoy the profits."

"Oh I will, Lady Melbourne," he assured her. If all such business could be conducted this cheaply he'd be twice as wealthy by now.

She gathered her reticule and Ashton followed her down the stairs to the door. He helped her put on her cloak before she turned to leave.

"It was interesting to meet you, Lord Lennox." She smiled that knowing smile again and he bowed over her hand, kissing it longer than was appropriate.

"And you, Lady Melbourne. I believe we may yet cross paths again." Their eyes met briefly and Ashton felt his world tilt on its axis. Lady Melbourne was going to be bad for his business.

When he opened the door for her, Charles stood there, hand raised as though to knock.

"Hello Ash, am I...er...interrupting?" His eyes darted between Ashton and Lady Melbourne.

"No." Both he and the lady replied in unison.

"Right, well, Ash, I need to speak to you straight away." Charles's stony gaze cut to the point. Something new had developed.

"It was...interesting to meet you," Lady Melbourne said and then hastened down the steps. He watched her depart for only a moment before Charles was dragging him by his good arm back inside.

"What is it?" Ashton asked.

Charles glanced about the house, as though searching

for spies in every corner. Ashton's worry deepened like a gnawing pit in his stomach.

"I was going through my correspondence with Lucien's mother. They'd been building up for some time. You know how she writes to me about Lysa."

"Yes." Charles made few attempts to reply back to Lucien's mother since the letters more often than not included offers of marriage to Lucien's sister, which would never have gone over well with anyone for any number of reasons.

"Well, I noticed a strange pattern in her letters. She's been through several footmen in the last few months. Six in all. She writes about accidents, broken legs, being thrown from a horse, a few of them just up and left without any reason. I wouldn't have noticed except that I read all of the letters in one sitting and it struck me."

Ashton frowned. "What struck you?"

"The pattern, Ash. *The pattern.*" He slapped a handful of letters against Ashton's chest. "She said the last footman hasn't had any of the problems the others had and that the curse might finally be lifted."

"And you don't believe it is a series of coincidental accidents," Ashton said, seeing where this was going. "You think he took out the other footman to gain a secure position at the Hall?"

"Exactly." Charles paced the entryway, and his eyes again searched around them. "The question is why Lucien's house if Cedric is the target. Perhaps it was Lucien who was the target all along? The carriage did attempt to run him over after all. Either way, we need to warn them."

"You're absolutely right," Ashton agreed. "But we must be careful. After our message to them about the cat, if we show up without cause, the man might act rashly. We should send Lucien a letter but address it to his mother. If the man is under Hugo's control he'd likely be instructed to open any mail addressed to Lucien or Cedric. Best to do this carefully."

"Good plan," Charles said.

Ashton winced as his arm panged. "I'll have you write the letter, if you don't mind."

He led Charles to his study and prayed their letter didn't come too late.

CHAPTER 26

*C*edric stretched stiffly in his chair by Audrey's bedside and rubbed the tight muscles in his neck with a weary hand. His sister was curled up in her bed fast asleep. Her delicate features and troubled expression made her appear like a fairy queen whose woes had followed her deep into the sacred realm of dreams.

Holding her had brought back horrific memories of years long past. He couldn't protect her from this, couldn't save her from all the hurts in the world. In many ways, he'd been both father and mother to her and Horatia after losing their parents, and perhaps the greatest cost had been that there was no one to hold him as he silently grieved.

The memories of last evening struck him all over again and Cedric shut his eyes. He'd been fond of Muff.

The cat had been one of the last connections he and his sisters had of their parents before the accident.

The accident. How many years would pass before the sting of his parents' deaths would subside? A man could only endure so much before it finally broke him.

Audrey shifted restlessly and awoke to find Cedric staring straight through her, his mind still far away.

"Cedric?" Her voice was a little hoarse. She'd cried herself to sleep last night after he'd made her eat dinner and collapsed with exhaustion. A weak smile revealed she was doing her best to come to terms with events. She'd taken the death hard but had already begun to move on. *Good girl*, he thought silently.

"What is it, sweetheart?" He sat up straighter in his chair. Audrey smiled at him, but it was sad and wistful.

"I'm sorry that I've been so much trouble for you lately." She pushed back her covers and sat up to face him.

"You're a woman, Audrey. Troublemaking is the forté of your gender, like convincing Charles to go along with your scheme and thinking it wouldn't anger me. I don't mind, except when I end up strangling my best friend over it. We ought to talk about that, you know." Cedric found himself smiling despite himself.

"I suppose we ought to," Audrey agreed.

"Why didn't you come to me? You could have told me that you wished to marry. I had no idea you were in such a state of desperation."

"It is different for women, Cedric. I think that because

Mama is not here that it is harder for you to understand. I want to marry. I want a husband and a life beyond Curzon Street. I dread a future like Horatia's."

Cedric slid to the edge of his chair. "And what future is that?"

"She's almost one and twenty and yet she will never marry because she's—" Audrey clapped a hand over her mouth.

The suddenness of her move worried Cedric. "Because she's what?"

"Oh I mustn't say. She wouldn't want me to betray her confidence."

Cedric was on his feet and looming over her. "You'd better tell me everything or I won't be very generous over the next few months for your shopping allowances."

Audrey scoffed. "Betray my sister for new gowns? Don't be silly."

"What if I doubled your allowance next month if you did?"

"Bribery? Never!"

"And what if I send you away to a place where there are no men of marriageable age?"

Audrey's eyes narrowed to slits, glowering up at him. "You play a cruel game, Cedric. I will tell you, but if Horatia finds out you learned it from me, I will find the next man on the street, be he a lamplighter or chimney sweep, and I shall run off to Scotland with him."

Cedric smiled. "You'd never marry a chimney sweep.

The soot would ruin your fine gowns. Now, about Horatia? You know I only want to make her happy. Tell me and I will see that it is kept between us." His used his best cajoling brotherly voice, yet his sister seemed unmoved.

"Cedric, I shouldn't tell you. You'll get angry, and nothing can come of it regardless. Just forget I said anything." She pursed her lips as though resigned never to speak again.

"Do I ever get angry at you or Horatia? I know I threatened your suitors, but have I ever shown a temper with you or your sister?"

She cocked a brow, as though internally debating the matter. Finally with a heavy sigh, she relented.

"I suppose no more than any other brother might. But if I tell you, you mustn't overreact. She won't ever marry because she's still in love with Lucien. She's never loved or wanted anyone else."

Cedric's throat went uncomfortably dry. "Lucien?"

He'd known that long ago Horatia had developed a child's affection for Lucien, but he thought that had ended long ago. Now it all made sense. Horatia being upset every time Lucien was even mentioned, her odd behavior on the rare occasions when they'd been forced to be in the same room.

"You are sure she still loves him?"

"Yes and I believe that Lucien may be starting to return her feelings."

This was worse than he could have imagined. Lucien

was like a brother, but if he was entertaining thoughts of an amorous nature towards Horatia... The League's rule existed for a reason. The last thing he or the others wanted was to fight over someone's sister, or pick up the pieces should the courtship sour. He could entertain thoughts of letting Audrey marry Jonathan because that man was young and didn't carry the weight of the sins the rest of the League did. But Horatia marrying Lucien was out of the question.

That man had a taste for wicked pleasures and Cedric would die before he let Horatia play a role in those dark fantasies. He could have any woman in the world, but not Horatia. Horatia deserved a gentleman who would care for and love her for the reserved and deeply loyal woman she was. She did not need to be burned in the wake of Lucien's fleeting passions.

Cedric shuddered as he recalled his discussion with Lucien in the billiard room the day before. Lucien had spoken of his changed feelings towards Horatia and foolishly Cedric had assumed his friend viewed her merely as a sister once again.

"What proof do you have of his feelings towards her?" Cedric asked.

"I'm not supposed to say..."

"Audrey," Cedric growled.

"Lucien bought her a gown for Christmas. It arrived yesterday from London."

"What sort of gown?"

"A lovely evening one to replace the one that was ruined. I helped him order it, since I have the best fashion sense in London."

"Naturally." Cedric's sarcasm was lost on his sister.

"But you mustn't be angry, Cedric. Nothing will come of it but...wouldn't it be wonderful if Lucien and Horatia were married?" Audrey smiled and clasped her hands.

The mere thought of Lucien in bed with his sister made a veil of red descend over Cedric's vision.

"Wonderful? Dash it all, Audrey! You're too bloody innocent. Lucien's not the kind to marry. None of us are, but *especially* not him." She didn't understand. Lucien would toss Horatia aside when the fires of passion burned down to embers. He'd seen it many times before, though always with women who found such terms agreeable. Horatia was no such woman.

"Is that any way to speak of your friend?" Audrey's eyes widened as though startled by his dark prediction.

"He's a friend, but he's also a devil. As am I. I know him only too well, and I know he won't marry her."

"You're wrong. Godric married Emily and he is much the same as the rest of you."

"Emily was different... She was a perfect match for Godric."

"And who's to say that Horatia is not Lucien's perfect match?" Audrey asked.

"If she is I dread to think what that says about our sister," Cedric muttered.

"You think that would mean she's a wicked, wanton woman, like Evangeline Mirabeau?" Audrey giggled at Cedric's horrified expression.

"Something like that. Certainly others would think that of her."

"Oh nonsense, Cedric. No one would think that of Horatia. She's far too sensible to do anything rash or romantic. She's Horatia," Audrey said as if that explained it all, as though there was no reason to worry.

"If Lucien is determined to have her, he won't let her be sensible. That's the entire point behind seduction. Men use passion to rob gentle bred ladies of their good sense. Just like Charles could have when he pretended to compromise you. He could have taken advantage of you, kitten."

"Firstly, brother dearest, *I* kissed *him*." The words caught Cedric unprepared. "And I had to do a great deal of chasing to achieve even that. Secondly, he knew you'd be angry. I had to beg him to help me no matter the cost. And thirdly, I was not nearly so swayed from rationality by kissing him as I was by kissing Jonathan."

Cedric froze in his pacing. "Jonathan? You mean to tell me that you've kissed him already? Is there anyone in Mayfair you haven't kissed?" he growled. His sisters were running amok like Whitechapel harlots. How long had they been doing this to him? Didn't they know it was his job to protect them, even if it meant protecting them from themselves?

Cedric collapsed back into his chair. "God in heaven. I think I may die from the shock of your exploits long before I reach old age."

Audrey watched him, warily. "Are you very angry with me?" Her voice wavered and Cedric winced.

"I'm not angry. But I am upset to learn you've become so determined on the matter. I want the truth now. Are you certain it is Jonathan you want to marry?"

Audrey gave a quick excited nod.

"Do you even know him? Audrey, you've only met him this September. I won't have you marrying a man for shallow reasons."

"How can I ever know a man when you threaten them all with pistols at dawn?"

Cedric huffed. "You exaggerate."

"Do I?" She raised one delicate brow.

He squirmed a little at her accusation. "Yes, it was only one time. The others fled before I could get that far in my shouting."

"And you feel this is helping your argument?"

"I like Jonathan, kitten, I do. The man cuts a fine figure, but that's no reason for marriage. You ought to marry for love." Cedric couldn't believe what he was saying. Somewhere along the way he'd managed to become his father. The words sounded like his.

The late Viscount Sheridan had been a noble man and he'd conducted himself with the highest levels of propriety and decorum. But buried beneath that he'd had a heart of gold that made him wise. It seemed some of his father's wisdom had developed in him, even if it was a little late.

"You're right, of course. But I know the way I feel around him, Cedric. I feel as though my life before him was merely an intake of breath before the true living begins."

"Oh God, you've been reading those dreadful gothic novels again."

"I have not!"

But the look in her eyes was so puzzling to him. It was as though she saw something he could not, a place that filled her with wonder and dreams. "I want to know him," she said. "I want to learn everything about him. But I cannot do that if you do not give me the chance. Will you consider him if I can convince him to court me?"

"If he needs convincing to pursue you, then he does not deserve you. But I will speak to him, and mention your interest. If he agrees, we shall arrange for you to see more of each other. Perhaps you might land a husband after all." He wouldn't have trusted any of his other friends with his sister. But Jonathan was new to their circle and didn't seem to be remotely as cavalier with his affections as his brother Godric had been at his age. There was something serious in the young man that Cedric found calming, far from the wilder valet he'd once been. It was as though Jonathan's new position in life had matured him rather than giving him airs.

"Oh thank you, Cedric!" Audrey slipped out from her covers and ran to him, wrapping her arms about his neck and hugging him.

"I will warn you that not all people in this world have the sweet and loving heart you do. If you believe you can withstand the gossip, then you may proceed."

She grinned impishly. "I think I can handle society and its gossip."

As always, he was completely at a loss as to how to say no to her. The troublesome little sprite was his world, just as Horatia was.

"You're welcome, my dear. Just promise me no more rash behavior. I need to handle this matter with Horatia and I can only survive one sisterly catastrophe at a time."

Audrey stifled a giggle as she released him. "I promise to behave."

"Why don't I believe you?" Cedric said with a theatrical sigh. "Why don't you get dressed and I shall return to take you down to breakfast." Cedric took his leave to give Audrey ample time to change while he went to his own chamber to freshen up. After that he had to find Horatia and see just how deeply her affections ran for Lucien, and whether the trouble was as bad as he feared.

Cedric had only just finished washing his face when he heard footsteps in the hall outside his bedchamber. He pulled on his boots hastily and went to open his door. Horatia was heading towards her room. She looked tired and rumpled and she wore the same gown as she had on last night. Worry ate away at him as he strode down the hall, catching her as she opened her bedroom door.

"May I come in, Horatia?" he asked softly. She nodded and let him follow her inside. "You did not sleep here?"

"No. After hearing about Muff, I rather lost my mind. It brought too many memories. I went out into the gardens and lost myself. I fell twice I think, and if Lucien hadn't found me I might have frozen to death. He rescued me, took me to the gardener's cottage and warmed me up by the fire then watched over me while I slept."

"My God," Cedric managed to say, torn between what she'd been through and the fact that Lucien had been with her all night.

"I had hoped I'd feel better or safer today..." She did not have to finish her sentence for him to know she did not.

Her tone was laced with pain of the heart. Cedric had spent last night holding one crying sister and he did not want to repeat the experience. But he was a brother first and a selfish rogue second.

"Come here." He opened his arms and Horatia buried her face in his chest. She did not weep, the tears seemed to have drained from her long before. He rubbed one hand gently over her upper back in a soothing motion while stroking her hair.

"You don't always have to be so strong. Grief only rewards those who accept it, not those who fight it."

Lucien had taught him this long ago, when Cedric had been convinced his life would end.

"You're right. But then who will be strong for you?" She gave a hiccupy laugh and pulled back to look up at him. "You are such a good brother, Cedric." She gently extricated herself from his embrace and he let her go.

Horatia approached her vanity and laughed at her mussed, wild, appearance. "Heavens, I look dreadful."

"Horatia, I'm afraid we must talk about something."

"Oh dear. I never like it when you use that tone. It makes me nervous." She tried to tease but her heart was not in it.

"You said Lucien found you and he stayed with you and watched over you last night."

"Yes," she answered cautiously.

"With another man, I might demand marriage if I felt he might have taken advantage of you."

"But not Lucien?" she asked, reading his tone correctly.

"No. That's why I am here. I know you still harbor some strong feelings for him and it has made me wonder whether Lucien has used them against you."

"Cedric, what exactly are you asking me?" Horatia demanded in frustrated exhaustion.

"Has he used you ill? You must tell me at once. I cannot allow him to do so."

"No. He has not." Horatia was slow to answer, but Cedric could not tell if she was deceiving him or not.

"I would not be angry with you if he had. Your feelings for him put you at a disadvantage. They make you vulnerable and he is cruel enough to—"

"Lucien is not cruel," Horatia protested. "He is your friend!"

"And I know him far better than you. Must I remind you of his treatment of you for the last seven years? He's done nothing but spurn you at every turn. Why you feel anything for him is beyond me."

"Cedric, if he changed—if he returned my feelings, if he cared about me, would you allow us to marry?" Horatia was never tentative, never hesitant about anything, yet now her very being seemed fragile and delicate.

"It would not matter what his feelings or affections were. I could never allow it," Cedric said bluntly.

"But why? Would it not be more to your liking to have a close friend as a brother-in-law?" Again she spoke with that damned hesitancy.

"Pick any man in all of England, but not *him*. I won't allow any sister of mine to be subjected to his desires. You know nothing about his amorous past, the countless mistresses, the nights at brothels. Not as I do. Even if I could overlook all of that, I could not forget how he treated you all these years, nor stop fearing that he might do it again later on. I am the head of our family. If I say you cannot marry Lucien, then you will accept my judgment and move on. Find a man more worthy of you."

"Why are you so quick to condemn him? Lucien has only ever supported you." Her words stung and Cedric wished he could silence her. "Need I remind you he was the one who brought me home that day when Mama and Papa died? He was the one who saved me, Cedric, and consoled you! To me that means something and if you are blind enough not to see his worth then please leave my room at once. We have nothing further to say to one another." Horatia marched over to her bedroom door and waited for him to leave.

He stopped halfway in the hall, studying her. Did she think that she could go against his commands? Surely she wouldn't be so brazen. He had to make it clear, she couldn't be with Lucien. That was final.

"You don't know him like I do, Horatia. He does things to his women that...well, I don't want to happen to you."

Her sudden blush had his anger rise like a tidal wave.

"What does it matter to you? What if I like the way I feel when I'm with him?"

Cedric pointed a finger at her. "You know nothing of his true self. As a friend, I can tolerate his behavior, even understand it, and I know there are those who would be more agreeable to his tastes. But you as a wife would not know happiness with him."

Horatia's eyes darkened with anger. "Not know happiness? Cedric, I *love* him. With every breath in my body, I belong to him and he to me. You cannot change that. It is done."

Did that mean what he thought? Had Horatia and Lucien…?

"My God," he breathed, stepping back. "You've been with him, haven't you?"

She didn't blink. Didn't say a word. She just gave one small but firm nod and his heart sank. If only she knew what Lucien was like, how he enjoyed tying up his women to the bed and dominating them and more. Horatia wasn't the sort of woman to want that in her life. But she was besotted. How could he break the spell?

"I meant what I said, Horatia. You will not marry him and if you think to let him drag you off to Gretna Green you will no longer be welcome in my house or my estates. You will be a stranger to me. Is that understood?"

It was a bluff, he could never disown her…but he couldn't have her thinking he would allow her to marry such a man.

"You have such a cold heart. No, I take that back. You have no heart at all," Horatia whispered sadly, her dark brown eyes misting with tears as she shut the door.

"Pardon me, my lord, do you require anything?" a footman asked as he walked out of a chamber close by, carrying fresh linens.

"Actually, yes." He paused studying the footman. "Have you seen Miss Sheridan going off alone with Lord Rochester at any point since we arrived?"

The footman hesitated, licked his lips nervously. "I'm sorry, sir, but it wouldn't be appropriate to speak of such matters. I hope you understand."

"I do. Thank you." The footman had as much as told him that Horatia and Lucien were meeting in secret.

There was nothing he could say to make his sister understand why she couldn't be with Lucien. She was ensnared in his trap, and few options remained to him. Everything Cedric had done was to protect her, even if it was from his own friends. It was only then, when he saw a passing footman carrying holly boughs, that he remembered today was Christmas Eve.

CHAPTER 27

$\mathcal{T}$he dining room was uncomfortably quiet that morning. Horatia ate only because she did not know what else to do. And even this she prolonged by prodding her food from one side of her plate to the other. Lady Rochester tried to engage her in conversation but Horatia's heart was too bruised to answer Lady Rochester's polite inquiries with much enthusiasm.

Horatia's gaze was torn between her brother at the far end of the table and Lucien who sat two seats away. It should have been a wonderful, joyous morning. She was a woman now, had crossed that threshold from innocent maiden to sensual goddess in Lucien's arms last night, yet she felt robbed of her happiness. Cedric's decree that she must choose left an unsettling pit in her stomach.

She raised her eyes from her plate to find Lucien watching her every move. All of the pain of her brother's words seem to fade. She made her decision. She would give Lucien time, let him decide how he felt. If in the end he wanted her then she would be with him. She loved Cedric and Audrey but someday Audrey would marry. Perhaps even Cedric would marry. If she chose them, she'd end up alone. And denying Lucien was like denying her body from breathing.

Lady Rochester at last broke that uncomfortable silence. "As you all know, tonight is Christmas Eve. In order to lighten our spirits, I believe we ought to exchange gifts this evening after dinner. Is that agreeable?" There were murmurs of assent and refreshed smiles. Horatia caught Lucien's eye and he offered her a secretive smile that warmed her blood. Footmen came to collect the plates and everyone rose to go about their day.

Horatia lingered in the hallway watching the flurry of activity with amusement until a footman approached her.

"Pardon me, Miss Sheridan. His lordship bade me to deliver this note to you and to show you a secret way to reach him when you are ready." He slid a slip of paper into her hand discreetly.

"Thank you, Gordon." She took shelter in a nearby alcove to read the note in peace.

Come to our cottage, my little stargazer.

Horatia's body began to hum with the promise of that single line.

Gordon cleared his throat. "If need be, I've been

instructed to show you a passageway that would get you outside without the rest of the house being aware of it."

"Yes, I would appreciate that." She retrieved her cloak and made her way to the passageway that led to the gardens. She glanced over her shoulder to make sure she was not being followed, then quickly made her way to the distant gardener's cottage. The chimney of the cottage already puffed with fresh smoke, an inviting place of refuge. She found the door unlocked and the sight inside made her pulse race. Crimson petals littered the entry way and down the hall to the bedroom. The scent of orchids and other flowers filled her senses.

"Lucien?" she called out nervously.

"In the bedroom, love. Come to me." His sensual voice spurred her onward. She found him waiting in a chair by the fire as she entered the room. The flowers she'd smelled coming inside covered every surface. Horatia felt guilty even stepping on the petals that surrounded her lover and the bed like a crimson moat.

"How did you manage all of this?" she asked in admiration. "How did you find the time?"

"After I escorted you back to the hall, I roped a few footmen into helping me raid my mother's hothouse for the best flowers and had them brought here. You deserve for it to be warm and sunny and full of flowers, but I'm afraid this is the best I can manage in the middle of an English winter." Lucien stood, but she sensed the nervousness in him, as though he feared she would not appreciate his efforts.

"Oh Lucien, it is so beautiful!" She gave a bright and honest smile as she dropped her cloak on the floor, causing petals to ripple outward. She tiptoed her way across to him, gently put a hand on his chest and shoved him back down into his chair. His breath quickened when she slid onto his lap and wrapped her arms about his neck. Lucien waited as she leaned into him, rewarding him with a kiss. He growled in soft pleasure as her lips met his, but he ended the kiss too quickly.

"I have a present for you." He gestured towards the bed. It was only then that Horatia spied the large box sitting in the center of it.

"But we are to open our presents tonight," she reminded him in what she hoped was an admonishing tone. He merely dropped his head and nibbled her throat until she was ready to agree to anything he might ask.

"This gift is one I cannot give to you in front of others. Go ahead, my love. Open it now."

He gently set her on her feet and propelled her towards the bed. Horatia lifted the top off the cream box and peeled back the thin paper to reveal the most beautiful gown she'd ever seen. It was then that she remembered what he'd told her before—that he'd bought her a gown to replace the one that had been ruined.

The idea of the gown, which she'd once believed Lucien had bought to strike back at Waverly's attack, had a vastly different meaning now. She pulled out the gown and held it up to see it in its full glory. A melody of red and green silk with Belgian lace and delicate embroidery unfolded before her. A sprig of faux mistletoe decorated the décolletage in an almost scandalous manner. Lucien certainly had a hand in creating this, that was certain.

"Well?" Lucien asked, standing behind her. Heat emanated off him in intoxicating waves. Horatia briefly shut her eyes, savoring this private moment of paradise.

"It is too expensive. You ought not to have spent so much on me." Despite her chastising she clutched the gown to her chest and turned to face him, making it clear she would not willingly give back the gift.

Lucien's lips slid into a crooked smile. "If you believe it too valuable...I can always allow you to repay me in favors."

"Hmm...and what would these favors be, exactly?" Horatia wanted to sound like a cool and confident woman bargaining her charms, but she was unable to hide her desire.

"For one gown, I will charge you this morning and afternoon between the sheets. I demand tangled limbs, moans of pleasure and wild abandon." He plucked the dress from her hands, folded it and nestled it back into the box with a tenderness that had Horatia's body weak-kneed with pleasure, then set it on the floor out of the way.

"You wish to be paid now?" Horatia half-giggled until

she saw the predatory look on his face. The savage lust in his eyes knocked the air from her lungs.

"Surrender to me now, Horatia. Let me have you a thousand ways, a thousand times." It was as close to pleading as Lucien had ever come and it aroused her in a way she had not expected.

She craved the power to make him plead, not from pain, but from desire and the need to control this passion, allowing it to slip only when she chose to. It was how he'd made her feel that night at the Midnight Garden and she wanted to experience it herself, before giving in to him again. When he looked at her like that it was like she was the last woman he would ever kiss, the only woman who would ever light the fire in his eyes and perhaps one day his heart…

"If you want me, it is you who will surrender to me, I think. I will have control." Suddenly she was holding out a hand and demanding the red silk she knew he kept on him. In a wordless look of surprise he turned the ribbons over to her. She pointed to his shirt and vest.

"Remove them," she commanded.

Lucien did so, but Horatia raised a hand. "Not too quickly now." Lucien's expression was dark and unreadable as she slowed down his movements. "Your boots next." Again he obeyed without a word, careful to take his time. Once he was clad only in his trousers, which hugged his muscled thighs like lovers, Horatia pointed to the bed.

"Lie on your back. Spread your arms."

He did as she commanded, and Horatia bit her lip as she watched the muscles of his back ripple like the sleek coat of a panther. He laid back and waited for her to come to him. With surprisingly steady hands she took one of his wrists and secured it to one bedpost. She brushed a few fingertips along his bicep, and his muscles twitched beneath her as she moved around to secure his other wrist. She left his legs free so he might have some mobility but no chance of flipping them over to be on top. He tested the bonds experimentally, his eyes still inscrutable.

When Horatia was satisfied that he could not get free, she positioned herself at the end of the bed and began to undress herself. Thankfully the gown she wore buttoned down the front. Lucien's tongue slipped out to wet his lips and Horatia imagined that tongue licking her but only if she allowed herself to be within reach. She had never felt so powerful, so aware of her hold over a man before.

With Lucien this felt right; she could do no wrong with him and he would never judge her again for sins not of her making. It was a freeing thought, to know that he was here with her and they were unburdened by the darkness of their past.

Once the gown was unbuttoned, she peeled it off her shoulders and slid it down off her hips in a teasingly slow move that had Lucien testing the strength of his bonds and bucking against the mattress. She dropped the gown to the floor and started to remove her stays and petticoats. Lucien's face flushed as she stood there, wearing nothing more than her chemise. Her breasts felt heavy and the nipples budded against the sheer fabric. Horatia caressed herself, enjoying the feel of her own hands along her body as much as the way it tortured Lucien.

She'd learned much about lovemaking in the few hours he'd had to teach her. They'd talked late into the night about the things a man and woman could do together. Horatia was intent on exploring some of those things now.

"Let me touch you, love," he begged. "Let me cup those perfect breasts."

"Silence, my lord."

She walked to the edge of the bed and climbed up between his spread legs. Horatia crawled over his body until she reached his mouth and she kissed him, thrusting her tongue deep, but withdrawing before he could catch it with his lips. Then she moved to his left ear, sucking on his lobe. Lucien groaned and writhed beneath her. She could feel the tension in his body, the need to capture her with his arms, but he was unable to do so. Lucien, the Marquess of Rochester, was at her mercy and it was good, so good.

"Be still, my lord, or you will be punished." She bit his neck playfully.

"Oh God!" he hissed. His erection strained between

"I've only ever wanted your heart," she replied. Lucien smiled tenderly and feathered kisses along her jaw. But now she was shy and unsure. "All these years, when you've been with other women? Could you ever be satisfied with just me? How can I be enough?" She was terrified of how he might answer.

"I can't rid myself of my past, love, but know this—you've never been far from my heart or mind. Even when I was determined to be cold to you, you made it hard to do. It is impossible to be without you now. When I'm with you I cannot be sated, when you leave me I want you back at my side. I miss the scent of your skin, the silky texture of your hair against my lips, the blinding smile you hide from the world so often with your shyness. I crave your stories of the stars and your loyalty to those you love. I'm not sure the poets agree what love is, but I think I may have, somehow along the way, fallen in love with you. And I fear I've fallen hard. Can I trust you with my heart, Horatia?" Lucien's voice was shaky and had nothing to do with their recent explosion of passion.

"Oh Lucien..." She kissed him deeply. "Consider your heart safe in my hands." He slanted his mouth over hers, tongue delving between her lips. When Horatia was finally able to breathe again she remembered that not all was well.

"Cedric knows that we are involved. He gave me an ultimatum. It was to choose between you or my family. I cannot have both. He will never welcome me home again if I choose you." She tried to explain as calmly as possible but her throat constricted with sadness. What sense did it make for her brother to deny her this? She knew life was not fair, far better than most, but shouldn't her brother try and even the unfairness out with goodness in her life? Or at the least he should not deny her the right to make herself happy.

Lucien frowned. "I will speak to him. It isn't fair for you to choose. Neither of us should have to choose between our love for each other and him." Lucien pulled back the covers for them to slide underneath so that they could be warmer. Once she was tucked against his side, warm and drowsy in his embrace, he buried his lips in her hair, breathing in her scent.

"If we have to choose," said Horatia, "I choose you, Lucien. I will always choose you." She nuzzled his neck before sleep claimed her. She did not hear Lucien's quiet reply.

"And I you, my little stargazer. But I will do everything within my power to see you won't have to."

CHAPTER 28

*H*alf an hour before Christmas Eve dinner, Lucien paced nervously inside the vast Russell library, waiting for Cedric to arrive. Gone were the last remnants of his misplaced coldness towards Horatia. All that was left was a deep seed of love. He'd spent years salting his soul trying to prevent that seed from taking root. But Horatia had become his sun, his water, and fed that deep seed. Petals were unfurling, roots coiling deep in his heart. He was going to have a long talk with his friend and Cedric would see the light and let Horatia be with him and that was that. There was no going back; he'd crossed the final bridge and burned it to ashes.

The library door opened and Cedric entered, looking as cold as the empty suit of armor that guarded it.

"I received your summons." His friend seemed to choose his words carefully.

Lucien tried to smile, but his nerves were on edge. "I did not mean to 'summon' you. I wished to discuss something of importance." His stomach felt as though someone had unleashed a bevy of butterflies. It was almost laughable to be so frightened, like a child standing up to their teacher.

Cedric shut the library door and approached Lucien with measured steps, hands clasped behind his back. "Here I am. What do you wish to talk about?"

Cedric's body language did not bode well, not at all.

"Over the past couple of months I've undergone a change of heart. A deep one. A very deep one." It was not the most flattering or elegant phrasing, but he had to begin this dreaded conversation somehow.

"I hadn't noticed." Cedric's voice held a fair amount of suspicion.

"It was not something I wanted anyone to see, Cedric. Look, what I am trying to tell you…" The words were there, but Cedric's hard eyes stilled them on Lucien's tongue, daring him to ask for something he had no right to ask for. Lucien drew a shaky breath before continuing.

"I seek your permission to marry Horatia." How unlike him, but he had to maintain his control for this brief moment and formality was the simplest way to go.

"So it's true then? You have your eyes set on my sister?"

Lucien knew Cedric in the way only true friends could and recognized that familiar edge of danger in Cedric's tone.

"I love her, Cedric..."

"Stop! You *do not* love her. You may love her body and the pleasure it gives but she will not be one more lady in the line of women you leave behind brokenhearted. Not my Horatia." Cedric's fists clenched at his side. Even twenty feet apart Lucien did not feel safe.

"Easy, Cedric. I am not that man anymore. Let me explain—"

"I will not listen to your lies, Lucien." Cedric stormed over and shoved a finger deep into Lucien's chest. "Save it for the next chit you fancy! You are breaking the rules our League was built on. I demand that you stay away from Horatia. That you won't even *look* at her."

"No." Lucien was weary of controlling himself. Cedric would listen to him, even if he had to bind him to a chair.

Cedric's eyes narrowed. "What?"

"I said no. We agreed to the second rule because we did not trust each other with the fairer sex, and rightfully so. But time changes us all. I love Horatia and I wish to wed her. I want a passel of children and her love in my life for the rest of my days. I have asked her to marry me and she has agreed. I came to you for the sake of our friendship and because you are her family. I do not *need* your permission to have her, because I already do." It was the worst possible thing to say and Lucien realized it too late.

Cedric's fist drove into Lucien's stomach, staggering him back. Cedric followed and landed another solid blow to Lucien's chest, so hard that he fell back and struck a bookshelf.

"How *dare* you lay claim to her! She is not yours to take!" Cedric swung another fist and Lucien was struck yet again as he was cornered against the shelf.

"And she is not yours to lock away! Horatia always has and always will be her own person. She gifted me with her heart and though I do not even begin to deserve her, she wants me and no one else. So I will have her as my wife and do my best to be worthy. You may not support her decision, but by God you will not punish her for loving me." Lucien's body shook with rage as Cedric pulled him back and threw another fist into him. Cedric stumbled into one of the library's suits of armor, knocking it over with a clang and clatter.

"You've already had her, you blackguard?"

Lucien said nothing.

"She's warmed your bed. She could be with your child even now!" The accusation stung Lucien more from the truth than anything else. Cedric knew him too well.

"Yes," Lucien said. "And if there is a babe growing in her now, the thought fills me with a love I cannot begin to understand."

"You say that now. You may even believe it. But it

does not matter. I know how you are, how cold you've been not just to her, but to other women. I don't care if my sister is your only chance at salvation, you will not have her. Not while I still draw breath."

The threat hit Lucien like a bolt of lightning. His senses frazzled as once more Cedric assaulted him with pummeling fists, again beating him back against the bookshelf. Lucien did not fight back. It would do no good.

"What do you mean by that?" Lucien asked.

Cedric puffed up his chest, as though addressing a condemned man. "I demand satisfaction, as is my right. Tomorrow at dawn. Choose a second and your preferred weapon."

"I will not duel with you, Cedric." Lucien could not believe it could come to this. The League often joked about Cedric being capable of such things, but none believed it.

"You will, or I will summon the rest of the League here and we will determine how to put you straight for breaking the second rule."

Lucien knew Cedric would be relentless on the matter, even if the others objected. The thought made his blood run cold. "Very well. I will be in the northern field at dawn with my second. I will bring my weapon of choice."

"Good." Cedric's eyes were filled with both anger and regret, but he said nothing more and turned to leave.

Lucien wanted to unsay the words that had brought them to this point, but Cedric was gone, and Lucien was alone in the library. Pain surged through him, reminders of all of the blows his friend had laid on him.

He stood next to the bookshelf for what felt like an eternity, catching his breath until he realized he was not alone. His sister, Lysandra, came out from behind the shelf he leaned against.

"How long have you been there?" He tried to sound harsh, but his words came out toneless.

Lysandra brushed a fingertip across her eyes, wiping tears from their corners. "Oh Lucien!"

She ran to him and he crumpled weakly in her arms. Falling to his knees on the wood floor, Lysandra was dragged down with him, still cradling him as he gasped for breath. What madness was this? To love Horatia and in the process lose Cedric? It wasn't fair and he shouldn't have to choose.

"There, there," Lysandra said, stroking his hair in the way he'd done countless times for her. After a few minutes, he was able to control himself once more.

"You mustn't tell a soul, Lysa. No one must know what has happened here. Do you understand?"

"I do. Mother will never forgive you for fighting a duel on Christmas."

"I may not be around to suffer her ill humor." Lucien had no fear of death, even at his friend's hand, but the thought of all those years wasted without Horatia clenched his heart like nothing else.

"Dueling is illegal. You don't have to go through with it."

"It's a matter of honor. Of love."

"What good are those words on a tombstone?"

"Cedric won't let up just because I say no. He'll brand me a coward on top of everything else. Horatia cannot marry a coward. And though marrying a coward is not illegal, it should be."

"You're being ridiculous, and you cannot deflect a bullet with your wit."

Lucien gave pause at Lysandra's words. "Yes... Duels are ridiculous, aren't they? No matter. We do what we must, even when it is ridiculous." He looked over the mess the one sided battle had left in its wake. An idea began to form, and most certainly a ridiculous one.

"So you are going to shoot him?" Lysandra asked.

"I love him like a brother. So far I've never shot any of my real brothers, and I won't start with Cedric. He may be too foolish to understand the truth, but come what may, I will not fire my pistol at him."

HORATIA WAS the most beautiful woman in the room that night after dinner. Lucien noticed this with a deep pang in his heart, regret and longing for a future he might never have now, left him quiet. All had enjoyed a wonderful feast marred only by Cedric and Lucien's silence towards one another. Now, family and friends were in the Russell ballroom dancing to a hired string quartet that performed Christmas music. The entire evening took on a greater importance to Lucien than ever before.

He danced with all of the ladies once, but kept returning to Horatia, as though keeping her in his arms would ensure that the night wouldn't end and dawn wouldn't have a chance to come. Cedric, for his part, kept his distance, allowing him this night like a final wish before the gallows.

Lucien's hand rested on the small of her back. He could feel the warmth of her body beneath his palm. Her gloved hand rested on his broad shoulder, fingers lightly curling in a tender possessiveness. Horatia wore his gown and it fit her perfectly, the embroidered silks clung to her in a way he wished he could. She held only radiant smiles tonight, and all sadness was banished by the merriment of the Christmas season. She had never looked lovelier in his eyes and he told her so.

"I am happy, Lucien. You made me so." She tightened her grip on his shoulder and his hand during their endless waltz.

"Would that I could always make you so happy, my love," he murmured too softly for her to hear over the music.

When at last the music faded Lady Rochester clapped her hands together.

"All right everyone, enough dancing. It is time for presents!" The announcement was followed by hearty cheers from the younger people in the ballroom. The group proceeded to the large parlor just off the ballroom where a roaring fire greeted them and refreshments of small Christmas puddings and freshly made wassail was ready to be drunk. Lucien's mind was not on Christmas puddings however. He did his best to ignore the concerned looks his sister kept shooting from across the room.

Just let me enjoy these last few hours...please, he beseeched fate helplessly.

Lucien felt almost reckless now, wanting to hold Horatia in his arms without a care as to who saw them. God, how he wanted her, how he loved her. Horatia seemed emboldened by the evening as they moved to a small settee. Under the waves of red silk from her gown his hand found hers and he gripped it like a man dying of thirst would a goblet of water.

From across the room Cedric's eyes were sharp, but he made no move against them. Lucien's body ached with the reminder of Cedric's righteous fury. Each breath, each twist of his body was a reminder of the animosity that had stolen Cedric's friendship from him like a cruel thief. It was agony, this choice which was no choice at all.

"Here, Lucien. This is for you," Horatia said in a breathless voice.

She looked as though she feared it would not be to his liking. Lucien smiled at her, thankful for the distraction as he took the package and opened it. In his lap he found a book titled *Astronomy and Mythology*. It was a history of the tales behind the constellations.

Grinning like the lovestruck fool he was, he opened the inside cover to find an inscription—*Happy Christmas, Lucien, may we forever share the stars*. He had never been one for poetry, but that single line had his heart both soaring and breaking. After the coming dawn there would be no more stars, no more tales, no more love… not without the cost of losing his best friend. The chances of dying in the duel were not as great as some made it out to be. That was the effect of pride on those who took part. But the truth was regardless of the outcome it would be devastating because it would tear the families apart. Horatia would lose him or her brother. No one would emerge from this unscathed.

"There's more." Horatia prodded with a cheeky smile as she pointed to the center of the book. He tugged a long slender strip of crimson silk out from the center pages. Too long for a bookmark, it was embroidered with silver stars and crescent moons.

"I thought you might find other uses for that." Horatia nibbled her lower lip with a gleam in her eyes. Damn the woman, she was perfect. Too bloody perfect.

The attention of the others in the room was diverted by Lucinda and Lysandra admiring Audrey's new fawn gloves.

"I love you," he mouthed silently

"I love you too," Horatia mouthed back.

"And this is your gift," Lucien said quietly, sliding her a small package behind the shelter of her skirts.

"But you already gave me mine," she said.

"When it comes to you, my love, I cannot seem to control myself." Lucien smiled as she began to unwrap the small gift, uncovering a velvet pouch. With a curious look she loosened the drawstrings and tipped it over. A slender bracelet of sapphires encircled by diamonds fell into her lap. Horatia's hands flew to her mouth.

"It was my grandmother's on my mother's side. She gave it to me when I was fifteen. She told me to give it to the woman who held my heart. I remember I laughed, telling her no one would ever have my heart, but the crafty old woman knew me better than I did myself. She told me to keep it and one day I'd know who to give it to.

"That night in the Midnight Garden when you spoke of the stars…I knew that this was meant for you. Even when I raged at you that night I still knew that you had to have this bracelet. You are the keeper of my heart. Take this gift and wear it when you think of me. These jewels are as close as I can get to stealing the stars and adorning you with them." Lucien took her right hand and gently secured the bracelet around her wrist.

Horatia marveled at the stunning glint of the gems in the firelight before Lucien slid her glove over the bracelet and covered it. Horatia gazed back at him wordlessly. She had never looked more beautiful, more wonderful. The angels paled in comparison, and no saints possessed brighter halos of innocence and purity of soul than his darling sweet Horatia.

"Lucien." She tried to say more but he could hear the break in her voice. She was overjoyed, filled with love and it humbled him.

When the last of the presents had been unwrapped, Sir John began to belt out carols in a deep rich baritone. His son, Avery and Lawrence all joined in while Lysandra and Audrey dissolved into giggles whenever the four men bungled the words. Linus stood by the fire fiddling with a woolen, navy blue scarf he'd received from Lucinda Cavendish. She joined him by the fire and with a small smile pushed his hands away and set about adjusting his scarf herself. Linus gazed down at her in open desire and admiration. Only Lucien seemed to notice when Linus set a hand on the young woman's waist and pulled her a few inches closer to him.

Hot cider was brought by a maid and once more conversation settled about the room like the distant hum of bees on a summer day.

"I wish it could always be like this," Horatia sighed dreamily.

Lucien agreed. There was nothing more wonderful

than being warm and drowsy in a fire lit parlor surrounded by one's family and friends while snow laced the world outside.

"I do too." Lucien tightened his hold on Horatia's hand and drank in the sight of her and his own family—the twinkle of his sister's eyes, and the mischievous grins of his brothers. Even the reluctant grin of Cedric who was allowing Audrey to fuss over him while he tried on his new red hunting coat.

It was well past midnight when everyone decided to go to bed and the party reluctantly dispersed. Lucien retreated to his room and let his valet, Felix, prepare him for bed. Felix tried to hide a yawn and gave Lucien a weary smile as he went off to the servants' quarters. Lucien donned his nightclothes and was in the process of wrapping his dressing gown about his bruised body when there was a knock on his bedroom door.

He went to open it and found a nightgown clad Horatia peering up at him in the dim light of the hallway.

"May I come in?" She slipped past him before he could answer and went straight for his bed, climbing in between the turned down covers.

"What about Ursula? Won't she worry about you being gone?" He closed the door to his bedroom.

"She knows where I am and that she is to keep her silence on my whereabouts. I think she likes you, even if she does think you're a rogue."

"I am a rogue." He stiffened his spine and mock scowled at her.

"Of course you are," she answered in a tone one used to placate a fussy child and patted the spot on the sheets beside her. "Your bed is icy, my lord, come and warm me up." She spoke like a princess wanting her devoted knight to heed her every wish. And Lucien was that knight.

"Yes, my lady." He bowed with a mocking grin and she threw a pillow at him.

"It will take more than pillows to stop me, love." He blew out the remaining candles before peeling off his robe. He didn't want Horatia to see the bruises her brother had wrought on his body.

"Now, about warming you up." Lucien tugged her into his arms beneath the covers.

What followed was a sort of lovemaking he'd never done before. No restraints, no delving into darker passions. He was tender and slow, and he poured his soul into every kiss and gave her his heart with every caress. Horatia cried out again and again beneath him. Lucien painted her face in his mind, ecstasy ravishing her features in the moonlight. He wanted to capture the beauty that was Horatia's alone.

This…he thought as he finally allowed himself to reach his release close to dawn in her arms, *this is worth dying for*. He briefly shut his eyes, hoping to catch an hour of sleep before Felix came to wake him.

CHAPTER 29

"It is time, my lord," Felix whispered, rousing Lucien from his bittersweet dreams. With great care he disentangled his body from Horatia's. She remained asleep, but she spread one arm out unconsciously seeking his vanished warmth and Lucien felt her loss like a blow. He dared not touch her, dared not get too close or he'd wake her and never be able to leave.

Lucien donned a pair of trousers, then hastily pulled on a shirt and green waistcoat. Without bothering with a cravat, he pulled on his boots and left the room. With a single look back at his bed Lucien silently bid farewell.

"Sleep, my dear, and dream of the stars."

He slipped down the hall until he reached Lawrence's bedroom. He found the door unlocked and saw Lawrence lay sprawled on his stomach, entirely naked from what

Lucien could see. He approached his brother's bed and shook his shoulder.

"Wake up, Lawrence."

Lawrence swatted a hand in Lucien's general direction.

"Five more minutes, Tom." Tom was Lawrence's valet. Lawrence tried to roll over and face away from him. Lucien returned the favor by smacking the back of his brother's head.

"Get up, Lawrence. I have need of you."

"Hmph...Lucien?"

"Come on. I need you to come with me to the North field straight away."

"The North field? What on earth for?" Lawrence sat up, rubbing his eyes and blinking.

"I have an appointment with a pistol," Lucien replied. That got Lawrence's attention and he leapt out of bed.

"What?"

"Get dressed and I will explain along the way." Lucien stood impatiently by the door as Lawrence threw on his clothes. Only when they were outside in the hall did Lucien explain about the duel.

"You are seriously going to duel Sheridan? I don't believe it. Not you two."

"Believe it, Lawrence. I blame Mother. If she hadn't worked towards forcing my hand with Horatia I might have been able to introduce the idea of courting Horatia to Cedric slowly without the volatile reaction."

Lawrence winced. "This is my fault. I can explain it to Sheridan. Maybe he'll see reason and not continue with this nonsense."

Lucien kept walking, his brother keeping pace. "Better that I alone face his wrath. I'm hoping he'll have cooled down during the night. If not…"

They walked quietly through the halls and Lucien paused just outside the library doors, handing Lawrence his great coat.

"Wait here, I need one more thing before we go."

When they reached the northern most field, where Cedric waited along with a confused and drowsy Gregory Cavendish. Lawrence and Gregory shared concerned glances as Lucien held out a boxed pair of pistols. Gregory and Lawrence assumed the duty of inspecting the weapons for any faults or tampering. Once the seconds determined the pistols were in fine working order, the men stepped back. Cedric and Lucien each took a pistol and then faced each other. The silence between them was only enhanced by their cloudy puffs of breath in the pale predawn light.

"Last chance to call this off, gentlemen." Gregory waited, but neither side attempted to put a stop to the duel.

Cedric shifted on his feet, his lips parted as though he wanted to speak, but then gave a little shake of his head.

"Twenty paces each," Cedric said.

"Agreed," Lucien replied. His heart screamed inside

his chest as he turned and began to measure out his paces. *Please God, let him come to his senses.* He made sure to take slow, measured steps, wincing each time the small clinks and creaks betrayed his best hope for surviving this should sanity not deliver him.

When the two were forty paces apart they raised their pistols in salute, waiting. Lucien slid his index finger out of the metal loop that enclosed the trigger, so that if he was hit he would not involuntarily fire his weapon.

The cold air shot through him like fire, his every sense on high alert. The smell of dead grass and the fell of crisp snow beneath his boots, the biting chill of the air and the endless gray skies melding with vast fields of virgin snow. *How sad that this last vision is so cold and lifeless.*

"You will fire at the call of three," Gregory called out, his tone carrying across the field.

"One..."

Back down, you fool, Lucien thought, and angled his body sideways to give Cedric as little of a target to aim at as possible.

"Two..."

Cedric dropped his pistol down to aim. Lucien dropped his arm farther, aiming his pistol instead towards his feet. Lucien's mind flashed across every moment of last night. He willed himself to summon his last ounce of emotional strength to stand firm for Horatia.

"Three…"

Cedric's hand visibly shook, then he cursed and fired. *Ptang!*

The bullet struck Lucien's shoulder and ricocheted, grazing his head. Lucien sighed with relief, even though the pain was agonizing. He hadn't died. The pain lessened slightly. Good, he was going to be fine, what was a flesh wound after all?

"You must return fire," Lawrence called out grudgingly. There were rules to these things.

Lucien fired his pistol into the ground. It was done.

As if the act had somehow released him, his body suddenly felt light and weak. He collapsed to the ground, clanking loudly. Maybe his head wound was more serious than he thought.

"You bloody fool!" Cedric tossed his pistol at Gregory before rushing over to where Lucien lay.

"Help me get this off." Lucien dug his hands into his coat, hoping to remove the metal armor plates underneath.

"Good God, what on earth…" Gregory asked as he caught sight of the armor on Lucien's shoulder, running down the length of his arm.

"That is what you retrieved from the library?" Lawrence examined his head. "Really, Lucien, where do you get these ideas? That's almost as bad as the time you snuck of out of Lady Godfrey's house right past her husband, dressed as a footman."

With a pained chuckle, Lucien nodded. "Perhaps. But that had also saved my life. Cedric's a fine shot and I didn't want to risk it." He glanced down at his shoulder.

Crimson stained the shiny metal where blood dripped from his temple. "Though I may have miscalculated somewhat." He looked to Cedric. "You damned fool. You actually fired!"

"Why didn't you fire back?" Cedric's voice was filled with despair. Was the wound even worse than he thought?

"I did fire back."

"Yes. Into the ground. You should have shot me."

"And what would that accomplish?" Lucien sighed. "I wagered my life that you would back out, or misfire. I'd hoped you would reconsider or calm yourself before it came to this. The armor was a desperate plan in case all that failed. It seemed I was right to do so."

Cedric looked pained. "I didn't mean to fire at all. I meant to stare you down until you yielded. When you lowered your pistol it unnerved me, and my hand...it shook."

Lucien's smile withered and he grew serious. "No matter what you think, I meant what I said. I love Horatia more than anything...but I could never kill my closest friend, nor the brother of my greatest love." Lucien tried to ignore the burning pain in his head. It felt like someone was branding his skull.

"You…you really love her?" Cedric asked. The pain in his eyes wounded Lucien more than the bullet.

"She is everything to me. Always has been. I just couldn't face that before. I tried to push her away." Lucien winced. "I don't deserve her." He shut his eyes as pain overcame him. A cold darkness swept over his limbs, numbing him to any other sensations.

"Help me get him up!" Cedric shouted at their seconds.

Lucien opened his eyes and tried to laugh. "I always knew she'd be the death of me," he said before he went numb again.

"You die on me and I'll kill you," Cedric growled as Lucien's eyelids fell heavily shut once more.

"Not planning on it," he said, but his spiraling vision warned him otherwise.

Memories of Horatia clouded his mind as he sought to focus on the best moments he'd had with her. But death was cruel he supposed, because only the sad and awful moments rose to his mind. Shouting at her in the Midnight Garden. His harsh words, forced kisses and scathing glances. *Such a damned fool I was*, he thought as he was swallowed by darkness.

HORATIA WOKE to an empty bed and frowned. Something was wrong. A sense of foreboding rippled through her like the remnants of a nightmare teasing the edges of her waking mind. She slid out of bed and slipped her shift and dressing gown back on. She wanted to seek out Lucien immediately but it seemed better to be fully dressed, should she have to canvas the huge mansion to find him. She trod down the hall and slipped inside her room.

She selected a gown that buttoned down the front, so as to avoid summoning Ursula. A moment after fastening the last button, she heard the distant crack of a gunshot. Horatia bolted to her window, which faced the northern field. She saw four distant shapes and a second crack cut across the field. One of the figures collapsed to the ground.

A duel! Why hadn't she questioned Lucien? She'd sensed something was amiss last night, but she had ignored it. Why had she done that? In her panic she barely heard the door open behind her.

"A terrible thing, is it not, Miss Sheridan?" a voice said softly from just over her shoulder. She tried to scream as an arm banded about her neck, choking her while a hand clamped over her mouth. "But I'm afraid I'm now running short on time and there is still much to do." The voice was strangely familiar. But even as Horatia thrashed against her captor she still could not see his face.

"I never would have guessed a quiet little chit like you would drive men to duel. Perhaps I will taste you for myself, just to see what the fuss is about." A tongue flitted around the shell of her ear. Horatia tried to claw at his arm, but it only squeezed her throat tighter. Black and gray spots blotted her vision as she fought to breathe.

"Fiery little hellcat. Didn't expect that from the likes of you."

Horatia saw a brief opportunity and abandoned her attempt to claw his arm. Instead she pushed her head forward and then threw it back, colliding her skull with his. Her attacker cursed and loosened his hold. Horatia dropped to her knees, escaping the arm wrapped around her neck. She turned just in time to see the face of the man who'd assaulted her.

"You!" she breathed in shock.

A blow struck her temple, and Horatia saw no more.

CEDRIC CURSED as he and Lawrence carried Lucien's body between them across the field and into the house. Gregory had sprinted ahead to alert the house and have someone ride to Hexby. As Cedric and Lawrence were nearing the stables they learned that someone was Gregory himself.

"I'm off for the doctor," he shouted and streaked past them on a dappled gray stallion. Avery and Sir John were the first two people to meet them at the front door.

"Good God!" Avery gasped at the bloody wound on Lucien's head and Cedric's grief-stricken expression.

"You were dueling?" Sir John growled. "Fools." He relieved Lawrence of Lucien's feet to help carry the unconscious Marquess up the stairs to an empty bedroom. The second Lucien was on the bed Lady Rochester burst into the room, fire in her eyes.

"Is he dead?" she asked, panic creeping into her.

"The blow glanced his skull," Lawrence said. "He may still live."

"May? Oh, he will not die. I want to kill him myself and he will not deny me that." But when she caught sight of her firstborn bleeding on the bed, she crumpled to her knees. Avery caught his mother before she could faint dead away.

"Get her out of her here, lad," Sir John barked. Avery obeyed, half-carrying his mother out of the room. Sir John turned his attention back to Lucien and started to rip off his shirt and remove the armor to see the damage better. The men winced at the bruises that ranged from Lucien's collarbone down to his hips.

"Who in the bloody hell did that?" Lawrence asked.

"I did," Cedric's said, void of emotion. "We fought last evening before dinner."

"What on earth possessed you to engage in fisticuffs and then a duel?" Sir John growled in such a way that he established himself the dominant male in the room of young foolish boys.

"He bedded my sister," Cedric defended, but there was little heat in his tone.

"You're a damned fool, Sheridan. Lucien loves her," Lawrence said.

"I realize that...now," Cedric admitted.

"Now may be too late," Lawrence shot back.

"You think I don't regret it?" Cedric snapped like a wounded animal and Lawrence saw the despair in his eyes. "I didn't even want to shoot him but my hand shook so badly and I..."

"Then why duel at all?" Lawrence asked.

"I'd hoped he'd back down. I was too afraid to trust him with my sister's heart. I could not let her be hurt. Not again."

"I think you ought to go and wake your sister, Sheridan. She should be prepared for the worst." Sir John put a steady hand on Cedric's shoulder and pushed him towards the door.

"You're right. Horatia must know." He left the room where Lucien lay bleeding and unconscious. What could he possibly say to her?

"Cedric?" Audrey's timid voice cut through his grief. She and Lucinda Cavendish were at the other end of the hall, clad only in nightgowns and robes.

"Where is Horatia?" he asked as they met halfway.

"I haven't seen her. Is it true? You shot Lucien in a duel?" Audrey's voice was tremulous and her eyes on the verge of tears.

"Yes."

"It's all my fault!" Audrey wailed. "I shouldn't have told you about them. Lucien will die and Horatia will never be happy and you will be hung for murder!" She reached for Cedric, seeking comfort from him but Cedric angled her towards Lucinda.

"I'm sorry. It is far more important that I find Horatia right now," he apologized. He had to put Horatia before Audrey today of all days.

She wasn't in her room. The bed was unmade and empty, and her nightgown abandoned on the floor. Her wardrobe was open and Cedric guessed she must have dressed before leaving. He turned to search for her elsewhere but a slip of paper caught his eye resting on her pillow. He retrieved it and read it hastily.

To the victor of the duel: Congratulations! Your prize awaits you and you alone at the gardener's cottage.

There was no name signed. The ambiguous wording was much like the note after the carriage incident. A threat veiled in civility. He did not know who had his sister, but knew who had to be pulling that man's strings. With a curse, Cedric crumpled the note and tossed it to the floor before running out the door. He prayed he could get there in time.

The house was in a buzz as servants flitted through the halls. Cedric tore past them to the stairs and out the back door to the gardens. Lucien's fate was out of his hands now, but he could still help Horatia.

He had no plan and no weapon. It had to be a trap, he knew, yet somehow it felt like the devil's due. When at last he reached the cottage his breath was ragged. He practically wrenched the door from its frame as he stormed inside.

The cottage was dark and quiet but he heard a pained whimper down the hall. Cedric immediately regretted the noise he'd made in entering. No doubt his sister's abductor knew he was here. There was a muffled shriek and Cedric rushed headlong down the hall.

He burst inside and found Horatia crumpled in a heap on the floor next to the bed. Rose petals strewn the floor and bed around her, mixing with the blood on her lip and the slashes on her arms. A man stood with a pistol in one hand and a knife in the other. He raised the pistol at Cedric's chest.

"So glad that you could join us, Lord Sheridan. Do have a seat. That chair." The man pointed to a chair by Horatia.

Before him stood one of Rochester's footmen, Gordon, dressed in the green livery of Rochester Hall. The same servant who had indirectly confirmed to him that Lucien and Horatia had been stealing away together.

"Sit down. Now," Gordon said, cocking the pistol.

"Cedric, get out of here!" Horatia hissed.

"I'm not leaving you." Cedric did not sit down, but he made no move to leave.

Gordon calmly swung the pistol towards Horatia.

"The situation is quite simple. You will sit in that chair, Sheridan, or I will splatter the wall with her brains."

Cedric slowly took a seat and waited. Gordon kicked a coil of rope towards Horatia.

"Bind his hands and feet to the chair. Bind him tight, or else." Horatia took the rope with shaky hands and got to her feet.

"It's all right," Cedric whispered. "Just do as he says." Cedric remained outwardly calm, but the fury in his eyes warned her that he had not given up yet. Horatia tied the rope around his boots and wrists. Cedric stretched and flexed against his bonds once she was done and the murderous look he gave Gordon made the footman smile.

"To be honest, this is not how I wanted to handle this commission at all. If it was up to me, I'd have killed you your first day here and been off before anyone woke. But I'm afraid my instructions were quite specific on a number of points, such as prolonging your discomfort."

"Who hired you?" Cedric demanded.

"I believe you know," Gordon replied simply. "And if you don't, well, it won't really matter much longer. Now, Miss Sheridan, be so kind as to lie down on the bed. I wish to enjoy you while your brother watches. It is Christmas, after all."

Horatia stumbled away from the bed in horror.

"Don't you touch her!" Cedric shouted, yanking on

the ropes. "You have me already, just finish me and be done with it."

Gordon put on a theatrical performance of confusion. "Oh? I'm sorry. You must have misunderstood. My instructions regarding prolonged discomfort and death were for your sister. I was instructed not to kill you unless absolutely necessary." Gordon started towards Horatia, a gleam in his cold gray eyes.

"Run! For God's sake run!" he shouted at his sister.

HORATIA MADE it halfway down the hall before Gordon caught up with her. He grabbed her by the hair and yanked her backward. She shrieked as Gordon pulled the knife back against her throat, drawing a trickle of blood. Horatia ceased fighting him then, and he dragged her back into the bedroom.

"Please. You may do with me what you will...but do not make my brother watch."

"I believe my employer would prefer it if he did." Gordon shoved Horatia onto the bed. She grunted in pain and rolled onto her back just as Gordon charged towards her.

"Lucien will kill you," she promised.

He only laughed. "I very much doubt he will. I'll be long gone before he comes here, assuming he survives at all. You really mustn't worry over him much though, it is you that you should be concerned about."

"How bad was the wound?" Horatia asked Cedric. "How badly did you hurt him?"

"I am not sure. When I left the house he was unconscious and bleeding heavily," Cedric said, looking away.

Gordon smirked at Horatia. She was silent for a long minute eyeing the dying embers in the fireplace. "It seems the hellcat has lost her hellion ways. How easily defeated you are."

Then she got to her feet and to both Cedric and Gordon's confusion she added a few logs to the fire.

"What are you doing?" Gordon asked suspiciously. "Back over here, now."

Her face was so bleak and dispassionate that Gordon glanced at Cedric as though ascertaining whether there was some plan at work here between the siblings. But Cedric's face only burned with shame and defeat.

Horatia whirled on him with the poker just as Gordon raised his pistol. The shot went wide as the sharp tip of the poker raked his chest. She struck his arm with the poker before he could pull out his knife. Gordon cried out in pain as his arm bent unnaturally, but before she could land a second blow he wrenched the poker from her with his good arm.

"That was very stupid." Gordon struck her across the head with the poker. Stars burst across her eyes before everything went dark.

GORDON FROWNED DOWN AT HORATIA. He tore off a length of her dress and fashioned himself a hasty sling.

"Well, there's no point in taking her now. In truth, I have no wish to linger here any longer. But a contract is a contract. But now that we're alone, I have to ask. Whatever did you do to earn such enmity? What sin earns a man this level of personal attention?"

Cedric said nothing. He didn't give a damn what the man had in store for him. He focused solely on his sister and the way she laid in a crumpled heap against the wall.

With no answer forthcoming, Gordon strode over to the fireplace. He used the poker to drag a log out of the fireplace and onto the floor. Slowly flames began to lick at the edges of the floor. Then he came over to Cedric and with his good arm cut his bindings. Before Cedric could fight him, Gordon rammed the pistol into his stomach.

"Move. I want you to walk out of this cottage ahead of me. I may need you if others have arrived."

"I'm not leaving my sister," Cedric snarled.

"Yes, you are, or I put a bullet through you and you won't be able to save anyone. You still have one sister left. Are you going to leave her as well?"

Fear exploded through Cedric, but he wouldn't give up on Horatia. He would *never* give up on her.

"Horatia! Horatia wake up!" he hollered as he was

pulled away. The flames from the log began to creep along the floor and up the curtains of the window.

Horatia did not stir. Blood trickled from her forehead. She had to be alive, she had to be! While the small fire danced, the crimson rose petals lit up one by one, flames devouring them in flashes like fireflies. As they exited the house, Gordon stumbled on the bottom step.

Cedric turned and grappled with him over the pistol. Cedric shoved against the footman's broken arm, causing him to cry out and drop the weapon. Cedric kicked it away and pushed the man back. He had mere seconds to either fight the villain and turn the tables, or to run back into the cottage to save his sister.

The choice was clear.

He dove back into the darkened doorway, rushing headlong towards the fire.

CHAPTER 30

Thoughts drifted through the murky waters of Lucien's mind, jumbled and hazy. Horatia's soft smiles and shivery sighs, Cedric's haunted stare as he raised a pistol at him.

His eyes wouldn't open and he couldn't move.

"Lawrence, try this," a feminine voice said.

Something sharp penetrated Lucien's nose and shot straight to his brain. His eyes flew open and he surged upright, a pounding headache and pain in his side nearly making him cry out. Smelling salts. One never got used to them.

Lucinda and Lawrence along with Sir John all stood watching him, eyes wide and worried.

"Cedric!" he shouted. Fear for his friend exploded into him as he remembered the duel. He was alive? Where was he now? His bedroom.

"Easy, Lucien, he's fine." Lawrence tried to still him with a firm hand but Lucien knocked it away. One thought formed more clearly now. He'd been too damned distracted to pay attention until now.

"Let me up, damn you! Where is Cedric? Where's Horatia?" He fought to be free of the tangling bed linens and fell to the floor. Pain tore through his head and he felt a large bandage bound around his head where the bullet had struck him. Sir John gripped his good arm and hauled him up onto his feet, angling him back towards the bed.

"You need to rest, Lucien," Lawrence said.

Lucien cursed and clutched a hand to his head but kept walking towards the door.

Avery and Linus ran into the room from the hallway.

"The gardener's cottage is on fire!" Avery shouted. "We need to get buckets and water. Everyone come with me to the kitchens."

"Has anyone see Horatia?" Lucien bellowed as everyone rushed towards the kitchens.

"No…" Audrey came running to him, breathless. "Her room was empty but there was this." She pressed a scrap of paper in his hands and he hastily scanned it.

"She's been kidnapped!"

The words on the page confirmed his worst fears. Horatia had been taken as bait to lure either him or Cedric to the cottage.

"Damn, we may be too late! Tell the others!" Lucien

took off at a run. He had to get to the cottage! He nearly fell down the stairs in his haste as people were rushing past him to find buckets to fill. When he burst out into the gardens he saw inky black smoke in the distance.

"Please be alive," he breathed as he raced towards the cottage. The question he couldn't answer was who had done this? It had to be someone on the staff, he knew it. No stranger had appeared out of nowhere, this was the act of someone who'd waited in the shadows for the right moment.

When Lucien was within twenty feet of the cottage he saw the house's new footman exiting from the front door, forcing Cedric in front of him with a pistol aimed at him. Gordon tripped and the two men struggled before Cedric fled back into the burning cottage.

The footman stared at Lucien. "I thought you were dead, Rochester. Good for you." Lucien took a step forward, intending to restrain the fiend, but Gordon raised a finger on his good arm. "Your friend went back inside to rescue your lady love. I didn't come here to kill him, but the fool will likely die all the same. What do you think?"

Gordon sidestepped Lucien and walked on past, but Lucien didn't care. Cedric and Horatia were inside the burning cottage. He plunged inside the smoky interior without a second thought, dropping as low as he could, and covering his face with his blood soaked shirt.

"Cedric! Horatia!" he shouted.

"Lucien?" A ragged voice answered from the end of the hall, followed by a hoarse cough.

"Cedric!" Lucien ran down to the open bedroom. He was repelled by the heat of the flames before him. Coughing, he waved his hand in the air, trying to shift the coiling smoke and he glimpsed Cedric, on the floor, barely conscious, and Horatia was much closer to the fire, crumpled on the floor.

"Get her out of here," Cedric groaned.

"I'm too damn selfish to give up either of you," Lucien shouted. He first ran to Horatia, dragging her body far away from the sprawling flames, then helped Cedric up. "I should think that as my friend, you should know me better by now."

"I'll try to follow," Cedric coughed, staggering for the door. "Go. Get her out of here."

Lucien knelt and lifted the unconscious woman in his arms, biting back the pain that still lanced through his head. Horatia's body was drenched in sweat; the limp feel of her in his arms made him sick with dread.

"Just keep moving," Lucien said through gritted teeth as he started for the door.

He met Cedric's gaze across the hazy expanse of the room. They both knew he wouldn't make it out on his own. Something wrenched in Lucien's heart as he witnessed the grim resignation in his friend's eyes.

"Take care of her for me," Cedric's voice was barely audible above the groaning of the house around them.

Lucien managed a nod and tightened his grip on Horatia as he carried her out. When he reached the door he ran a good distance away from the cottage before falling to his knees. A small crowd of servants and guests were forming a bucket line, throwing pails of water on the far side of the cottage where the blaze was largest.

Horatia rolled out of Lucien's arms and onto the snowy ground, leaving a sooty trail of black in her wake. He bent over her and cupped her face between his shaking hands and kissed her. She stirred beneath him, then coughed violently.

"Lucien?"

"I love you. Never forget that," he said, kissing her once more before he ripped himself away and started back into the cottage.

"Lucien!" Horatia cried out.

He paused at the entrance to the cottage, looking back, then plunged into the swirling smoke.

Lucien put his bloody sleeve back up over his face and ducked as low as he could. He was halfway down the hall when the beams overhead shrieked. One of them shifted and crashed down behind him as he crossed the threshold of the bedroom. He found Cedric slumped on the ground before him.

Lucien swatted a few flames that had latched onto his leg. The fire burned him, but he stamped the flames out and crawled over to Cedric.

Another beam crashed down by the fireplace. Sparks

shot up around the two men and Lucien shut his eyes and flinched away from the flames until the heat receded. A moment after he'd hoisted Cedric up, a massive chunk of the ceiling fell and struck Cedric from behind, sending Lucien toppling to the ground, the beam on top of them both. Lucien yelped in pain as the beam trapped his legs and pinned Cedric down by his back. Lucien clawed at the wood, even though flaming splinters dug into his raw palms. He glanced up, hoping to find anything that might help him when he saw a shadow at the end of the hallway.

"Leave us!" he screamed in desperation. "The roof is coming down!"

But the shadow drew closer, revealing itself as Horatia wrapped in a wet heavy cloak. She hopped over flaming wood and stones until she was kneeling by Lucien's legs and using the wet cloak to cover the flames, heaved at the beam with all her might. Lucien dragged himself out and he and Horatia both worked to pull the debris off of Cedric.

They each grabbed one of Cedric's arms and carried him towards the exit. More than once the flames and smoke almost won, but finally the three stumbled out of the cottage with Cedric just as the entire roof collapsed. Relief and pain swept through Lucien as the last bit of adrenaline in him finally expired.

He collapsed next to Cedric and was lost to the world.

CHAPTER 31

*H*oratia lay curled up against Lucien's body as
he slept in his bed. No one dared to point out
the impropriety of it and if they had Horatia would have
screamed. As it was, everyone was very polite, even the
doctor from Hexby, whom Gregory had returned with
ten minutes after she, Lucien and Cedric had escaped the
cottage.

Lucien's injury from the duel had indeed been minor,
a scratch. The doctor had assured them that head
wounds, even grazes tended to bleed profusely. The
concussion had been of far more concern, but that too
had passed. Unless Lucien suffered an unexpected infection, he would be fine. Horatia hadn't left Lucien's side
since they'd returned to the house, other than to quickly
bathe and change. Now the doctor was attending to
Cedric, who was resting in the room across the hall.

Horatia stroked Lucien's hair back from his forehead and placed a delicate kiss to his brow.

"I cannot believe that Gordon escaped," she whispered. The idea that the man who had tried to kill her was still out there was terrifying.

"He won't be back," Lucien said with such certainty that she pulled away a little to stare at him.

"How do you know?"

"We know who he is and what he was hired to do. We are safe from him." The implied *but not entirely safe* hung heavy in the air.

"Horatia? The doctor would like to speak to you," Lady Rochester said quietly from the doorway. Her eyes settled on Horatia and Lucien, but she didn't say anything, a sad smile crossing her lips.

Poor Lady Rochester was pale and the lines around her eyes, which had once been only there from joy and laughter, seemed to age her with concern over her son.

"Is everything all right?" Horatia asked, sitting up.

"He...the doctor has news regarding your brother."

Horatia slid from the bed and steadied herself. "Bad news?"

Lady Rochester's hesitation worried Horatia. "Yes. He wishes to speak to you and Audrey alone. Cedric is sleeping right now. The doctor will see you in his room."

Horatia couldn't seem to move. Her body felt as though it had turned to marble. She couldn't take much more of this. It was as though her entire body was strung like a harp's strings and she was seconds away from snapping.

Horatia crossed the hall and found Audrey and the doctor waiting for her in the other room. She shut the door behind her.

"You have news?" She was unable to look away from the sleeping form of her brother.

The gray-haired doctor cleared his throat. "Yes. It seems that Lord Sheridan has suffered a very serious injury to the head. I'm afraid that he has lost his sight...completely."

Audrey clung to a bedpost for support. Tears began to roll down her cheeks but she said nothing.

"He's blind?" Horatia asked.

"I am not sure if the condition is permanent, but I thought I should advise you immediately so that you might prepare for the worst. Life for someone without sight can be very difficult, but made easier by the support of one's family..."

The doctor droned on but Horatia ceased listening. Her head turned back towards Cedric. A strip of gauze had been wound around his head, over his eyes.

Blind. Her brother was blind. Her own vision seemed to spot and darken before she remembered to breathe and her vision cleared.

"Thank you, doctor," she said. The doctor then left her and Audrey alone for a while.

"Audrey...why don't you go have some tea brought for

us?" Horatia suggested, and her bleary-eyed sister dashed out of the room. It would be best for Audrey to have her time to cry. Horatia could not think logically with her sister in the same room. She sat down on the edge of the bed and nearly jumped when Cedric spoke.

"Don't cry, Horatia. Please. I'll have enough of that from Audrey." Cedric shoved at the bandage, pushing it away from his face as he opened his eyes and gazed in her general direction, but there was an unsettling blankness in his gaze that ripped open Horatia's very soul. How much of a person's life existed behind their eyes? So much expression, emotion, and understanding was lost to Cedric now. She bit her lip to keep from weeping.

"I can't stand to have my eyes covered, even if I can't see. Come closer. Let me have your hand," Cedric said gently, his right hand seeking the comfort of hers. Horatia threw herself against her brother's chest and he wrapped his arms about her. He kissed the top of her head and held her tight. That simple, sweet act tore her open. There was no stopping the tears. Funny thing that comfort often made her cry. It was as though she was only strong when alone, or perhaps it was that she only trusted those she loved to allow herself such feelings. Who would care for Cedric? He would have her and Audrey...but it wouldn't be enough.

Her brother's hand stroked her hair. She tucked her head into his shoulder as she'd done when she was younger, only this time she hoped it was him who was comforted.

"Please forgive me, Horatia," his voice broke. "I've made so many mistakes of late. I did not trust your judgment and I did not have faith in Lucien's heart. He asked me to believe in his love for you but I couldn't. I have failed you both and it has cost us all a great deal."

"Don't say that," Horatia began but Cedric shushed her.

"I must, Horatia. The truth is that Lucien loves you and he deserves you for a wife. I give my blessing freely. Any man who is stubborn enough to care about both of us even when the world is burning down around him... that man is allowed to marry my sister."

"Oh Cedric."

Guilt warred with her joy over being able to marry Lucien. It wasn't fair to feel such happiness when her brother faced a lifetime of darkness.

"I asked you not to cry," he said, his hands wiping tears from her face.

"May I cry from happiness?" she asked.

"I suppose I can suffer tears of joy." Cedric chuckled. "You will be happy with him. Lucien, I mean?"

"Yes. He loves me and when I am with him I feel free. Gloriously free to just be myself. I love him so much." She wished Cedric could see the truth of it in her eyes, but knew it carried in her voice as well

"Then there is nothing more to do but place the banns

in the papers and ready St. George's. Your marriage to Lucien won't be as bad as I feared. He is one of my closest friends after all and now to be a brother-in-law." Cedric laughed as though genuinely amused. "What an odd notion that is. But it is no longer an unwelcome one."

"Will you walk me down the aisle?" Horatia asked after a moment.

"You wish a blind man leading you to the alter? Sounds like a bad omen, my dear."

Horatia hugged her brother and pretended not to see the tears streak down his face. In that moment, she would have given her life in exchange for his sight.

"You don't have to lead me. Just hold my arm and trust me to guide you. You've always cared for me. Now let me care for you."

Cedric's smiled trembled. "Then guide me, because I will most certainly be there to give you away."

"You could never give me away. We are stuck with each other. In marrying Lucien I don't believe you'll ever be rid of either of us again." Horatia sighed, thinking of how happy Christmas Eve the night before had been. "Happy Christmas, Cedric."

Her brother chuckled. "I hope to God next year we have the dullest holiday ever."

Audrey returned with a maid bearing a tea tray, her eyes still red and puffy.

"Anyone care for some tea?" she asked with a falsely bright tone that might have fooled a small child.

Cedric moved to sit up. "I would love some."

When he released Horatia, she joined her sister to help with the tea tray. Audrey's hands trembled so badly that Horatia took the offered cup and saucer before it rattled to pieces. Horatia prepared Cedric's tea just as he liked before she returned to the bed and reached for his hands. She placed the cup in his open palms and he slowly raised it to his lips. He sipped carefully so as not to spill.

"Well...that was easier than I expected. Thank heaven for small favors," Cedric remarked. The maid returned and addressed Horatia.

"His lordship is awake and is asking for you, ma'am."

Horatia looked at her brother's face, and even though he could not see her, he must have sensed her gaze upon him.

"Well, what are you waiting for? Go and see the man." Cedric shooed her out of the room. "Lucien abhors tardiness."

Horatia rushed back across the hall into Lucien's bedchamber. He was sitting up, his bare chest bandaged around his lower waist. His hazel eyes lit up like topaz stones when he saw her.

"Thank God you're all right," she said.

He held his arms out for her and she curled up in his embrace as though she'd never left him. He grunted and winced.

"That might be overstating my condition a little." He chuckled.

Lucien kissed her gently, a compassionate expression of his love, but it soon burned hotter, threatening to consume them both. After a long delicious moment he freed her lips and just held her close.

"Cedric has given us his blessing. If you still want me…" Horatia was suddenly uncertain. Maybe Lucien would not want her because of all the trouble she'd been. Duels and assassins were not exactly easy obstacles to dodge.

"After all I've endured to have you? If you think I'll just let you escape after that, you are quite mistaken. I plan to marry you as soon as possible and if that requires tying you to my bed I most certainly will." Lucien's hands slid down her back to cup her bottom teasingly. Horatia tried not to grin.

"You already have tied me to your bed, and I quite enjoyed that experience. Should I feign escape to ensure that you do it again?" She stroked his chest, relishing the feel of his warm skin. She would never get over how easy it was to be with him, to tease and play in a way she'd always longed for.

"That sounds like a game I should certainly like to play, as soon as I am no longer at the mercy of my mother." Lucien winced. "Or the doctor."

"You had better heal soon, darling, because I am in

desperate need of you." Horatia brushed her lips lightly across his. "All of you..."

"And what of Cedric?" Lucien asked Horatia. "No one has told me how he is."

Horatia tensed in his arms, and a darkness fell over her.

"What's wrong?" His heart lodged in his throat as he saw tears glimmering in the corners of her eyes.

She bit her lip and looked away. When she still didn't answer, he caught her chin and turned her face back towards his.

"What is it, my love? Just tell me."

Her shaky nod tore at him. "Cedric is alive but...he is blind."

"Blind? God in heaven!" Lucien cursed. He couldn't begin to comprehend the torture of that affliction. To never see anything ever again? Lucien's arms tightened about Horatia.

"Is there nothing we can do?" he asked her.

"The doctor does not know if it is temporary or permanent. We need to be there for him. Support him. Life will be difficult for him from now on and he will need his family and friends to see him through this."

"You are always so brave, my love. And you are right. He will need us now more than ever." Lucien shut his eyes and held Horatia, to let her know that he would never let her go again.

"You know, when I went out to the field this morning, I thought to myself that my greatest regret was all the time I wasted without you," he whispered into her soft brown hair.

"Don't worry, Lucien. I plan to make up for it." Horatia kissed him with all the love she'd been holding for him and him alone.

When their mouths parted, he cupped the back of her head, pressing his forehead to hers.

He was like a man viewing his first sunrise and seeing its striking beauty, that was how it felt to know he and Horatia would be happy. He was awestruck knowing how fortunate and blessed he was to have her in his life and in his heart. They had fought through the very fires of hell itself to be together and now they deserved joy, great joy.

Perhaps it wasn't so bad, to be a rake redeemed.

He smiled and stole another kiss from his love.

There are only good things to come, he silently promised her with his lips and with his heart.

EPILOGUE

*A*nne Chessley always seemed to forget how to breathe whenever she was near Viscount Sheridan. With short breaths she watched him walk down the aisle in St. George's. Light pierced the stained glass at the front of the church, showering a rainbow of colors onto the altar and the people gathered in the pews.

Miss Sheridan and her brother moved arm in arm down the aisle. His free hand gripped a cane that he swept over the floor ahead of them. Music echoed off the walls and floated to the ceiling in a roar of wondrous sound. At the front of the church, near the altar, the Marquess of Rochester waited to receive his bride.

A wedding of the ages. A rake reformed—or so the *Quizzing Glass* had reported—and a quiet, beautiful woman, blossoming with love. Anne felt a little ache in her chest as she wished to be so fortunate.

All too soon her attention was pulled back to Cedric. Even thinking of him made her so happy. Yet sadness lingered at the edges of her joy like shadows. Cedric's dark eyes roved over the crowds, unseeing. Anne fisted her fingers in her handkerchief.

Blind. The man she'd spent many dreams with during the night was blind.

Her father leaned down to whisper in her ear. "Brave man, that Sheridan. Always liked him before, but now, well, he's damned courageous."

Anne agreed. She closed her eyes, wondering if she would be as brave as him to walk down the aisle without being able to see?

No. The very thought of it terrified her. To be that helpless…that dependent. How did he bear it? She wasn't that brave. Cedric had no choice. He had to face that eternal darkness every second of every hour of every day. A shudder wracked her body and she moved closer to her father. He put an arm around her shoulders. He was such a good man, a good father.

Anne knew how lucky she was to have him. Her mother had died so long ago, but her death hadn't broken him. He'd doubled his love for Anne and they had become inseparable. It was a good thing she never intended to marry. She could not bear the thought of leaving her poor papa alone.

Her eyes found Cedric again, unable to look away from him for long. She adored the way he offered his sister a sheepish smile and kissed her cheek before stepping back to allow her to join Lord Rochester. Lord Lennox stepped up from the front pew, whispered something to Cedric and then with a guiding hand, helped him find his way back to his pew to sit.

The sight moved Anne. The League of Rogues had always fascinated her with their scandalous ways, but what she admired was their kindness towards each other. Like a large family. She only wished she could be a part of it. Alas, that path was not for her. She wasn't like Emily, the Duchess of Essex or Horatia, the soon-to-be Lady Rochester.

The ceremony itself was a blur for Anne. Instead she had focused on Cedric. The way his chestnut hair was a tad too long and curled at the ends. He was so handsome to look at, and yet somehow his personality, even his soul, came out through his expressions as well.

Cedric was different. There was a warmth to his smiles. The faint laugh lines around his eyes and mouth would crinkle when he grinned and laughed. Watching him, adoring him, knowing he would never belong to her was bittersweet. It was rather like stumbling upon a painting in a secret gallery. She could look, admire, love from afar but never step through the painted canvas into that world.

If only you were mine, Cedric. If only I was yours...

~

CEDRIC LEANED against the railing of the last wooden pew at the back of the church, speaking with the final guests as they trickled out and onto the steps outside. Lucien and Horatia had already gone on ahead in a carriage to Lucien's townhouse to prepare for the wedding breakfast.

A chasm opened up in Cedric's chest at the thought of returning home to find Horatia's empty bedchamber. It would be just Audrey and him for now...and Mittens of course. The poor old cat missed her littermate Muff terribly. The first few weeks following his death she wandered the house at all hours, crying, yet never heard Muff's answering call.

After a month she'd given up and taken to stalking Cedric at night, finding him wherever he was and eventually settled down to sleep, whether it was his bed, a settee in the parlor or elsewhere. At first he'd hated her direct attentions, especially the way she'd pounce on him without warning, claws digging into him as she kneaded herself into a blissful state of contentedness. But once he'd grown used to Mittens' impromptu nightly appearances he'd settled in with her and relished the warmth of her small body and the steady purr she made. The sound was perhaps the most comforting aspect of the arrangement. It reassured him that nothing loomed out of the darkness to harm him when he could not see it. His enemies would have no chance of sneaking up on him, not while Mittens manned her post.

Audrey slipped her hand in his, pulling his attention back to their guests.

"Lord Chessley! Anne!" Audrey greeted eagerly.

"Miss Sheridan." Lord Chessley's deep baritone voice was full of amusement. "For now you are indeed Miss Sheridan, since your sister is now married. What a lovely ceremony, wasn't it? Anne and I were thankful you thought to invite us."

"Of course!" Audrey replied without hesitation.

"Yes, we were very happy to come," Anne said.

Cedric's breath hitched. He'd always loved the sound of her voice, warm like a glass of fine brandy.

"Thank you so much for inviting us. Your sister looked so beautiful. I can tell she and Lord Rochester will be very happy."

Audrey laughed. "They had better be, given all that has happened."

Cedric detected the note of anxiety in his sister's tone and gently nudged her ribs to remind her to be silent. The news of his blindness had been unavoidable. However, the matter of how he'd lost his sight—other than 'in a fire'—was a matter best left unremarked upon returning after the holidays. If only he could shake the nightmares, rid himself of the horrors of the lost memories. What was worse was knowing that Charles suffered the same sort of dreams, had for years now. He relived drowning in the River Cam far too often. Could a man ever come back from that? Perhaps not.

"Well, Anne and I must be going. Thank you again for allowing us to come. Lord Sheridan, Miss Sheridan." Lord Chessley bid his goodbyes.

Cedric extended his hand, shaking the other's and then he waited for Anne to take his hand as well. A moment of hesitation, then Anne slid her gloved fingers into his grasp, which he raised to his lips, brushing a soft kiss on the backs of her knuckles. A tendril of longing spun in him, like a fine gossamer thread and as delicate as a bloom after a harsh frost.

In another life he would have claimed her for a dance at the ball where they had first met. In another life he might have been the first and only man to kiss her lips, to see her smile and hear her laugh.

In another life, she could have been mine…

Hugo Waverly waited inside his coach just outside the church. The door opened and Daniel Shefford slid in. Waverly rapped his cane on the roof and the coach started forward. He settled the cane on his lap, a gloved finger running over the silver head. Once he'd had a cane with lion's head. A gift from his father, a gift that Cedric Sheridan had stolen from him when they'd been at Cambridge. Now his cane bore a wolf's head. The creature's teeth were bared in a silent, menacing snarl. For that was how he saw himself. A wolf amidst a flock of insipid sheep. It was only a matter of time before he feasted upon his prey.

"What have you to report?" he asked Shefford.

"Mostly good news. Gordon made it to your ship in Brighton. He's heading out first thing for Spain. He'll be of good use there because he is fluent in the language."

"Excellent." Hugo hadn't been too disappointed by the report of Gordon's failure to kill Horatia Sheridan. After all, the true purpose had been achieved. The League knew that their loved ones were no more safe than they were themselves. The exercise had been a fruitful one because it revealed the League's weaknesses. Ones he could exploit over time until he was ready. And he couldn't deny the pain he caused along the way was pleasurable. Like a cat beating a mouse senseless but staving off the death blow, fascinated with the stunned little creature lying limp beneath its paws.

"Sir, Avery Russell has been active in our office these last few months. Should we reassign him elsewhere while we engage in this current business?"

"No, leave Russell where he is. We can use him to keep an eye on his brother. He might even become useful to us later. I want you to focus on our Brighton connections. There's a small bit of an underground slave trade that I wish to remove from the port."

"Slaves?" Shefford scowled.

"Yes."

"Very good, sir."

Waverly settled back in his seat, his mind ever turning with possibilities.

"How was the wedding by the way?" he asked Shefford.

Shefford shrugged. "Nice, I suppose. I don't much care for them. Since Sheridan has lost his sight, he's become a source of pity by most of the *ton*. They avoid him when possible."

"Do they now?" Waverly couldn't repress a smile. What a delightful little turn that had been, to learn of Sheridan's blindness. A fitting end for the thief. The fact that the *ton* had turned their backs on him was an added reward.

"I believe there is one who overlooks his condition. A woman named Anne Chessley. She and Sheridan were speaking just before I left."

He'd heard of the Chessleys. Her father was a baron, a wealthy one. That situation would bear watching. He would not let Sheridan have a bride. He didn't deserve happiness. Perhaps he could make use of the slavery situation in Brighton before he had it shut down. Weren't there always markets abroad for genteel bred ladies with fair skin? If Sheridan ever married, it wouldn't be for long.

THE END

· · ·

*Be sure to turn the page to see Exclusive Art of Horatia and Lucien waltzing!

Thanks for reading *His Wicked Seduction.* I hope you enjoyed it!

Never Miss a New Book by FOLLOWING ME at:
- Book Bub

- Newsletter

IF YOU'D LIKE to read the first three chapters from *Her Wicked Proposal,* the first book in this series, please turn the page.

A
LEAGUE OF
ROGUES
NOVEL

HER *Wicked*
Proposal

LAUREN SMITH

CHAPTER 1

*L*eague Rule Number 5:
A man's best lover is a spirited lady, but one should treat spirited ladies the way one would a wild horse, with a firm hold and gentle voice.

EXCERPT from *The Quizzing Glass Gazette*, April 21, 1821, The Lady Society Column:

LADY SOCIETY IS IN MOURNING. The dangerous rakehell Viscount Sheridan has been rendered blind. She cannot help but miss those dark brown eyes that scorched more than one innocent young lady's heart as he watched them from the shadows of a ballroom. Oh, my dear Viscount Sheridan, won't you come out into society again? Lady Society is issuing you a challenge. Do not hide from her, or else she will unearth those secrets you hold most dear.

Perchance there is a lady who might yet tempt your sightless eyes and convince you to live again. Would you not like a woman once more to warm your bed? A woman to tame your wicked heart?

LONDON, *April 1821*

Using his silver lion's head cane, Cedric, Viscount Sheridan, rapped it harshly against the cobblestones of the winding path in his London townhouse garden as he tried to navigate his way to the fountain. All around him the world was a winter gray. Yet his other senses assured him it was spring. Sunlight warmed his face and arms where he'd rolled up his sleeves. A flower-scented breeze tickled his nose and tousled his hair. Cedric took seven measured steps, counting them in his head.

Seven steps to the center of the garden, then five steps to... He caught the tip of his boot on a raised stone, stumbled and collided with the ground. He stifled a cry as stones bit into his palms and the bones of his knees cracked.

Panting, every muscle tensed, he lay on the ground for a long moment, fighting off the waves of shame and the childish urge to whimper with the pain. His eyesight hadn't been the only thing he'd lost. It seemed sense and balance had abandoned him as well.

Finally he picked himself up, patted the ground

around himself to find his cane and rose unsteadily to his feet. He was a grown man of two and thirty—he could *and would* bear this pain as any well-bred gentleman was expected to.

It was a small mercy none of his servants were around to witness this moment of weakness.

Once more. Five steps to the fountain, he reminded himself, and taking care to lift his feet higher, he avoided any more raised stones. He should know this path by now, as he had walked it a hundred times. Yet he still couldn't see it as clearly in his head as he knew he should. When the tip of his cane rapped lightly on the stone fountain's base, he bent over and reached out to find the ledge and, with a great sigh of relief, sat down.

Every hour of every day, from the moment he rose for the day until he retired to bed, he lived in constant fear of toppling precious family heirlooms, embarrassing himself in front of his friends or family, or worse, causing further damage to his body. It was a cruel twist of fate to have once been a virile man afraid of nothing, and reduced to someone who woke each morning only to remember he was forever trapped in darkness.

Too often in the last few weeks, he'd sat at his desk, head buried in his hands, the heels of his palms pressed deep into his eyes as he tried to bring back the vision he desperately needed.

His despair was too strong, and he couldn't summon the will to care.

Thank God for this garden. Peace, quiet, no one to see him in this state. Moments like this were a blessing. There were no social callers, no awkward visits from people who didn't understand the trials of being blind. Out in his garden, he could exist without worries, without anxiety. The fresh air, warm sun and the sounds of birds and insects made him feel alive again, as much as a broken man could. The temptation to remain outside forever was a strong one, but his hands burned from being scraped raw and he'd have to come inside to sleep and eat.

A bee hummed somewhere to his right, probably skimming the budding flowers. The twitter of birds in a nearby tree teased his ears, filling the silence with a delicate trill that was distinct and clear. He could make out every note, each singular melody and the changes in tempo and pitch as the birds talked to one another.

No more could he focus on the tiny details of sight, like the faces of his sisters and his friends as they laughed and talked, or the way wind would stir the trees into rippling waves of emerald in the summer, or the way a woman's mouth turned that perfect shade of red when kissed by a lover. Sounds, scents and touch were his only companions now. He clung to the sound of Audrey's delicate giggles, and the softness of Horatia's hand when she held his while guiding him around.

The light steps of a footman on gravel disturbed him from his thoughts. The sure-footed steps had to be

Benjamin Abbot, one of the older footmen. He'd learned so much about his servants in the last few months. The maids by their voices and the sounds of their skirts, the footmen by their heavier steps. Each servant was unique. It was one of the things he'd learned to value most after losing his sight. He'd always had a good relationship with his servants before, but now he relied on them more than ever.

"There is a young lady here to see you, my lord."

"Oh?" Cedric didn't bother looking in Benjamin's direction. There seemed little point in looking at a person if one could not see them. "Did this lady give you a name?" he asked the footman.

"Miss Chessley. Baron Chessley's daughter," the footman replied.

Cedric drew in a sharp breath.

Anne is here? Why?

He'd been with many women over the years, seducing his way from one bed to the next. But not with Anne Chessley. She was different. She'd intrigued him, resisted him, and challenged him. A veritable ice maiden in her ivory tower, yet each time he caught her eye, for a brief second heat would flare, so bright and hot it made him hungry for her. She was a challenge, and he'd always been one for a good challenge.

Last year he'd courted her, but she hadn't let him near enough for even one kiss. He'd spent a fortune on sending lavish bouquets and had purchased opera box seats facing her father's box in order to watch her enjoy the music from across the theater. And yet she had remained unattainable. Always polite, but never truly open. After months of trying, Cedric had been forced to admit defeat. She would never surrender to him or his attempts at seduction.

And then he'd lost his sight. Any thought of marriage now was inconceivable. While his fortune was still a draw for some eligible ladies, he could no longer stomach the macabre dance of courtship. Not when all he heard were the rude whispers of the ladies behind their fans about his condition. He wanted no such revulsion or pity from his future wife.

Anne would certainly pity him, or be discomforted by his newfound clumsiness. She was too cold-hearted to care whether he could make it five feet without hurting himself or damaging something around him. He couldn't fathom what she'd be doing here of all places, not when she'd spent so much time avoiding him. Furthermore, she was not one for social calls and wouldn't dare pay one to him. Add to that the news he'd recently heard regarding her, and he couldn't imagine why she was here.

Last week when his friend Lucien and his sister Horatia had come by for their weekly visit, Cedric had learned that Baron Chessley, Anne's father, had died in his sleep. Anne was now a wealthy heiress and had no need of anyone, let alone Cedric. Which brought him back to that infernal question—*Why had she come?*

Was she so ravaged by the grief of losing her only living relative that she was coming to him for solace? He doubted it. What could he offer a woman like her? He was half a man, broken, damaged. A bloody fool.

He forced his face into a businesslike façade. He would treat her the same way he treated all the young ladies he came across since he'd lost his sight, with polite distance. His pride demanded he maintain the upper hand, especially with Anne. She must never know that he still desired her, still craved her with a madness that escaped logic.

Visions of her gray eyes played tricks on his mind. To remember her so vividly, the pale pink lips that curved in a smile only when she dropped her guard, and the way her nose crinkled when she disagreed with him. His chest constricted at the memories of their often passionate discussions on horses, their shared interest. It was the only way he'd ever gotten her to respond to him, by drawing her out through her strong opinions. The icy little hellion loved to argue, and he'd taken great delight in provoking her to blushes.

Damn. I've become a sentimental fool.

The footman coughed politely, reminding Cedric he was waiting.

"Please bring her to me," he instructed.

It was too much of a waste of time to find his way back inside now. Far easier to have her brought to him in the gardens instead. The weather was fine, and he knew

Anne well enough to know that she enjoyed the outdoors.

The footman's steps retreated, and a minute later Cedric picked up the sound of a lady's booted steps on the garden path. He heard her gasp when she came close enough to see him.

"My lord! You're bleeding!" Anne rushed over. Her scent hit him, an alluring scent of orchids that was uniquely hers. He sensed the warmth of her hands close to his own as she joined him at the fountain. She clasped his palms and gently touched his stinging skin. He'd become so used to the cuts and scrapes that he barely noticed them anymore.

She clasped his palms and gently touched his stinging hands. He repressed a shiver. Without sight, all he had left to make sense of the world were touch, taste and smell. Anne's touch lit a hint of fire beneath his skin.

"Bleeding?" he asked dumbly, too wrapped up with the sensation of silk skirts brushing his shins. His hurt hands long forgotten. Excitement burned in his veins, and that old urge to seduce rose to the surface. He couldn't recall a time when she'd been this close to him of her own accord.

"Yes, my lord. There are bits of gravel in your palms. Did you…" She hesitated to continue.

His need for her withered at the pity in her tone. "Did I fall? Yes," he answered curtly. He'd never needed pity, and he didn't want it now, certainly not from her. He puffed out his chest and scowled in her direction. An unsettling silence filled the air between them. Anne always had the power to put him on edge, make every muscle coil and tense. What expression was she wearing on that face of hers? Were those delicate brows he remembered arching above her lovely eyes with surprise, or set in a frown? Damnation, he wished he could see her.

"Would you let me help you?" Anne asked quietly.

"How?" Skepticism filled Cedric's tone.

Rather than reply she tugged her gloves off and grasped his hands, putting them into the cold, crisp water of the fountain, and her fingers gently rubbed and scrubbed at his stinging palms. Then she brought his hands back up.

"Do you have a handkerchief?" she asked.

"In my breast pocket," he said. He felt her hand delve into the pocket of his vest and retrieve it. The simple action was strangely erotic and sent his pulse fluttering. He was always the one to slide a hand under a lady's bodice, or skirt. It was quite a different experience to have a lady's hand moving under his clothes. He could feel the warmth of her skin close to his chest. With an inward grin, he relished the sensation of her soft hands invading his clothes.

When she found his handkerchief, she patted his hands dry and then held his palms up. Her warm breath glided over his skin in a soft pattern as she blew gently on his cuts to dry them.

"I don't think they will bleed further. You must take care not to do anything rough to them for a few days so you won't excite the cuts again."

Her scolding tone caught him off guard and shattered the warm bubble of desire around him. "Thank you, ma'am," he replied stiffly, more from shock than anything. "Pardon my bluntness, but why have you come?" The burning question *why* still plagued him.

Anne was silent for a long while before speaking. When she did, her hands pulled away from his, severing their contact.

"I am sure you've heard about my father."

"I have," Cedric said softly. "He was a good man, and I do not say that about most men of my acquaintance. You have my deepest sympathies and condolences."

Pain lanced through him, sharp and sudden behind his ribs. *His own parents' coffins being lowered into twin graves. His two little sisters clutching his arms on either side, their cherubic faces stained with tears.* Those were memories he did not want, memories he fought every day to keep buried.

"Thank you." Her voice was steady, but he knew how strong Anne was and it made him proud of her. At the same time, he wanted to draw her close and whisper soft, sweet things in her ear, to comfort her.

That shocked him. Since when was he the sort of man

to comfort? He was a rakehell, a seducer and rogue of the worst sort. Not one who cuddled a woman to his body.

"It is actually his death which has brought me to you."

"Oh? I can't imagine how..."

"If you forgive me for my bluntness, my lord, the truth of the matter is that I need to marry. My father's death has left me wealthy and unfortunately more of a target for the fortune hunters of the *ton* than I would have liked."

He didn't miss the tinge of desperation in her voice. As long as he'd known her, she'd always shied from the public eye, and the burden of being an heiress must have been a great one.

"And what has this to do with me?" Cedric asked. Surely she didn't think...it was too much to hope that she would ask him to court her again.

"I need a husband, and most of the eligible men seeking a bride are not what I would ever consider to be suitable matches. I came here...hoping that perhaps..." Her hands grasped his, and the action startled him, but he kept calm and gently held on to her.

What did she hope? His chest tightened. "Speak your mind, Miss Chessley," Cedric demanded, perhaps a little too strongly. Her grip on his hands loosened, and his hands dropped into his lap.

"Perhaps this was a mistake. I shouldn't have bothered you," Anne muttered apologetically. He heard her rise to leave.

Cedric stood with her and reached blindly in her direction, hoping to catch her wrist to halt her. Instead his hand curled around the flare of a womanly full hip. Rather than release her, he dug his fingers in, just hard enough to halt her escape. A startled gasp came from the sudden contact.

"Tell me what you came to say, please," he half-pleaded, not wanting her to go.

He'd spent so much time alone of late, which he'd thought he preferred given his condition. But Anne's company was welcome. It reminded him of better times, yet it left no sting of his lost sight. Rather it lit a fire in his blood, reminding him of the way he used to tease her and how she'd resisted him with her delightful verbal sparring. He restrained himself from a grin when she did not try to escape his hold.

"I came to ask you if you would consider marriage... to me." The last two words were a breathless whisper so faint, he wondered if he'd imagined them.

"You want to marry me?"

He could have Anne at last! Yet he'd sworn to himself that marriage wasn't possible, that any woman who tied herself to him would never be happy with a damaged shell of a man. How could Anne think he would be a good choice? If she thought she could be his wife in name only, she was mistaken.

If he and Anne married, he would get her beneath him in a bed and find the heaven he knew awaited him there.

If marriage was the only avenue in which he could find paradise, then he would have the banns read immediately. Still, if he knew Anne, which he did, there had to be a catch.

"Yes. Well…'want' is perhaps a strong word. But I would marry you if you asked me."

"Why me?" If she had her pick of fortune hunters and other young bucks, why would she settle for a blind, pathetic fool? It made little sense.

"Of all the men I've met, you have remained interested in me and have no desire to pursue me for my fortune since it is well known yours is far greater than mine. I am under no illusion of the true reason for your interest. My father's stallions would become yours, of course, should we marry. You would be free to breed your own mares with them. I thought perhaps that might entice you. I would be willing to work with you on the breeding, since it is a shared interest. I also believe we could grow to like each other well enough to get along. You have my father's approval as well as Emily's, and that assures me of your character."

Cedric laughed to himself. Even with his rakish reputation among the *ton* and rumors in the papers, her father had approved of him? They'd met often at Tattersalls to discuss fine horseflesh. He and the late baron had agreed on nearly everything, except politics, but those debates had been lively and well-argued on both sides over glasses of port at clubs like White's.

A deep pang struck him then at the sudden sense of loss of the baron. He'd let his blindness become a reason to wallow in his own darkness and hadn't even given much thought to how Anne must feel. Her father, a man she was very close to since she'd lost her mother so young.

And she came to me for protection from fortune hunters...

The thought made him feel warm in a place deep inside that had been left cold these many long months since he'd lost his sight.

"You would honestly marry me? I must warn you, Miss Chessley, I am no longer the charmer I once was. My life has become...complicated." The admission hurt him like a blow, but it was unavoidable. She had the right to know what she would face if she married him.

"I know, my lord. I had a favorite spaniel that went blind when I was a child. I know the hardships you face." Her voice was still a touch breathless.

"I don't think comparing me to a dog is quite helping your case, Miss Chessley." He laughed wryly before becoming more serious. "I don't respond well to pity, and if we married I would be your husband in full. I am sure you know what that means. Therefore, you should see yourself out."

A short gasp escaped her, but he couldn't tell if it was shock or outrage. Bloody hell, he couldn't read her, not the way he used to. A faint tremor moved through her,

and he felt it through his hand that still rested possessively on her hip.

"I would offer to escort you to the door, but it takes
me a while to find my way out of the gardens once I get
here." Despite his telling her to leave, he didn't remove
his hold on her.

Fight me, Anne. Don't go.

He hated telling her to leave, but he knew how it
would be between them. She would remain icy, he would
remain blind, and neither of them would ever figure out
what to do with one another outside the bedroom. Such a
concern might not have bothered him before, a part of
him had always expected a marriage in name only, but
since the happy marriages of his two close friends, he'd
discovered he longed for more than sensual satisfaction
with his wife, should he ever take one.

At first he'd brushed it off as sentimentality, but being
surrounded by couples in love had altered his perceptions,
and as he reviewed his childhood with more frequency
since the accident, he remembered the easy relationship
of his parents. He realized that a large part of him had
always yearned for something similar. He wanted what
his friends and parents had: love *and* friendship. He used
to laugh about such things, as though they were the naïve
aspirations of poets, but now he needed them.

"I am aware that you would be entitled to your rights
as a husband. I would not deny you." It was stiffly and

bravely delivered, and she still did not back away from him or demand he stop touching her.

Cedric's lips twitched. He had enough memory of her to know what expression accompanied that tone of voice. Her chin would be raised, her high cheekbones rosy with embarrassment and her lovely eyes flashing with unspoken indignation. His hand dropped from her hip, but he did not hear her leave. She remained close, the sound of her breath teasing his ears.

"You may agree to lie limp beneath me, but I do not want that in a wife. I desire a willing bedmate, something you made clear to me last spring that you would never be."

"People change," she answered.

"Perhaps, but a woman's nature often does not. You were always fashioned of ice, Miss Chessley, and I have no intention of worsening my already crumbling life by freezing to death in your bed. Simply evading fortune hunters is not enough for you to seek me out. Do you think me stupid as well as blind?"

He felt the air shift before the slap hit him full across his face. The attack sparked a fire of arousal in him rather than anger. Maybe he could melt her after all.

"How *dare* you speak like that!" Anne hissed.

"I apologize if the truth hurts, but I am weary of the pretense of civilities. Now, please leave or else I may spout further truths that may be upsetting to you."

"You ruthless cad!" Anne moved to strike him again, but he had the advantage of anticipating her reaction.

By luck alone, he caught her wrist and jerked her body against him. His other hand settled upon her shoulder and moved along to cup the nape of her neck. He held her still in his strong grip and moved gently toward her face. He was able to find her cheek and kiss a soft path to her lips. Once he found it, he abandoned all pretense of tenderness and ravaged her mouth.

She trembled in his embrace, her own tongue retreating from his at first. But he continued his campaign, rubbing his fingers on her neck in a soothing fashion until she relaxed against him. The swell of triumph he felt when her tongue slipped between his lips was glorious. And then Cedric withdrew, stepping back from her, his breath coming fast.

"If you can swear to respond like that to me in bed, then I will ask you to marry me." It was a challenge he didn't expect her to rise to, but he prayed she would. His desire for her, one he'd harbored for years, protecting the low banked fire, now sparked into a slowly building inferno. If only she could agree to open herself to him...

"I...can." Her husky, breathless response tugged at his baser side, his lower parts hardening with need. She continued to speak, unaware of the effect she was having on him. "What I mean to say is you kiss much better than I expected."

"You swear then? To respond in such a way each time I come to you?" Cedric pressed.

"I swear," Anne promised, but Cedric heard the hesitancy in her voice.

He gentled his hold on her and tried to soften his voice. "I will not ever force you, if that is your concern. But I will warn you my appetite for pleasure is voracious." He flashed her a smile he'd broken many hearts with and only wished he could see her reaction to it.

"I would rather handle your appetites, my lord, than suffer one more night at a ball having to dance with those fools who see me as no more than a pile of gold in a ball gown," Anne declared.

Cedric nearly laughed. There was the spitfire he remembered, the one who rose to every challenge he issued. Maybe it was only a feeble imagining that she'd come to him out of pity or the belief that he wouldn't press her for a full marital relationship now that he was blind. He was a betting man by nature, and he'd wager, given her response, that she loved to spar with him just as much as he liked to with her. Perhaps there was a chance for them after all.

"I suppose that settles it. I shall endeavor to do this properly then." Cedric reached out to find the edge of the fountain's base and used it as a steady force to get down on one knee. He reached out a hand in her direction.

"Please give me your hand, Miss Chessley." He gripped her offered hand in his own, feeling the faint edges of mild calluses, a hand belonging to a woman whose world involved horses. She wasn't wearing gloves. Strange, he hadn't noticed it until now.

"Miss Chessley, would you do me the grand honor of being my wife?" He smiled, the absurdity of the moment too amusing to remain bottled up. It was a tragedy he couldn't see her eyes. Would their gray depths sparkle with passion or be murky with uncertainty?

"Yes, my lord," Anne replied, breathless again.

Cedric wondered whether his smile had affected Anne. He rose with her help and searched for his cane. She put it in his hands, and he felt her grip tighten as he smiled again.

Had his smile affected her? Or was she genuinely happy he'd proposed? God, he wished he could see. Too long he'd relied on the language of the eyes. Now he was lost, a clumsy man with only his ears and hands to guide him.

"Excellent. When would you prefer to announce this? I believe it is tradition to wait six months, until you are allowed to go into half-mourning."

A panicked hand latched on to his sleeve. "No! I wish to marry within the week. The season is in full swing, and a quick marriage will end the numerous assaults on Chessley Manor by the bachelors of London."

The pitch of her voice changed as she spoke of fortune hunters, and he wondered if that was the truth. Still, he would not question her if she was coming to him.

The idea of being married held an appeal he hadn't thought possible before. He wouldn't be alone. Not anymore. Her voice would break through the darkness and keep him from falling into despair.

Still, there would be consequences. "You know the *ton* will have our heads over the scandal. They'll assume you're with child, or imagine worse motives for such haste."

"I didn't think you were the sort to fear scandal, my lord." Her challenging tone had him biting back another laugh. How well the lady knew him! They really would suit after all, he had faith now.

"Of course not. I thrive on it. I was unaware that you shared my...*lust* for attention." He wished he could have seen her face. Did she blush at his suggestive words?

"I may not *lust* for it, as you put it, but I don't fear it." Her tone suggested truth. He'd have heard her uneven breaths or a tremor in her voice had she been lying.

"You would prefer then that I procure a special license?"

"Yes, if it is not too much trouble," Anne said.

"Very well. I will write to you tomorrow."

"Thank you, my lord." Anne's hands tightened in his as she leaned forward and brushed her lips on his cheek in a ghost of a kiss. Passion fought with tenderness inside him at the unexpected contact. She remained close by. "Would you like me to guide you back to the house?"

It was he who hesitated this time. Dare he agree and

admit his fear of stumbling? Or would refusing upset her? Damnation, he wished he understood women better. He'd lived with his sisters for years and was intelligent enough to admit he knew next to nothing about the feminine species or their complex and often unfathomable views of humankind. Perhaps it was wiser to accept her offer than to upset her. "Yes. That would be good of you."

Cedric was surprised when she tucked her arm in his and they proceeded along the cobblestoned path in silence. But it was not a rigid silence like he expected. Something between them had changed. He only wished he knew what it meant. But he would soon find out. They were to wed, after all. How odd that he was torn between dread and fascination.

CHAPTER 2

"I think it only fitting that he's been deprived of sight, devil that he is. May he never fix his lecherous gaze on another virtuous woman ever again," Lord Upton announced to the men in the main card room of Berkley's, an elite gentlemen's club. There were several murmurs of agreement on this, but an equal number of disgruntled mutters.

Cedric entered the card room, fighting off the natural panic of being in a room where he felt intensely vulnerable. "Stow it, Upton. I'm blind, not deaf. Do not make me call you out."

His cane swung back and forth across the carpet as he navigated his way through the tables. He could not see Lord Upton's face, but the disquiet in the area of where he heard Upton's voice was telling. Cedric smiled and waited for his friend Ashton Lennox to join him.

"Cedric?"

He flinched at the sudden sound of his friend's voice. Ashton had a way of walking softly as a cat.

Although Cedric could no longer see, he remembered well enough how Ashton looked. Tall, pale blond hair and sharp blue eyes. Ashton was one of his closest friends and the one Cedric trusted most to help him survive without his sight. Ash had always been more patient than the other League members, and he needed that dependable patience to help him muddle through now. He could imagine the intense gaze his friend fixed on him at that moment. Even in a world of darkness, he still sensed when he was being watched.

"It's fine. Upton is a damned fool, that is all." He discreetly gripped Ashton's right arm and let Ashton lead him toward the private parlor that was reserved for him and his friends. Although his pride demanded he make his way on his own, reason reminded him that if he were to be so foolish as to walk without someone to guide him, he'd likely trip and give that bastard Lord Upton just what he wanted from Cedric, to be the laughingstock of the room.

Sleep with a man's daughter one time and don't marry her...he acts like I burned down his house.

Cedric's ears picked up on the sneer in Upton's voice, which seemed far too close for comfort. "Dueling with a blind man? His honor is not worth that foolish endeavor."

Cedric stiffened and cursed his remaining senses,

which had heightened in awareness since his loss of sight, especially his hearing.

"Pay him no heed," Ashton said coolly.

"Unfortunately, he's right. I'd have to have my second point my pistol in the right direction, and even then the shot would be unlikely." He let this slip in his usually sardonic tone, but the truth of it ate away at his insides.

That was perhaps one of the worst things about losing his sight and having his balance diminished. He could no longer ride, shoot, or hunt. He couldn't do *anything* he used to do. Even going to his gentlemen's club had become a nuisance. He felt exposed without one of his friends accompanying him. Over the past several months he'd learned to recognize men based on their voices and the way they walked, but it wasn't enough to feel secure when he was out and about in London. Every sense was heightened, yet his concern that he could be attacked remained just as high. Having his sight last December hadn't saved him from danger, and now he was even more vulnerable.

An assassin almost certainly hired by Sir Hugo Waverly had tried to kill him last Christmas. The assassin had almost succeeded, and it was because of this Cedric had lost his sight. Trapped in a burning cottage with his sister Horatia, he truly thought they were going to die. At the last moment, Lucien Russell, the Marquess of Rochester, had found them and dragged them both bodily from the burning building as flames leapt around them. The last thing Cedric remembered was the sound of a wood beam groaning as it broke from the ceiling and collapsed on his head, forcing him into this world of darkness.

The doctor who had seen to him had been unable to determine whether his condition would be permanent. But Cedric had accepted it as such after the first two months passed. Cedric had opened his eyes each morning to a slate of gray; every night he'd forgotten in his sleep that his eyes were sightless, and every morning he awoke anew to the agony of his loss.

At first he'd suffered from a stifling panic, but he'd forced himself to calm down with slow, deep breaths. What followed then was an aching sadness, a helplessness that made him furious and terrified. He was resigned to darkness and to living life at a slow pace, doing little with himself until yesterday when he'd received Anne in the garden.

It was Anne's visit that had him calling a meeting of his closest friends, known to most of London through the society papers as the League of Rogues. The League consisted of Godric, the Duke of Essex; his half brother, Jonathan St. Laurent; Lucien, the Marquess of Rochester; Charles, the Earl of Lonsdale; Ashton, Baron Lennox; and himself.

Cedric felt Ashton's muscles in his arm shift as Ashton opened the door to the private parlor. The rumble of familiar voices surrounded him as he and Ashton entered the room.

"Good to see you, Cedric," Godric said somewhere to Cedric's left. Godric had somehow managed to leave the arms of his sweet wife, Emily, to join them at the club.

He remembered how Godric had convinced the League to abduct the poor woman last year when her uncle had embezzled money from Godric. She was meant to be a pawn in a larger game, only it turned out Emily was far better at moving the pieces. That abduction had landed Godric with a wife who had been up to the challenge of taming him. Cedric grinned. Nothing had been the same for the League since Emily had become a part of their lives.

"Is everyone here?" Cedric listened to the shuffle of boots and the rustle of clothing as the men took their seats nearby.

"All here," Lucien announced. That red-headed devil had recently married Cedric's sister, Horatia, even facing a duel with Cedric to do so. More than once it had occurred to him that his blindness might somehow be God's punishment for his stubbornness on the matter.

Cedric trusted these five men with his life. With the exception of Jonathan, they had survived countless close calls with death and been a party to many scandals in the *ton*. But above all they were friends, and it was as friends that he needed them the most now.

"What's this you said in your note about news?" Jonathan asked.

"Can someone pour me a scotch and push me toward a chair?" he asked with a half-joking smile. His friends chuckled.

Ashton urged him a few steps forward, and Cedric's knees brushed the firm cushion of a chair. He took a seat and set his cane down on the floor.

"First, before we hear what Cedric has to say, I have some news of my own," Lucien said, his voice a little breathless with excitement. "Is it all right if I speak, Cedric?" His voice carried some secret weight, at least to Cedric's heightened hearing. What could make Lucien, one of the boldest men he'd ever known, become timid?

Cedric nodded.

"Horatia and I...well...we are expecting. The doctor confirmed it this morning."

"A baby?" Cedric sat up, elated at the thought. He then thought of Anne and himself. Would they someday be announcing such news? Was he ready to be a father? Instinct said no, but his heart still stirred at the thought.

"Yes. The doctor said she has been with child for two months now. We can expect the child in November." The pride and warmth in Lucien's tone was obvious.

Four months ago Cedric had been appalled and infuriated when his friend, a rakehell who could make Lucifer himself blush, and Cedric's sister had become lovers. It had felt like he'd lost his sister, a companion he'd relied on so much, and one of the two people in his life it was his duty to protect from rogues with wicked reputations. Now it was one of the most wonderful things in the world to know that his friend and sister were so in love and so happy with each other. Secretly, he'd feared that a marriage between them would put some distance between him and Lucien, but it hadn't.

Cedric and Lucien's friendship had been through a rough patch last December, but Cedric couldn't deny the truth. Lucien loved his sister with a depth Cedric hadn't thought possible. And soon Lucien would love the child who was on the way. Envy slithered inside Cedric, curling and twisting. He wanted a marriage like that, with love and children.

He sighed wearily. *Lord, I'm getting sentimental.* Time and circumstance had changed them all, it seemed.

The cheers and teasing commenced all around Cedric as the warmth of his friends cloaked him.

"Congratulations!" Charles and Ashton said from either side of Cedric.

"A baby Russell," Jonathan marveled with a devious chuckle. "Your mother must be pleased as punch, Lucien."

Cedric was unable to stop his grin. "I'm to be an uncle then?"

Lucien laughed. "Many times over, I hope."

Cedric glowered. "Have a care, man, that's my sister you married, not a broodmare."

"Very well, I'll let Horatia decide the number of children. But *you* will have to deal with my mother when she doesn't get her ten desired grandchildren."

"Now," Jonathan prompted. "Let us hear your news, Cedric."

"Oh...right. Well, Ashton and I have just come from the Doctors' Commons where I procured a special marriage license. I'm to be married within the week."

There was a spewing sound and brandy sprayed over Cedric's face.

"Bloody hell! Who did that?"

"Apologies," said Charles. "You just caught me off guard. Did I hear you correctly?"

Cedric removed his handkerchief from his pocket and mopped his face, trying not to scowl in Charles's direction.

"Married to *whom?*" Lucien asked, his tone echoing Charles's disbelief.

"Anne Chessley." He waited for any sort of reaction, but he hadn't expected the silence he met instead. What were they doing? Staring at him with gaping mouths or glancing at each other in concern? *Damn my eyes.* A chair creaked nearby as someone shifted in their seat.

"What? No congratulations?" Cedric tried to joke, but his grin faltered as the silenced continued.

Finally Ashton broke the quiet. "I think they are merely surprised as you gave up on courting Anne last year."

Lucien cut in. "And she is supposed to be in mourning for her father."

"Marriage next week seems extremely scandalous, even for gentlemen like us," Ashton added.

Godric spoke up, his tone gentle. "Ashton makes a fair point. Not that I care one whit about what society considers scandalous. Not when there are true injustices in the world. I am deuced glad to hear you are marrying Anne. I know Emily will be ecstatic to hear you and Anne finally settled down together. She was always convinced that you cared more about Anne than you let on."

"The only reason I'm not congratulating you, old boy, is because you've now evened the odds of sane men versus married men in this room." Charles's droll tone set Cedric's teeth on edge. "Ash, Jonathan and I will have to hold out against being leg-shackled."

Cedric snorted at this. Charles and marriage went as well together as...well...Charles and a convent full of nuns—which, in other words, was not well at all.

"Anyone else care to question my judgment in marrying Anne?" Cedric asked defensively.

"I am not questioning your judgment," Ashton replied, "but I am most curious as to how it came about. I agreed to take you to obtain a special license, but until now you've been close-lipped on the matter of why."

Cedric sighed. It was a question that had been plaguing him since Anne came to see him the day before. With any others he would not breathe a word of his true feelings, nor explain what had transpired with Anne the day before. But the League had different rules. They shared the darkest of secrets without a second thought, such was the depth of their trust in one another.

"As you know, Anne is now the heiress to her father's estate since he passed away. Apparently the young bucks and fortune hunters are already in relentless pursuit of her fortune. She sought me out and proposed a scheme of sorts."

"A scheme?" Godric sounded intrigued by Cedric's choice of words. The last time the League had involved themselves in a scheme, they'd taken part in a messy abduction, and Godric ended up married.

"Yes, she asked me to ask her to marry her."

"Hold on, you're telling me that Anne, the ice maiden, asked you to propose to her?" Charles didn't sound convinced.

"She's *not* an ice maiden," Cedric growled.

"Weren't you the one who named her that?" Charles reminded him.

Cedric clenched his fists. "I was mistaken. I expect all of you to respect my wish that she never be addressed that way in *or* out of her hearing again."

"Of course, old boy, whatever you say," Charles agreed.

"So finish the story," Jonathan prodded.

Cedric gave a little shrug. "It is that and nothing more.

She suggested the scheme, and I agreed and got down on one knee and asked her to be my wife."

There was another interminable period of silence that seemed almost to deafen his sensitive eardrums as he waited for his friends to speak. Even the other conversations in the room had died down, as if the men in the room were straining to overhear what was going on in their little corner.

"But *why* did you agree to ask her?" Godric inquired, the only one brave enough to shatter the quiet.

He steeled himself and spoke, soft but firm. "Not one of you in this room can comprehend what it has been like for me. I cannot live as I used to, cannot pursue the life I once had. But when Anne came to me, I realized that she may be my one and only chance left to live."

The silence in the room now filled with tension. With that awful silence suffocating him, he started to speak. His friends had to understand why he'd agreed to Anne's offer.

"She has agreed to marry me despite all the things I cannot give her. I cannot praise her for her loveliness. I cannot take her to balls and dance with her. I cannot even go riding with her. That she has come to me over these other men seeking her hand, it lessens the sting of my current condition. I believe, given time, that we may be able to make ourselves decently happy together."

"Decently happy? Cedric, you deserve love, great love,

not decent," Godric replied with surprisingly deep emotion. Lucien murmured his agreement with this.

Cedric shook his head. It was so easy for them to believe that. They had both been lucky to find women who loved them. He was not so fortunate. His past was shadowed with far too many regrets and poor decisions. Fate held no such love for him, and decent was in itself a gift.

"It is kind that you think so, Godric, but I do not agree. I've hurt both my family and my friends too often of late and have been a selfish bastard most of my life." He held up a hand to silence the murmurs of disagreement. "I plan to marry Anne in a week, and I wish you all to attend." He let the invitation slip out a little more quietly, suddenly afraid that his friends would desert him.

"I shall be there," Ashton said, putting a hand on Cedric's shoulder.

"Horatia would have my guts for garters if we missed it." Lucien's reply made Cedric snort. His little sister would no doubt have Lucien trussed up in the finest clothes of her choosing and sitting on the first row of the church pew. *If only I could have my sight back for one moment to see that.*

Godric and Jonathan assured him they too would come.

Charles was the last to speak. With an exaggerated sigh he said, "I *suppose* I ought to go, if only to make sure you don't trip and knock out the archbishop. That sort of thing is likely to bring lightning down on us all, and Christ knows I've got enough bolts of wrath thrown at me every day."

A rough pat on the shoulder shook Cedric as Godric spoke. "In honor of your announcement, would I be able to tempt you to dine with us tonight? Emily will send Anne an invitation as well. It would be good to have everyone together again."

"If you wish. Just send word to me when dinner is and I shall be there." Cedric fumbled for his cane where he'd set it down. Another hand touched his as it found the cane and pressed it into his palm.

"Thank you," Cedric said.

"You're welcome." Jonathan cleared his throat. "And how does Miss Audrey fare, if I might ask? I was told she and Lady Russell are currently in France?"

"Yes. They are somewhere near Nice the last I heard," Cedric said.

He had sent his youngest sister, Audrey, on a European tour with Lucien's mother just a few weeks after Lucien and Horatia married in early January. Audrey was eighteen and a pretty, vivacious girl. She'd managed to do well growing up without their parents, having only Cedric as her guardian. This year should have been her second season, but Cedric's blindness had left him unable to escort her to balls and parties, her lifeblood for entertainment. Audrey had been moping about for nearly two months, and he'd felt like he'd lamed a favorite horse. She needed to be out in the world, experiencing life, so he'd asked Lucien's mother to take Audrey abroad to Europe for half a year.

Next year would be soon enough to unleash Audrey onto the world. She was innocent and naïve, but also determined to get a husband, a deadly combination for her virtue and Cedric's nerves. Therefore, he had proposed her trip with the promise that as soon as she returned he would have a potential husband waiting for her. He would collect a smattering of men he approved of and would present them to her and let her choose.

It turned out Audrey's absence had been a blow to Cedric's social tendencies. He missed her morning chatter about the latest Parisian fashions over breakfast, missed her insistence that they go driving in Hyde Park in his phaeton so she might see the handsome bucks of London. He missed her hugs and the patter of her slippers on the stairs. He'd sworn long ago that his sisters were a damned nuisance, but he'd since eaten those words and enjoyed the pair of sisters he'd been gifted with and had stopped cursing his luck for having no brothers. Horatia and Audrey were everything to him, the only family he had left. Horatia's marriage and Audrey's trip had left him very alone in his townhouse.

"Well, I had best be off. Er…Ash, would you assist me to the carriage?" Asking for help wounded his already battered pride, but the embarrassment of asking his friends was lessening slowly. They did not offer pity, and once he realized this, he was thankful. They merely helped him, and that meant a thousand words he'd never say to them.

"Of course." Cedric felt Ashton's hand take his arm and guide him toward the door.

"I'll send word on dinner to everyone," Godric called out cheerfully before the parlor door swung open.

"Now, where shall we go?" Ashton asked Cedric politely. He never seemed to mind accompanying Cedric on his errands about London.

Cedric grinned. "To see my future bride."

CHAPTER 3

$\mathcal{A}$nne Chessley stood in the entryway of her townhouse on Regent Street. Her back and neck were tense as she fought to remain poised and cool, hoping to hide her racing heart and the creeping flush in her cheeks. Had it only been yesterday that she foolishly sought out Viscount Sheridan and convinced him to propose to her?

God, please don't let this be a mistake. What if he didn't come? What if he changed his mind and didn't go through with the wedding? Anne shoved the thoughts aside, though not easily.

How much difference one day can make, she thought. Since her father had passed the week before, sleep had eluded her, but last night...she'd drifted to sleep with thoughts of Cedric and that wicked kiss he'd given her.

No, not given, *shared*. As much as it embarrassed her to admit it, she'd kissed him back.

Anne smoothed her black crepe gown over her hips and sighed. The ripples of the stiff fabric were an uncomfortable reminder of her mourning and her grief. Her father, Archibald Chessley, was dead, and she was alone in the world.

She was too logical not to be aware that part of her still denied he was dead. She had witnessed his lifeless body when she'd found him in his chair in the library, cold as marble, after a chambermaid had rushed to her bedroom to tell her he was gone.

The emptiness of her home had cut her deeply and driven her to action. She couldn't stand the silence anymore. A part of her still expected him to emerge from his study, cigar smoke wafting from him, or to have him join her outside and offer to go riding together in Hyde Park. It had just been the two of them since she was four when her mother, Julia, had died from pneumonia.

And mere days after his death, she'd been forced to endure suitor after suitor leaving their cards on silver trays, hoping she'd give them a chance to court her. All for her blasted inheritance. If they acted this way while she was still in mourning, the fortune hunters would become more determined to compromise her, even at the risk of scandal, in order to coerce her into marriage. Such a marriage was an unimaginable fate that she needed to avoid at all costs. She could only think of one person who wouldn't care about her money and whom she could stand to marry. Viscount Sheridan.

She smiled faintly. He was a tall, handsome gentleman with brown hair and warm brown eyes. A stubborn jaw and aquiline nose gave him a rebellious and imperious look, but his full, sensual lips revealed his humorous streak. She loved to watch him grin. His smiles always sent her pulse dancing and erased her rational thoughts.

She'd gone to him because she knew she could be honest with him, let him know the truth about why she needed to marry with haste. What she hadn't realized until last night, when she'd returned to an empty house, was how desperate and lonely she was. No more late-night conversations by the fire with her father, no morning breakfast chatter. Just deafening silence.

She assumed that a man like Cedric would not understand her wish to marry out of loneliness and it might not engender his sympathy. Yet he was the only man she could stand the thought of marrying. They shared a surprising number of interests, and could likely make a go of it, if he went through with it.

It was why rushing to him had seemed so natural. He always had something of interest to say, even when he wasn't trying to shock or seduce her. Being around him, she'd never felt alone.

But seeing him yesterday had been unexpectedly painful. He'd been sitting by the fountain, hands cut and bleeding, trousers and shirt dirty all along the front. It had been obvious he'd fallen shortly before she'd arrived. Seeing the blood on his hands and the almost casual way he'd forgotten about it jolted her heart. It seemed he'd grown used to falling, to getting hurt. No one should be in such constant pain that they grew accustomed to it like that.

Anne had wanted to wrap her arms about the wounded viscount's neck and comfort him, but she resisted. They knew so little of each other, and he didn't know her well enough to see the difference between pity and compassion. He would despise her if he thought she pitied him. She only desired to comfort a man who had been deeply hurt. She couldn't begin to imagine what he might have endured since he'd lost his sight.

It had been ages since she'd seen him. All the balls she attended, the dinner parties, were empty without him there. He'd closeted himself up in his house and no longer participated in life. It was as though he'd given up, and something about that made her chest tighten. A man like him should be experiencing life, not closeted at home. Perhaps if they married he could find some peace and she would ease the sting of her lonely heart by keeping him company, perhaps even easing him into some activities again.

Yes, I'll convince him to live again. Why that mattered so much, she didn't want to consider too deeply.

So here she stood, waiting for him to arrive so they could discuss the details of their new life together. But try as she might to focus on the future, her mind kept reliving their kiss from yesterday. In all of his seductions last spring he'd never kissed her. He'd teased and hinted about it, but she'd politely rebuffed him each time. Then yesterday he'd taken control and changed her life with one fiery meeting of their mouths. After that Anne knew she *would* marry him. The hunger tinged with desperation in his kiss sent her spiraling with mirrored longing. It was as though something ancient and soul deep had stirred to life, and she couldn't deny the urge to satisfy that hunger any longer.

It hadn't been her first kiss. Her first had been taken—stolen—by a man she despised. A man who still frightened her. And he'd stolen more than just a kiss. He'd taken something that she could never reclaim. At only eighteen years old, she'd lost any right to a marriage like her friends. Any potential bridegroom would have realized she was no longer a virgin, and the scandal it created would be unbearable.

She would have to tell Cedric, but not yet. Not until after they were married. It felt wrong to conceal such an important truth from him, but she couldn't risk losing his agreement to their union.

She'd learned firsthand that men had but one goal, to pleasure themselves, often at a woman's expense. But Cedric's kiss had promised something different. It had teased, then instructed and then encouraged her to seek her own pleasure from him. He'd then said that he would only marry her if she promised to respond to him like that. He wanted a willing bed partner, a willing lover.

To Anne that meant he wanted a woman who would seek her pleasure back and not expect the man to leave when he alone was satisfied. That kiss told her Cedric would be a generous lover, one who would care for her passion in return. As nervous as she was about her future wifely duties, somehow that kiss had rekindled a fire that had died when she was eighteen. That was why she had agreed to this.

Horse hooves pounded on the driveway and the clatter of carriage wheels jolted Anne out of her musings. Cedric was here. Her heart gave a traitorous flutter, and her hands trembled.

She hastened away from the door and ran up the stairs to the parlor, where she checked her appearance in the small framed looking glass. She studied her face with a frown. Her cheeks, too sallow from her grief in the past week, made her look exhausted to the point of ghoulish. With a muttered curse she pinched her cheeks, hoping to liven up her coloring. Then she smoothed her brown hair back, relieved to see the hints of gold still there when the sunlight hit it just right. Her hair made her passably pretty, as did her eyes, but she was nothing compared to the ladies she'd seen Cedric spend time with over the years. True beauties.

She sighed, her heart stinging. Then she froze.

What am I doing? He cannot even see me.

She could probably wear a cloth sack and he'd never know unless he touched her...

But he *would* touch her. The very thought of how he might do that made her body flush and suddenly she was a little dizzy. Taking a seat in a wingback chair in the parlor close to the front entrance, she waited. A minute or so later a footman announced Baron Lennox and Viscount Sheridan's arrival. As she had been expecting him, she'd given the footman orders to bring them to the parlor directly.

Lord Ashton Lennox entered first, his left arm dropping from Cedric's side as though neither man wanted her to see he'd been guiding Cedric like a child on leading strings. Anne rose at once and smiled at them as she approached. She took Cedric's outstretched hand and without a word led him to a chair.

"I am glad to see you are in good health, Lord Lennox," Anne remarked.

Ashton chuckled pleasantly. "Thank you. I ought to have made my apologies again for the nature of our last meeting." Anne had to admit, Lennox was quite dashing when he wasn't gazing at someone with that frightening intensity she so often saw him use. It was as though he was analyzing everyone and everything around him—for what purpose, she could only guess.

"I take it you have fully recovered?" Anne asked, thinking back to last December when she'd seen Ashton at Emily's house, bleeding from a gunshot. He'd been wounded while he and Godric had been at a house of ill-repute. Given the time of day, and the happily married status of the Duke of Essex, Anne suspected there was something more behind why the men had gone to the Midnight Garden midmorning, and it had nothing to do with bedding women.

It was an awkward thing to see Lennox again after she'd seen him bare-chested. Under other circumstances that might have been considered compromising. Thankfully, they'd been at the Duke of Essex's house and Emily wouldn't have breathed a word to anyone about what happened. Still, Anne wasn't going to forget seeing Ashton's bare, muscled chest, wound or no. It made her wonder what Cedric's bare chest would look like…

Heat crept into her cheeks. When Ashton raised a brow, she glanced away until he spoke.

"I have, thank you. May I offer my condolences on your father's passing?" Ashton was ever the gentleman, and Anne smiled warmly at him.

"Thank you. He is greatly missed. And how are you, Lord Sheridan?" Anne turned to Cedric, who had been silently facing her. His once vibrant and warm brown eyes were blank, but the rest of his face held the nuances of his expressions. He looked intense and focused with his brows knit together. She couldn't help but wonder what he was thinking about.

"I am well, and you?" he replied.

"Very well." Damn, this was all too formal. But what

had she expected? She had put so much effort into pushing him away the last few years that bridging that gap to form a friendship seemed almost impossible. She also feared that if she showed any warmth toward him he'd treat her motives with suspicion and not trust her when she asked for his help.

Cedric cleared his throat. "As my letter informed you, I have procured the special license and set a date at St. George's five days hence. Is that amenable to you? I do not wish to rush you if you need time to have a gown made or..." His voice trailed off.

It was clear he had no knowledge of a woman's requirements for a wedding. Fortunately for the both of them, she was going to wear a gown she already owned and did not desire any unnecessary amount of fanfare.

"A Saturday wedding will be lovely," Anne assured him.

The subtle lines of tension about his mouth relaxed. "Good. That is good. Oh, I mustn't forget. Godric has invited me to dine with him this evening, and I believe Emily will be sending you an invitation shortly. I hope you will consent to come."

She was surprised by his eagerness, though he quickly struggled to veil it in his expression.

"I will be happy to come, of course," she answered.

Emily St. Laurent, the Duchess of Essex, was Anne's close friend. When Anne had been eighteen, she'd had her come-out in London and met Emily's mother. The lovely Mrs. Parr had helped her enter society smoothly. Anne had vowed to return the favor for Mrs. Parr's daughter when Emily's parents had been lost at sea over a year ago.

Of course, Anne had little actual time introducing Emily to London because Godric, Cedric, and the other rogues he called his friends had abducted the poor girl on her second night coming out in London society.

None of that mattered now, however. Emily had tamed the darkly handsome Godric, and the two were so madly in love that Anne was often sad and jealous when she had to be around them. Admitting that wasn't something she was proud of, but it was the truth. She did envy her friend for her happiness, but she was also glad Emily was so blessed.

Tonight she could dine with them and enjoy the glow of her own upcoming wedding. She and Cedric may not be in love, but they seemed to share an equal eagerness for their marriage and that in itself was a pleasant surprise.

"Oh, Cedric, I've just realized I've left my riding gloves in the carriage. I will go and fetch them." Ashton rose quickly and departed the room, leaving Cedric and Anne alone.

"Did he just make up an excuse to abandon me?" Cedric started. Anne stifled an uncharacteristic giggle.

"I believe he did…"

"Does he think we're too stupid to realize he came in

a coach and therefore has no need for riding gloves?" Cedric stood up as he spoke and held out a hand toward her. "May I sit with you?"

"Oh. I'm in a chair. If you wish, I could come to you on the settee?" Anne offered.

"I would like that." He sat back down and waited for her to join him.

Anne took a seat next to him and was startled when Cedric reached into his coat pocket for a small velvet box.

"This was one of my mother's favorite rings. I would like for it to be yours." He opened the box and Anne gasped. The ring was lovely. A stone was nestled there, a gem that seemed to change color in the light.

"It's beautiful! What gemstone is that?" Anne asked.

"It's a very rare gem found in Russia. It changes colors by reflecting whatever shades are closest to it. It reminded me of your eyes. I think I chose it for that reason rather than buy you a new ring. Do you like it?"

"Yes." Her voice was a little broken. She felt her eyes welling with tears. He'd remembered her gray eyes and the odd way they reflected colors. For some reason that alone put her on the verge of crying.

"Shall I put it on for you?" Cedric offered.

"Please." She put her hand on top of one of his and he took it, his thumb stroking the length of each of her fingers, as though counting them before he reached her ring finger. Then he plucked the ring from the velvet box and slid it on her finger. It fit perfectly, she noted with a shy happiness.

"I..." Cedric shrugged off his words and Anne had the feeling he wanted to say something more, but they were not friends, not lovers and not married. They were mere acquaintances, which felt enough like strangers for all intents and purposes, and she supposed he didn't feel comfortable speaking freely with her yet.

"Thank you for the ring, my lord."

"Anne, we're about to get married...please call me Cedric." The plaintive note in his voice made her agree.

She tried the name aloud. "Cedric." She'd said it often enough around Emily but never in Cedric's presence. She liked the sound of it almost as much as she liked the sound of her own name on his lips. It brought unbidden desires to her mind. Would he whisper her name hoarsely in the darkness as he came to claim her? Would he roar it like a lion? After her only experience of intimacy with a man, she'd been hurt and frightened, but now she was intrigued and excited. She was physically responding to the mere thought of Cedric bedding her.

Cedric seemed to reconsider his silence and opened his mouth to speak when a footman at the parlor door interrupted him.

"There's an invitation for you, madam, and I have a message for Lord Sheridan from Lord Lennox. He regrets that he must take the carriage and see to a personal matter immediately."

"He what?" The look of panic on Cedric's face was startling. Anne realized the dread he must have felt at being forced to travel the city alone. It must be dangerous too.

"Thank you, John. I'll take the message." Anne quickly rose and took the offered note and the footman left.

"Is everything all right?" Anne asked Cedric as he got to his feet. His eyes stared vaguely in the direction of the door, anxiety plain on his face.

"He left me..." Cedric's voice, although a low masculine timbre, still held the frightened waver of a little boy.

Anne's chest tightened at the sight of him, the mighty rake fallen so low. Rather than revel in Cedric's plight as she might have once, she felt only compassion. He'd agreed to rescue her from her situation, and it was only fair that she do the same for him. But she would have to do it in a manner that was less obvious. Anne knew enough about men to know that they hated being taken care of like children.

"If Lord Lennox does not return with your coach in a few hours, I would be most appreciative if you would accompany me in mine to the St. Laurent house for dinner. It would be most convenient. I don't wish to trouble my lady's maid to accompany me just for the brief duration of a carriage ride."

Cedric looked calmer, her suggestion working wonders on his anxiety. His shoulders, which had been bunched up tight, dropped back down and he took a deep breath.

"I would be delighted, but as you can see…I am not in my evening clothes. I need to return to my house to change."

"I do not take long to prepare. I could be ready in an hour, and we could take my carriage to your house before we continue." Anne prayed he could hear the hope in her tone.

"That would be…acceptable," he answered after a moment.

"I appreciate that you can offer me an escort. Now would you care to wait here in the parlor while I go and get dressed for this evening?"

"Is that the proper thing? I must confess I'm dreadful at following the rules of propriety. I would much rather stand in your bedchamber listening to the sounds of silk rustling against your skin as you slip the gown on…but I am certain that you would not allow that." Cedric chuckled. "You might think I've faked my blindness these past few months just for that opportunity." His sensual lips were parted for his laughter, and Anne could feel herself blushing madly. Thank goodness he couldn't see her face.

"I've struck my fair lady speechless!" he teased as Anne scowled at him. His lady? Not yet. Lucky for him he could not see her, otherwise he would have realized he was in trouble.

"Are you always going to be so..." Anne trailed off, lacking a word that could encompass his behavior.

"Wicked?" he suggested with a cocky grin.

"Yes," Anne replied as she started to walk past him. Cedric's hand reached out and bumped her forearm before his hand anchored itself to her wrist.

"What are you doing?" Anne demanded as he reeled her into his embrace.

"I thought it was customary to seal an engagement with a kiss."

Anne's body flared treacherously to life at his words, but she resisted.

"You kissed me yesterday. Besides, kissing is only for the wedding," Anne argued, jerking against the steely muscled arms that locked around her waist, securing her against him.

"Only the wedding? I don't know who instructed you in the ways of desire, but they were either a fool or an idiot," Cedric said in a husky voice.

Anne stared up at his brown eyes focused distantly on her face, as though he knew instinctively how tall she was. He shifted one of his hands from her waist and let it slide up along the black crepe gown she wore. The heel of his palm brushed the side of her left breast and she shivered.

Cedric's eyes narrowed as he repeated the motion, moving his palm a few inches inward, stroking the crepe fabric only few inches away from the tip of her breast. To her mortified fascination her nipples hardened, as though desperate for his touch. Anne tried to pull away, but Cedric's intense look held her in place as his hand resumed its original path up her side and along her shoulder. His fingertips ran a slow line up her throat and along the line of her jaw to reach her chin.

Anne felt as though she was an uncharted foreign land. Cedric's fingertips were memorizing the contours of her country for his own private map. When he discovered her lips he traced them, and then parted them with the pad of his thumb. Anne reacted without thinking and nipped him with her teeth.

"Bite me anywhere, anytime, my little hellion," he purred as his head descended toward hers.

Anne was only too aware that she was imprisoned by the strength of his arms. She was no tiny, delicate creature. Anne had a full figure with muscles and curves she'd often despised, but she'd never before taken for granted her natural strength. Being unable to escape Cedric was both infuriating and strangely arousing. He would never force her to his bed, he'd said, but it was obvious he wasn't about to sit idly by and wait for her to come to him. He took her by surprise and established his dominance over her like a stud stallion with a broodmare. She knew he would not stop until he'd mated his body to hers. The dark turn of her thoughts was obliterated by the meeting of their mouths.

Cedric tasted her gently for the first few seconds, as

though learning the shape of her mouth, before he let loose his rough passion. He dug a hand into her hair, fisting his fingers in her coiffure, and tugged, forcing her head to fall back and leave her mouth and neck at his mercy.

Anne's hands were trapped at her sides, clenched into fists, then unclenched as Cedric's mouth sucked on her earlobe, then moved to the sensitive skin just beneath it. She fought off a shiver as tingles shot down the length of her spine as his lips moved in slow, hot kisses.

"Melt for me, love," he encouraged between breaths. Anne felt the instinctive need to obey, but her mind threw up a red flag in warning.

"Can't." Her voice was breathless as she fought the pleasure she could feel rising deep inside her.

"Yes, you can...be wicked with me, Anne."

Cedric's hands in her hair loosened and cupped her neck, holding her still so his mouth could wander back to hers.

"Open your mouth," he commanded before slanting his mouth over hers again. She refused to open, and he slid his fingers around her left breast and pinched her nipple sharply. The sensation shot a fierce desire straight to her womb. She gasped. Cedric swallowed the sound of her shock with a deep growl of satisfaction as his tongue invaded her newly opened lips.

Anne jerked in his grasp, but he refused to surrender his control of her. He kneaded her breast, cupping it, shaping it with his strong hand. Anne's knees buckled rebelliously.

Cedric released her as abruptly as he'd captured her. "I will tame you yet."

Anne pulled away, putting several feet of distance between them. Once they were married she would have to be careful; she couldn't allow him to paw at her and control her with her own passions. She'd vowed to come to his bed willingly, but now she feared she'd been too brave to assume she could manage it without losing herself. When Cedric kissed her it seemed to undo her from the inside out. When his lips meshed with hers she felt time rewind itself to that first night she'd seen him.

She'd been so young and foolish then, ready for love and marriage and a sweet life. Anne shook her head to clear it of sad memories and noticed Cedric flash her a mocking smile full of satisfaction.

"No doubt when we marry you think to take up the habit of hiding from me, Anne, but know this—I may be blind, but my other senses leave me quite capable of finding you. Each move you make I'll hear the rustle of your skirt, or catch the lingering scent of your perfume. I will make you mine all the more fiercely. Now go and change for dinner before I decide to scandalize you and follow you to your chambers."

Anne needed no second warning. She was out of the parlor and rushing up to her room in seconds, but she couldn't escape the echo of his laughter. They'd fought a battle of wills, and she only realized now that she had lost. Cedric was far more cunning than she'd assumed. He was not outwardly a scholarly type or a businessman, but he had a wealth of carnal knowledge that had put her at a disadvantage today.

I must always be on guard, she told herself.

As Anne dressed in the sanctuary of her bedchamber, she selected a gown of russet brown that had golden embroidery on the puffed sleeves and hem. It was a gown more suited to autumn with its hues more pumpkin than like flowers, which fashion dictated during the spring. She knew she should have stayed in her mourning blacks, but the thought of a lovely evening wasted in that awful black crepe was an unpleasant one.

Her father wouldn't have wanted her to wear black for long; he'd never approved of the conventions of mourning.

Grief attends to itself in its own time, in its own way, her father had often said. *It neither expects nor desires formality.* The dinner at the St. Laurent townhouse was private in nature, and Anne felt confident that Emily would not demand she wear black.

After Anne dressed she called in her lady's maid, Imogene, who looked briefly startled at Anne's choice of gown, but knew better than to comment on it.

"What would you like for me to do with your hair?" Imogene asked as she eyed the tangled mess of Anne's coiffure. Anne blushed.

"Something loose perhaps?"

"That would be wise. Since I foresee much mussing in your future." Imogene winked. The pair, close in age, had been as close as servant and mistress could be for the last four years. Imogene teased her mercilessly whenever she thought she could get away with it.

"Is it that obvious?" Anne asked sullenly.

"That your fiancé sees through that wall of manners you put up? Yes. The staff are most excited about your upcoming nuptials, if I may be so bold to say." Imogene smoothed a hand over her dark hair that was pulled back in a subdued but still fashionable knot before she set to work on Anne's hair.

"Bold, yes, but please continue. What do they say? About my decision." Anne was very close to her staff here; she'd known all of them since she was a child. And she was concerned that her haste in marriage might damage their opinion of her.

Imogene began pulling pins out of Anne's hair and started brushing it with a silver-backed comb. "Well, we know you're supposed to wait and all, but most of us have seen those vultures circling around the house, and none of us blame you one bit for speeding things up. You couldn't have chosen a better man. We ladies like the viscount. He's most appealing to the eye, with a fine pair of legs on him and a smile to melt butter…"

Imogene sighed dreamily, clearly performing for her benefit. Anne bit her lip to keep from laughing.

"And the young lads admire him for reasons I'd not like to say in front of your ladyship. The older men here recognize his influence and wealth. Your father could not have hoped for a better match, God rest his soul. The viscount will do well by you, treat you like the lady you are."

Imogene's hands worked their magic, twisting and twining until Anne's hair was gathered at the back to keep it out of her face, but the light brown waves still made a lovely fall of bright rich color loose enough that Cedric could still thread his fingers through it without ruining the pins holding her hair up.

"Thank you, Imogene, it's lovely as always." Anne patted Imogene's hand, which rested lightly on her right shoulder.

Imogene giggled. "Are you ready? I'm sure your young buck is eager to make off with you."

Anne laughed, despite the furious blush Imogene's words brought forth. "Imogene, I swear!"

CEDRIC COCKED his head while he waited in the parlor, listening to the sound of Anne's laughter. It was light yet slightly husky, a laugh better heard in bed after her lover had pleasured her until she was limp and sated.

Cedric smiled. *Soon I will be that man.* The kiss he'd given her today had been unplanned, but no less satisfying. She shouldn't have bitten him. For some reason that had made him as hard as a marble statue, and it had taken all his strength to keep from throwing her onto the settee and showing her how much he liked to bite back. She wouldn't have fought him for very long, but she was still too resistant to him. She would have used his actions to paint him the villain.

It was better to wait, to seduce slowly. Being both parent and brother to his two sisters, he'd been exposed to the secrets of the feminine mind enough to know how Anne would react. Women were intelligent creatures, and they had to be courted and seduced properly to be won over and not merely subjugated.

Cedric ran a hand through his hair, enveloping himself in the brief memory of that last kiss. Her skin felt as smooth as satin, her hair soft as silk and her mouth— *God the taste!*—sweet, wet and unbelievably hot. He hoped that she would eventually put that mouth on other places, preferably below his waist. Sensation during lovemaking had intensified after losing his sight, and the thought of Anne's hot mouth around him there... An irrepressible grin twisted his lips at the thought.

Each kiss he took from her was rich in the promise of passion yet to come. He would woo her with whispered words, sensual caresses and drugging kisses until she was no longer able to resist him. He wanted her to beg for him, to need him as desperately as he needed her.

He had once thrived on his sexual conquests, and he'd

had his share of mistresses over the years, but Anne was different. Winning her seemed a different level of achievement altogether. But it was going to be so much harder to win her over when he couldn't even see her. It was a challenge, but one he was willing to rise to.

He could track her without his sight. The scent of wild orchids left an impression in the air like the invisible essence of a fairy queen. And the sounds... His imagination dined on the whisper of her skirts on the carpets until it was as sweet to hear as a lover's gasp of pleasure, creating a vision in his mind of her raising those skirts just for him and baring milky smooth thighs virgin to his touch.

God, I've been too long without a woman, he thought glumly and shifted on the settee as his groin tightened and his trousers stretched.

Instead he focused on how he was going to murder Ashton for leaving him here. He'd make that blond-haired fiend pay. Ashton was supposed to protect him and guide him, not abandon him in a house with unfamiliar terrain. It had taken him weeks to learn the lay of his own house, count all the steps and memorize the floor plans and furniture arrangements.

Being at Anne's without his friend's guidance was frightening. He would never forgive the man for the terror he felt when the footman had announced Ashton's departure. The fear had practically immobilized him until Anne had spoken. Had it not been for her, he might have collapsed or lunged for the door and hurt himself again.

But Anne had assessed his panic and calmed him, distracted him. They were not even married, yet she already seemed to know how to cope with his condition. He sensed no pity, nor contempt or disgust in her tone when she spoke to him. Her reluctance to touch him or welcome his embrace had nothing at all to do with his blindness.

The same could not be said for his former mistress Portia. Just three weeks after his accident he had returned to London and summoned her, hoping to banish his sorrows in the comfort of her body. Portia had come, eager for his company as well, but when he could not praise her beauty she'd grown bored. She seemed irritated at his clumsy touch. When he'd once been powerful and mastering over her body, he now touched tenderly, hesitantly, unsure of himself. The worst part of the evening had been when he'd tripped over the edge of an upturned carpet and fallen flat on his face. Pain had exploded in his body, and she had dared to laugh. Still, he had gotten up and tried to erase the moment with a wry joke at his own expense.

When he offered her a glass of wine he'd missed her outstretched hand and spilled it on her gown. She'd shrieked like the devil's own and slapped him. Unable to see her blow coming, he'd been unprepared for the sharpness of her hit and he'd stumbled back in surprise.

This had only worsened his already teetering balance and sent him sprawling on the floor. He'd cracked his head on the baseboard of his bed and lay half-conscious at her feet, broken in every way that mattered.

And to add to his misery, she'd stood there and shouted at him. "Who could ever sleep with a broken excuse of a man like you? You can't even see your boots to put them on! I wouldn't let you bed me if you were the last man in all of England!" And then she'd gone. His valet had heard the commotion and rushed to his aid.

What sort of man am I? Portia had been right. He was as helpless as a babe. A man no longer. The truth of that was just as emotionally crippling as his blindness was physically. He'd wanted to die.

It was a thought he'd never spoken aloud to anyone and hadn't acted upon because too many people he loved would be hurt by such a coward's way out. Yet it didn't change his feelings, or the sense of desperation and helplessness that made him wish to end everything, the pain, the shame, all of it.

Until Anne. She had come to him, hiding her plea for marriage to him behind that cool bravado she'd always had. Her bravery had been the deciding factor for him. If she was willing to give married life a try, then so was he.

Besides, how hard could marriage be?

Grab Cedric's book now HERE to see how it ends!
Turn the page to see my other available titles!

OTHER TITLES BY LAUREN SMITH

Historical
The League of Rogues Series
Wicked Designs
His Wicked Seduction
Her Wicked Proposal
Wicked Rivals
Her Wicked Longing
His Wicked Embrace (coming soon)
The Earl of Pembroke (coming soon)
His Wicked Secret (coming soon)
The Seduction Series
The Duelist's Seduction
The Rakehell's Seduction
The Rogue's Seduction (coming soon)
Standalone Stories

Tempted by A Rogue
Sins and Scandals
An Earl By Any Other Name
A Gentleman Never Surrenders
A Scottish Lord for Christmas

Contemporary
The Surrender Series
The Gilded Cuff
The Gilded Cage
The Gilded Chain
Her British Stepbrother
Forbidden: Her British Stepbrother
Seduction: Her British Stepbrother
Climax: Her British Stepbrother

Paranormal
Dark Seductions Series
The Shadows of Stormclyffe Hall
The Love Bites Series
The Bite of Winter
Brotherhood of the Blood Moon Series
Blood Moon on the Rise (coming soon)
Brothers of Ash and Fire
Grigori: A Royal Dragon Romance
Mikhail: A Royal Dragon Romance
Rurik: A Royal Dragon Romance

Sci-Fi Romance
Cyborg Genesis Series
Across the Stars (coming soon)

ACKNOWLEDGMENTS

I'd like to thank my editor, Noah Chinn for being a wicked mad plot genius. You are the best thing to ever happen to me and my manuscripts. I would also like to thank my Regency Romance Critique group; you ladies have been through countless drafts on my various stories and have supported me the way the best of friends always do. Lastly, I'd like to thank the readers who were so excited to read the first book in the League of Rogues Series and who have patiently waited for Lucien's story. I hope you all enjoy the book! Your support means everything to me and the League!

ABOUT THE AUTHOR

Lauren Smith is an Oklahoma attorney by day, author by night who pens adventurous and edgy romance stories by the light of her smart phone flashlight app. She knew she was destined to be a romance writer when she attempted to re-write the entire *Titanic* movie just to save Jack from drowning. Connecting with readers by writing emotionally moving, realistic and sexy romances no matter what time period is her passion. She's won multiple awards in several romance subgenres including: New England Reader's Choice Awards, Greater Detroit BookSeller's Best Awards, and a Semi-Finalist award for the Mary Wollstonecraft Shelley Award.

To connect with Lauren visit her at:
www.laurensmithbooks.com
lauren@laurensmithbooks.com

Made in the USA
Las Vegas, NV
23 March 2024